PLUM BUN

Black Women Writers Series

PLUM BUN

A NOVEL WITHOUT A MORAL

Jessie Redmon FAUSET

Introduction by Deborah McDowell

"To Market, to Market
To buy a Plum Bun;
Home again, Home again,
Market is done."

BEACON PRESS, BOSTON

Beacon Press
25 Beacon Street
Boston, Massachusetts 02108-2892
www.beacon.org

Beacon Press books
are published under the auspices of
the Unitarian Universalist Association of Congregations.

First published in 1929 by Frederick A. Stokes Company, New York

Introduction © 1990 by Deborah McDowell
First published as a Beacon paperback in 1990
All rights reserved
Printed in the United States of America

04 03 02   8 7 6 5 4 3

Library of Congress Cataloging-in-Publication Data
Fauset, Jessie Redmon.
Plum bun : a novel without a moral / Jessie Redmon Fauset;
with an introduction by Deborah McDowell.
p. cm.
Black women writers
Originally published: New York:
Frederick A. Stokes Company, 1929.
ISBN 0-8070-0919-9
I. Title.
PS3511.A864P57   1990
813'.52 20   90-52590

To
MY FATHER AND MOTHER
REDMON AND ANNA FAUSET

CONTENTS

INTRODUCTION: REGULATING MIDWIVES

Deborah McDowell

WHENEVER I cite Jessie Fauset as a writer of the Harlem Renaissance, I get a predictable response: Who is he? If those familiar with the movement know that Jessie was a she, their knowledge of her tends to be restricted to a handful of generalizations. Most of these issue from long-standing misinformation about Fauset's supposed background as an "Old Philadelphian" of wealth and status. Reading from life to art, even Fauset's most charitable readers have generally concluded that she was simply an apologist for the black middle class, and that her most important role in the Harlem Renaissance was that of a midwife. Langston Hughes's famous statement in his autobiography *The Big Sea* might well be said to have served as her epitaph. He groups her with two others who "midwifed the so-called New Negro literature into being."

Like midwives throughout history, Fauset played a role reserved for women—in particular, for those who failed to conform to their socially assigned roles as women. Midwifery has long been a controversial profession. Its devaluation in modern times has been directly proportionate to the growth of

ix

technology and the elevation of the medical profession as a sphere reserved for men. As a midwife to the Harlem Renaissance, Fauset played the now depreciated role of one who assists at a birth but is otherwise considered inessential to it.

Yet Fauset's contribution was vital to the Harlem Renaissance as it is popularly understood, despite the movement's dominance by male writers. In *Color, Sex, and Poetry*, Gloria Hull observes that though women certainly participated fully in the movement, broad social factors—most prominently men's negative attitudes toward women and male-formulated aesthetic norms and expectations —worked to exclude and marginalize its women writers. Those norms and expectations served a regulating function that Fauset was able to sidestep, if not ignore.

Crisis magazine gave temporary license and support to Fauset's independence during the period from 1919 to 1926, when she was its literary editor. She took the position at the height of the magazine's circulation and during the period of its most intense involvement in the arts. Hired to promote this first flush of artistic endeavor, Fauset proved an astute and responsive advocate of others' work. As editor she published (some for the first time) those writers who went on to become the most prominent figures of the Harlem movement— Claude McKay, Jean Toomer, Anne Spencer, and, arguably the most famous, Langston Hughes. It was Fauset who accepted Hughes's most anthologized poem, "The Negro Speaks of Rivers." In a letter to Hughes, following her acceptance of more of his poems, she wrote, "You assuredly have the true poetic touch, the divine afflatus, which will someday carry you far."[1] Hughes later won distinction as poet laureate of Harlem, and eventually of African-Americans everywhere.

Although Hughes was the best known of the writers whom she encouraged, Fauset was equally important to the career of Jean Toomer, whose work she considered "marked proof of an art and of a contribution to literature which will be distinctly Negroid and without propaganda." Impressed especially with his poem "Song of the Son," she praised its "studied and practiced" technique and advised Toomer to "read voraciously, not only the moderns but the ancients. Get some translations of the Greek poets. Get together enough French to be able to read the imagist poetry of France."

Fauset's editorial stance had nothing to do with pedantry or dilettantism. She understood, however, that provincialism could be a dragrope around a writer's neck. Her impatience with narrow conceptions of art was especially evident in her interest in comparative black literatures. She both translated and reviewed translations of French West Indian writing, appreciating as only a translator can that few works bear resetting in another tongue. Her review of the translation of René Maran's celebrated novel *Batouala* is a judicious and nuanced piece of criticism, alert to both the translation's technical achievements and its failings.

Fauset reflected her disdain for the provincial not only in her editorial practices but also in her own writing. Her travel essays—especially "This Way to the Flea Market," "Dark Algiers the White," "Impressions of the Second Pan African Conference," and "What Europe Thought of the Pan African Conference"—indicate a literary career with considerable range and a writer with sharp political acuity and deep social commitment. Despite the range and radical nature of her interests and commitments, however, Jessie Fauset is grouped invariably and disparagingly with the writers of the Harlem Renaissance classified as the "Rear Guard," the "traditional," "imitative" writers who, in an effort to earn white critical approval, avoided technical and thematic innovations, retreating instead to the safety of outworn literary conventions. That assessment, generally made on the basis of Fauset's fiction, is far more accurate as a judgment of her poetry. Never collected in a single volume, her poems were published mainly in *The Crisis* and in such important anthologies of the period as James Weldon Johnson's *The Book of American Negro Poetry*. Though the emphasis in Harlem Renaissance writing was professedly on things "Negro," Fauset's poetry, with few exceptions, was both conventional in form and curiously silent on questions of race. Except for two or three experimental pieces, her roughly two dozen published poems are unremarkable imitations of Western poetic conventions in spirit, form, and theme.

Some critics have been more severe in their assessments of Fauset's poetry, especially of its "Western" predilections, impugning in the process her consciousness of and commitment to her own race. Viewed from a different perspective, however, Fauset's "universal" (read Westernized) lyrics of love and nature can be said to problematize the very ideas and categories of "Western" and its constructed opposite, "black." Behind all of Fauset's work both as editor and writer is a sensibility, catholic and global in its reach, that complicates simplistic orthodoxies. For her, "blackness" was not synonymous with Afro-American, but included black people worldwide.

Arthur Davis's assessment of Fauset's poetry is, in the end, closest to the mark. In his estimation her lyrics were "light and sophisticated. . . . neither good enough to become an impressive part of the canon of New Poetry or bad enough to be over-looked entirely."[2] It is reasonable to conjecture, given Fauset's keen editorial eye, that she herself might have held a similarly balanced view of her poetry. In any case, she wrote almost no poems after the middle 1920s. A letter written to Joel Spingarn about that same time suggests that she might even have been considering giving up her writing altogether.

In a 26 January 1926 letter to Spingarn, then vice president of the NAACP, Jessie Fauset asked for his assistance in securing employment. About to end her roughly seven-year stint as literary editor of *The Crisis*, the cultural arm of the NAACP, she enumerated her preferences:

1 To be a publisher's reader (if remunerative enough).
2 To be a social secretary in a private family, prefer-ably for a woman.
3 To be connected with one of the foundations here in New York.

She concluded that "in the case of publisher's reader, if the question of color should come up, I could of course work at home."

This matter-of-fact letter shows Fauset combin-ing an enterprising spirit with a sober, no-nonsense recognition of the realities of occupational segregation. Fauset's training and credentials, which she outlined for Spingarn—A.B., A.M., Phi Beta Kappa, and fluent French polished through study at the Sorbonne—did little over the years to dissolve the occupational barriers she encountered throughout her career. Upon her graduation from Philadelphia High School for Girls in 1900, it was assumed that she would go to college, but as her biographer notes, "Precedent in Pennsylvania for a black woman in college was . . . in 1900 invisible." After many unsuccessful attempts to gain admission to Bryn Mawr College, Fauset received a scholarship to Cornell University, where she enrolled in 1901. Although Cornell's records are incomplete, it is believed that Fauset was the first black woman to matriculate there. Graduating in 1905, Fauset found that her color kept her from finding a teaching position in her hometown of Philadelphia. She noted once in an interview: "When I graduated from training school, I found the high schools barred to me because of my color. Philadelphia, birthplace of Independence and City of Brotherly Love—I have never quite been able to reconcile theory with fact."

As it turned out, Fauset did not become a "publisher's reader," at least not in the strictest sense. She did, however, closely monitor publishers' attitudes toward black writing. She was particularly alert to their lurking prejudices against any writing that failed to satisfy the demand for the "different," the "distinct," and the "indigenous" in black art. These were usually codes for what came to be called the cult of the primitive exotic—in large part the construction and fantasy of white intellectuals—and Fauset was brave enough to resist it. *Plum Bun* was to be her *pièce de resistance*.

. . . . .

On its face *Plum Bun* (1929) seems to be just another novel of racial passing.[3] It has all the generic features of the passing novel: a mulatto protagonist, seeking to avoid the constraints of color prejudice in America, decides to cross the color line and pass for white, a deception attended with many anxieties and frequently penetrated. After learning that life on the other side is not without its hardships, the heroine, Angela Murray, develops an appreciation for black life and culture, and returns "home," psychically if not physically, to the black community.

While *Plum Bun* certainly displays the most salient features of the novel-of-passing, to read it simply as such is to miss its complex treatment of the intricacies of gender oppression, as well as the irony and subtlety of its artistic technique. *Plum Bun* is a richly textured and ingeniously designed narrative, containing plots within plots and texts within texts that comment upon one another in intricate combinations. Within this tapestry the passing plot constitutes just one thread, albeit an important one, woven into the novel's overarching frame—that of the *bildungsroman* or novel of development.

While the passing plot forms a major phase in Angela Murray's coming-of-age, in the narrative's configuration it cannot be separated from the marriage plot, which constitutes the structural core of the novel. Angela's obsession with getting married

is frustrated by the exigencies of sex-role stereo-
typing and the limitations of her own romantic assumptions. Although she still plans to marry at the
novel's end, it is not because she believes marriage
to be "the most desirable end for a woman." Instead, she has attained a hard-headed realism regarding the position of women, particularly women
of color, in the United States.

Combining passing and marriage as dual plots
in a novel of female development serves to under-
line Fauset's prevailing theme: the unequal power
relationships in American society. These two plots
could not be more appropriate in a narrative about
power, for both passing and marriage are attempts
—at times naive and fantasy-ridden—by blacks
and women to overcome the structural inequalities
that disempower them. Both marriage and passing
are means by which these two disenfranchised
groups hope to gain access to power. As the narrative makes clear, their expectations are frequently
unfulfilled.

This tension between expectation and fulfillment is introduced in the epigraph that gives
the novel its title and that structures its five sec-
tions ("Home," "Market," "Plum Bun," "Home
Again," and "Market is Done"):

> To Market, To Market,
> To Buy a Plum Bun;
> Home again, Home again,
> Market is done.

The fulfilled expectation of the speaker in the nursery rhyme stands in ironic contrast to the foiled
expectations of Angela Murray. Further, as Ian

xvi

McInnes notes astutely, "If the nursery rhyme epigraph is part of the white male narrative of hope and fulfillment, it is also part of the white male narrative of political and economic opportunism. The only character in the novel who actually buys much of anything, for instance, is Roger Fielding. The verse is thus sexually as well as racially ironic."[4]

As befits a novel of female development and power asymmetries, the opening of the narrative reads like a classic fairy tale. Fauset begins by describing, largely through her protagonist's eyes, the address on Opal Street in Philadelphia where Angela lives: it is an "unpretentious little street lined with unpretentious little houses, inhabited. . . . by unpretentious little people. . . . In one of these houses dwelt a father, a mother and two daughters." Continuing a pattern she began in an early novella, *The Sleeper Wakes* (1920), Fauset focuses on the powerful role fairy tales play in conditioning women to idealize marriage and romantic love.

Reading fairy tales to Angela and her sister, Virginia, their mother adds, " 'And they lived happily ever after, just like your father and me.' " The narrative necessarily gives a racial inflection to the fairy-tale plot, for Angela's mother follows this generic ending with a different and realistic injunction: Angela and her sister must become "schoolteachers and independent" so as to escape the degrading and exploitative conditions she once suffered as a ladies' maid. But for much of the narrative this practical imperative, based on the realities of most black women's lives, wars with Angela's frenzied pursuit of a different and dominant cultural fantasy in which women are rescued by wealthy men and secondarily share in their power.

Nowhere is this fantasy more strikingly illustrated than in the following passage:

> She remembered an expression 'free, white and twenty-one,'—this was what it meant then, this sense of owning the world. . . . 'If I were a man' she said, 'I could be president,' and laughed at herself for the 'if' itself proclaimed a limitation. But that inconsistency bothered her little; she did not want to be a man. *Power*, greatness, authority, these were fitting and proper for men; but there were sweeter, more beautiful gifts for women, and *power* of a certain kind too. Such a *power* she would like to exert in this glittering new world, so full of mysteries and promise. If she could afford it she would have a salon, a drawing-room where men and women should come and pour themselves out to her sympathy and magnetism. To accomplish this she must have money and influence; indeed since she was so young she would need even protection; perhaps it would it better to marry . . . a white man. The thought came to her suddenly out of the void; she had never thought of this possibility before. . . . She knew that men had a better time of it than women, coloured men than coloured women, white men than white women . . . it would be fun, great fun to capture *power* and protection in addition to the freedom and independence which she had so long coveted and which now lay in her hand [emphasis added].

This passage captures vividly the novel's central concern with the forms and sources of power, which are gender-, race-, and class-specific. While white men can become president, wielding the power and authority that that office affords, women must settle for a second-hand power—power experienced vicariously through their husbands. That

these husbands must be white underscores the na-
ïveté of such a fantasy for black women. The passage hints, moreover, at what will be a developing
connection in the novel: the causal link between
money and power and the white male prerogative
of monopolizing both. Angela recognizes these relations of power and fantasizes about enjoying her
share by marrying. What she will actually encounter in her relationship with Roger Fielding, the
wealthy white man, is a replay of the racial pre-
history of concubinage and sexual exploitation. Angela leaves the memory of that history behind her
in Philadelphia, and her attempts at fulfillment
with Roger in New York—imaged as a contest of
wills—illuminate glaringly how unmatched she is.

Ironically, while Angela fights to reach her goal
she doesn't realize that Roger is not after marriage
but rather a bohemian-inspired "free love."[5] Their
trips to the market are for two radically different
commodities. For her, the plum is power and influence attainable only through marriage to a wealthy
white man. For him, the plum is sex, to be bought
and consumed. Angela's game play for marriage is
Roger's foreplay for sex. Finally and ironically,
Angela tries to "buy" in a society that only allows
her to "sell."[6]

Appropriately, the novel's critique of the relations between money, sex, and power gathers force
in its core chapters, "Market" and "Plum Bun."
Juxtaposed next to each other, in both chapters
commercial and sexual imagery dominates. There
are repeated references to withholding and giving,
terms with both sexual and economic connotations.
Martha cautions Angela not to "withhold too
much. Give a little." The materialist imagery de-

velops in contrast to Angela's perceptions that her "life is rounding out like a fairy tale" and that her relationship with Roger is "the finest flower of chivalry and devotion." She is confident that Roger "love[s] her and would want to marry her, for it never occurred to her that men bestowed such attentions on a *passing fancy*" (emphasis added).

Angela's relationship with Roger exemplifies critic Nancy Hartsock's characterization of the commodities exchanged in the courtship market as "sexual gratification and 'firm commitments' (presumably marriage)."[7] To gain his desired end, sex, Roger uses his wealth. "Anything . . . that money can buy, I can get and I can give," he tells Angela. This proposition elicits a counter proposition from Angela who, despite her sexual fastidiousness, considers resorting to the use of the only weapon she has—sex, the power of the "weak." She reasons that "men paid a big price for their desires. Her price would be marriage." Of course, Angela soon discovers her powerlessness to command that price. The novelty of their passion worn off, Roger ends the relationship.

While Roger's departure fosters in Angela a more worldly-wise attitude about male/female relations, it does not destroy the pattern of dependency that her relationship with him encouraged. For a time she convinces herself that, as a woman, she needs the "safety" and "assurance" that marriage putatively affords. It is important, however, that the novel postpones the fulfillment of that desire. Despite Angela's best efforts to marry first Roger, then Anthony Cross, she is thwarted, for it becomes clear that she must first be self-sufficient before entering a relationship with a man.

Angela's self-sufficiency is, significantly, uncovered and sustained by work, and her work becomes empowering. While all of her experiences with power have hitherto been formed by the relational, involving a dialectic of dominance and submission, after her affair with Roger power becomes associated in her mind with individual capacity or the power to act independently. Angela's self-development begins in earnest when she becomes gainfully employed as a designer for a fashion journal while continuing to refine her portrait painting.

Consistent with the romantic conventions on which it draws, the novel ends as Angela is planning to marry. But she has developed an independence and autonomy that needs ratification neither from men nor marriage. She is now ready to enter a marriage in which both partners are "strong individualists, molten and blended in a design which fail[s] to obscure their emphatic personalities."

.   .   .   .   .

In concentrating on the social relations of power, in criticizing the norms of female socialization and the sexual double-standard, in endorsing female independence beyond traditional definitions of womanhood, *Plum Bun* displays a progressiveness and daring that few critics have noted. As in so many novels written by women, blacks, and other members of "literary subcultures," indirect strategies and narrative disguise become necessary covers for rebellious and subversive concerns. Such writers often employ literary and social conventions that function as a mask behind which lie decidedly unconventional critiques.

Inherently self-reflexive, *Plum Bun*, like the protagonist whose story it tells, is passing. It passes for another novel of passing, for a modern fairy tale of age-old concerns. While white skin is Angela's mask, Fauset's deft manipulation of familiar literary genres and conventions is the narrative's mask. Although *Plum Bun* borrows elements from the passing novel, the fairy tale, and the women's romance, it eludes classification.

The passing plot affords Fauset a subtle vehicle through which to critique the naive act of passing, but also to analyze the paradoxes of color prejudice in America. Because of its literary doubleness, misunderstandings of the function of class, race, and color in her work abound. Even her most sympathetic readers see Fauset as ideologically conservative with respect to racial history and class dynamics and unconscious of "her own internalized race prejudice." Again, such readings miss the ironic complexity embedded in the passing plot. If such works as Plum Bun do imply a "hierarchy based on color," that hierarchy resides not in the value system of the novels themselves but in the social structures and patterns they dramatize and encode.[8]

All of Fauset's novels comprehend the extent to which social hierarchies are color-coded, both within and between the races, a coding that interacts with America's basic attitudes toward racial intermixture. It is interesting to note that *Plum Bun* appeared at the end of a decade in which both lynchings and urban riots were on the rise and in which theories and ideologies of race proliferated. While many of these theories were motivated by a desire to restrict immigration on racial grounds, they were appropriated by agents of white supremacy. Such works as Lothrop Stoddard's *The Rising Tide of Color*,[9] Madison Grant's *The Passing of the Great Race*, Clinton Burr's *American Race Heritage*, and Alfred Wiggam's *The Fruit of the Family Tree* all attempted to define race in strictly biological terms.

In *Plum Bun, There Is Confusion* (1924), and *The Chinaberry Tree* (1931), Fauset challenged the irrationalities of the American attempt to classify races biologically and dramatized race as a cultural construct. The figure of the mulatto who could pass for white exposed the basis of that irrationality in prejudice. To argue, as does Arthur P. Davis, that Fauset's novels attempt to show "white America . . . that, except for superficial differences of color . . . upper-class Negroes [were] just like the better class whites"[10] is to read Fauset's novels as superficially as white supremacists read race.

The passing plot enabled Fauset to attack the system of racial classification as it operated in the patronage system and the publishing industry, both of which held fixed ideas about the "proper" subject matter for black writers. Although *Plum Bun* is not simply an allegory, it is not unreasonable to suggest that the novel is a response to this prevailing rigidity of patrons and publishers.[11] It comments specifically on the Harlem Renaissance and the literary straitjacketing that pervaded the movement, violating many writers' artistic integrity and autonomy.

    .   .   .   .   .

No examination of the Harlem Renaissance is complete without a consideration of the economics and politics of the literary marketplace at that time—in particular, of the complex arrangements that often obtained between black writers and their patrons and publishers. Because these writers were so new to the commercial arts, "they were necessarily dependent; they had no force or leverage [either] within the publishing or the critical establishments," as Nathan Huggins rightly notes. "Opinion was against black artists," he continues, and thus "they needed supporters and advocates, defense and encouragement from those who were supposed to know." The question increasingly became, however, "whose sensibilities, tastes, and interests were being patronized?"[12] For the most part, it was the white patrons and publishers who demanded what the age as a whole demanded: the treatment of Negroes as exemplars of primitivism.

Mrs. Rufus Osgood Mason made such a demand on Langston Hughes. She served as his patron for a number of years; the power play in their relationship captures the dynamics that often prevailed between patron and writer during this period. "Concerning Negroes, [Mrs. Mason] felt that they were America's great link with the primitive, and that they had something very precious to give to the Western world," as Hughes put it in his autobiography. He continued, "She wanted me to be primitive and know and feel the intuitions of the primitive. But, unfortunately, I did not feel the rhythms of the primitive surging through me, and so I could not live and write as though I did."[13]

Hughes was not the only black writer who felt this pressure. Even those who refused to submit to the pressures toward primitivism debated the issue in literary reviews and symposia throughout the period. Many maintained that the demand for

the treatment of primitive exotics was the demand
for a depiction of the black "underworld" and thus
a desire for control over black representation. One
such symposium ran in *The Crisis* from March to
December 1926 and was entitled, "The Negro in
Art: How Shall He Be Portrayed?" The questions posed by the editor, W. E. B. DuBois, interpreted the publishing industry's demand for the
"primitive/exotic" as the demand for the depiction
of black sexuality. DuBois asked a variety of writers—both white and black—to respond to such
questions as: "Is not the continual portrayal of the
sordid, foolish and criminal among Negroes con-
vincing the world that this and this alone . . . is
really and essentially Negroid . . . and preventing
white artists from knowing any other types and preventing black artists from daring to paint them?"
"Is there not a real danger that young colored
writers will be tempted to follow the popular trend
in portraying Negro character in the underworld
rather than seeking to paint the truth about themselves and their own social class?"

Jessie Fauset responded by arguing emphati-
cally that following the popular trend of portraying the black "underworld" was a "grave danger"
for black writers. If they followed the crowd, she
added, they risked creating "a literary insincerity
both insidious and abominable." In choosing not
to pander to this branch of popular taste, Fauset
exercised both courage and integrity and remained
faithful to her own artistic objectives, which had
little currency in a publishing industry obsessed
with sensationalism and high profits.

For contrast we need look no further than the
commercial success of Carl Van Vechten's novel

Nigger Heaven (1926) and Claude McKay's *Home to Harlem* (1928). While both these books attempted to strike a balance between portrayals of the black intelligentsia and the black underworld, critics argued that the latter dominated and accounted for the books' high sales. *Nigger Heaven* sold 100,000 copies immediately, went through thirteen reprints, and was translated into French, Swedish, Russian, and Japanese. Widely considered the first and most popular novel to depict the "lower strata" of the black community, *Nigger Heaven* allegedly created the demand in the publishing industry for works by and about blacks with a similar emphasis. Though McKay denied the influence of Van Vechten's novel on his own, the emphasis in *Home to Harlem* on sex and sensationalism, on the exoticism of the Harlem cabaret scene, has linked the novel in critics' minds to *Nigger Heaven*. *Home to Harlem* reached the New York *Herald Tribune* bestseller list, which amounted to "literary prostitution" according to Marcus Garvey. To DuBois, the novel catered to that "prurient demand" by "a certain decadent section of the white American world" for black characters given to "lascivious sexual promiscuity."[14]

In this book market, black writers had few options: they could do the bidding of publishers and patrons or encounter great difficulties getting published, as did Fauset when she ventured publication outside of *The Crisis*. She battled the major New York publishing firms that stifled her creative freedom by prescribing and proscribing her literary province. She criticized publishers for not being "better sport[s] about work that did not succumb to current fashion." Most, she argued, have an "*idee fixe*," adding that "they even more than the public . . . persist in considering only certain types of Negroes interesting and if an author presents a variant they fear that the public either won't believe it or won't stand for it."[15] Fauset was right. "White readers just don't expect Negroes to be like this," wrote the first publisher to see and reject the manuscript of Fauset's first novel, *There Is Confusion*. Other publishers followed suit. Only a promised preface by a white writer, Zona Gale, persuaded Frederick Stokes Company to publish Fauset's third novel, *The Chinaberry Tree*.

Despite rejections and difficulties, Fauset refused to satisfy the demands of the publishing establishment. Though she knew that the power to pass judgment on her work rested with the white male literary establishment, she refused to compromise her own artistic vision. In the process she took pleasure, at least in *Plum Bun*, in teasing commercial expectation. Although there are no explicitly sexual scenes in the novel, it brims with innuendoes. Fauset capitalizes on the multivalent sexual implications of her title. The suggestions in "bun" or "tail" are clear, as are those in Roger's name. Fauset must have heard the classic blues singers of the 1920s—Gertrude "Ma" Rainey and Bessie Smith, for example—and the double-entendres of their lyrics gave her an additional lesson in literary duplicity. Perhaps the most common metaphor in these lyrics is that equating sex with food. Consider the following popular lyric:

> Jelly roll, jelly roll ain't so hard to find,
> There's a baker shop in town bakes it brown like mine,
> I got a sweet jelly, a lovin' sweet jelly roll,
> If you taste my jelly it'll satisfy your worried soul.

While none of the sexual suggestions of "plum bun" are lost upon Fauset, she bypasses their sensational aspects in favor of a clear-sighted examination of the politics of sex. Those readers going to the literary market expecting their plum bun—sex and sensationalism, Van Vechten style—were unfulfilled.

The "Van Vechtenites" were not the only readers whose expectations were unfulfilled. While the genre of passing helped to mask Fauset's digs at the publishing industry, the romance trappings of her novel helped, similarly, to mask her criticism of the image of women and the idealization of romantic love that such genres privilege. The audience for books idealizing romantic love was at least as strong as for those in search of erotic sensationalism. Thornton Wilder's Pulitzer Prize-winning novel *The Bridge of San Luis Rey*, for example, paralleled Van Vechten's *Nigger Heaven* and Claude McKay's *Home to Harlem* in commercial success and popular appeal. Within ninety days of its publication the novel had sold 100,000 copies, becoming the best-selling book of 1928.

I am not suggesting that Fauset's novel is a specific critique of Wilder's, but rather of the cultural valorization of romance that it embodied. If read closely, the novel's evocation of the fairy tale and the romance will inevitably seem designed for satiric purposes. Stunned at Roger's offer to set her up in a "lovenest," Angela thinks, "So this was her castle, her fortress of protection, her refuge." He finally seduces her in front of the fireplace on a stormy evening, complete with driving rain and beating wind—all cliches of romantic entrapment. "He swept her up in his arms, cradling her in them like a baby with her face beneath his own. 'You know that we were meant for each other, that we belong to each other!' " Such stock language and scenes recur and are undercut and satirized in the novel, although the satire has not been readily detected. In revising the conventions of women's romance and the fairy tale, Fauset employs a specific strategy described by critics as the use of familiar and normative conventions or "horizons of expectation" in unfamiliar and unconventional configurations in order to point up the deficiences of those norms. In so doing, writers alter, expand, and possibly transform the reader's expectations to allow for what was formerly unexpected and unacceptable. *Plum Bun* baits the reader with a range of familiar expectations about women and blacks, found both in and out of literature, but then refuses to fulfill them, particularly those that conform to the culturally coded exegeses of race and gender.

From the beginning of her career, Fauset insisted that the U.S. publishing system had created a complex of ideologies of race, in fiction and nonfiction alike, that necessitated control by black writers of portrayals of black people. She was skeptical about whether whites could "write evenly on the racial situation in America" and once admitted to an interviewer that she began to write fiction in earnest when T. S. Stribling's novel *Birthright* failed, in her estimation, to depict blacks authentically. In those times belief in the possibilities of "authentic" representation was strong and widely accepted, and thus Fauset could assert confidently, "Here is an audience waiting to hear the truth about us. Let we who are better qualified to present that truth than any white writer try to do so."

While Fauset had come to accept that most white publishers doubted her qualifications for representing "blackness," ironically most blacks doubted them as well. Her novels were typically regarded as "vapidly genteel lace curtain romances." In one of the most condescending appraisals, Claude McKay described Fauset as "prim and dainty as a primrose," and added that "her novels [were] quite as fastidious and precious."

Unfortunately, responses like McKay's were all too frequent, stemming primarily from a tendency during and since the Harlem Renaissance to deify the proletarian or "folk" tradition and to demonize the middle class. Wilson J. Moses is one of the few critics to observe with disapproval that this "proletarian/bohemian interpretation" of the art of the movement "has been granted a sort of moral superiority over any other framework of analysis in black literary and intellectual history."

Within this critical tendency to slight anyone associated with black middle-class existence, Fauset has always been an easy target. She was caught in a shift in black literary aesthetics, as well as a shift in Afro-American strategies of social reform. While Fauset's attachment to the priorities of liberal reform struck many readers, then and now, as an insular and thus inadequate strategy of social change, one could say that Fauset chose the terms of her enclosure, swerving away from the finality and fixity of racial classification as well as the class and caste of gender and genre alike.

Notes

1. Arnold Rampersad, *The Life of Langston Hughes, Volume I: 1902–1941* (New York: Oxford University Press, 1986), p. 70.
2. Arthur P. Davis, *From the Dark Tower* (Washington, D. C.: Howard University Press, 1974), p. 93.
3. The novel of passing is a genre that has preoccupied Afro-American writers throughout their literary history. *Plum Bun* joins the roster that includes such pre–Harlem Renaissance novels as William Wells Brown's *Clotel* (1853), Charles Chesnutt's *The House Behind the Cedars* (1900), and James Weldon Johnson's *The Autobiography of an Ex-Colored Man* (1912). Fauset returned to the genre again and again, beginning with her early short stories "Emmy" and "The Sleeper Wakes," published in *The Crisis,* and continuing in her last novel, *Comedy, American Style* (1933). The novel of passing was also popular among other novelists of the period, including Walter White's *Flight* (1926) and Nella Larsen's *Passing* (1929).
4. Ian MacInnes, "Closure and the Fiction of Female Development." Unpublished essay.
5. The free-love movement, which began in the 1870s, was common among Greenwich Village intellectuals in the 1920s. They opposed legal and clerical marriage, which, in their estimation, stifled love. See Linda Gordon, *Woman's Body, Woman's Right* (New York: Penguin, 1974).
6. I adapt this point from Ian MacInnes in the essay noted above.
7. *Money, Sex and Power: Toward a Feminist Historical Materialism* (New York: Longman, 1983), p. 155.
8. Rafia Zafar. Unpublished manuscript.
9. Stoddard also wrote regularly for such popular magazines as *Collier's* and *Saturday Evening Post.*
10. Davis, *From the Dark Tower,* p. 90.
11. It is significant that early in her artistic career Angela considers becoming a portrait painter, but she resists the thought because "she hated the idea of the position in which she would be placed, fearfully placating and flattering possible patrons, hurrying through with an order because she needed the cheque, accepting patronage and condescension."
12. *Harlem Renaissance* (New York: Oxford University Press, 1971), p. 128.
13. *The Big Sea* (New York: Hill and Wang, 1940), pp. 316, 325.

14. *Voices of a Black Nation: Political Journalism in the Harlem Renaissance,* ed. Theodore Vincent (San Francisco: Ramparts Press, 1973), pp. 352–60.

15. "The Negro in Art: How Shall He Be Portrayed." *The Crisis,* 32 (June 1926), 72. Zora Neale Hurston, Fauset's contemporary, would write later that "publishers and producers are cool to the idea" of literature "about the higher emotions and love of upper-class Negroes and the minorities in general. . . . It is assumed that all non Anglo-Saxons are uncomplicated stereotypes. . . ." See "What White Publishers Won't Print," rpt. in *I Love Myself When I am Laughing,* ed. Alice Walker (New York: The Feminist Press, 1979), pp. 169–73.

Suggestions for Further Reading

Ammons, Elizabeth. "New Literary History: Edith Wharton and Jessie Redmon Fauset," *College English* 14 (1987): 207–218.

Anderson, Jervis. *This Was Harlem.* New York: Farrar Straus Giroux, 1981.

Braithwaite, William Stanley. "The Novels of Jessie Fauset." In *The Black Novelist,* ed. Robert Hemenway. Columbus, Ohio: Charles Merrill, 1970, pp. 46–54.

Carby, Hazel. *Reconstructing Womanhood: The Emergence of the Afro-American Woman Novelist.* New York: Oxford University Press, 1987.

Christian, Barbara. *Black Women Novelists: The Development of a Tradition, 1892–1976.* Connecticut: Greenwood Press, 1980.

Feeney, Joseph T., S. J. "A Sardonic Unconventional Jessie Fauset: The Double Structure and Double Vision of Her Novels," *College Language Association Journal* 22 (June 1979: 365–382.

———. "Black Childhood as Ironic: A Nursery Rhyme Transformed in Jessie Fauset's Novel *Plum Bun." Minority Voices* 4 (Fall 1980): 65–69.

Huggins, Nathan I. *Harlem Renaissance.* New York: Oxford University Press, 1970.

Johnson, Abby Arthur. "Literary Midwife: Jessie Redmon Fauset and the Harlem Renaissance." *Phylon,* volume 39: 143–53.

Lewis, David Levering. *When Harlem Was In Vogue.* New York: Knopf, 1981.

McDowell, Deborah E. "The Neglected Dimension of Jessie Redmon Fauset." *Afro-Americans in New York Life and History* (July 1981): 33–49.

Sims, Janet L. "Jessie Redmon Fauset (1885–1961): A Selected Annotated Bibliography." *Black American Literature Forum* 14 (Winter 1980): 147–152.

Starkey, Marion. "Jessie Fauset." *Southern Workman* (May 1932): 217–220.

Sylvander, Carolyn Wedin. *Jessie Redmon Fauset, Black American Writer.* Troy, New York: The Whitson Publishing Company, 1981.

HOME

CHAPTER I

OPAL STREET, as streets go, is no jewel of the first water. It is merely an imitation, and none too good at that. Narrow, unsparkling, uninviting, it stretches meekly off from dull Jefferson Street to the dingy, drab market which forms the north side of Oxford Street. It has no mystery, no allure, either of exclusiveness or of downright depravity; its usages are plainly significant,—an unpretentious little street lined with unpretentious little houses, inhabited for the most part by unpretentious little people.

The dwellings are three stories high, and contain six boxes called by courtesy, rooms—a "parlour", a midget of a dining-room, a larger kitchen and, above, a front bedroom seemingly large only because it extends for the full width of the house, a mere shadow of a bathroom, and another back bedroom with windows whose possibilities are spoiled by their outlook on sad and diminutive back-yards. And above these two, still two others built in similar wise.

In one of these houses dwelt a father, a mother and two daughters. Here, as often happens in a home sheltering two generations, opposite, unevenly matched emotions faced each other. In the houses of the rich the satisfied ambition of the older generation is faced by the overwhelming ambition of the younger. Or the elders may find themselves brought in opposition to the blank indifference and ennui of youth engendered by the realization that there remain no more worlds to conquer; their fathers having already taken all. In houses on Opal Street these niceties of distinction are hardly to be found; there is a more direct and concrete contrast. The satisfied ambition of maturity is a foil for the restless despair of youth.

Affairs in the Murray household were advancing towards this stage; yet not a soul in that family of four could have foretold its coming. To Junius and Mattie Murray, who had known poverty and homelessness, the little house on Opal Street represented the *ne plus ultra* of ambition; to their daughter Angela it seemed the dingiest, drabbest chrysalis that had ever fettered the wings of a brilliant butterfly. The stories which Junius and Mattie told of difficulties overcome, of the arduous learning of trades, of the pitiful scraping together of infinitesimal savings, would have made a latter-day Iliad, but to Angela they were merely a description of a life which she at any cost would avoid living. Somewhere in the world were paths which lead to broad thoroughfares, large, bright houses, delicate niceties of existence. Those paths Angela meant to find and frequent. At a very early age she had observed that the good things of life are unevenly distributed; merit is not always rewarded; hard labour does not necessarily entail adequate recompense. Certain fortuitous endowments, great physical beauty, unusual strength, a certain unswerving singleness of mind, —gifts bestowed quite blindly and disproportionately by the forces which control life,—these were

12

the qualities which contributed toward a glowing
and pleasant existence.

Angela had no high purpose in life; unlike her
sister Virginia, who meant some day to invent a
marvellous method for teaching the pianoforte,
Angela felt no impulse to discover, or to perfect.
True she thought she might become eventually a
distinguished painter, but that was because she
felt within herself an ability to depict which as far
as it went was correct and promising. Her eye for
line and for expression was already good and she
had a nice feeling for colour. Moreover she possessed the instinct for self-appraisal which taught
her that she had much to learn. And she was sure
that the knowledge once gained would flower in
her case to perfection. But her gift was not for
her the end of existence; rather it was an adjunct
to a life which was to know light, pleasure, gaiety
and freedom.

Freedom! That was the note which Angela
heard oftenest in the melody of living which was
to be hers. With a wildness that fell just short of
unreasonableness she hated restraint. Her father's
earlier days as coachman in a private family, his
later successful, independent years as boss carpenter, her mother's youth spent as maid to a
famous actress, all this was to Angela a manifestation of the sort of thing which happens to those
enchained it might be by duty, by poverty, by
weakness or by colour.

Colour or rather the lack of it seemed to the
child the one absolute prerequisite to the life of
which she was always dreaming. One might break
loose from a too hampering sense of duty; poverty could be overcome; physicians conquered

weakness; but colour, the mere possession of a black or a white skin, that was clearly one of those fortuitous endowments of the gods. Gratitude was no strong ingredient in this girl's nature, yet very often early she began thanking Fate for the chance which in that household of four had bestowed on her the heritage of her mother's fair skin. She might so easily have been, like her father, black, or have received the melange which had resulted in Virginia's rosy bronzeness and her deeply waving black hair. But Angela had received not only her mother's creamy complexion and her soft cloudy, chestnut hair, but she had taken from Junius the aquiline nose, the gift of some remote Indian ancestor which gave to his face and his eldest daughter's that touch of chiselled immobility.

∙ ∙ ∙ ∙ ∙

It was from her mother that Angela learned the possibilities for joy and freedom which seemed to her inherent in mere whiteness. No one would have been more amazed than that same mother if she could have guessed how her daughter interpreted her actions. Certainly Mrs. Murray did not attribute what she considered her happy, busy, sheltered life on tiny Opal Street to the accident of her colour; she attributed it to her black husband whom she had been glad and proud to marry. It is equally certain that that white skin of hers had not saved her from occasional contumely and insult. The famous actress for whom she had worked was aware of Mattie's mixed blood and, boasting temperament rather than refinement, had often dubbed her "white nigger."

Angela's mother employed her colour very much as she practised certain winning usages of smile and voice to obtain indulgences which meant much to her and which took nothing from anyone else. Then, too, she was possessed of a keener sense of humour than her daughter; it amused her when by herself to take lunch at an exclusive restaurant whose patrons would have been panic-stricken if they had divined the presence of a "coloured" woman no matter how little her appearance differed from theirs. It was with no idea of disclaiming her own that she sat in orchestra seats which Philadelphia denied to coloured patrons. But when Junius or indeed any other dark friend accompanied her she was the first to announce that she liked to sit in the balcony or gallery, as indeed she did; her infrequent occupation of orchestra seats was due merely to a mischievous determination to flout a silly and unjust law.

Her years with the actress had left their mark, a perfectly harmless and rather charming one. At least so it seemed to Junius, whose weakness was for the qualities known as "essentially feminine." Mrs. Murray loved pretty clothes, she liked shops devoted to the service of women; she enjoyed being even on the fringe of a fashionable gathering. A satisfaction that was almost ecstatic seized her when she drank tea in the midst of modishly gowned women in a stylish tea-room. It pleased her to stand in the foyer of a great hotel or of the Academy of Music and to be part of the whirling, humming, palpitating gaiety. She had no desire to be of these people, but she liked to look on; it amused and thrilled and kept alive some unquenchable instinct for life which thrived within her. To walk through Wanamaker's on Saturday, to stroll from Fifteenth to Ninth Street on Chestnut, to have her tea in the Bellevue Stratford, to stand in the lobby of the St. James' fitting on immaculate gloves; all innocent, childish pleasures pursued without malice or envy contrived to cast a glamour over Monday's washing and Tuesday's ironing, the scrubbing of kitchen and bathroom and the fashioning of children's clothes. She was endowed with a humorous and pungent method of presentation; Junius, who had had the wit not to interfere with these little excursions and the sympathy to take them at their face value, preferred one of his wife's sparkling accounts of a Saturday's adventure in "passing" to all the tall stories told by cronies at his lodge.

Much of this pleasure, harmless and charming though it was, would have been impossible with a dark skin.

In these first years of marriage, Mattie, busied with the house and the two babies had given up those excursions. Later, when the children had grown and Junius had reached the stage where he could afford to give himself a half-holiday on Saturdays, the two parents inaugurated a plan of action which eventually became a fixed programme. Each took a child, and Junius went off to a beloved but long since suspended pastime of exploring old Philadelphia, whereas Mattie embarked once more on her social adventures. It is true that Mattie accompanied by brown Virginia could not move quite as freely as when with Angela. But her maternal instincts were sound; her children, their feelings and their faith

in her meant much more than the pleasure which
she would have been first to call unnecessary and
silly.   As it happened the children themselves
quite unconsciously solved the dilemma; Virginia
found shopping tiring and stupid, Angela returned
from her father's adventuring worn and bored.
Gradually the rule was formed that Angela accompanied her mother and Virginia her father.

.   .   .   .   .

On such fortuities does life depend.   Little
Angela Murray, hurrying through Saturday
morning's scrubbing of steps in order that she
might have her bath at one and be with her
mother on Chestnut Street at two, never realized
that her mother took her pleasure among all
these pale people because it was there that she
happened to find it.   It never occurred to her that
the delight which her mother obviously showed
in meeting friends on Sunday morning when the
whole united Murray family came out of church
was the same as she showed on Chestnut Street
the previous Saturday, because she was finding
the qualities which her heart craved, bustle, excitement and fashion.   The daughter could not
guess that if the economic status or the racial gen-
ius of coloured people had permitted them to run
modish hotels or vast and popular department
stores her mother would have been there.   She
drew for herself certain clearly formed conclu-
sions which her subconscious mind thus codified:
First, that the great rewards of life—riches,
glamour, pleasure,—are for white-skinned people
only.   Secondly, that Junius and Virginia were

denied these privileges because they were dark; here her reasoning bore at least an element of verisimilitude but she missed the essential fact that her father and sister did not care for this type of pleasure. The effect of her fallaciousness was to cause her to feel a faint pity for her unfortunate relatives and also to feel that coloured people were to be considered fortunate only in the proportion in which they measured up to the physical standards of white people.

One Saturday excursion left a far-reaching impression. Mrs. Murray and Angela had spent a successful and interesting afternoon. They had browsed among the contents of the small exclusive shops in Walnut Street; they had had soda at Adams' on Broad Street and they were standing finally in the portico of the Walton Hotel deciding with fashionable and idle elegance what they should do next. A thin stream of people constantly passing threw an occasional glance at the quietly modish pair, the well-dressed, assured woman and the refined and no less assured daughter. The door-man knew them; it was one of Mrs. Murray's pleasures to proffer him a small tip, much appreciated since it was uncalled for. This was the atmosphere which she loved. Angela had put on her gloves and was waiting for her mother, who was drawing on her own with great care, when she glimpsed in the laughing, hurrying Saturday throng the figures of her father and of Virginia. They were close enough for her mother, who saw them too, to touch them by merely descending a few steps and stretching out her arm. In a second the pair had vanished. Angela saw her mother's face change—with trepidation she thought. She remarked: "It's a good thing Papa didn't see us, you'd have had to speak to him, wouldn't you?" But her mother, giving her a distracted glance, made no reply.

That night, after the girls were in bed, Mattie, perched on the arm of her husband's chair, told him about it. "I was at my old game of play-acting again to-day, June, passing you know, and darling, you and Virginia went by within arm's reach and we never spoke to you. I'm so ashamed."

But Junius consoled her. Long before their marriage he had known of his Mattie's weakness and its essential harmlessness. "My dear girl, I told you long ago that where no principle was involved, your passing means nothing to me. It's just a little joke; I don't think you'd be ashamed to acknowledge your old husband anywhere if it were necessary."

"I'd do that if people were mistaking me for a queen," she assured him fondly. But she was silent, not quite satisfied. "After all," she said with her charming frankness, "it isn't you, dear, who make me feel guilty. I really am ashamed to think that I let Virginia pass by without a word. I think I should feel very badly if she were to know it. I don't believe I'll ever let myself be quite as silly as that again."

But of this determination Angela, dreaming excitedly of Saturdays spent in turning her small olive face firmly away from peering black countenances was, unhappily, unaware.

CHAPTER II

SATURDAY came to be the day of the week for Angela, but her sister Virginia preferred Sundays. She loved the atmosphere of golden sanctity which seemed to hover with a sweet glory about the stodgy, shabby little dwelling. Usually she came downstairs first so as to enjoy by herself the blessed "Sunday feeling" which, she used to declare, would have made it possible for her to recognize the day if she had awakened to it even in China. She was only twelve at this time, yet she had already developed a singular aptitude and liking for the care of the home, and this her mother gratefully fostered. Gradually the custom was formed of turning over to her small hands all the duties of Sunday morning; they were to her a ritual. First the kettle must be started boiling, then the pavement swept. Her father's paper must be carried up and left outside his door. Virginia found a nameless and sweet satisfaction in performing these services.

She prepared the Sunday breakfast which was always the same,—bacon and eggs, strong coffee with good cream for Junius, chocolate for the other three and muffins. After the kettle had boiled and the muffins were mixed it took exactly half an hour to complete preparations. Virginia always went about these matters in the same way.

She set the muffins in the oven, pursing her lips and frowning a little just as she had seen her mother do; then she went to the foot of the narrow, enclosed staircase and called "hoo-hoo" with a soft rising inflection,—"last call to dinner," her father termed it. And finally, just for those last few minutes before the family descended she went into the box of a parlour and played hymns, old-fashioned and stately tunes,—"How firm a foundation," "The spacious firmament on high," "Am I a soldier of the Cross." Her father's inflexible bass, booming down the stairs, her mother's faint alto in thirds mingled with her own sweet treble; a shaft of sunlight, faint and watery in winter, strong and golden in summer, shimmering through the room in the morning dusk completed for the little girl a sensation of happiness which lay perilously near tears.

.   .   .   .   .

After breakfast came the bustle of preparing for church. Junius of course had come down in complete readiness; but the others must change their dresses; Virginia had mislaid her Sunday hair-ribbon again; Angela had discovered a rip in her best gloves and could not be induced to go down until it had been mended. "Wait for me just a minute, Jinny dear, I can't go out looking like this, can I?" She did not like going to church, at least not to their church, but she did care about her appearance and she liked the luxuriousness of being "dressed up" on two successive days. At last the little procession filed out, Mattie hoping that they would not be late, she did hate it so;

Angela thinking that this was a stupid way to spend Sunday and wondering at just what period of one's life existence began to shape itself as *you* wanted it. Her father's thoughts were inchoate; expressed they would have revealed a patriarchal aspect almost biblical. He had been a poor boy, homeless, a nobody, yet somehow he had contrived in his mid-forties to attain to the status of a respectable citizen, house-owner, a good provider. He possessed a charming wife and two fine daughters, and as was befitting he was accompanying them to the house of the Lord. As for Virginia, no one to see her in her little red hat and her mother's cut-over blue coat could have divined how near she was to bursting with happiness. Father, mother and children, well-dressed, well-fed, united, going to church on a beautiful Sunday morning; there was an immense cosmic rightness about all this which she sensed rather than realized. She envied no one the incident of finer clothes or a larger home; this unity was the core of happiness, all other satisfactions must radiate from this one; greater happiness could be only a matter of degree but never of essence. When she grew up she meant to live the same kind of life; she would marry a man exactly like her father and she would conduct her home exactly as did her mother. Only she would pray very hard every day for five children, two boys and two girls and then a last little one,—it was hard for her to decide whether this should be a boy or a girl,—which should stay small for a long, long time. And on Sundays they would all go to church.

Intent on her dreaming she rarely heard the sermon. It was different with the hymns, for they

22

constituted the main part of the service for her
father, and she meant to play them again for
him later in the happy, golden afternoon or the
grey dusk of early evening. But first there were
acquaintances to greet, friends of her parents who
called them by their first names and who, in
speaking of Virginia and Angela still said: "And
these are the babies; my, how they grow! It
doesn't seem as though it could be you, Mattie
Ford, grown up and with children!"

On Communion Sundays the service was very
late, and Angela would grow restless and twist
about in her seat, but the younger girl loved the
sudden, mystic hush which seemed to descend on
the congregation. Her mother's sweetly merry
face took on a certain childish solemnity, her father's stern profile softened into beatific expec-
tancy. In the exquisite diction of the sacramental
service there were certain words, certain phrases
that almost made the child faint; the minister had
a faint burr in his voice and somehow this lent a
peculiar underlying resonance to his intonation;
he half spoke, half chanted and when, picking up
the wafer he began "For in the night" and then
broke it, Virginia could have cried out with the
ecstasy which filled her. She felt that those who
partook of the bread and wine were somehow
transfigured; her mother and father wore an expression of ineffable content as they returned to
their seats and there was one woman, a middle-
aged, mischief-making person, who returned from
taking the sacrament, walking down the aisle, her
hands clasped loosely in front of her and her face
so absolutely uplifted that Virginia used to hasten
to get within earshot of her after the church was

dismissed, sure that her first words must savour
of something mystic and holy. But her assumption proved always to be ill-founded.

.   .   .   .   .

The afternoon and the evening repeated the
morning's charm but in a different key. Usually a
few acquaintances dropped in; the parlour and
dining-room were full for an hour or more of
pleasant, harmless chatter. Mr. Henson, the po-
liceman, a tall, yellow man with freckles on his
nose and red "bad hair" would clap Mr. Murray
on the back and exclaim "I tell you what, June,"
—which always seemed to Virginia a remarkably
daring way in which to address her tall, dignified
father. Matthew Henson, a boy of sixteen,
would inevitably be hovering about Angela who
found him insufferably boresome and made no
effort to hide her ennui. Mrs. Murray passed
around rather hard cookies and delicious currant
wine, talking stitches and patterns meanwhile
with two or three friends of her youth with a
frequent injection of "Mame, do you remember!"

Presently the house, emptied of all but the
family, grew still again, dusk and the lamp light
across the street alternately panelling the walls.
Mrs. Murray murmured something about fixing
a bite to eat, "I'll leave it in the kitchen if anybody wants it." Angela reflected aloud that she
had still to get her Algebra or History or French
as the case might be, but nobody moved. What
they were really waiting for was for Virginia to
start to play and finally she would cross the nar-

row absurdity of a room and stretching out her
slim, brown hands would begin her version, a
glorified one, of the hymns which they had sung
in church that morning, and then the old favour-
ites which she had played before breakfast. Even
Angela, somewhat remote and difficult at first,
fell into this evening mood and asked for a special
tune or a repetition: "I like the way you play
that, Jinny." For an hour or more they were as
close and united as it is possible for a family to
be.

At eight o'clock or thereabouts Junius said exactly as though it had not been in his thoughts
all evening: "Play the 'Dying Christian', daughter." And Virginia, her treble sounding very
childish and shrill against her father's deep, unyielding bass, began Pope's masterpiece on the
death of a true believer. The magnificently sol-
emn words: "Vital spark of heavenly flame," the
strangely appropriate minor music filled the little
house with an awesome beauty which was almost
palpable. It affected Angela so that in sheer
self-defence she would go out in the kitchen and
eat her share of the cold supper set by her mother.
But Mattie, although she never sang this piece,
remained while her husband and daughter sang
on. Death triumphant and mighty had no fears
for her. It was inevitable, she knew, but she would
never have to face it alone. When her husband
died, she would die too, she was sure of it; and
if death came to her first it would be only a little
while before Junius would be there stretching
out his hand and guiding her through all the
rough, strange places just as years ago, when he
had been a coachman to the actress for whom she

25

worked, he had stretched out his good, honest hand and had saved her from a dangerous and equivocal position. She wiped away happy and grateful tears.

"The world recedes, it disappears," sang Virginia. But it made no difference how far it drifted away as long as the four of them were together; and they would always be together, her father and mother and she and Angela. With her visual mind she saw them proceeding endlessly through space; there were her parents, arm in arm, and she and—but to-night and other nights she could not see Angela; it grieved her to lose sight thus of her sister, she knew she must be there, but grope as she might she could not find her. And then quite suddenly Angela was there again, but a different Angela, not quite the same as in the beginning of the picture.

And suddenly she realized that she was doing four things at once and each of them with all the intentness which she could muster; she was singing, she was playing, she was searching for Angela and she was grieving because Angela as she knew her was lost forever.

"Oh Death, oh Death, where is thy sting!" the hymn ended triumphantly,—she and the piano as usual came out a little ahead of Junius which was always funny. She said, "Where's Angela?" and knew what the answer would be. "I'm tired, mummy! I guess I'll go to bed."

"You ought to, you got up so early and you've been going all day."

Kissing her parents good-night she mounted the stairs languidly, her whole being pervaded with the fervid yet delicate rapture of the day.

26

CHAPTER III

MONDAY morning brought the return of the busy, happy week. It meant wash-day for Mattie, for she and Junius had never been able to raise their ménage to the status either of a maid or of putting out the wash. But this lack meant nothing to her,—she had been married fifteen years and still had the ability to enjoy the satisfaction of having a home in which she had full sway instead of being at the beck and call of others. She was old enough to remember a day when poverty for a coloured girl connoted one of three things: going out to service, working as ladies' maid, or taking a genteel but poorly paid position as seamstress with one of the families of the rich and great on Rittenhouse Square, out West Walnut Street or in one of the numerous impeccable, aristocratic suburbs of Philadelphia.

She had tried her hand at all three of these possibilities, had known what it meant to rise at five o'clock, start the laundry work for a patronizing indifferent family of people who spoke of her in her hearing as "the girl" or remarked of her in a slightly lower but still audible tone as being rather better than the usual run of niggers,—"She never steals, I'd trust her with anything and she isn't what you'd call lazy either." For this family she had prepared breakfast, gone back to her wash-

27

ing, served lunch, had taken down the clothes,
sprinkled and folded them, had gone upstairs and
made three beds, not including her own and then
had returned to the kitchen to prepare dinner.
At night she nodded over the dishes and finally
stumbling up to the third floor fell into her un-
made bed, sometimes not even fully undressed.
And Tuesday morning she would begin on the
long and tedious strain of ironing. For this she
received four dollars a week with the privilege of
every other Sunday and every Thursday off. But
she could have no callers.

As a seamstress, life had been a little more en-
durable but more precarious. The wages were
better while they lasted, she had a small but comfortable room; her meals were brought up to her
on a tray and the young girls of the households
in which she was employed treated her with a
careless kindness which while it still had its element of patronage was not offensive. But such
families had a disconcerting habit of closing their
households and departing for months at a time,
and there was Mattie stranded and perilously trying to make ends meet by taking in sewing. But
her clientèle was composed of girls as poor as
she, who either did their own dressmaking or
could afford to pay only the merest trifle for her
really exquisite and meticulous work.

·   ·   ·   ·   ·

The situation with the actress had really been
the best in many, in almost all, respects. But
it presented its pitfalls. Mattie was young, pretty
and innocent; the actress was young, beautiful

28

and sophisticated. She had been married twice
and had been the heroine of many affairs; maid-
enly modesty, virtue for its own sake, were qualities long since forgotten; high ideals and personal
self-respect were too abstract for her slightly
coarsened mind to visualize, and at any rate they
were incomprehensible and even absurd in a servant, and in a coloured servant to boot She knew
that in spite of Mattie's white skin there was
black blood in her veins; in fact she would not
have taken the girl on had she not been coloured;
all her servants must be coloured, for hers was a
carelessly conducted household, and she felt dimly
that all coloured people are thickly streaked with
immorality. They were naturally loose, she reasoned, when she thought about it at all. "Look
at the number of mixed bloods among them; look
at Mattie herself for that matter, a perfectly
white nigger if ever there was one. I'll bet her
mother wasn't any better than she should be."

When the girl had come to her with tears in
her eyes and begged her not to send her as mes-
senger to the house of a certain Haynes Brokinaw, politician and well-known man about town,
Madame had laughed out loud. "How ridiculous! He'll treat you all right. I should like to
know what a girl like you expects. And anyway,
if I don't care, why should you? Now run along
with the note and don't bother me about this
again. I hire you to do what I want, not to do
as you want." She was not even jealous,— of a
coloured working girl! And anyway, constancy
was no virtue in her eyes; she did not possess it
herself and she valued it little in others.

Mattie was in despair. She was receiving

29

twenty-five dollars a month, her board, and a comfortable, pleasant room. She was seeing something of the world and learning of its amenities. It was during this period that she learned how very pleasant indeed life could be for a person possessing only a very little extra money and a white skin. But the special attraction which her present position held for her was that every day she had a certain amount of time to call her own, for she was Madame's personal servant; in no wise was she connected with the routine of keeping the house. If Madame elected to spend the whole day away from home, Mattie, once she had arranged for the evening toilette, was free to act and to go where she pleased.

And now here was this impasse looming up with Brokinaw. More than once Mattie had felt his covetous eyes on her; she had dreaded going to his rooms from the very beginning. She had even told his butler, "I'll be back in half an hour for the answer;" and she would not wait in the great square hall as he had indicated for there she was sure that danger lurked. But the third time Brokinaw was standing in the hall. "Just come into my study," he told her, "while I read this and write the answer." And he had looked at her with his cold, green eyes and had asked her why she was so out of breath. "There's no need to rush so, child; stay here and rest. I'm in no hurry, I assure you. Are you really coloured? You know, I've seen lots of white girls not as pretty as you. Sit here and tell me all about your mother,—and your father. Do—do you remember him?" His whole bearing reeked with intention.

Within a week Madame was sending her again
and she had suggested fearfully the new coachman. "No," said Madame. "It's Wednesday,
his night off, and I wouldn't send him anyway;
coachmen are too hard to keep nowadays; you're
all getting so independent." Mattie had come
down from her room and walked slowly, slowly to
the corner where the new coachman, tall and black
and grave, was just hailing a car. She ran to him
and jerked down the arm which he had just lifted
to seize the railing. "Oh, Mr. Murray," she
stammered. He had been so astonished and so
kind. Her halting explanation done, he took the
note in silence and delivered it, and the next
night and for many nights thereafter they walked
through the silent, beautiful square, and Junius
had told her haltingly and with fear that he loved
her. She threw her arms about his neck: "And
I love you too."

"You don't mind my being so dark then? Lots
of coloured girls I know wouldn't look at a black
man."

But it was partly on account of his colour that
she loved him; in her eyes his colour meant safety. "Why should I mind?" she asked with one of
her rare outbursts of bitterness, "my own colour
has never brought me anything but insult and
trouble."

The other servants, it appeared, had told him
that sometimes she—he hesitated—"passed."

"Yes, yes, of course I do," she explained it
eagerly, "but never to them. And anyway when
I am alone what can I do? I can't label myself.
And if I'm hungry or tired and I'm near a place
where they don't want coloured people, why

31

should I observe their silly old rules, rules that
are unnatural and unjust,—because the world was
made for everybody, wasn't it, Junius?"

She had told him then how hard and joyless
her girlhood life had been,—she had known such
dreadful poverty and she had been hard put to it
to keep herself together. But since she had come
to live with Madame Sylvio she had glimpsed,
thanks to her mistress's careless kindness, something of the life of comparative ease and beauty
and refinement which one could easily taste if he
possessed just a modicum of extra money and the
prerequisite of a white skin.

"I've only done it for fun but I won't do it any
more if it displeases you. I'd much rather live
in the smallest house in the world with you, Junius, than be wandering around as I have so often,
lonely and unknown in hotels and restaurants."
Her sweetness disarmed him. There was no reason in the world why she should give up her harmless pleasure unless, he added rather sternly, some
genuine principle were involved.

It was the happiest moment of her life when
Junius had gone to Madame and told her that
both he and Mattie were leaving. "We are going
to be married," he announced proudly. The actress had been sorry to lose her, and wanted to
give her a hundred dollars, but the tall, black
coachman would not let his wife accept it. "She
is to have only what she earned," he said in stern
refusal. He hated Madame Sylvio for having
thrown the girl in the way of Haynes Brokinaw.

They had married and gone straight into the
little house on Opal Street which later was to become their own. Mattie her husband considered

a perfect woman, sweet, industrious, affectionate and illogical. But to her he was God.

When Angela and Virginia were little children and their mother used to read them fairy tales she would add to the ending, "And so they lived happily ever after, just like your father and me."

All this was passing happily through her mind on this Monday morning. Junius was working somewhere in the neighbourhood; his shop was down on Bainbridge Street, but he tried to devote Mondays and Tuesdays to work up town so that he could run in and help Mattie on these trying days. Before the advent of the washing machine he used to dart in and out two or three time in the course of a morning to lend a hand to the heavy sheets and the bed-spreads. Now those articles were taken care of in the laundry, but Junius still kept up the pleasant fiction.

Virginia attended school just around the corner, and presently she would come in too, not so much to get her own lunch as to prepare it for her mother. She possessed her father's attitude toward Mattie as someone who must be helped, indulged and protected. Moreover she had an unusually keen sense of gratitude toward her father and mother for their kindness and their unselfish ambitions for their children. Jinny never tired of hearing of the difficult childhood of her parents. She knew of no story quite so thrilling as the account of their early trials and difficulties. She thought it wonderfully sweet of them to plan, as they constantly did, better things for their daughters. "My girls shall never come through my experiences," Mattie would say firmly. They were both to be school-teachers and independent.

33

It is true that neither of them felt any special leaning toward this calling. Angela frankly despised it, but she supposed she must make her living some way. The salary was fairly good—in fact, very good for a poor girl—and there would be the long summer vacation. At fourteen she knew already how much money she would save during those first two or three years and how she would spend those summer vacations. But although she proffered this much information to her family she kept her plans to herself. Mattie often pondered on this lack of openness in her older daughter. Virginia was absolutely transparent. She did not think she would care for teaching either, that is, not for teaching in the ordinary sense. But she realized that for the present that was the best profession which her parents could have chosen for them. She would spend her summers learning all she could about methods of teaching music.

"And a lot of good it will do you," Angela scoffed. "You know perfectly well that there are no coloured teachers of music in the public schools here in Philadelphia." But Jinny thought it possible that there might be. "When Mamma was coming along there were very few coloured teachers at all, and now it looks as though there'd be plenty of chance for us. And anyway you never know your luck."

By four o'clock the day's work was over and Mattie free to do as she pleased. This was her idle hour. The girls would get dinner, a Monday version of whatever the main course had been the day before. Their mother was on no account to be disturbed or importuned. To-day as usual she sat in the Morris chair in the dining-room, dividing her time between the Sunday paper and the girls' chatter. It was one of her most cherished experiences,—this sense of a day's hard labour far behind her, the happy voices of her girls, her joyous expectation of her husband's home-coming. Usually the children made a game of their preparations, recalling some nonsense of their early childhood days when it had been their delight to dress up as ladies. Virginia would approach Angela: "Pardon me, is this Mrs. Henrietta Jones?" And Angela, drawing herself up haughtily would reply: "Er,—really you have the advantage of me." Then Virginia: "Oh pardon! I thought you were Mrs. Jones and I had heard my friend Mrs. Smith speak of you so often and since you were in the neighbourhood and passing, I was going to ask you in to have some ice-cream." The game of course being that Angela should immediately drop her haughtiness and proceed for the sake of the goodies to ingratiate herself into her neighbour's esteem. It was a poor joke, long since worn thin, but the two girls still used the greeting and for some reason it had became part of the Monday ritual of preparing the supper.

But to-night Angela's response lacked spontaneity. She was absorbed and reserved, even a little sulky. Deftly and swiftly she moved about her work, however, and no one who had not attended regularly on those Monday evening preparations could have guessed that there was anything on her mind other than complete absorption in the problem of cutting the bread or garnishing the warmed over roast beef. But Mattie was aware of the quality of brooding in her intense

35

concentration. She had seen it before in her daughter but to-night, though to her practised eye it was more apparent than ever, she could not put her hand on it. Angela's response, if asked what was the matter, would be "Oh, nothing." It came to her suddenly that her older daughter was growing up; in a couple of months she would be fifteen. Children were often absorbed and moody when they were in their teens, too engaged in finding themselves to care about their effect on others. She must see to it that the girl had plenty of rest; perhaps school had been too strenuous for her to-day; she thought the high school programme very badly arranged, five hours one right after the other were much too long. "Angela, child, I think you'd better not be long out of bed to-night; you look very tired to me."

Angela nodded. But her father came in then and in the little hubbub that arose about his homecoming and the final preparations for supper her listlessness went without further remark.

CHAPTER IV

THE third storey front was Angela's bedroom. She was glad of its loneliness and security to-night,—even if her mother had not suggested her going to bed early she would have sought its shelter immediately after supper. Study for its own sake held no attractions for her; she did not care for any of her subjects really except Drawing and French. And when she was drawing she did not consider that she was studying, it was too naturally a means of self-expression. As for French, she did have to study that with great care, for languages did not come to her with any great readiness, but there was an element of fine lady-ism about the beautiful, logical tongue that made her in accordance with some secret subconscious ambition resolve to make it her own.

The other subjects, History, English, and Physical Geography, were not drudgery, for she had a fair enough mind; but then they were not attractive either, and she was lacking in Virginia's dogged resignation to unwelcome duties. Even when Jinny was a little girl she had been known to say manfully in the face of an uncongenial task: "Well I dotta det it done." Angela was not like that. But to-night she was concentrating with all her power on her work. During the day she had been badly hurt; she had received a wound whose

37

depth and violence she would not reveal even to her parents,—because, and this only increased the pain, young as she was she knew that there was nothing they could do about it. There was nothing to be done but to get over it. Only she was not developed enough to state this stoicism to herself. She was like a little pet cat that had once formed part of their household; its leg had been badly torn by a passing dog and the poor thing had dragged itself into the house and lain on its cushion patiently, waiting stolidly for this unfamiliar agony to subside. So Angela waited for the hurt in her mind to cease.

But across the history dates on the printed page and through the stately lines of Lycidas she kept seeing Mary Hastings' accusing face, hearing Mary Hastings' accusing voice:

"Coloured! Angela, you never told me that you were coloured!"

And then her own voice in tragic but proud bewilderment. "Tell you that I was coloured! Why of course I never told you that I was coloured. Why should I?"

.   .   .   .   .

She had been so proud of Mary Hastings' friendship. In the dark and tortured spaces of her difficult life it had been a lovely, hidden refuge. It had been an experience so rarely sweet that she had hardly spoken of it even to Virginia. The other girls in her classes had meant nothing to her. At least she had schooled herself to have them mean nothing. Some of them she had known since early childhood; they had lived in her neighbourhood and had gone to the graded schools with her. They had known that she was coloured, for they had seen her with Virginia, and sometimes her tall, black father had come to fetch her home on a rainy day. There had been pleasant enough contacts and intimacies; in the quiet of Jefferson Street they had played "The Farmer in the Dell," and "Here come three jolly, jolly sailor-boys;" dark retreats of the old market had afforded endless satisfaction for "Hide and Go Seek." She and those other children had gone shopping arm in arm for school supplies, threading their way in and out of the bustle and confusion that were Columbia Avenue.

As she grew older many of these intimacies lessened, in some cases ceased altogether. But she was never conscious of being left completely alone; there was always some one with whom to eat lunch or who was going her way after school. It was not until she reached the high school that she began to realize how solitary her life was becoming. There were no other coloured girls in her class but there had been only two or three during her school-life, and if there had been any she would not necessarily have confined herself to them; that this might be a good thing to do in sheer self-defence would hardly have occurred to her. But this problem did not confront her; what did confront her was that the very girls with whom she had grown up were evading her; when she went to the Assembly none of them sat next to her unless no other seat were vacant; little groups toward which she drifted during lunch, inexplicably dissolved to re-form in another portion of the room. Sometimes a girl in this new group

39

threw her a backward glance charged either with a mean amusement or with annoyance.

Angela was proud; she did not need such a hint more than once, but she was bewildered and hurt. She took stories to school to read at recess, or wandered into the drawing laboratory and touched up her designs. Miss Barrington thought her an unusually industrious student.

And then in the middle of the term Mary Hastings had come, a slender, well-bred girl of fifteen. She was rather stupid in her work, in fact she shone in nothing but French and good manners. Undeniably she had an air, and her accent was remarkable. The other pupils, giggling, produced certain uncouth and unheard of sounds, but Mary said in French: "No, I have lent my knife to the brother-in-law of the gardener but here is my cane," quite as though the idiotic phrase were part of an imaginary conversation which she was conducting and appreciating. "She really knows what she's talking about," little Esther Bayliss commented, and added that Mary's family had lost some money and they had had to send her to public school. But it was some time before this knowledge, dispensed by Esther with mysterious yet absolute authenticity, became generally known. Meanwhile Mary was left to her own devices while the class with complete but tacit unanimity "tried her out." Mary, unaware of this, looked with her near-sighted, slightly supercilious gaze about the room at recess and seeing only one girl, and that girl Angela, who approached in dress, manner and deportment her own rather set ideas, had taken her lunch over to the other pupil's desk

and said: "Come on, let's eat together while you
tell me who everybody is."

Angela took the invitation as simply as the
other had offered. "That little girl in the pur-
plish dress is Esther Bayliss and the tall one in
the thick glasses——"

Mary, sitting with her back to the feeding
groups, never troubled to look around. "I don't
mean the girls. I expect I'll know them soon
enough when I get around to it. I mean the teachers. Do you have to dig for them?" She liked
Angela and she showed it plainly and directly.
Her home was in some remote fastness of West
Philadelphia which she could reach with comparative swiftness by taking the car at Spring Garden
Street. Instead she walked half way home with
her new friend, up Seventeenth Street as far as
Girard Avenue where, after a final exchange of
school matters and farewells, she took the car,
leaving Angela to her happy, satisfied thoughts.
And presently she began to know more than happiness and satisfaction, she was knowing the extreme gratification of being the chosen companion
ion of a popular and important girl, for Mary,
although not quick at her studies, was a power in
everything else. She dressed well, she had plenty
of pocket money, she could play the latest marches
in the gymnasium, she received a certain indefinable but flattering attention from the teachers,
and she could make things "go." The school
paper was moribund and Mary knew how to re-
suscitate it; she brought in advertisements from
her father's business; she made her married sisters obtain subscriptions. Without being obtru-

sive or over-bearing, without condescension and without toadying she was the leader of her class. And with it all she stuck to Angela. She accepted popularity because it was thrust upon her, but she was friendly with Angela because the latter suited her.

Angela was happy. She had a friend and the friendship brought her unexpected advantages. She was no longer left out of groups because there could be no class plans without Mary and Mary would remain nowhere for any length of time without Angela. So to save time and argument, and also to avoid offending the regent, Angela was always included. Not that she cared much about this, but she did like Mary; as is the way of a "fidus Achates," she gave her friendship whole-heartedly. And it was gratifying to be in the midst of things.

· · · · ·

In April the school magazine announced a new departure. Henceforth the editorial staff was to be composed of two representatives from each class; of these one was to be the chief representative chosen by vote of the class, the other was to be assistant, selected by the chief. The chief representative, said the announcement pompously, would sit in at executive meetings and have a voice in the policy of the paper. The assistant would solicit and collect subscriptions, collect fees, receive and report complaints and in brief, said Esther Bayliss, "do all the dirty work." But she coveted the position and title for all that.

Angela's class held a brief meeting after school

and elected Mary Hastings as representative without a dissenting vote. "No," said Angela holding up a last rather grimy bit of paper. "Here is one for Esther Bayliss." Two or three of the girls giggled; everyone knew that she must have voted for herself; indeed it had been she who had insisted on taking a ballot rather than a vote by acclaim. Mary was already on her feet. She had been sure of the result of the election, would have been astonished indeed had it turned out any other way. "Well, girls," she began in her rather high, refined voice, "I wish to thank you for the—er—confidence you have bestowed, that is, placed in me and I'm sure you all know I'll do my best to keep the old paper going. And while I'm about it I might just as well announce that I'm choosing Angela Murray for my assistant."

There was a moment's silence. The girls who had thought about it at all had known that if Mary were elected, as assuredly she would be, this meant also the election of Angela. And those who had taken no thought saw no reason to object to her appointment. And anyway there was nothing to be done. But Esther Bayliss pushed forward: "I don't know how it is with the rest of you, but I should have to think twice before I'd trust my subscription money to a coloured girl."

Mary said in utter astonishment: "Coloured, why what are you talking about? Who's coloured?"

"Angela, Angela Murray, that's who's coloured. At least she used to be when we all went to school at Eighteenth and Oxford."

Mary said again: "Coloured!" And then, "Angela, you never told me you were coloured!"

Angela's voice was as amazed as her own: "Tell
you that I was coloured! Why of course I never
told you that I was coloured! Why should I?"

"There," said Esther, "see she never told Mary
that she was coloured. What wouldn't she have
done with our money!"

.   .   .   .   .

Angela had picked up her books and strolled
out the door. But she flew down the north staircase and out the Brandywine Street entrance and
so to Sixteenth Street where she would meet no
one she knew, especially at this belated hour. At
home there would be work to do, her lessons to
get and the long, long hours of the night must
pass before she would have to face again the hurt
and humiliation of the classroom; before she
would have to steel her heart and her nerves to
drop Mary Hastings before Mary Hastings could
drop her. No one, no one, Mary least of all,
should guess how completely she had been wounded. Mary and her shrinking bewilderment! Mary
and her exclamation: "Coloured!" This was a
curious business, this colour. It was the one god
apparently to whom you could sacrifice everything. On account of it her mother had neglected
to greet her own husband on the street. Mary
Hastings could let it come between her and her
friend.

In the morning she was at school early; the
girls should all see her there and their individual
attitude should be her attitude. She would remember each one's greetings, would store it away for
future guidance. Some of the girls were especially

44

careful to speak to her, one or two gave her a
meaning smile, or so she took it, and turned away.
Some did not speak at all. When Mary Hastings
came in Angela rose and sauntered unseeing and
unheeding deliberately past her through the doorway, across the hall to Miss Barrington's laboratory. As she returned she passed Mary's desk,
and the girl lifted troubled but not unfriendly eyes
to meet her own; Angela met the glance fully but
without recognition. She thought to herself:
"Coloured! If they had said to me Mary Hastings is a voodoo, I'd have answered, 'What of it?
She's my friend.' "

.   .   .   .   .

Before June Mary Hastings came up to her and
asked her to wait after school. Angela who had
been neither avoiding nor seeking her gave a cool
nod. They walked out of the French classroom
together. When they reached the corner Mary
spoke:
"Oh, Angela, let's be friends again. It doesn't
really make any difference. See, I don't care any
more."
"But that's what I don't understand. Why
should it have made any difference in the first
place? I'm just the same as I was before you
knew I was coloured and just the same afterwards.
Why should it ever have made any difference at
all?"
"I don't know, I'm sure. I was just surprised.
It was all so unexpected."
"What was unexpected?"
"Oh, I don't know. I can't explain it. But
let's be friends."

45

"Well," said Angela slowly, "I'm willing, but I don't think it will ever be the same again."

It wasn't. Some element, spontaneity, trustfulness was lacking. Mary, who had never thought of speaking of colour, was suddenly conscious that here was a subject which she must not discuss. She was less frank, at times even restrained. Angela, too young to define her thoughts, yet felt vaguely: "She failed me once,—I was her friend, —yet she failed me for something with which I had nothing to do. She's just as likely to do it again. It's in her."

Definitely she said to herself, "Mary withdrew herself not because I was coloured but because she didn't know I was coloured. Therefore if she had never known I was coloured she would always have been my friend. We would have kept on having our good times together." And she began to wonder which was the more important, a patent insistence on the fact of colour or an acceptance of the good things of life which could come to you in America if either you were not coloured or the fact of your racial connections was not made known.

During the summer Mary Hastings' family, it appeared, recovered their fallen fortunes. At any rate she did not return to school in the fall and Angela never saw her again.

CHAPTER V

VIRGINIA came rushing in. "Angela, where's Mummy?"

"Out. What's all the excitement?"

"I've been appointed. Isn't it great? Won't Mother and Dad be delighted! Right at the beginning of the year too, so I won't have to wait. The official notice isn't out yet but I know it's all right. Miss Herren wants me to report to-morrow. Isn't it perfectly marvellous! Here I graduate from the Normal in June and in the second week of school in September I've got my perfectly good job. Darling child, it's very much better, as you may have heard me observe before, to be born lucky than rich. But I am lucky and I'll be rich too. Think of that salary for my very own! With both of us working, Mummy won't have to want for a thing, nor Father either. Mummy won't have to do a lick of work if she doesn't want to. Well, what have you got to say about it, old Rain-in-the-Face? Or perhaps this isn't Mrs. Henrietta Jones whom I'm addressing of?"

Angela giggled, then raised an imaginary lorg-nette. "Er,—really I think you have the advantage of me. Well, I was thinking how fortunate you were to get your appointment right off the bat and how you'll hate it now that you have got it."

She herself, appointed two years previously,

47

had had no such luck. Strictly speaking there are
no coloured schools as such in Philadelphia. Yet,
by an unwritten law, although coloured children
may be taught by white teachers, white children
must never receive knowledge at the hands of coloured instructors. As the number of coloured
Normal School graduates is steadily increasing,
the city gets around this difficulty by manning a
school in a district thickly populated by Negroes,
with a coloured principal and a coloured teaching
force. Coloured children living in that district
must thereupon attend that school. But no attention is paid to the white children who leave this
same district for the next nearest white or
"mixed" school.

Angela had been sixth on the list of coloured
graduates. Five had been appointed, but there
was no vacancy for her, and for several months
she was idle with here and there a day, perhaps a
week of substituting. She could not be appointed
in any but a coloured school, and she was not supposed to substitute in any but this kind of class-
room. Then her father discovered that a young
white woman was teaching in a coloured school.
He made some searching inquiries and was met
with the complacent rejoinder that as soon as a
vacancy occurred in a white school, Miss Mc-
Sweeney would be transferred there and his
daughter could have her place.

Just as she had anticipated, Angela did not want
the job after she received it. She had expected
to loathe teaching little children and her expectation, it turned out, was perfectly well grounded.
Perhaps she might like to teach drawing to grown-
ups; she would certainly like to have a try at it.

48

Meanwhile it was nice to be independent, to be holding a lady-like, respectable position so different from her mother's early days, to be able to have pretty clothes and to help with the house, in brief to be drawing an appreciably adequate and steady salary. For one thing it made it possible for her to take up work at the Philadelphia Academy of Fine Arts at Broad and Cherry.

·   ·   ·   ·   ·

Jinny was in excellent spirits at dinner. "Now, Mummy darling, you really shall walk in silk attire and siller hae to spare." Angela's appointment had done away with the drudgery of wash-day. "We'll get Hettie Daniels to come in Saturdays and clean up. I won't have to scrub the front steps any more and everything will be feasting and fun." Pushing aside her plate she rushed over to her father, climbed on his knee and flung her lovely bronze arms around his neck. She still adored him, still thought him the finest man in the world; she still wanted her husband to be just exactly like him; he would not be so tall nor would he be quite as dark. Matthew Henson was of only medium height and was a sort of reddish yellow and he distinctly was not as handsome as her father. Indeed Virginia thought, with a pang of shame at her disloyalty, that it would have been a fine thing if he could exchange his lighter skin for her father's colour if in so doing it he might have gained her father's thick, coarsely grained but beautifully curling, open black hair. Matthew had inherited his father's thick, tight, "bad" hair. Only, thank heaven, it was darker.

49

Junius tucked his slender daughter back in the hollow of his arm.

"Well, baby, you want something off my plate?" As a child Virginia had been a notorious beggar.

"Darling! I was thinking that now you could buy Mr. Hallowell's car. He's got his eye on a Cadillac, Kate says, and he'd be willing to let Henry Ford go for a song."

Junius was pleased, but he thought he ought to protest. "Do I look as old as all that? I might be able to buy the actual car, now that my girls are getting so monied, but the upkeep, I understand, is pretty steep."

"Oh, nonsense," said Mattie. "Go on and get it, June. Think how nice it will be riding out North Broad Street in the evenings."

And Angela added kindly: "I think you owe it to yourself to get it, Dad. Jinny and I'll carry the house till you get it paid for."

"Well, there's no reason of course why I——" he corrected himself, "why we shouldn't have a car if we want it." He saw himself spending happy moments digging in the little car's inmost mysteries. He would buy new parts, change the engine perhaps, paint it and overhaul her generally. And he might just as well indulge himself. The little house was long since paid for; he was well insured, and his two daughters were grown up and taking care of themselves. He slid Jinny off his knee.

"I believe I'll run over to the Hallowells now and see what Tom'll take for that car. Catch him before he goes down town in it."

Virginia called after him. "Just think! May-

be this time next week you'll be going down town
in it."

. . . . . .

She was very happy. Life was turning out just
right. She was young, she was twenty, she was
about to earn her own living,—"to be about to
live"—she said, happily quoting a Latin construction which had always intrigued her. Her
mother would never have to work again; her father would have a Henry Ford; she herself would
get a new, good music teacher and would also
take up the study of methods at the University of
Pennsylvania.

Angela could hear her downstairs talking to
Matthew Henson whose ring she had just answered. "Only think, Matt, I've been appointed."

"Great!" said Matthew. "Is Angela in? Do
you think she'd like to go to the movies with me
to-night? She was too tired last time. Run up
and ask her, there's a good girl."

Angela sighed. She didn't want to go out with
Matthew; he wearied her so. And besides people
always looked at her so strangely. She wished
he would take it into his head to come and see
Jinny.

. . . . . .

Sunday was still a happy day. Already an air
of prosperity, of having arrived beyond the striving point, had settled over the family. Mr. Murray's negotiations with Tom Hallowell had been
most successful. The Ford, a little four-seater
coupé, compact and sturdy, had changed hands.

Its former owner came around on Sunday to give Junius a lesson. The entire household piled in, for both girls were possessed of the modern slenderness. They rode out Jefferson Street and far, far out Ridge Avenue to the Wissahickon and on to Chestnut Hill. From time to time, when the traffic was thin, Junius took the wheel, anticipating Tom's instructions with the readiness of the born mechanic. They came back laughing and happy and pardonably proud. The dense, tender glow of the late afternoon September sun flooded the little parlour, the dining-room was dusky and the kitchen was redolent of scents of ginger bread and spiced preserves. After supper there were no lessons to get. "It'll be years before I forget all that stuff I learned in practice school," said Jinny gaily.

Later on some boys came in; Matthew Henson inevitably, peering dissatisfied through the autumn gloom for Angela and immediately content when he saw her; Arthur Sawyer, who had just entered the School of Pedagogy and was a little ashamed of it, for he considered teaching work fit only for women. "But I've got to make a living somehow, ain't I? And I won't go into that post-office!"

"What's the matter with the post-office?" Henson asked indignantly. He had just been appointed. In reality he did not fancy the work himself, but he did not want it decried before Angela.

"Tell me what better or surer job is there for a coloured man in Philadelphia?"

"Nothing," said Sawyer promptly, "not a thing in the world except school teaching. But that's just what I object to. I'm sick of planning my

52

life with regard to being coloured. I'm not a bit ashamed of my race. I don't mind in the least that once we were slaves. Every race in the world has at some time occupied a servile position. But I do mind having to take it into consideration every time I want to eat outside of my home, every time I enter a theatre, every time I think of a profession.

"But you do have to take it into consideration," said Jinny softly. "At present it's one of the facts of our living, just as lameness or near-sightedness might be for a white man."

The inevitable race discussion was on.

"Ah, but there you're all off, Miss Virginia." A tall, lanky, rather supercilious youth spoke up from the corner. He had been known to them all their lives as Franky Porter, but he had taken lately to publishing poems in the Philadelphia *Tribunal* which he signed F. Seymour Porter. "Really you're all off, for you speak as though colour itself were a deformity. Whereas, as Miss Angela being an artist knows, colour may really be a very beautiful thing, mayn't it?"

"Oh don't drag me into your old discussion," Angela answered crossly. "I'm sick of this whole race business if you ask me. And don't call me Miss Angela. Call me Angela as you've all done all our lives or else call me Miss Murray. No, I don't think being coloured in America is a beautiful thing. I think it's nothing short of a curse."

"Well," said Porter slowly, "I think its being or not being a curse rests with you. You've got to decide whether or not you're going to let it interfere with personal development and to that extent it may be harmful or it may be an incentive.

53

I take it that Sawyer here, who even when we were all kids always wanted to be an engineer, will transmute his colour either into a bane or a blessing according to whether he lets it make him hide his natural tendencies under the bushel of school-teaching or become an inspiration toward making him the very best kind of engineer that there ever was so that people will just have to take him for what he is and overlook the fact of colour."

"That's it," said Jinny. "You know, being coloured often does spur you on."

"And that's what I object to," Angela answered perversely. "I'm sick of this business of always being below or above a certain norm. Doesn't anyone think that we have a right to be happy simply, naturally?"

·   ·   ·   ·   ·

Gradually they drifted into music. Virginia played a few popular songs and presently the old beautiful airs of all time, "Drink to me only with thine eyes" and "Sweet and Low." Arthur Sawyer had a soft, melting tenor and Angela a rather good alto; Virginia and the other boys carried the air while Junius boomed his deep, unyielding bass. The lovely melodies and the peace of the happy, tranquil household crept over them, and presently they exchanged farewells and the young men passed wearied and contented out into the dark confines of Opal Street. Angela and Mattie went upstairs, but Virginia and her father stayed below and sang very softly so as not to disturb the sleeping street; a few hymns and finally the majestic strains of "The Dying Christian" floated up. Mrs. Murray had complained of feeling tired. "I think I'll just lie a moment on your bed, Angela, until your father comes up." But her daughter noticed that she had not relaxed, instead she was straining forward a little and Angela realized that she was trying to catch every note of her husband's virile, hearty voice.

She said, "You heard what we were all talking about before the boys left. You and father don't ever bother to discuss such matters, do you?"

Her mother seemed to strain past the sound of her voice. "Not any more; oh, of course we used to talk about such things, but you get so taken up with the problem of living, just life itself you know, that by and by being coloured or not is just one thing more or less that you have to contend with. But of course there have been times when colour was the starting point of our discussions. I remember how when you and Jinny were little things and she was always running to the piano and you were scribbling all over the walls, —many's the time I've slapped your little fingers for that, Angela,—we used to spend half the night talking about you, your father and I. I wanted you to be great artists but Junius said: 'No, we'll give them a good, plain education and set them in the way of earning a sure and honest living; then if they've got it in them to travel over all the rocks that'll be in their way as coloured girls, they'll manage, never you fear.' And he was right." The music downstairs ceased and she lay back, relaxed and drowsy. "Your father's always right."

Much of this was news to Angela, and she

would have liked to learn more about those early nocturnal discussions. But she only said, smiling, "You're still crazy about father, aren't you, dar- ling?"

Her mother was wide awake in an instant. "Crazy! I'd give my life for him!"

·   ·   ·   ·   ·

The Saturday excursions were long since a thing of the past; Henry Ford had changed that. Also the extra work which the girls had taken upon themselves in addition to their teaching,— Angela at the Academy, Virginia at the Universi- ty,—made Saturday afternoon a too sorely needed period of relaxation to be spent in the old familiar fashion. Still there were times when Angela in search of a new frock or intent on the exploration of a picture gallery asked her mother to accompany her. And at such times the two indulged in their former custom of having tea and a comfortable hour's chat in the luxurious com- fort of some exclusive tea-room or hotel. Mattie, older and not quite so lightly stepping in these days of comparative ease as in those other times when a week's arduous duties lay behind her, still responded joyously to the call of fashion and grooming, the air of "good living" which per- vaded these places. Moreover she herself was able to contribute to this atmosphere. Her daughters insisted on presenting her with the graceful and dainty clothes which she loved, and they were equally insistent on her wearing them. "No use hanging them in a closet," said Jinny blithely. All her prophecies had come true—her mother had the services of a maid whenever she needed them, she went clad for the most part "in silk attire," and she had "siller to spare" and to spend.

She was down town spending it now. The Ladies' Auxiliary of her church was to give a reception after Lent, and Mattie meant to hold her own with the best of them. "We're getting to be old ladies," she said a bit wistfully, "but we'll make you young ones look at us once or twice just the same." Angela replied that she was sure of that. "And I know one or two little secrets for the complexion that will make it impossible for you to call yourself old."

But those her mother knew already. However she expressed a willingness to accept Angela's offer. She loved to be fussed over, and of late Angela had shown a tendency to rival even Jinny in this particular. The older girl was beginning to lose some of her restlessness. Life was pretty hum-drum, but it was comfortable and pleasant; her family life was ideal and her time at the art school delightful. The instructor was interested in her progress, and one or two of the girls had shown a desire for real intimacy. These intimations she had not followed up very closely, but she was seeing enough of a larger, freer world to make her chafe less at the restrictions which somehow seemed to bind in her own group. As a result of even this slight satisfaction of her cravings, she was indulging less and less in brooding and introspection, although at no time was she able to adapt herself to living with the complete spontaneity so characteristic of Jinny.

But she was young, and life would somehow twist and shape itself to her subconscious yearnings, just as it had done for her mother, she thought, following Mattie in and out of shops, delivering opinions and lending herself to all the exigencies which shopping imposed. It was not an occupation which she particularly enjoyed, but, like her mother, she adored the atmosphere and its accompaniment of well-dressed and luxuriously stationed women. No one could tell, no one would have thought for a moment that she and her mother had come from tiny Opal Street; no one could have dreamed of their racial connections. "And if Jinny were here," she thought, slowly selecting another cake, "she really would be just as capable of fitting into all this as mother and I; but they wouldn't let her light." And again she let herself dwell on the fallaciousness of a social system which stretched appearance so far beyond being.

From the tea-room they emerged into the damp greyness of the March afternoon. The streets were slushy and slimy; the sky above sodden and dull. Mattie shivered and thought of the Morris chair in the minute but cosy dining-room of her home. She wanted to go to the "Y" on Catherine Street and there were two calls to make far down Fifteenth. But at last all this was accomplished. "Now we'll get the next car and before you know it you'll be home."

"You look tired, Mother," said Angela.

"I am tired," she acknowledged, and, suddenly sagging against her daughter, lost consciousness. About them a small crowd formed, and a man passing in an automobile kindly drove the two women to a hospital in Broad Street two blocks away. It was a hospital to which no coloured woman would ever have been admitted except to

char, but there was no such question to be raised
in the case of this patient. "She'll be all right
presently," the interne announced, "just a little
fainting spell brought on by over-exertion. Was
that your car you came in? It would be nice if
you could have one to get her home in."

"Oh, but I can," and in a moment Angela had
rushed to the telephone forgetting everything
except that her father was in his shop to-day and
therefore almost within reach and so was the car.

Not long after he came striding into the hospital, tall and black and rather shabby in his working clothes. He was greeted by the clerk with a
rather hostile, "Yes, and what do you want?"

Angela, hastening across the lobby to him,
halted at the intonation.

Junius was equal to the moment's demands.
"I'm Mrs. Murray's chauffeur," he announced,
hating the deception, but he would not have his
wife bundled out too soon. "Is she very badly
off, Miss Angela?"

His daughter hastened to reassure him. "No,
she'll be down in a few minutes now."

"And meanwhile you can wait outside," said
the attendant icily. She did not believe that black
people were exactly human; there was no place
for them in the scheme of life so far as she could
see.

Junius withdrew, and in a half hour's time the
young interne and the nurse came out supporting
his wan wife. He sprang to the pavement: "Lean
on me, Mrs. Murray."

But sobbing, she threw her arms about his
neck. "Oh Junius, Junius!"

He lifted her then, drew back for Angela and

mounting himself, drove away. The interne stepped back into the hospital raging about these damn white women and their nigger servants. Such women ought to be placed in a psycho-pathic ward and the niggers burned.

．　　　．　　　．　　　．　　　．

The girls got Mrs. Murray into the Morris chair and ran upstairs for pillows and wraps. When they returned Junius was in the chair and Mrs. Murray in his arms. "Oh, June, dear June, such a service of love."

"Do you suppose she's going to die?" whispered Jinny, stricken. What, she wondered, would become of her father.

But in a few days Mattie was fully recovered and more happy than ever in the reflorescence of love and tenderness which had sprung up between herself and Junius. Only Junius was not so well. He had had a slight touch of grippe during the winter and the half hour's loitering in the treacherous March weather, before the hospital, had not served to improve it. He was hoarse and feverish, though this he did not immediately admit. But a tearing pain in his chest compelled him one morning to suggest the doctor. In a panic Mattie sent for him. Junius really ill! She had never seen him in anything but the pink of condition. The doctor reluctantly admitted pneumonia—"a severe case but I think we can pull him through."

He suffered terribly—Mattie suffered with him, never leaving his bedside. On the fifth day he was delirious. His wife thought, "Surely God

60

isn't going to let him die without speaking to me again."

Toward evening he opened his eyes and saw her tender, stricken face. He smiled. "Dear Mattie," and then, "Jinny, I'd like to hear some music, 'Vital spark'——"

So his daughter went down to the little parlour and played and sang "The Dying Christian."

Angela thought, "Oh, isn't this terrible! Oh how can she?" Presently she called softly, "Jinny, Jinny come up."

Junius' hand was groping for Mattie's. She placed it in his. "Dear Mattie," he said, "Heaven opens on my eyes,——"

.　　.　　.　　.　　.　　.

The house was still with the awful stillness that follows a funeral. All the bustle and hurry were over; the end, the fulfilment toward which the family had been striving for the last three days was accomplished. The baked funeral meats had been removed; Virginia had seen to that. Angela was up in her room, staring dry-eyed before her; she loved her father, but not even for him could she endure this aching, formless pain of bereavement. She kept saying to herself fiercely: "I must get over this, I can't stand this. I'll go away."

Mrs. Murray sat in the old Morris chair in the dining-room. She stroked its arms with her plump, worn fingers; she laid her face again and again on its shabby back. One knew that she was remembering a dark, loved cheek. Jinny said, "Come upstairs and let me put you to bed, darling.

You're going to sleep with me, you know. You're going to comfort your little girl, aren't you, Mummy?" Then as there was no response, "Darling, you'll make yourself ill."

Her mother sat up suddenly. "Yes, that's what I want to do. Oh, Jinny, do you think I can make myself ill enough to follow him soon? My daughter, try to forgive me, but I must go to him. I can't live without him. I don't deserve a daughter like you, but,—don't let them hold me back. I want to die, I must die. Say you forgive me,——"

"Darling," and it was as though her husband rather than her daughter spoke, "whatever you want is what I want." By a supreme effort she held back her tears, but it was years before she forgot the picture of her mother sitting back in the old Morris chair, composing herself for death.

CHAPTER VI

AT the Academy matters progressed smoothly without the flawing of a ripple. Angela looked forward to the hours which she spent there and honestly regretted their passage. Her fellow students and the instructors were more than cordial, there was an actual sense of camaraderie among them. She had not mentioned the fact of her Negro strain, indeed she had no occasion to, but she did not believe that this fact if known would cause any change in attitude. Artists were noted for their broad-mindedness. They were the first persons in the world to judge a person for his worth rather than by any hall-mark. It is true that Miss Henderson, a young lady of undeniable colour, was not received with the same cordiality and attention which Angela was receiving, and this, too, despite the fact that the former's work showed undeniable talent, even originality. Angela thought that something in the young lady's personality precluded an approach to friendship; she seemed to be wary, almost offensively stand-offish. Certainly she never spoke unless spoken to; she had been known to spend a whole session without even glancing at a fellow student.

Angela herself had not arrived at any genuine intimacies. Two of the girls had asked her to their

homes but she had always refused; such invitations
would have to be returned with similar ones and
the presence of Jinny would entail explanations.
The invitation of Mr. Shields, the instructor, to
have tea at his wife's at home was another matter
and of this she gladly availed herself. She could
not tell to just what end she was striving. She did
not like teaching and longed to give it up. On the
other hand she must make her living. Mr. Shields
had suggested that she might be able to increase
both her earning capacity and her enjoyments
through a more practical application of her art.
There were directorships of drawing in the public
schools, positions in art schools and colleges, or,
since Angela frankly acknowledged her unwillingness to instruct, there was such a thing as
being buyer for the art section of a department
store.

"And anyway," said Mrs. Shields, "you never
know what may be in store for you if you just
have preparation." She and her husband were
both attracted to the pleasant-spoken, talented
girl. Angela possessed an undeniable air, and she
dressed well, even superlatively. Her parents'
death had meant the possession of half the house
and half of three thousand dollars' worth of insurance. Her salary was adequate, her expenses
light. Indeed even her present mode of living
gave her little cause for complaint except that her
racial affiliations narrowed her confines. But she
was restlessly conscious of a desire for broader
horizons. She confided something like this to her
new friends.

"Perfectly natural," they agreed. "There's no
telling where your tastes and talents will lead you,

64

—to Europe perhaps and surely to the formation
of new and interesting friendships. You'll find
artistic folk the broadest, most liberal people in
the world."

"There are possibilities of scholarships, too,"
Mr. Shields concluded more practically. The
Academy offered a few in competition. But there
were others more liberally endowed and practically without restriction.

. . . . .

Sundays on Opal Street bore still their aspect of
something different and special. Jinny sometimes
went to church, sometimes packed the car with a
group of laughing girls of her age and played
at her father's old game of exploring. Angela
preferred to stay in the house. She liked to
sleep late, get up for a leisurely bath and a
meticulous toilet. Afterwards she would turn
over her wardrobe, sorting and discarding;
read the week's forecast of theatres, concerts
and exhibits. And finally she would begin
sketching, usually ending up with a new view
of Hetty Daniels' head.

Hetty, who lived with them now in the triple
capacity, as she saw it, of housekeeper, companion,
and chaperone, loved to pose. It satisfied some
unquenchable vanity in her unloved, empty existence. She could not conceive of being sketched
because she was, in the artist's jargon, "interesting," "paintable," or "difficult." Models, as
she understood it, were chosen for their beauty.
Square and upright she sat, regaling Angela with
tales of the romantic adventures of some remote

period which was her youth. She could not be very old, the young girl thought; indeed, from some of her dates she must have been at least twelve years younger than her mother. Yet Mrs. Murray had carried with her to the end some irrefragable quality of girlishness which would keep her memory forever young.

Miss Daniels' great fetish was sex morality. "Then young fellers was always 'round me thick ez bees; wasn't any night they wasn't more fellows in my kitchen then you an' Jinny ever has in yore parlour. But I never listened to none of the' talk, jist held out agin 'em and kept my pearl of great price untarnished. I aimed then and I'm continual to aim to be a verjous woman."

Her unslaked yearnings gleamed suddenly out of her eyes, transforming her usually rather expressionless face into something wild and avid. The dark brown immobile mask of her skin made an excellent foil for the vividness of an emotion which was so apparent, so palpable that it seemed like something superimposed upon the background of her countenance.

"If I could just get that look for Mr. Shields," Angela said half aloud to herself, "I bet I could get any of their old scholarships. . . . So you had lots more beaux than we have, Hetty? Well you wouldn't have to go far to outdo us there."

The same half dozen young men still visited the Murray household on Sundays. None of them except Matthew Henson came as a suitor; the others looked in partly from habit, partly, Jinny used to say, for the sake of Hetty Daniels' good

66

ginger bread, but more than for any other reason
for the sake of having a comfortable place in
which to argue and someone with whom to conduct the argument.

"They certainly do argue;" Angela grumbled a
little, but she didn't care. Matthew was usually
the leader in their illimitable discussions, but she
much preferred him at this than at his clumsy
and distasteful love-making. Of course she could
go out, but there was no place for her to visit and
no companions for her to visit with. If she made
calls there would be merely a replica of what she
was finding in her own household. It was true
that in the ultra-modern set Sunday dancing was
being taken up. But she and Virginia did not
fit in here any too well. Her fancy envisaged a
comfortable drawing-room (there *were* folks who
used that term), peopled with distinguished men
and women who did things, wrote and painted and
acted,—people with a broad, cultural background
behind them, or, lacking that, with the originality
of thought and speech which comes from failing,
deliberately failing, to conform to the pattern.
Somewhere, she supposed, there must be coloured
people like that. But she didn't know any of them.
She knew there were people in Philadelphia
who had left far, far behind them the economic
class to which her father and mother belonged. But their thoughts, their actions were
still cramped and confined; they were sitting in
their new, even luxurious quarters, still mental
parvenus, still discussing the eternal race question
even as these boys here.

To-night they were hard at it again with a new
phase which Angela, who usually sat only half

attentive in their midst, did not remember ever having heard touched before. Seymour Porter had started the ball by forcing their attention to one of his poems. It was not a bad poem; as modern verse goes it possessed a touch distinctly above the mediocre.

"Why don't you stop that stuff and get down to brass tacks, Porter?" Matthew snarled. "You'll be of much more service to your race as a good dentist than as a half-baked poet." Henson happened to know that the amount of study which the young poet did at the University kept him just barely registered in the dental college.

Porter ran his hand over his beautifully groomed hair. He had worn a stocking cap in his room all the early part of the day to enable him to perform this gesture without disaster. "There you go, Henson,—service to the race and all the rest of it. Doesn't it ever occur to you that the race is made up of individuals and you can't conserve the good of the whole unless you establish that of each part? It is better for me to be a first rate dentist and be a cabined and confined personality or a half-baked poet, as you'd call it, and be myself?"

Henson reasoned that a coloured American must take into account that he is usually living in a hostile community. "If you're only a half-baked poet they'll think that you're a representative of your race and that we're all equally no account. But if you're a fine dentist, they won't think, it's true, that we're all as skilled as you, but they will respect you and concede that probably there're a few more like

68

you. Inconsistent, but that's the way they argue."

Arthur Sawyer objected to this constant yielding to an invisible censorship. "If you're coloured you've just got to straddle a bit; you've got to consider both racial and individual integrity. I've got to be sure of a living right now. So in order not to bring the charge of vagrancy against my family I'm going to teach until I've saved enough money to study engineering in comfort."

"And when you get through?" Matthew asked politely.

"When I get through, if this city has come to its senses, I'll get a big job with Baldwin. If not I'll go to South America and take out naturalization papers."

"But you can't do that," cried Jinny, "we'd need you more than ever if you had all that training. You know what I think? We've all of us got to make up our minds to the sacrifice of something. I mean something more than just the ordinary sacrifices in life, not so much for the sake of the next generation as for the sake of some principle, for the sake of some immaterial quality like pride or intense self-respect or even a saving complacency; a spiritual tonic which the race needs perhaps just as much as the body might need iron or whatever it does need to give the proper kind of resistance. There are some things which an individual might want, but which he'd just have to give up forever for the sake of the more important whole."

"It beats me," said Sawyer indulgently, "how a little thing like you can catch hold of such a big thought. I don't know about a man's giving up his heart's desire forever, though, just because he's coloured. That seems to me a pretty large order."

"Large order or not," Henson caught him up, "she comes mighty near being right. What do you think, Angela?"

"Just the same as I've always thought. I don't see any sense in living unless you're going to be happy."

.   .   .   .   .

Angela took the sketch of Hetty Daniels to school. "What an interesting type!" said Gertrude Quale, the girl next to her. "Such cosmic and tragic unhappiness in that face. What is she, not an American?"

"Oh yes she is. She's an old coloured woman who's worked in our family for years and she was born right here in Philadelphia."

"Oh coloured! Well, of course I suppose you would call her an American though I never think of darkies as Americans. Coloured, —yes that would account for that unhappiness in her face. I suppose they all mind it awfully."

It was the afternoon for the life class. The model came in, a short, rather slender young woman with a faintly pretty, shrewdish face full of a certain dark, mean character. Angela glanced at her thoughtfully, full of pleasant anticipation. She liked to work for character, preferred it even to beauty. The model caught her eye, looked away and again turned her full gaze upon her

with an insistent, slightly incredulous stare. It
was Esther Bayliss who had once been in the High
School with Angela. She had left not long
after Mary Hastings' return to her boarding
school.

Angela saw no reason why she should speak
to her and presently, engrossed in the portrayal
of the round, yet pointed little face, forgot the
girl's identity. But Esther kept her eyes fixed
on her former school-mate with a sort of intense,
angry brooding so absorbing that she forgot her
pose and Mr. Shields spoke to her two or three
times. On the third occasion he said not unkindly, "You'll have to hold your pose better
than this, Miss Bayliss, or we won't be able to
keep you on."

"I don't want you to keep me on." She spoke
with an amazing vindictiveness. "I haven't got
to the point yet where I'm going to lower myself
to pose for a coloured girl."

He looked around the room in amazement;
no, Miss Henderson wasn't there, she never came
to this class he remembered. "Well after that
we couldn't keep you anyway. We're not taking
orders from our models. But there's no coloured
girl here."

"Oh yes there is, unless she's changed her
name." She laughed spitefully. "Isn't that Angela Murray over there next to that Jew girl?"
In spite of himself, Shields nodded. "Well, she's
coloured though she wouldn't let you know. But
I know. I went to school with her in North
Philadelphia. And I tell you I wouldn't stay
to pose for her not if you were to pay me ten
times what I'm getting. Sitting there drawing

from me just as though she were as good as a
white girl!"

Astonished and disconcerted, he told his wife
about it. "But I can't think she's really coloured,
Mabel. Why she looks and acts just like a white
girl. She dresses in better taste than anybody in
the room. But that little wretch of a model
insisted that she was coloured."

"Well she just can't be. Do you suppose I
don't know a coloured woman when I see one?
I can tell 'em a mile off."

It seemed to him a vital and yet such a dis-
graceful matter. "If she is coloured she should
have told me. I'd certainly like to know, but
hang it all, I can't ask her, for suppose she should
be white in spite of what that little beast of a
model said?" He found her address in the regis-
try and overcome one afternoon with shamed
curiosity drove up to Opal Street and slowly past
her house. Jinny was coming in from school and
Hetty Daniels on her way to market greeted her
on the lower step. Then Virginia put the key in
the lock and passed inside. "She is coloured," he
told his wife, "for no white girl in her senses
would be rooming with coloured people."

"I should say not! Coloured, is she? Well,
she shan't come here again, Henry."

Angela approached him after class on Saturday. "How is Mrs. Shields? I can't get out
to see her this week but I'll be sure to run in
next."

He blurted out miserably, "But, Miss Murray,
you never told me that you were coloured."

She felt as though she were rehearsing a
well-known part in a play. "Coloured! Of

course I never told you that I was coloured.
Why should I?"

.   .   .   .   .   .

But apparently there was some reason why she
should tell it; she sat in her room in utter dejection
trying to reason it out. Just as in the old days
she had not discussed the matter with Jinny, for
what could the latter do? She wondered if
her mother had ever met with any such experiences. Was there something inherently wrong
in "passing?"
Her mother had never seemed to consider it as
anything but a lark. And on the one occasion,
that terrible day in the hospital when passing or
not passing might have meant the difference
between good will and unpleasantness, her mother
had deliberately given the whole show away. But
her mother, she had long since begun to realize,
had not considered this business of colour or
the lack of it as pertaining intimately to her
personal happiness. She was perfectly satisfied,
absolutely content whether she was part of that
white world with Angela or up on little Opal
Street with her dark family and friends. Whereas it seemed to Angela that all the things which
she most wanted were wrapped up with white
people. All the good things were theirs. Not,
some coldly reasoning instinct within was saying, because they were white. But because for
the present they had power and the badge of
that power was whiteness, very like the colours
on the escutcheon of a powerful house. She
possessed the badge, and unless there was

73

someone to tell she could possess the power for which it stood.

Hetty Daniels shrilled up: "Mr. Henson's down here to see you."

Tiresome though his presence was, she almost welcomed him to-night, and even accepted his eager invitation to go to see a picture. "It's in a little gem of a theatre, Angela. You'll like the surroundings almost as much as the picture, and that's very good. Sawyer and I saw it about two weeks ago. I thought then that I'd like to take you."

She knew that this was his indirect method of telling her that they would meet with no difficulty in the matter of admission; a comforting assurance for Philadelphia theatres, as Angela knew, could be very unpleasant to would-be coloured patrons. Henson offered to telephone for a taxi while she was getting on her street clothes, and she permitted the unnecessary extravagance for she hated the conjectures on the faces of passengers in the street cars; conjecture, she felt in her sensitiveness, which she could only set right by being unusually kind and friendly in her manner to Henson. And this produced undesirable effects on him. She had gone out with him more often in the Ford, which permitted a modicum of privacy. But Jinny was off in the little car to-night.

At Broad and Ridge Avenue the taxi was held up; it was twenty-five minutes after eight when they reached the theatre. Matthew gave Angela a bill. "Do you mind getting the tickets while I settle for the cab?" he asked nervously. He did not want her to miss even the advertisements. This, he almost prayed, would be a perfect night.

Cramming the change into his pocket, he rushed into the lobby and joined Angela, who, almost as excited as he, for she liked a good picture, handed the tickets to the attendant. He returned the stubs. "All right, good seats there to your left," The theatre was only one storey. He glanced at Matthew.

"Here, here, where do you think you're going?"

Matthew answered unsuspecting: "It's all right. The young lady gave you the tickets."

"Yes, but not for you; she can go in, but you can't." He handed him the torn ticket, turned and took one of the stubs from Angela, and thrust that in the young man's unwilling hand. "Go over there and get your refund."

"But," said Matthew and Angela could feel his very manhood sickening under the silly humiliation of the moment, "there must be some mistake; I sat in this same theatre less than three weeks ago."

"Well, you won't sit in there to-night; the management's changed hands since then, and we're not selling tickets to coloured people." He glanced at Angela a little uncertainly. "The young lady can come in——"

Angela threw her ticket on the floor. "Oh, come Matthew, come."

Outside he said stiffly, "I'll get a taxi, we'll go somewhere else."

"No, no! We wouldn't enjoy it. Let's go home and we don't need a taxi. We can get the Sixteenth Street car right at the corner."

75

She was very kind to him in the car; she was so sorry for him, suddenly conscious of the pain which must be his at being stripped before the girl he loved of his masculine right to protect, to appear the hero.

She let him open the two doors for her but stopped him in the box of a hall. "I think I'll say good-night now, Matthew; I'm more tired than I realized. But,—but it was an adventure, wasn't it?"

His eyes adored her, his hand caught hers: "Angela, I'd have given all I hope to possess to have been able to prevent it; you know I never dreamed of letting you in for such humiliation. Oh how are we ever going to get this thing straight?"

"Well, it wasn't your fault." Unexpectedly she lifted her delicate face to his, so stricken and freckled and woebegone, and kissed him, lifted her hand and actually stroked his reddish, stiff, "bad" hair.

Like a man in a dream he walked down the street wondering how long it would be before they married.

.   .   .   .   .

Angela, waking in the middle of the night and reviewing to herself the events of the day, said aloud: "This is the end," and fell asleep again.

The little back room was still Jinny's, but Angela, in order to give the third storey front to Hetty Daniels, had moved into the room which had once been her mother's. She and Virginia had placed the respective head-boards of their narrow, virginal beds against the dividing wall so that they could lie in bed and talk to each other through the communicating door-way, their voices making a circuit from speaker to listener in what Jinny called a hair-pin curve.

Angela called in as soon as she heard her sister moving, "Jinny, listen. I'm going away."

Her sister, still half asleep, lay intensely quiet for another second, trying to pick up the continuity of this dream. Then her senses came to her.

"What'd you say, Angela?"

"I said I was going away. I'm going to leave Philadelphia, give up school teaching, break away from our loving friends and acquaintances, and bust up the whole shooting match."

"Haven't gone crazy, have you?"

"No, I think I'm just beginning to come to my senses. I'm sick, sick, sick of seeing what I want dangled right before my eyes and then of having it snatched away from me and all of it through no fault of my own."

"Darling, you know I haven't the faintest idea of what you're driving at."

"Well, I'll tell you." Out came the whole story, an accumulation of the slights, real and fancied, which her colour had engendered throughout her lifetime; though even then she did not tell of that first hurt through Mary Hastings. That would always linger in some remote, impenetrable fastness of her mind, for wounded trust was there as well as wounded pride and love. "And these two last happenings with Matthew and Mr.

77

Shields are just too much; besides they've shown
me the way."

"Shown you what way?"

Virginia had arisen and thrown an old rose
kimono around her. She had inherited her
father's thick and rather coarsely waving black
hair, enhanced by her mother's softness. She
was slender, yet rounded; her cheeks were flushed
with sleep and excitement. Her eyes shone. As
she sat in the brilliant wrap, cross-legged at the
foot of her sister's narrow bed, she made the
latter think of a striking dainty, colourful robin.

"Well you see as long as the Shields thought I
was white they were willing to help me to all the
glories of the promised land. And the doorman
last night,—he couldn't tell what I was, but he
could tell about Matthew, so he put him out;
just as the Shields are getting ready in another
way to put me out. But as long as they didn't
know it didn't matter. Which means it isn't being coloured that makes the difference, it's letting
it be known. Do you see?

"So I've thought and thought. I guess really
I've had it in my mind for a long time, but last
night it seemed to stand right out in my consciousness. Why should I shut myself off from
all the things I want most,—clever people, people
who do things, Art,—" her voice spelt it with a
capital,—"travel and a lot of things which are
in the world for everybody really but which only
white people, as far as I can see, get their hands
on. I mean scholarships and special funds,
patronage. Oh Jinny, you don't know, I don't
think you can understand the things I want to
see and know. You're not like me——"

"I don't know why I'm not," said Jinny looking more like a robin than ever. Her bright eyes dwelt on her sister. "After all, the same blood flows in my veins and in the same proportion. Sure you're not laying too much stress on something only temporarily inconvenient?"

"But it isn't temporarily inconvenient; it's happening to me every day. And it isn't as though it were something that I could help. Look how Mr. Shields stressed the fact that I hadn't told him I was coloured. And see how it changed his attitude toward me; you can't think how different his manner was. Yet as long as he didn't know, there was nothing he wasn't willing and glad, glad to do for me. Now he might be willing but he'll not be glad though I need his assistance more than some white girl who will find a dozen people to help her just because she is white." Some faint disapproval in her sister's face halted her for a moment. "What's the matter? You certainly don't think I ought to say first thing: 'I'm Angela Murray. I know I look white but I'm coloured and expect to be treated accordingly!' Now do you?"

"No," said Jinny, "of course that's absurd. Only I don't think you ought to mind quite so hard when they do find out the facts. It seems sort of an insult to yourself. And then, too, it makes you lose a good chance to do something for—for all of us who can't look like you but who really have the same combination of blood that you have."

"Oh that's some more of your and Matthew Henson's philosophy. Now be practical, Jinny;

79

after all I am both white and Negro and look
white.   Why shouldn't I declare for the one that
will bring me the greatest happiness, prosperity
and respect?"

"No reason in the world except that since in
this country public opinion is against any infusion
of black blood it would seem an awfully decent
thing to put yourself, even in the face of appearances, on the side of black blood and say: 'Look
here, this is what a mixture of black and white
really means!'"

Angela was silent and Virginia, feeling suddenly
very young, almost childish in the presence of
this issue, took a turn about the room.   She
halted beside her sister.

"Just what is it you want to do, Angela?
Evidently you have some plan."

She had.   Her idea was to sell the house
and to divide the proceeds.   With her share
of this and her half of the insurance she
would go to New York or to Chicago, certainly
to some place where she could by no chance
be known, and launch out "into a freer, fuller
life."

"And leave me!" said Jinny astonished.   Somehow it had not dawned on her that the two would
actually separate.   She did not know what she
had thought, but certainly not that.   The tears
ran down her cheeks.

Angela, unable to endure either her own pain
or the sight of it in others, had all of a man's
dislike for tears.

"Don't be absurd, Jinny!   How could I live
the way I want to if you're with me.   We'd keep
on loving each other and seeing one another from

time to time, but we might just as well face the
facts. Some of those girls in the art school used
to ask me to their homes; it would have meant
opportunity, a broader outlook, but I never dared
accept because I knew I couldn't return the
invitation."

Under that Jinny winced a little, but she spoke
with spirit. "After that, Angela dear, I'm
beginning to think that you *have* more white
blood in your veins than I, and it was that extra
amount which made it possible for you to make
that remark." She trailed back to her room and
when Hetty Daniels announced breakfast she
found that a bad headache required a longer
stay in bed.

．　　　．　　　．　　　．　　　．

For many years the memory of those next few
weeks lingered in Virginia's mind beside that
other tragic memory of her mother's deliberate
submission to death. But Angela was almost
tremulous with happiness and anticipation. Almost as though by magic her affairs were arranging themselves. She was to have the three thousand dollars and Jinny was to be the sole possessor
of the house. Junius had paid far less than this
sum for it, but it had undoubtedly increased in
value. "It's a fair enough investment for you,
Miss Virginia," Mr. Hallowell remarked gruffly.
He had disapproved heartily of this summary
division, would have disapproved more thoroughly
and openly if he had had any idea of the reasons
behind it. But the girls had told no one, not
even him, of their plans. "Some sisters' quarrel,

I suppose," he commented to his wife. "I've never seen any coloured people yet, relatives that is, who could stand the joint possession of a little money."

A late Easter was casting its charm over the city when Angela trim, even elegant, in her conventional tailored suit, stood in the dining-room of the little house waiting for her taxi. She had burned her bridges behind her, had resigned from school, severed her connection with the Academy, and had permitted an impression to spread that she was going West to visit indefinitely a distant cousin of her mother's. In reality she was going to New York. She had covered her tracks very well, she thought; none of her friends was to see her off; indeed, none of them knew the exact hour of her departure. She was even leaving from the North Philadelphia station so that none of the porters of the main depôt, friends perhaps of the boys who came to her house, and, through some far flung communal instinct familiar to coloured people, acquainted with her by sight, would be able to tell of her going. Jinny, until she heard of this, had meant to accompany her to the station, but Angela's precaution palpably scotched this idea; she made no comment when Virginia announced that it would be impossible for her to see her sister off. An indefinable steeliness was creeping upon them.

Yet when the taxi stood rumbling and snorting outside, Angela, her heart suddenly mounting to her throat, her eyes smarting, put her arm tightly about her sister who clung to her frankly crying. But she only said: "Now, Jinny, there's nothing to cry about. You'll be coming to New York soon. First thing I know you'll be walking up to me: 'Pardon me! Isn't this Mrs. Henrietta Jones?' "

Virginia tried to laugh, "And you'll be saying: 'Really you have the advantage of me.' Oh, Angela, don't leave me!"

The cabby was honking impatiently. "I must, darling. Good-bye, Virginia. You'll hear from me right away."

She ran down the steps, glanced happily back. But her sister had already closed the door.

MARKET

CHAPTER I

FIFTH AVENUE is a canyon; its towering buildings dwarf the importance of the people hurrying
through its narrow confines. But Fourteenth
Street is a river, impersonally flowing, broad-
bosomed, with strange and devious craft covering
its expanse. To Angela the famous avenue seemed
but one manifestation of living, but Fourteenth
Street was the rendezvous of life itself. Here for
those first few weeks after her arrival in New
York she wandered, almost prowled, intent upon
the jostling shops, the hurrying, pushing people,
above all intent upon the faces of those people
with their showings of grief, pride, gaiety, greed,
joy, ambition, content. There was little enough of
this last. These men and women were living at a
sharper pitch of intensity than those she had observed in Philadelphia. The few coloured people
whom she saw were different too; they possessed
an independence of carriage, a purposefulness, an
assurance in their manner that pleased her. But
she could not see that any of these people, black
or white, were any happier than those whom she
had observed all her life.

But *she* was happier; she was living on the crest
of a wave of excitement and satisfaction which
would never wane, never break, never be spent.
She was seeing the world, she was getting ac-

87

quainted with life in her own way without restrictions or restraint; she was young, she was
temporarily independent, she was intelligent, she
was white. She remembered an expression "free,
white and twenty-one,"—this was what it meant
then, this sense of owning the world, this realization that other things being equal, all things were
possible. "If I were a man," she said, "I could be
president," and laughed at herself for the "if" itself proclaimed a limitation. But that inconsis-
tency bothered her little; she did not want to be
a man. Power, greatness, authority, these were
fitting and proper for men; but there were sweeter, more beautiful gifts for women, and power of
a certain kind too. Such a power she would like
to exert in this glittering new world, so full of
mysteries and promise. If she could afford it she
would have a salon, a drawing-room where men
and women, not necessarily great, but real, alive,
free and untrammelled in manner and thought,
should come and pour themselves out to her sympathy and magnetism. To accomplish this she
must have money and influence; indeed since she
was so young she would need even protection;
perhaps it would be better to marry . . . a white
man. The thought came to her suddenly out of
the void; she had never thought of this possibility before. If she were to do this, do it suitably,
then all that richness, all that fullness of life which
she so ardently craved would be doubly hers. She
knew that men had a better time of it than women,
coloured men than coloured women, white men
than white momen. Not that she envied them.
Only it would be fun, great fun to capture power
and protection in addition to the freedom and

independence which she had so long coveted and which now lay in her hand.

But, she smiled to herself, she had no way of approaching these ends. She knew no one in New York; she could conceive of no manner in which she was likely to form desirable acquaintances; at present her home consisted of the four walls of the smallest room in Union Square Hotel. She had gone there the second day after her arrival, having spent an expensive twenty-four hours at the Astor. Later she came to realize that there were infinitely cheaper habitations to be had, but she could not tear herself away from Fourteenth Street. It was Spring, and the Square was full of rusty specimens of mankind who sat on the benches, as did Angela herself, for hours at a stretch, as though they thought the invigorating air and the mellow sun would work some magical burgeoning on their garments such as was worked on the trees. But though these latter changed, the garments changed not nor did their owners. They remained the same, drooping, discouraged down and outers. "I am seeing life," thought Angela, "this is the way people live," and never realized that some of these people looking curiously, speculatively at her wondered what had been her portion to bring her thus early to this unsavoury company.

"A great picture!" she thought. "I'll make a great picture of these people some day and call them 'Fourteenth Street types'." And suddenly a vast sadness invaded her; she wondered if there were people more alive, more sentient to the joy, the adventure of living, even than she, to whom she would also be a "type." But she

could not believe this. She was at once almost
irreconcilably too concentrated and too objective.
Her living during these days was so intense, so
almost solidified, as though her desire to live as
she did and she herself were so one and the same
thing that it would have been practically impossible for another onlooker like herself to insert
the point of his discrimination into her firm
panoply of satisfaction. So she continued to
browse along her chosen thoroughfare, stopping
most often in the Square or before a piano
store on the same street. There was in this shop
a player-piano which was usually in action, and
as the front glass had been removed the increased
clearness of the strains brought a steady, patient,
apparently insatiable group of listeners to a standstill. They were mostly men, and as they were
far less given, Angela observed, to concealing their
feelings than women, it was easy to follow
their emotional gamut. Jazz made them smile
but with a certain wistfulness—if only they had
time for dancing now, just now when the mood
was on them! The young woman looking at the
gathering of shabby pedestrians, worn business
men and ruminative errand boys felt for them a
pity not untinged with satisfaction. *She* had taken
what she wanted while the mood was on her.
Love songs, particularly those of the sorrowful
ballad variety brought to these unmindful faces
a strained regret. But there was one expression
which Angela could only half interpret. It drifted
on to those listening countenances usually at
the playing of old Irish and Scottish tunes. She
noticed then an acuter attitude of attention, the
eyes took on a look of inwardness of utter remote-

ness. A passer-by engrossed in thought caught
a strain and at once his gait and expression fell
under the spell. The listeners might be as varied
as fifteen people may be, yet for the moment they
would be caught in a common, almost cosmic
nostalgia. If the next piece were jazz that
particular crowd would disperse, its members
going on their meditative ways, blessed or cursed
with heaven knew what memories which must
not to be disturbed by the strident jangling of the
latest popular song.

"Homesick," Angela used to say to herself.
And she would feel so, too, though she hardly
knew for what,—certainly not for Philadelphia
and that other life which now seemed so
removed as to have been impossible. And
she made notes in her sketch book to enable
her some day to make a great picture of these
"types" too.

. . . . . .

Of course she was being unconscionably idle;
but as her days were filled to overflowing with
the impact of new impressions, this signified
nothing. She could not guess what life would
bring her. For the moment it seemed to her both
wise and amusing to sit with idle hands and see
what would happen. By a not inexplicable turn
of mind she took to going very frequently to the
cinema where most things did happen. She
found herself studying the screen with a strained
and ardent intensity, losing the slight patronizing
scepticism which had once been hers with regard
to the adventures of these shadowy heroes and

heroines; so utterly unforeseen a turn had her own
experiences taken.   This time last year she had
never dreamed of, had hardly dared to long for
a life as free and as full as hers was now and was
promising to be.   Yet here she was on the thresh-
hold of a career totally different from anything
that a scenario writer could envisage.   Oh yes,
she knew that hundreds, indeed thousands of
white coloured people "went over to the other
side," but that was just the point, she knew the
fact without knowing hitherto any of the possibilities of the adventure.   Already Philadelphia
and her trials were receding into the distance.
Would these people, she wondered, glancing
about her in the soft gloom of the beautiful theatre, begrudge her, if they knew, her cherished
freedom and sense of unrestraint?   If she were to
say to this next woman for instance, "I'm coloured," would she show the occasional dog-in-the-
manger attitude of certain white Americans and
refuse to sit by her or make a complaint to the
usher?   But she had no intention of making such
an announcement.   So she spent many happy, irresponsible, amused hours in the marvellous houses on Broadway or in the dark commonplaceness
of her beloved Fourteenth Street.   There was a
theatre, too, on Seventh Avenue just at the edge
of the Village, which she came to frequent, not so
much for the sake of the plays, which were the
same as elsewhere, as for the sake of the audience, a curiously intimate sort of audience made
of numerous still more intimate groups.   Their
members seemed both purposeful and leisurely.
When she came here her loneliness palled on
her,   however.   All   unaware   her   face ·took

on the wistfulness of the men gazing in the music store. She wished she knew some of these pleasant people.

.   .   .   .   .

It came to her that she was neglecting her Art. "And it was for that that I broke away from everything and came to New York. I must hunt up some classes." This she felt was not quite true, then the real cause rushed up to the surface of her mind: "And perhaps I'll meet some people."

She enrolled in one of the art classes in Cooper Union. This, after all, she felt would be the real beginning of her adventure. For here she must make acquaintances and one of them, perhaps several, must produce some effect on her life, perhaps alter its whole tenor. And for the first time she would be seen, would be met against her new background or rather, against no background. No boyish stowaway on a ship had a greater exuberance in going forth to meet the unknown than had Angela as she entered her class that first afternoon. In the room were five people, working steadily and chatting in an extremely desultory way. The instructor, one of the five, motioned her to a seat whose position made her one of the group. He set up her easel and as she arranged her material she glanced shyly but keenly about her. For the first time she realized how lonely she had been. She thought with a joy which surprised herself: "Within a week I'll be chatting with them too; perhaps going to lunch or to tea with one of them." She arranged herself for a better view. The young woman nearest her, the possessor of a great mop of tawny hair and smiling clear, slate-grey eyes glanced up at her and nodded, "Am I in your way?" Except for her hair and eyes she was nondescript. A little beyond sat a coloured girl of medium height and build, very dark, very clean, very reserved. Angela, studying her with inner secret knowledge, could feel her constantly withdrawn from her companions. Her refinement was conspicuous but her reserve more so; when asked she passed and received erasers and other articles but she herself did no borrowing nor did she initiate any conversation. Her squarish head capped with a mass of unnaturally straight and unnaturally burnished hair possessed a kind of ugly beauty. Angela could not tell whether her features were good but blurred and blunted by the soft night of her skin or really ugly with an ugliness lost and plunged in that skin's deep concealment. Two students were still slightly behind her. She wondered how she could best contrive to see them.

Someone said: "Hi, there! Miss New One, have *you* got a decent eraser? all mine are on the blink." Not so sure whether or not the term applied to herself she turned to meet the singularly intent gaze of a slender girl with blue eyes, light chestnut hair and cheeks fairly blazing with some unguessed excitement. Angela smiled and offered her eraser.

"It ought to be decent, it's new."

"Yes, it's a very good one; many thanks. I'll try not to trouble you again. My name's Paulette Lister, what's yours?"

"Angèle Mory." She had changed it thus

slightly when she came to New York. Some
troubling sense of loyalty to her father and mother
had made it impossible for her to do away with it
altogether.

"Mory," said a young man who had been
working just beyond Paulette; "that's Spanish.
Are you by any chance?"

"I don't think so."

"He is," said Paulette. "His name is
Anthony Cruz—isn't that a lovely name? But
he changed it to Cross because no American would
ever pronounce the z right, and he didn't want to
be taken for a widow's cruse."

"That's a shameful joke," said Cross, "but
since I made it up, I think you might give me a
chance to spring it, Miss Lister. A poor thing
but mine own. You might have a heart."

"Get even with her, why don't you, by introducing her as Miss Blister?" asked Angela, highly
diverted by the foolish talk.

Several people came in then, and she discovered
that she had been half an hour too early, the class
was just beginning. She glanced about at the
newcomers, a beautiful Jewess with a pearly skin
and a head positively foaming with curls, a tall
Scandinavian, an obvious German, several more
Americans. Not one of them made the photograph on her mind equal to those made by the coloured girl whose name, she learned, was Rachel
Powell, the slate-eyed Martha Burden, Paulette
Lister and Anthony Cross. Her prediction came
true. With in a week she was on jestingly intimate terms with every one of them except Miss
Powell, who lent her belongings, borrowed nothing, and spoke only when she was spoken to.

At the end of ten days Miss Burden asked Angela to come and have lunch "at the same place where I go".

. . . . .

On an exquisite afternoon she went to Harlem. At One Hundred and Thirty-fifth street she left the 'bus and walked through from Seventh Avenue to Lenox, then up to One Hundred and Forty-seventh Street and back down Seventh Avenue to One Hundred and Thirty-ninth Street, through this to Eighth Avenue and then weaving back and forth between the two Avenues through Thirty-eighth, Thirty-seventh down to One Hundred and Thirty-fifth Street to Eighth Avenue where she took the Elevated and went back to the New York which she knew.

But she was amazed and impressed at this bustling, frolicking, busy, laughing great city within a greater one. She had never seen coloured life so thick, so varied, so complete. Moreover, just as this city reproduced in microcosm all the important features of any metropolis, so undoubtedly life up here was just the same, she thought dimly, as life anywhere else. Not all these people, she realized, glancing keenly at the throngs of black and brown, yellow and white faces about her were servants or underlings or end men. She saw a beautiful woman all brown and red dressed as exquisitely as anyone she had seen on Fifth Avenue. A man's sharp, high-bred face etched itself on her memory,—the face of a professional man perhaps,—it might be an artist. She doubted that; he might of course be a musician, but it was unlikely that he would be her kind of an artist, for how could he exist? Ah, there lay the great difference. In all material, even in all practical things these two worlds were alike, but in the production, the fostering of those ultimate manifestations, this world was lacking, for its people were without the means or the leisure to support them and enjoy. And these were the manifestations which she craved, together with the freedom to enjoy them. No, she was not sorry that she had chosen as she had, even though she could now realize that life viewed from the angle of Opal and Jefferson Streets in Philadelphia and that same life viewed from One Hundred and Thirty-fifth Street and Seventh Avenue in New York might present bewildering different facets.

Unquestionably there was something very fascinating, even terrible, about this stream of life, —it seemed to her to run thicker, more turgidly than that safe, sublimated existence in which her new friends had their being. It was deeper, more mightily moving even than the torrent of Fourteenth Street. Undoubtedly just as these people, —for she already saw them objectively, doubly so, once with her natural remoteness and once with the remoteness of her new estate,—just as these people could suffer more than others, just so they could enjoy themselves more. She watched the moiling groups on Lenox Avenue; the amazingly well-dressed and good-looking throngs of young men on Seventh Avenue at One Hundred and Thirty-seventh and Thirty-fifth Streets. They were gossiping, laughing, dickering, chaffing, combining the customs of the small town with the astonishing cosmopolitanism of their clothes and manners. Nowhere down town did she see life

like this. Oh, all this was fuller, richer, not finer
but richer with the difference in quality that there
is between velvet and silk. Harlem was a great
city, but after all it was a city within a city, and
she was glad, as she strained for last glimpses out
of the lurching "L" train, that she had cast in
her lot with the dwellers outside its dark and
serried tents.

CHAPTER II

"Where do you live?" asked Paulette, "when you're not here at school?"

Angela blushed as she told her.

"In a hotel? In Union Square? Child, are you a millionaire? Where did you come from? Don't you care anything about the delights of home? Mr. Cross, come closer. Here is this poor child living benightedly in a hotel when she might have two rooms at least in the Village for almost the same price."

Mr. Cross came closer but without saying anything. He was really, Angela thought, a very serious, almost sad young man. He had never continued long the bantering line with which he had first made her acquaintance.

She explained that she had not known where to go. "Often I've thought of moving, and of course I'm spending too much money, for what I get out of it,—I've the littlest room."

Paulette opened her eyes very wide which gave an onlooker the effect of seeing suddenly the blue sky very close at hand. Her cheeks took on a flaming tint. She was really a beautiful, even fascinating girl—or woman,—Angela never learned which, for she never knew her age. But her fascination did not rest on her looks, or at least it did not arise from that source; it was more

99

the result of her manner. She was so alive, so intense, so interested, if she were interested, that all her nerves, her emotions even were enlisted to accomplish the end which she might have in view. And withal she possessed the simplicity of a child. There was an unsuspected strength about her also that was oddly at variance with the rather striking fragility of her appearance, the trustingness of her gaze, the limpid unaffectedness of her manner. Mr. Cross, Angela thought negligently, must be in love with her; he was usually at her side when they sketched. But later she came to see that there was nothing at all between these two except a certain friendly appreciation tempered by a wary kindness on the part of Mr. Cross and a negligent generosity on the part of Paulette.

She displayed no negligence of generosity in her desire and eagerness to find Angela a suitable apartment. She did hold out, however, with amazing frankness for one "not too near me but also not too far away." But this pleased the girl, for she had been afraid that Paulette would insist on offering to share her own apartment and she would not have known how to refuse. She had the complete egoist's desire for solitude.

Paulette lived on Bank Street; she found for her new friend "a duck,—just a duck,—no other word will describe it,—of an apartment" on Jayne Street, two rooms, bath and kitchenette. There was also a tiny balcony giving on a mews. It was more than Angela should have afforded, but the ease with which her affairs were working out gave her an assurance, almost an arrogance of confidence. Besides she planned to save by getting her own meals. The place was already furnished, its former occupant was preparing to go to London for two or more years.

"Two years," Angela said gaily, "everything in the world can happen to me in that time. Oh I wonder what will have happened; what I will be like!" And she prepared to move in her slender store of possessions. Anthony, prompted, she suspected by Paulette, offered rather shyly to help her. It was a rainy day, there were several boxes after all, and taxis were scarce, though finally he captured one for her and came riding back in triumph with the driver. Afterwards a few books had to be arranged, pictures must be hung. She had an inspiration.

"You tend to all this and I'll get you the best dinner you ever tasted in your life." Memories of Monday night dinners on Opal Street flooded her memory. She served homely, filling dishes, "fit for a drayman," she teased him. There were corn-beef hash, roasted sweet potatoes, corn pudding, and, regardless of the hour, muffins. After supper she refused to let him help her with the dishes but had him rest in the big chair in the living-room while she laughed and talked with him from the kitchenette at a distance of two yards. Gradually, as he sat there smoking, the sadness and strain faded out of his thin, dark face, he laughed and jested like any other normal young man. When he bade her good-bye he let his slow dark gaze rest in hers for a long silent moment. She closed the door and stood laughing, arranging her hair before the mirror.

"Of course he's loads better looking, but something about him makes me think of Matthew

Henson.. But nothing doing, young-fellow-me-lad.
Spanish and I suppose terribly proud. I wonder
what he'd say if he really knew?"

.   .   .   .   .   .

She was to go to Paulette's to dinner. "Just
we two," stipulated Miss Lister. "Of course, I
could have a gang of men, but I think it will be
fun for us to get acquainted." Angela was
pleased; she was very fond of Paulette, she liked
her for her generous, capable self. And she was
not quite ready for meeting men. She must know
something more about these people with whom
she was spending her life. Anthony Cross had
been affable enough, but she was not sure that he,
with his curious sadness, his half-proud, half-sensi-
tive tendency to withdrawal, were a fair enough
type. However, in spite of Paulette's piotesta-
tions, there were three young men standing in her
large, dark living-room when Angela arrived.

"But you've got to go at once," said Paulette,
laughing but firm; "here is my friend,—isn't she
beautiful? We've too many things to discuss
without being bothered by you."

"Paulette has these fits of cruelty," said one
of the three, a short, stocky fellow with an ugly,
sensitive face. "She'd have made a good Nero.
But anyway I'm glad I stayed long enough to see
you. Don't let her hide you from us altogether."
Another man made a civil remark; the third one
standing back in the gloomy room said nothing,
but. the girl caught the impression of tallness and
blondness and of a pair of blue eyes which stared
at her intently. She felt awkward and showed it.

"See, you've made her shy," said Paulette accusingly. "I won't bother introducing them, Angèle, you'll meet them all too soon." Laughing, protesting, the men filed out, and their unwilling hostess closed the door on them with sincere lack of regret. "Men," she mused candidly. "Of course we can't get along without them any more than they can without us, but I get tired of them, —they're nearly all animals. I'd rather have a good woman friend any day." She sighed with genuine sincerity. "Yet my place is always full of men. Would you rather have your chops rare or well done? I like mine cooked to a cinder." Angela preferred hers well done. "Stay here and look around; see if I have anything to amuse you." Catching up an apron she vanished into some smaller and darker retreat which she called her kitchen.

The apartment consisted of the whole floor of a house on Bank Street, dark and constantly within the sound of the opening front door and the noises of the street. "But you don't have the damned stairs when you come in late at night," Paulette explained. The front room was, Angela supposed, the bedroom, though the only reason for this supposition was the appearance of a dressing-table and a wide, flat divan about one foot and a half from the floor, covered with black or purple velvet. The dressing-table was a good piece of mahogany, but the chairs were indifferently of the kitchen variety and of the sort which, magazines affirm, may be made out of a large packing box. In the living-room, where the little table was set, the same anomaly prevailed; the china was fine, even dainty, but the glasses were thick and the plating had begun to wear off the silver ware. On the other hand the pictures were unusual, none of the stereotyped things; instead Angela remarked a good copy of Brueghel's "Peasant Wedding," the head of Bernini and two etchings whose authors she did not know. The bookcase held two paper bound volumes of the poems of Béranger and Villon and a little black worn copy of Heine. But the other books were high-brow to the point of austerity: Ely, Shaw and Strindberg.

"Perhaps you'd like to wash your hands?" called Paulette. "There's a bathroom down the corridor there, you can't miss it. You may have some of my favourite lotion if you want it—up there on the shelf." Angela washed her hands and looked up for the lotion. Her eyes opened wide in amazement. Beside the bottle stood a man's shaving mug and brush and a case of razors.

The meal, "for you can't call it a dinner," the cook remarked candidly, was a success. The chops were tender though smoky; there were spinach, potatoes, tomato and lettuce salad, rolls, coffee and cheese. Its rugged quality surprised Angela not a little; it was more a meal for a working man than for a woman, above all, a woman of the faery quality of Paulette. "I get so tired," she said, lifting a huge mouthful, "if I don't eat heartily; besides it ruins my temper to go hungry." Her whole attitude toward the meal was so masculine and her appearance so daintily feminine that Angela burst out laughing, explaining with much amusement the cause of her merriment. "I hope you don't mind," she ended, "for

of course you are conspicuously feminine. There's
nothing of the man about you."

To her surprise Paulette resented this last
statement. "There is a great deal of the man
about me. I've learned that a woman is a fool
who lets her feminity stand in the way of what
she wants. I've made a philosophy of it. I see
what I want; I use my wiles as a woman to get
it, and I employ the qualities of men, tenacity and
ruthlessness, to keep it. And when I'm through
with it, I throw it away just as they do. Consequently I have no regrets and no encumbrances."

A packet of cigarettes lay open on the table
and she motioned to her friend to have one.
Angela refused, and sat watching her inhale in
deep respirations, she had never seen a woman
more completely at ease, more assuredly mistress
of herself and of her fate. When they had begun
eating Paulette had poured out two cocktails, toss-
ing hers off immediately and finishing Angela's, too,
when the latter, finding it too much like machine
oil for her taste, had set it down scarcely diminished. "You'll get used to them if you go about
with these men. You'll be drinking along with
the rest of us."

She had practically no curiosity and on the other
hand no reticences. And she had met with every
conceivable experience, had visited France, Ger-
many and Sweden; she was now contemplating a
trip to Italy and might go to Russia; she would
go now, in fact, if it were not that a friend of
hers, Jack Hudson, was about to go there, too,
and as she was on the verge of having an affair
with him she thought she'd better wait. She
didn't relish the prospect of such an event in a

foreign land, it put you too much at the man's
mercy. An affair, if you were going to have one,
was much better conducted on your own *pied à
terre*.

"An affair?" gasped Angela.

"Yes,— why, haven't you ever had a lover?"

"A lover?"

"Goodness me, are you a poll parrot? Why
yes, a lover. I've had"—she hesitated before the
other's complete amazement,—"I've had more
than one, I can tell you."

"And you've no intention of marrying?"

"Oh I don't say that; but what's the use of
tying yourself up now while you're young? And
then, too, this way you don't always have them
around your feet; you can always leave them or
they'll leave you. But it's better for you to leave
them first. It insures your pride." With her
babyish face and her sweet, high voice she was like
a child babling precociously. Yet she seemed
bathed in intensity. But later she began to talk
of her books and of her pictures, of her work and
on all these subjects she spoke with the same sub-
dued excitement; her eyes flashed, her cheeks
grew scarlet, all experience meant life to her in
various manifestations. She had been on a newspaper, one of the New York dailies; she had done
press-agenting. At present she was illustrating
for a fashion magazine. There was no end to
her versatilities.

Angela said she must go.

"But you'll come again soon, won't you,
Angèle?"

A wistfulness crept into her voice. "I do so
want a woman friend. When a woman really is

your friend she's so dependable and she's not expecting anything in return." She saw her guest
to the door. "We could have some wonderful
times. Good-night, Angèle." Like a child she
lifted her face to be kissed.

Angela's first thought as she walked down the
dark street was for the unfamiliar name by which
Paulette had called her. For though she had
signed herself very often as Angèle, no one as yet
used it. Her old familiar formula came to her:
"I wonder what she would think if she knew."
But of one thing she was sure: if Paulette had been
in her place she would have acted in exactly the
same way. "She would have seen what she wanted
and would have taken it," she murmured and
fell to thinking of the various confidences which
Paulette had bestowed upon her,—though so
frank and unreserved were her remarks that "confidences" was hardly the name to apply to them.
Certainly, Angela thought, she was in a new
world and with new people. Beyond question
some of the coloured people of her acquaintance
must have lived in a manner which would not
bear inspection, but she could not think of one
who would thus have discussed it calmly with
either friend or stranger. Wondering what it
would be like to conduct oneself absolutely according to one's own laws, she turned into the dark
little vestibule on Jayne Street. As usual the Jewish girl who lived above her was standing blurred
in the thick blackness of the hall, and as usual
Angela did not realize this until, touching the button and turning on the light, she caught sight of
Miss Salting straining her face upwards to receive
her lover's kiss.

CHAPTER III

From the pinnacle of her satisfaction in her studies, in her new friends and in the joke which she was having upon custom and tradition she looked across the class-room at Miss Powell who preserved her attitude of dignified reserve. Angela thought she would try to break it down; on Wednesday she asked the coloured girl to have lunch with her and was pleased to have the invitation accepted. She had no intention of taking the girl up as a matter either of patronage or of loyalty. But she thought it would be nice to offer her the ordinary amenities which their common student life made natural and possible. Miss Powell it appeared ate generally in an Automat or in a cafeteria, but Angela knew of a nice tea-room. "It's rather arty, but they do serve a good meal and it's cheap." Unfortunately on Wednesday she had to leave before noon; she told Miss Powell to meet her at the little restaurant. "Go in and get a table and wait for me, but I'm sure I'll be there as soon as you will." After all she was late, but, what was worse, she found to her dismay that Miss Powell, instead of entering the tea-room, had been awaiting her across the street. There were no tables and the two had to wait almost fifteen minutes before being served.

"Why on earth didn't you go in?" asked Angela a trifle impatiently, "you could have held the table." Miss Powell answered imperturbably: "Because I didn't know how they would receive me if I went in by myself." Angela could not pretend to misunderstand her. "Oh, I think they would have been all right," she murmured, blushing at her stupidity. How quickly she had forgotton those fears and uncertainties. She had never experienced this sort of difficulty herself, but she certainly knew of them from Virginia and others.

The lunch was not a particularly pleasant one. Either Miss Powell was actually dull or she had made a resolve never to let herself go in the presence of white people; perhaps she feared being misunderstood, perhaps she saw in such encounters a lurking attempt at sociological investigations; she would lend herself to no such procedure, that much was plain. Angela could feel her effort to charm, to invite confidence, glance upon and fall back from this impenetrable armour. She had been amazed to find both Paulette and Martha Burden already gaining their living by their sketches. Miss Burden indeed was a caricaturist of no mean local reputation; Anthony Cross was frankly a commercial artist, though he hoped some day to be a recognized painter of portraits. She was curious to learn of Miss Powell's prospects. Inquiry revealed that the young lady had one secret aspiration; to win or earn enough money to go to France and then after that, she said with sudden ardour, "anything could happen." To this end she had worked, saved, scraped, gone without pleasures and clothes. Her work was creditable, indeed above the average, but not sufficiently imbued, Angela thought, with the divine promise to warrant this sublimation of normal desires.

Miss Powell seemed to read her thought. "And then it gives me a chance to show America that one of us can stick; that we have some idea above the ordinary humdrum of existence."

She made no attempt to return the luncheon but she sent Angela one day a bunch of beautiful jonquils,—made no further attempt at friendship. To one versed in the psychology of this proud, sensitive people the reason·was perfectly plain. "You've been awfully nice to me and I appreciate it but don't think I'm going to thrust myself upon you. Your ways and mine lie along different paths."

·   ·   ·   ·   ·

Such contacts, such interpretations and investigations were making up her life, a life that for her was interesting and absorbing, but which had its perils and uncertainties. She had no purpose, for it was absurd for her, even with her ability, to consider Art an end. She was using it now deliberately, as she had always used it vaguely, to get in touch with interesting people and with a more attractive atmosphere. And she was spending money too fast; she had been in New York eight months, and she had already spent a thousand dollars. At this rate her little fortune which had seemed at first inexhaustible would last her less than two years; at best, eighteen months more. Then she must face,—what? Teaching again? Never, she'd had enough of that. Perhaps she could earn her living with her brush, doing menu cards, Christmas and birthday greetings, flowers, Pierrots and Pierrettes on satin pillow tops. She did not relish that. True there were the specialities of Paulette and of Martha Burden, but she lacked the deft sureness of the one and the slightly mordant philosophy underlying the work of the other. Her own specialty she felt sure lay along the line of reproducing, of interpreting on a face the emotion which lay back of that expression. She thought of her Fourteenth Street "types",— that would be the sort of work which she would really enjoy, that and the depicting of the countenance of a purse-proud but lonely man, of the silken inanity of a society girl, of the smiling despair of a harlot. Even in her own mind she hesitated before the use of that terrible word, but association was teaching her to call a spade a spade.

Yes, she might do worse than follow the example of Mr. Cross and become a portrait painter. But somehow she did not want to have to do this; necessity would, she was sure, spoil her touch; besides, she hated the idea of the position in which she would be placed, fearfully placating and flattering possible patrons, hurrying through with an order because she needed the cheque, accepting patronage and condescension. No, she hoped to be sought after, to have the circumstances which would permit her to pick and choose, to refuse if the whim pleased her. It should mean something to be painted by "Mory." People would say "I'm going to have my portrait done by 'Mory'." But all this would call for position, power, wealth. And again she said to herself . . . "I might marry—a white man.

Marriage is the easiest way for a woman to get those things, and white men have them." But she knew only one white man, Anthony Cross, and he would never have those qualities, at least not by his deliberate seeking. They might come eventually but only after long years. Long, long years of struggle with realities. There was a simple, genuine steadfastness in him that made her realize that he would seek for the expression of truth and of himself even at the cost of the trimmings of life. And she was ashamed, for she knew that for the vanities and gewgaws of a leisurely and irresponsible existence she would sacrifice her own talent, the integrity of her ability to interpret life, to write down a history with her brush.

．　　　　．　　　　．　　　　．　　　　．

Martha Burden was as strong and as pronounced a personage as Paulette; even stronger perhaps because she had the great gift of silence. Paulette, as Angela soon realized, lived in a state of constant defiance. "I don't care what people think," was her slogan; men and women appealed to her in proportion to the opposition which they, too, proclaimed for the established thing. Angela was surprised that she clung as persistently as she did to a friendship with a person as conventional and reactionary as herself. But Martha Burden was not like that. One could not tell whether or not she was thinking about other people's opinions. It was probable that the other people and their attitude never entered her mind. She was cool and slightly aloof, with the coolness

and aloofness of her slaty eyes and her thick,
tawny hair. Neither the slatiness nor the tawniness proclaimed warmth—only depth, depth and
again depth. It was impossible to realize what
she would be like if impassioned or deeply stirred
to anger. There would probably be something
implacable, god-like about her; she would be capable of a long, slow, steady burning of passion.
Few men would love Martha though many might
admire her. But a man once enchanted might
easily die for her.

Angela liked her house with its simple elegance,
its fine, soft curtains and steady, shaded glow of
light that stood somehow for home. She liked
her husband, Ladislas Starr, whom Martha produced without a shade of consciousness that this
was the first intimation she had given of being
married. They were strong individualists, molten
and blended in a design which failed to obscure
their emphatic personalities. Their apartment in
the Village was large and neat and sunny; it bore
no trace of palpable wealth, yet nothing conduc-
ing to comfort was lacking. Book-cases in the
dining-room and living-room spilled over; the
Nation, the *Mercury,* the *Crisis, a magazine of
the darker races,* left on the broad arm of an
easy chair, mutely invited; it was late autumn,
almost winter, but there were jars of fresh flowers. The bedroom where Angela went to remove
her wrap was dainty and restful.

The little gathering to which Martha had invited her was made up of members as strongly
individual as the host and hostess. They were all
specialists in their way, and specialists for the
most part in some offshoot of a calling or move-

ment which was itself already highly specialized.
Martha presented a psychiatrist, a war correspondent,—"I'm that only when there is a war
of course," he explained to Angela's openly respectful gaze,—a dramatist, a corporation lawyer, a white-faced, conspicuously beautiful poet
with a long evasive Russian name, two press
agents, a theatrical manager, an actress who
played only Shakespeare rôles, a teacher of defective children and a medical student who had
been a conscientious objector and had served a
long time at Leavenworth. He lapsed constantly
into a rapt self-communion from which he only
roused himself to utter fiery tirades against the
evils of society.

In spite of their highly specialized interests they
were all possessed of a common ground of knowledge in which such subjects as Russia, Consum-
ers' Leagues, and the coming presidential election
figured most largely. There was much laughter
and chaffing but no airiness, no persiflage. One
of the press agents, Mrs. Cecil, entered upon a
long discussion with the corporation lawyer on
a Bill pending before Congress; she knew as much
as he about the matter and held her own in a
long and almost bitter argument which only the
coming of refreshments broke up.

Just before the close of the argument two other
young men had come in, but Angela never learned
their vocation. Furthermore she was interested
in observing the young teacher of defective children. She was coloured; small and well-built,
exquisitely dressed, and of a beautiful tint, all
bronze and soft red, "like Jinny" thought Angela,
a little astonished to observe how the warmth of

her appearance overshadowed or rather over-
shone everyone else in the room. The tawniness
even of Miss Burden's hair went dead beside her.
The only thing to cope with her richness was the
classical beauty of the Russian poet's features.
He seemed unable to keep his eyes away from
her; was punctiliously attentive to her wants and
leaned forward several times during the long political discussion to whisper low spoken and apparently amusing comments. The young woman,
perfectly at ease in her deep chair, received his
attentions with a slightly detached, amused objectivity an objectivity which she had for everyone
in the room including Angela at whom she had
glanced once rather sharply. But the detachment
of her manner was totally different from Miss
Powell's sensitive dignity. Totally without self-
consciousness she let her warm dark eyes travel
from one face to another. She might have been
saying: "How far you are away from the things
that really matter, birth and death and hard, hard
work!" The Russian poet must have realized
this, for once Angela heard him say, leaning forward, "*You* think all this is futile, don't you?"

.   .   .   .   .

Martha motioned for her to wait a moment
until most of the other guests had gone, then she
came forward with one of the two young men who
had come in without introduction. "This is Roger
Fielding, he'll see you home."

He was tall and blond with deeply blue eyes
which smiled on her as he said: "Would you
like to walk or ride? It's raining a little."

Angela said she preferred to walk.

"All right then. Here, Starr, come across with that umbrella I lent you."

They went out into the thin, tingling rain of late Autumn. "I was surprised," said Roger, "to see you there with the high-brows. I didn't think you looked that way when I met you at Paulette's."

"We've met before? I'm—I'm sorry, but I don't seem to remember you."

"No I don't suppose you would. Well, we didn't exactly meet; I saw you one day at Paulette's. That's why I came this evening, because I heard you'd be here and I'd get a chance to see you again; but I was surprised because you didn't seem like that mouthy bunch. They make me tired taking life so plaguey seriously. Martha and her old high-brows!" he ended ungratefully.

Angela, a little taken back with the frankness of his desire to meet her, said she hadn't thought they were serious.

"Not think them serious? Great Scott! what kind of talk are you used to? You look as though you'd just come out of a Sunday-school! Do you prefer bible texts?"

But she could not explain to him the picture which she saw in her mind of men and women at her father's home in Opal Street,—the men talking painfully of rents, of lynchings, of building and loan associations; the women of child-bearing and the sacrifices which must be made to put Gertie through school, to educate Howard. "I don't mean for any of my children to go through what I did." And in later years in her own first maturity, young Henson and Sawyer and the others in the tiny parlour talking of ideals and inevitable sacrifices for the race; the burnt-offering of individualism for some dimly glimpsed racial whole. This was seriousness, even sombreness, with a great sickening vital upthrust of reality. But these other topics, peaks of civilization super-imposed upon peaks, she found, even though interesting, utterly futile.

They had reached the little hall now. "We must talk loud," she whispered.

"Why?" he asked, speaking obediently very loud indeed.

"Wait a minute; no, she's not there. The girl above me meets her young man here at night and just as sure as I forget her and come in quietly there they are in the midst of a kiss. I suspect she hates me."

In his young male sophistication he thought at first that this was a lead, but her air was so gay and so childishly guileless that he changed his opinion. "Though no girl in this day and time could be as simple and innocent as *she* looks."

But aloud he said, "Of course she doesn't hate you, nobody could do that. I assure you I don't."

She thought his gallantries very amusing. "Well, it relieves me to hear you say so; that'll keep me from worrying for one night at least." And withdrawing her hand from his retaining grasp, she ran upstairs.

.   .   .   .   .

A letter from Virginia lay inside the door. Getting ready for bed she read it in bits.

117

"Angela darling, wouldn't it be fun if I were to come to New York too? Of course you'd keep on living in your Village and I'd live in famous Harlem, but we'd both be in the same city, which is where two only sisters ought to be,—dumb I calls it to live apart the way we do. The man out at the U. of P. is crazy to have me take an exam. in music; it would be easy enough and much better pay than I get here. So there are two perfectly good reasons why I should come. He thinks I'll do him credit and I want to get away from this town."

Then between the lines the real reason betrayed itself:

"I do have such awful luck. Edna Brown had a party out in Merion not long ago and Matthew took me. And you know what riding in a train can do for me,—well that night of all nights I had to become car-sick. Matthew had been so nice. He came to see me the next morning, but, child, he's never been near me from that day to this. I suppose a man can't get over a girl's being such a sight as I was that night. Can't things be too hateful!"

Angela couldn't help murmuring: "Imagine anyone wanting old Matthew so badly that she's willing to break up her home to get over him. Now why couldn't he have liked her instead of me?"

And pondering on such mysteries she crept into bed. But she fell to thinking again about the evening she had spent with Martha and the people whom she had met. And again it seemed to her that they represented an almost alarmingly unnecessary class. If any great social cataclysm

were to happen they would surely be the first to
be swept out of the running. Only the real people
could survive. Even Paulette's mode of living,
it seemed to her, had something more forthright
and vital.

CHAPTER IV

In the morning she was awakened by the ringing of the telephone. The instrument was an extravagance, for, save for Anthony's, she received few calls and made practically none. But the woman from whom she had taken the apartment had persuaded her into keeping it. Still, as she had never indicted the change in ownership, its value was small. She lay there for a moment blinking drowsily in the thin but intensely gold sunshine of December thinking that her ears were deceiving her.

Finally she reached out a rosy arm, curled it about the edge of the door jamb and, reaching the little table that stood in the other room just on the other side of the door, set the instrument up in her bed. The apartment was so small that almost everything was within arm's reach.

"Hello," she murmured sleepily.

"Oh, I thought you must be there; I said to myself: 'She couldn't have left home this early.' What time do you go to that famous drawing class of yours anyway?"

"I beg your pardon! Who is this speaking, please?"

"Why, Roger, of course,—Roger Fielding. Don't say you've forgotten me already. This is Angèle, isn't it?"

"Yes this is Angèle Mory speaking, Mr. Fielding."

"Did I offend your Highness, Miss Mory? Will you have lunch with me to-day and let me tell you how sorry I am?"

But she was lunching with Anthony. "I have an engagement."

"Of course you have. Well, will you have tea, dinner, supper to-day,—breakfast and all the other meals to-morrow and so on for a week? You might just as well say 'yes' because I'll pester you till you do."

"I'm engaged for tea, too, but I'm not really as popular as I sound. That's my last engagement for this week; I'll be glad to have dinner with you."

"Right-oh! Now don't go back and finish up that beauty sleep, for if you're any more charming than you were last night I won't answer for myself. I'll be there at eight."

Inexperienced as she was, she was still able to recognize his method as a bit florid; she preferred, on the whole, Anthony's manner at lunch when he leaned forward and touching her hand very lightly said: "Isn't it great for us to be here! I'm so content, Angèle. Promise me you'll have lunch with me every day this week. I've had a streak of luck with my drawings."

She promised him, a little thrilled herself with his evident sincerity and with the niceness of the smile which so transfigured his dark, thin face, robbing it of its tenseness and strain.

Still something, some vanity, some vague premonition of adventure, led her to linger over her dressing for the dinner with Roger. There was never very much colour in her cheeks, but her skin was warm and white; there was vitality beneath her pallor; her hair was warm, too, long and thick and yet so fine that it gave her little head the effect of being surrounded by a nimbus of light; rather wayward, glancing, shifting light for there were little tendrils and wisps and curls in front and about the temples which no amount of coaxing could subdue. She touched up her mouth a little, not so much to redden it as to give a hint of the mondaine to her appearance. Her dress was flame-colour—Paulette had induced her to buy it,—of a plain, rather heavy beautiful glowing silk. The neck was high in back and girlishly modest in front. She had a string of good artificial pearls and two heavy silver bracelets. Thus she gave the effect of a flame herself; intense and opaque at the heart where her dress gleamed and shone, transparent and fragile where her white warm neck and face rose into the tenuous shadow of her hair. Her appearance excited herself.

Roger found her delightful. As to women he considered himself a connoisseur. This girl pleased him in many respects. She was young; she was, when lighted from within by some indescribable mechanism, even beautiful; she had charm and, what was for him even more important, she was puzzling. In repose, he noticed, studying her closely, her quiet look took on the resemblance of an arrested movement, a composure on tip-toe so to speak, as though she had been stopped in the swift transition from one mood to another. And back of that momentary cessation of action one could see a mind darting, quick, restless, indefatigable, observing, tabulating perhaps even mocking. She had for him the quality of the foreigner, but she gave this quality an objectivity as though he were the stranger and she the well-known established personage taking note of his peculiarities and apparently boundlessly diverted by them.

But of all this Angela was absolutely unaware. No wonder she was puzzling to Roger, for, in addition to the excitement which she—a young woman in the high tide of her youth, her health, and her beauty—would be feeling at receiving in the proper setting the devotion and attention which all women crave, she was swimming in the flood of excitement created by her unique position. Stolen waters are the sweetest. And Angela never forgot that they were stolen. She thought: "Here I am having everything that a girl ought to have just because I had sense enough to suit my actions to my appearance." The realization, the secret fun bubbling back in some hidden recess of her heart, brought colour to her cheeks, a certain temerity to her manner. Roger pondered on this quality. If she were reckless!

The dinner was perfect; it was served with elegance and beauty. Indeed she was surprised at the surroundings, the grandeur even of the hotel to which he had brought her. She had no idea of his means, but had supposed that his circumstances were about those of her other new friends; probably he was better off than Anthony, whose poverty she instinctively sensed, and she judged that his income, whatever it might be,

was not so perilous as Paulette's. But she would
have put him on the same footing as the Starrs.
This sort of expenditure, however, meant money,
"unless he really does like me and is splurging
this time just for me." The idea appealed
to her vanity and gave her a sense of power;
she looked at Roger with a warm smile. At
once his intent, considering gaze filmed; he was
already leaning toward her but he bent even
farther across the perfect little table and asked
in a low, eager tone: "Shall we stay here and
dance or go to your house and talk and smoke
a bit?"

"Oh we'll stay and dance; it would be so late
by the time we get home that we'd only have a
few minutes."

Presently the golden evening was over and
they were in the vestibule at Jayne Street. Roger
said very loudly: "Where's that push button?"
Then lower: "Well, your young lovers aren't
here to-night either. I'm beginning to think you
made that story up, Angèle."

She assured him, laughing, that she had told
the truth. "You come here some time and you'll
see them for yourself." But she wished she could
think of something more ordinary to say. His
hands held hers very tightly; they were very
strong and for the first time she noticed that the
veins stood up on them like cords. She tried to
pull her own away and he released them and,
taking her key, turned the lock in the inner door,
then stood looking down at her.

"Well I'm glad they're not here to-night to
take their revenge." And as he handed her back
the key he kissed her on the lips. His knowledge

of women based on many, many such experiences, told him that her swift retreat was absolutely unfeigned.

As on a former occasion she stood, after she had gained her room, considering herself in the glass. She had been kissed only once before, by Matthew Henson, and that kiss had been neither as casual nor as disturbing as this. She was thrilled, excited, and vaguely displeased. "He is fresh, I'll say that for him." And subsiding into the easy chair she thought for a long time of Anthony Cross and his deep respectful ardour.

In the morning there were flowers.

· · · · · ·

From the class-room she went with Paulette to deliver the latter's sketches. "Have tea to-day with me; we'll blow ourselves at the Ritz. This is the only time in the month that I have any money, so we'll make the best of it."

Angela looked about the warm, luxurious room at the serene, luxurious women, the super-groomed, super-deferential, tremendously confident men. She sighed. "I love all this, love it."

Paulette, busy blowing smoke-rings, nodded. "I blew sixteen that time. Watch me do it again. There's nothing really to this kind of life, you know."

"Oh don't blow smoke-rings! It's the only thing in the world that can spoil your looks. What do you mean there's nothing to it?"

"Well for a day-in-and-day-out existence, it just doesn't do. It's too boring. It's fun for you and me to drift in here twice a year when we've just had a nice, fat cheque which we've got to spend. But there's nothing to it for every day; it's too much like reaching the harbour where you would be. The tumult and the shouting are all over. I'd rather live just above the danger line down on little old Bank Street, and think up a way to make five hundred dollars so I could go to the French Riviera second class and bum around those little towns, Villefranche, Beaulieu, Cagnes,—you must see them, Angèle— and have a spanking affair with a real man with honest to God blood in his veins than to sit here and drink tea and listen to the nothings of all these tame tigers, trying you out, seeing how much it will take to buy you."

Angela was bewildered by this outburst. "I thought you said you didn't like affairs unless you could conduct them on your own *pied à terre.*"

"Did I? Well that was another time—not to-day. By the way, what would you say if I were to tell you that I'm going to Russia?"

She glanced at her friend with the bright shamelessness of a child, for she knew that Angela had heard of Jack Hudson's acceptance as newspaper correspondent in Moscow.

"I wouldn't say anything except that I'd much rather be here in the warmth and cleanliness of the Ritz than be in Moscow where I'm sure it will be cold and dirty."

"That's because you've never wanted anyone." Her face for a moment was all desire. Beautiful

but terrible too. "She actually looks like Hetty
Daniels," thought Angela in astonishment. Only,
alas, there was no longer any beauty in Hetty's
face.

"When you've set your heart on anybody or
on anything there'll be no telling what you'll
do, Angèle. For all your innocence you're as
deep, you'll be as desperate as Martha Burden
once you're started. I know your kind. Well, if
you must play around in the Ritz, etcet., etcet.,
I'll tell Roger Fielding. He's a good squire and
he can afford it."

"Why? Is he so rich?"

"Rich! If all the wealth that he—no, not he,
but his father—if all the wealth that old man
Fielding possesses were to be converted into silver
dollars there wouldn't be space enough in this
room, big as it is, to hold it."

Angela tried to envisage it. "And Roger, what
does he do?"

"Spend it. What is there for him to do?
Nothing except have a good time and keep
in his father's good graces. His father's some
kind of a personage and all that, you know,
crazy about his name and his posterity. Roger
doesn't dare get drunk and lie in the gutter
and he mustn't make a misalliance. Outside
of that the world's his oyster and he eats it
every day. There's a boy who gets everything
he wants."

"What do you mean by a misalliance? He's
not royalty."

"Spoken like a good American. No, he's not.
But he mustn't marry outside certain limits. No
chorus girl romances for his father. The old man

wouldn't care a rap about money but he would
insist on blue blood and the Mayflower. The
funny thing is that Roger, for all his appearing
so democratic, is that way too. But of course
he's been so run after the marvel is that he's
as unspoiled as he is. But it's the one thing
I can't stick in him. I don't mind a man's not
marrying me; but I can't forgive him if he
thinks I'm not good enough to marry him.
Any woman is better than the best of men."
Her face took on its intense, burning expression;
one would have said she was consumed with
excitement.

Angela nodded, only half-listening. Roger a
multi-millionaire! Roger who only two nights
ago had kissed and mumbled her fingers, his eyes
avid and yet so humble and beseeching!

"One thing, if you do start playing around
with Roger be careful. He's a good bit of a
rotter, and he doesn't care what he says or spends
to gain his ends." She laughed at the inquiry in
her friend's eyes. "No, I've never given Roger
five minutes' thought. But I know his kind.
They're dangerous. It's wrong for men to have
both money and power; they're bound to make
some woman suffer. Come on up the Avenue
with me and I'll buy a hat. I can't wear this
whang any longer. It's too small, looks like a
peanut on a barrel."

. . . . .

Angela was visual minded. She saw the days
of the week, the months of the year in little narrow
divisions of space. She saw the past years of her

128

life falling into separate, uneven compartments
whose ensemble made up her existence. Whenever
she looked back on this period from Christmas to
Easter she saw a bluish haze beginning in a white
mist and flaming into something red and terrible;
and across the bluish haze stretched the name:
Roger.

Roger! She had never seen anyone like him:
so gay, so beautiful, like a blond, glorious god, so
overwhelming, so persistent. She had not liked
him so much at first except as one likes the sun
or the sky or a singing bird, anything jolly and
free. There had been no touching points for their
minds. He knew nothing of life except what was
pleasurable; it is true his idea of the pleasurable
did not always coincide with hers. He had no
fears, no restraints, no worries. Yes, he had one;
he did not want to offend his father. He wanted
ardently and unswervingly his father's money.
He did not begrudge his senior a day, an hour, a
moment of life; about this he had a queer,
unselfish sincerity. The old financial war horse
had made his fortune by hard labour and pitiless
fighting. He had given Roger his being, the
entrée into a wonderful existence. Already he
bestowed upon him an annual sum which would
have kept several families in comfort. If Roger
had cared to save for two years he need never have
asked his father for another cent. With any kind
of luck he could have built up for himself a second
colossal fortune. But he did not care to do this.
He did not wish his father one instant's loss of
life or of its enjoyment. But he did want final
possession of those millions.

Angela liked him best when he talked about

"my dad;" he never mentioned the vastness
of his wealth, but by now she could not have
helped guessing even without Paulette's aid that
he was a wealthy man. She would not take
jewellery from him, but there was a steady
stream of flowers, fruit, candy, books, fine copies
of the old masters. She was afraid and ashamed
to express a longing in his presence. And with
all this his steady, constant attendance. And an
odd watchfulness which she felt but could not
explain.

"He must love me." she said to herself, thinking of his caresses. She had been unable to keep
him from kissing her. Her uneasiness had amused
and charmed him: he laughed at her Puritanism,
succeeded in shaming her out of it. "Child,
where have you lived? Why there's nothing in a
kiss. If I didn't kiss you I couldn't come to see
you. And I have to see you, Angèle!" His
voice grew deep; the expression in his eyes made
her own falter.

Yet he did not ask her to marry him. "But
I suppose it's because he can see I don't love
him yet." And she wondered what it would
be like to love. Even Jinny knew more about
this than she, for she had felt, perhaps still
did feel, a strong affection for Matthew Henson.
Well, anyway, if they married she would probably come to love him; most women learned
to love their husbands. At first after her conversation with Paulette about Roger she had
rather expected a diminution at any time of
his attention, for after all she was unknown; from
Roger's angle she would be more than outside
the pale. But she was sure now that he loved and

would want to marry her, for it never occurred
to her that men bestowed attentions such as these
on a passing fancy. She saw her life rounding out
like a fairy tale. Poor, coloured—coloured in
America; unknown, a nobody! And here at her
hand was the forward thrust shadow of love
and of great wealth. She would do lots of good
among coloured people; she would see that Miss
Powell, for instance, had her scholarship. Oh
she would hunt out girls and men like Seymour
Porter,—she had almost forgotten his name,—
or was it Arthur Sawyer?—and give them a taste
of life in its fullness and beauty such as they had
never dreamed of.

To-night she was to go out with Roger. She
wore her flame-coloured dress again; a pretty
green one was also hanging up in her closet, but
she wore the flame one because it lighted her up
from within—lighted not only her lovely, fine
body but her mind too. Her satisfaction with her
appearance let loose some inexplicable spring of
gaiety and merriment and simplicity so that she
seemed almost daring.

Roger, sitting opposite, tried to probe her
mood, tried to gauge the invitation of her manner
and its possibilities. She touched him once or
twice, familiarly; he thought almost possessively.
She seemed to be within reach now if along with
that accessibility she had recklessness. It was this
attribute which for the first time to-night he
thought to divine within her. If in addition to
her insatiable interest in life—for she was always
asking him about people and places,—she possessed this recklessness, then indeed he might put
to her a proposal which had been hanging on his

lips for weeks and months. Something innocent, pathetically untouched about her had hitherto kept him back. But if she had the requisite daring! They were dining in East Tenth Street in a small *café*—small contrasted with the Park Avenue Hotel to which he had first taken her. But about them stretched the glitter and perfection of crystal and silver, of marvellous napery and of obsequious service. Everything, Angela thought, looking about her, was translated. The slight odour of food was, she told Fielding, really an aroma: the mineral water which he was drinking because he could not help it and she because she could not learn to like wine, was nectar; the bread, the fish, the courses, were ambrosia. The food, too, in general was to be spoken of as viands.

"Vittles, translated," she said laughing.

"And you, you, too, are translated. Angèle, you are wonderful, you are charming," his lips answered but his senses beat and hammered. Intoxicated with the magic of the moment and the surroundings, she turned her smiling countenance a little nearer, and saw his face change, darken. A cloud over the sun.

"Excuse me," he said and walked hastily across the room back of her. In astonishment she turned and looked after him. At a table behind her three coloured people (under the direction of a puzzled and troubled waiter,) were about to take a table. Roger went up and spoke to the headwaiter authoritatively, even angrily. The latter glanced about the room, nodded obsequiously and crossing, addressed the little group. There was a hasty, slightly acrid discussion. Then the

three filed out, past Angela's table this time, their
heads high.

She turned back to her plate, her heart sick.
For her the evening was ended. Roger came back,
his face flushed, triumphant, "Well I put a spoke
in the wheel of those 'coons'! They forget
themselves so quickly, coming in here spoiling
white people's appetites. I told the manager if
they brought one of their damned suits I'd be
responsible. I wasn't going to have them here
with you, Angèle. I could tell that night at
Martha Burden's by the way you looked at that
girl that you had no time for darkies. I'll bet
you'd never been that near to one before in your
life, had you? Wonder where Martha picked
that one up."

She was silent, lifeless. He went on recounting
instances of how effectively he had "spoked the
wheel" of various coloured people. He had black-
balled Negroes in Harvard, aspirants for small
literary or honour societies. "I'd send 'em all
back to Africa if I could. There's been a darkey
up in Harlem's got the right idea, I understand;
though he must be a low brute to cave in on his
race that way; of course it's merely a matter of
money with him. He'd betray them all for a few
thousands. Gosh, if he could really pull it through
I don't know but what I'd be willing to finance
it."

To this tirade there were economic reasons to
oppose, tenets of justice, high ideals of humanity.
But she could think of none of them. Speechless,
she listened to him, her appetite fled.

"What's the matter, Angèle? Did it make you
sick to see them?"

133

"No, no not that. I—I don't mind them; you're mistaken about me and that girl at Martha Burden's. It's you, you're so violent. I didn't know you were that way!"

"And I've made you afraid of me? Oh, I don't want to do that." But he was flattered to think that he had affected her. "See here, let's get some air. I'll take you for a spin around the Park and then run you home."

But she did not want to go to the Park; she wanted to go home immediately. His little blue car was outside; in fifteen minutes they were at Jayne Street. She would not permit him to come inside, not even in the vestibule; she barely gave him her hand.

"But Angèle, you can't leave me like this; why what have I done? Did it frighten you because I swore a little? But I'd never swear at you. Don't go like this."

She was gone, leaving him staring and non-plussed on the sidewalk. Lighting a cigarette, he climbed back in his car. "Now what the devil!" He shifted his gears. "But she likes me. I'd have sworn she liked me to-night. Those damn niggers! I bet she's thinking about me this minute."

·   ·   ·   ·   ·

He would have lost his bet. She was thinking about the coloured people.

She could visualize them all so plainly; she could interpret their changing expressions as completely as though those changes lay before her in a book. There were a girl and two men, one

young, the other the father perhaps of either of
the other two. The fatherly-looking person, for
so her mind docketed him, bore an expression of
readiness for any outcome whatever. She knew
and understood the type. His experiences of
surprises engendered by this thing called prejudice
had been too vast for them to appear to him as
surprises. If they were served this was a lucky
day; if not he would refuse to let the incident
shake his stout spirit.

It was to the young man and the girl that her
interest went winging. In the mirror behind
Roger she had seen them entering the room and
she had thought: "Oh, here are some of them
fighting it out again. Oh God! please let them be
served, please don't let their evening be spoiled."
She was so happy herself and she knew that the
reception of fifty other *maîtres d' hôtel* could not
atone for a rebuff at the beginning of the game.
The young fellow was nervous, his face tense,—
thus might he have looked going to meet the
enemy's charge in the recent Great War; but
there the odds were even; here the cards were
already stacked against him. Presently his ex
pression would change for one of grimness,
determination and despair. Talk of a lawsuit
would follow; apparently did follow; still a lawsuit at best is a poor substitute for an evening's
fun.

But the girl, the girl in whose shoes she herself
might so easily have been! She was so clearly a
nice girl, with all that the phrase implies. To
Angela watching her intently and yet with the indifference of safety she recalled Virginia, so
slender, so appealing she was and so brave. So

135

very brave! Ah, that courage! It affected at
first a gay hardihood: "Oh I know it isn't cus-
tomary for people like us to come into this café,
but everything is going to be all right." It met
Angela's gaze with a steadiness before which
her own quailed, for she thought: "Oh, poor
thing! perhaps she thinks that I don't want her
either." And when the blow had fallen the
courage had had to be translated anew into a
comforting assurance. "Don't worry about me,
Jimmy," the watching guest could just hear her.
"Indeed, indeed it won't spoil the evening, I
should say not; there're plenty of places where
they'd be all right. We just happened to pick a
lemon."

The three had filed out, their heads high, their
gaze poised and level. But the net result of the
evening's adventure would be an increased cynicism in the elderly man, a growing bitterness for
the young fellow, and a new timidity in the girl,
who, even after they had passed into the street,
could not relieve her feelings, for she must comfort her baffled and goaded escort.

Angela wondered if she had been half as con-
soling to Matthew Henson,—was it just a short
year ago? And suddenly, sitting immobile in her
arm-chair, her evening cloak slipping unnoticed
to the floor, triumph began to mount in her. Life
could never cheat her as it had cheated that
coloured girl this evening, as it had once cheated
her in Philadelphia with Matthew. She was free,
free to taste life in all its fullness and sweetness,
in all its minutest details. By exercising sufficient
courage to employ the unique weapon which an
accident of heredity had placed in her grasp she

was able to master life. How she blessed her
mother for showing her the way! In a country
where colour or the lack of it meant the difference
between freedom and fetters how lucky she was!

But, she told herself, she was through with
Roger Fielding.

CHAPTER V

Now it was Spring, Spring in New York. Washington Square was a riot of greens that showed up bravely against the great red brick houses on its north side. The Arch viewed from Fifth Avenue seemed a gateway to Paradise. The long deep streets running the length of the city invited an exploration to the ends where pots of gold doubtless gleamed. On the short crosswise streets the April sun streamed in splendid banners of deep golden light.

In two weeks Angela had seen Roger only once. He telephoned every day, pleading, beseeching, entreating. On the one occasion when she did permit him to call there were almost tears in his eyes. "But, darling, what did I do? If you'd only tell me that. Perhaps I could explain away whatever it is that's come between us." But there was nothing to explain she told him gravely, it was just that he was harder, more cruel than she had expected; no, it wasn't the coloured people, she lied and felt her soul blushing, it was that now she knew him when he was angry or displeased, and she could see how ruthless, how determined he was to have things his way. His willingness to pay the costs of the possbile lawsuit had filled her with a sharp fear. What could one do against a man, against a group of men such as he and his

138

kind represented who would spend time and
money to maintain a prejudice based on a silly,
time-worn tradition?

Yet she found she did not want to lose sight
of him completely. The care, the attention, the
flattery with which he had surrounded her were
beginning to produce their effect. In the beautiful
but slightly wearying balminess of the Spring she
missed the blue car which had been constantly
at her call; eating a good but homely meal in
her little living-room with the cooking odours
fairly overwhelming her from the kitchenette, she
found herself longing unconsciously for the dainty
food, the fresh Spring delicacies which she knew
he would be only too glad to procure for her.
Shamefacedly she had to acknowledge that the
separation which she was so rigidly enforcing
meant a difference in her tiny exchequer, for it had
now been many months since she had regularly
taken her main meal by herself and at her own
expense.

To-day she was especially conscious of her
dependence upon him, for she was to spend the
afternoon in Van Cortlandt Park with Anthony.
There had been talk of subways and the Elevated.
Roger would have had the blue car at the door
and she would have driven out of Jayne Street in
state. Now it transpired that Anthony was to
deliver some drawings to a man, a tricky customer,
whom it was best to waylay if possible on Saturday
afternoon. Much as he regretted it he would
probably be a little late. Angela, therefore, to
save time must meet him at Seventy-second Street.
Roger would never have made a request like that;
he would have brought his lawyer or his business

man along in the car with him and, dismissing him with a curt "Well I'll see if I can finish this to-morrow," would have hastened to her with his best Walter Raleigh manner, and would have produced the cloak, too, if she would but say so. Perhaps she'd have to take him back. Doubtless later on she could manage his prejudices if only he would not speak. But how was she to accomplish that?

Still it was lovely being here with Anthony in the park, so green and fresh, so new with the recurring newness of Spring. Anthony touched her hand and said as he had once before, "I'm so content to be with you, Angel. I may call you Angel, mayn't I? You are that to me, you know. Oh if you only knew how happy it makes me to be content, to be satisfied like this. I could get down on my knees and thank God for it like a little boy." He looked like a little boy as he said it. "Happiness is a hard thing to find and harder still to keep."

She asked him idly, "Haven't you always been happy?"

His face underwent a startling change. Not only did the old sadness and strain come back on it, but a great bitterness such as she had never before seen.

"No," he said slowly as though thinking through long years of his life. "I haven't been happy for years, not since I was a little boy. Never once have I been happy nor even at ease until I met you."

But she did not want him to find his happiness in her. That way would only lead to greater un-happiness for him. So she said, to change the subject: "Could you tell me about it?"

But there was nothing to tell, he assured her, his face growing darker, grimmer. "Only my father was killed when I was a little boy, killed by his enemies. I've hated them ever since; I never stopped hating them until I met you." But this was just as dangerous a road as the other plus the possibilities of re-opening old wounds. So she only shivered and said vaguely, "Oh, that was terrible! Too terrible to talk about. I'm sorry, Anthony!" And then as a last desperate topic: "Are you ever going back to Brazil?" For she knew that he had come to the United States from Rio de Janeiro. He had spent Christmas at her house, and had shown her pictures of the great, beautiful city and of his mother, a slender, dark-eyed woman with a perpetual sadness in her eyes.

The conversation languished. She thought: "It must be terrible to be a man and to have these secret hates and horrors back of one." Some Spanish feud, a matter of hot blood and ready knives, a sudden stroke, and then this deadly memory for him.

"No," he said after a long pause. "I'm never going back to Brazil. I couldn't." He turned to her suddenly. "Tell me, Angel, what kind of girl are you, what do you think worth while? Could you, for the sake of love, for the sake of being loyal to the purposes and vows of someone you loved, bring yourself to endure privation and hardship and misunderstanding, hardship that would be none the less hard because it really could be avoided?"

She thought of her mother who had loved her father so dearly, and of the wash-days which she

141

had endured for him, the long years of household routine before she and Jinny had been old enough to help her first with their hands and then with their earnings. She thought of the little, dark, shabby house, of the made-over dresses and turned coats. And then she saw Roger and his wealth and his golden recklessness, his golden keys which could open the doors to beauty and ease and— decency! Oh, it wasn't decent for women to have to scrub and work and slave and bear children and sacrifice their looks and their pretty hands,— she saw her mother's hands as they had always looked on wash day, they had a white, boiled appearance. No, she would not fool herself nor Anthony. She was no sentimentalist. It was not likely that she, a girl who had left her little sister and her home to go out to seek life and happiness would throw it over for poverty,—hardship. If a man loved a woman how could he ask her that?

So she told him gently: "No, Anthony, I couldn't," and watched the blood drain from his face and the old look of unhappiness drift into his eyes.

He answered inadequately. "No, of course you couldn't." And turning over,—he had been sitting on the grass at her feet—he lay face downward on the scented turf. Presently he sat up and giving her a singularly sweet but wistful smile, said: "I almost touched happiness, Angèle. Did you by any chance ever happen to read Browning's 'Two in the Roman Campagna'?"

But she had read very little poetry except what had been required in her High School work, and certainly not Browning.

He began to interpret the fragile, difficult
beauty of the poem with its light but sure touch
on evanescent, indefinable feeling. He quoted:

> "How is it under our control
> To love or not to love?"

And again:

> "Infinite passion, and the pain
> Of infinite hearts that yearn."

They were silent for a long time. And again
she wondered how it would feel to love. He
watched the sun drop suddenly below some tree
tops and rose to his feet shivering a little as
though its disappearance had made him immediately cold.

" 'So the good moment goes.' Come, Angel,
we'll have to hasten. It's getting dark and it's
a long walk to the subway."

.   .   .   .   .

The memory of the afternoon stayed by her,
shrouding her thoughts, clinging to them like a
tenuous, adhering mantle. But she said to herself:
"There's no use thinking about that. I'm not
going to live that kind of life." And she knew
she wanted Roger and what he could give her and
the light and gladness which he always radiated.
She wanted none of Anthony's poverty and privation and secret vows,—he meant, she supposed,
some promise to devote himself to REAL ART,
—her visual mind saw it in capitals. Well, she
was sick of tragedy, she belonged to a tragic race.

143

"God knows it's time for one member of it to be having a little fun."

"Yes," she thought all through her class, painting furiously—for she had taken up her work in earnest since Christmas—"yes, I'll just make up my mind to it. I'll take Roger back and get married and settle down to a pleasant, safe, beautiful life." And useful. It should be very useful. Perhaps she'd win Roger around to helping coloured people. She'd look up all sorts of down-and-outers and give them a hand. And she'd help Anthony, at least she'd offer to help him; she didn't believe he would permit her.

Coming out of the building a thought occurred to her: "Take Roger back, but back to what? To his old status of admiring, familiar, generous friend? Just that and no more?" Here was her old problem again. She stopped short to consider it.

Martha Burden overtook her. "Planning the great masterpiece of the ages, Angèle? Better come along and work it out by my fireside. I can give you some tea. Are you coming?"

"Yes," said Angela, still absorbed.

"Well," said Martha after they had reached the house. "I've never seen any study as deep as that. Come out of it Angèle, you'll drown. You're not by any chance in love, are you?"

"No," she replied, "at least I don't know. But tell me, Martha, suppose—suppose I were in love with one of them, what do you do about it, how do you get them to propose?"

Martha lay back and laughed. "Such candour have I not met, no, not in all Flapperdom. Angèle, if I could answer that I'd be turning women away from my door and handing out my knowledge to the ones I did admit at a hundred dollars a throw."

"But there must be some way. Oh, of course, I know lots of them propose, but how do you get a proposal from the ones you want,—the,—the interesting ones?"

"You really want to know? The only answer I can give you is Humpty Dumpty's dictum to Alice about verbs and adjectives: 'It depends on which is the stronger'." She interpreted for her young guest was clearly mystified. "It depends on (A) whether you are strong enough to make him like you more than you like him; (B) whether if you really do like him more than he does you you can conceal it. In other words, so far as liking is concerned you must always be ahead of the game, you must always like or appear to like him a little less than he does you. And you must make him want you. But you mustn't give. Oh yes, I know that men are always wanting women to give, but they don't want the women to want to give. They want to take,—or at any rate to compel the giving."

"It sounds very complicated, like some subtle game."

A deep febrile light came into Martha's eyes. "It is a game, and the hardest game in the world for a woman, but the most fascinating; the hardest in which to strike a happy medium. You see, you have to be careful not to withhold too much and yet to give very little. If we don't give enough we lose them. If we give too much we lose ourselves. Oh, Angèle, God doesn't like women."

"But," said Angela thinking of her own mother, "there are some women who give all and men like them the better for it."

"Oh, yes, that's true. Those are the blessed among women. They ought to get down on their knees every day and thank God for permitting them to be their normal selves and not having to play a game." For a moment her still, proud face broke into deeps of pain. "Oh, Angèle, think of loving and never, never being able to show it until you're asked for it; think of living a game every hour of your life!" Her face quivered back to its normal immobility.

Angela walked home through the purple twilight musing no longer on her own case but on this unexpected revelation. "Well," she said, "I certainly shouldn't like to love like that." She thought of Anthony: "A woman could be her true self with him." But she had given him up.

.   .   .   .   .

If the thing to do were to play a game she would play one. Indeed she rather enjoyed the prospect. She was playing a game now, a game against public tradition on the one hand and family instinct on the other; the stakes were happiness and excitement, and almost anyone looking at the tricks which she had already taken would prophesy that she would be the winner. She decided to follow all the rules as laid down by Martha Burden and to add any workable ideas of her own. When Roger called again she was still unable to see him, but her voice was a shade less curt over the telephone; she did not cut him

off so abruptly. "I must not withhold too much,"
she reminded herself. He was quick to note the
subtle change in intonation. "But you're going
to let me come to see you soon, Angèle," he
pleaded. "You wouldn't hold out this way
against me forever. Say when I may come."

"Oh, one of these days; I must go now, Roger.
Good-bye."

After the third call she let him come to spend
Friday evening. She heard the blue car rumbling
in the street and a few minutes later he came
literally staggering into the living-room so laden
was he with packages. Flowers, heaps of spring
posies had come earlier in the day, lilacs, jonquils,
narcissi. Now this evening there were books and
candy, handkerchiefs,—"they were so dainty and
they looked just like you," he said fearfully, for
she had never taken an article of dress from him,
—two pictures, a palette and some fine brushes
and last a hamper of all sorts of delicacies.
"I thought if you didn't mind we'd have
supper here; it would be fun with just us
two."

How much he pleased her he could not divine;
it was the first time he had ever given a hint of
any desire for sheer domesticity. Anthony had
sought nothing better than to sit and smoke and
watch her flitting about in her absurd red or
violet apron. Matthew Henson had been speechless with ecstasy when on a winter night she had
allowed him to come into the kitchen while she
prepared for him a cup of cocoa. But Roger's
palate had been so flattered by the concoctions
of chefs famous in London, Paris and New York
that he had set no store by her simple cooking.

Indeed his inevitable comment had been: "Here, what do you want to get yourself all tired out for? Let's go to a restaurant. It's heaps less bother."

But to-night he, too, watched her with humble, delighted eyes. She realized that he was conscious of her every movement; once he tried to embrace her, but she whirled out of his reach without reproach but with decision. He subsided, too thankful to be once more in her presence to take any risks. And when he left he had kissed her hand.

She began going about with him again, but with condescension, with kindness. And with the new vision gained from her talk with Martha she could see his passion mounting. "Make him want you," —that was the second rule. It was clear that he did, no man could be as persevering as this otherwise. Still he did not speak. They were to meet that afternoon in front of the school to go "anywhere you want, dear, I'm yours to command." It was the first time that he had called for her at the building, and she came out a little early, for she did not want any of the three, Martha, Paulette, nor Anthony, to see whom she was meeting. It would be better to walk to the corner, she thought, they'd be just that much less likely to recognize him. She heard footsteps hurrying behind her, heard her name and turned to see Miss Powell, pleased and excited. She laid her hand on Angela's arm but the latter shook her off. Roger must not see her on familiar terms like this with a coloured girl for she felt that the afternoon portended something and she wanted no side issues. The coloured girl gave her a penetrating glance; then her habitual reserve settled down

148

blotting out the eagerness, leaving her face blurred and heavy. "I beg your pardon, Miss Mory, I'm sure," she murmured and stepped out into the tempestuous traffic of Fourth Avenue. Angela was sorry; she would make it up to-morrow, she thought, but she had not dismissed her a moment too soon for Roger came rushing up, his car resplendent and resplendent himself in a grey suit, soft grey hat and blue tie. Angela looked at him approvingly. "You look just like the men in the advertising pages of the Saturday Evening Post," she said, and the fact that he did not wince under the compliment proved the depth of his devotion, for every one of his outer garments, hat, shoes, and suit, had been made to measure.

They went to Concy Island. "The ocean will be there, but very few people and only a very few amusements," said Roger. They had a delightful time; they were like school children, easily and frankly amused; they entered all the booths that were open, ate pop-corn and hot dogs and other local dainties. And presently they were flying home under the double line of trees on Ocean Parkway and entering the bosky loveliness of Prospect Park. Roger slowed down a little.

"Oh," said Angela. "I love this car."

He bent toward her instantly. "Does it please you? Did you miss it when you made me stay away from you?"

She was afraid she had made a mistake: "Yes, but that's not why I let you come back."

"I know that. But you do like it, don't you, comfort and beauty and dainty surroundings?"

"Yes," she said solemnly, "I love them all."

He was silent then for a long, long time, his face a little set, a worried line on his forehead.

"Well now what's he thinking about?" she asked herself, watching his hands and their clever manipulation of the steering wheel though his thoughts, she knew, were not on that.

He turned to her with an air of having made up his mind. "Angèle, I want you to promise to spend a day out riding with me pretty soon. I— I have something I want to say to you." He was a worldly young man about town but he was actually mopping his brow. "I've got to go south for a week for my father,—he owns some timber down there with which he used to supply saw-mills but since the damned niggers have started running north it's been something of a weight on his hands. He wants me to go down and see whether it's worth his while to hold on to it any longer. It's so rarely that he asks anything of me along a business line that I'd hate to refuse him. But I'll be back the morning of the twenty-sixth. I'll have to spend the afternoon and evening with him out on Long Island but on the twenty-seventh could you go out with me?"

She said as though all this preamble portended nothing: "I couldn't give you the whole day, but I'd go in the afternoon."

"Oh," his face fell a little. "Well, the after-noon then. Only of course we won't be able to go far out. Perhaps you'd like me to arrange a lunch and we'd go to one of the Parks, Central or the Bronx, or Van Cortlandt,——"

"No, not Van Cortlandt," she told him. That park was sacred to Anthony Cross.

"Well, wherever you say. We can settle it

even that day. The main thing is that you'll
go."

She said to herself. "Aren't men funny! He
could have asked me five times over while he was
making all these arrangements." But she was
immensely relieved, even happy. She felt very
kindly toward him; perhaps she was in love after
all, only she was not the demonstrative kind. It
was too late for him to come in, but they sat in the
car in the dark security of Jayne Street and she
let him take her in his arms and kiss her again
and again. For the first time she returned his
kisses.

.   .   .   .   .

Weary but triumphant she mounted the stairs
almost stumbling from a sudden, overwhelming
fatigue. She had been under a strain! But it
was all over now; she had conquered, she had been
the stronger. She had secured not only him but
an assured future, wealth, protection, influence,
even power. She herself was power,—like the
women one reads about, like Cleopatra,— Cleo
patra's African origin intrigued her, it was a fitting comparison. Smiling, she took the last steep
stairs lightly, springily, suddenly reinvigorated.

As she opened the door a little heap of letters
struck her foot. Switching on the light she sat
in the easy chair and incuriously turned them over.
They were bills for the most part, she had had to
dress to keep herself dainty and desirable for
Roger. At the bottom of the heap was a letter
from Virginia. When she became Mrs. Roger
Fielding she would never have to worry about a

bill again; how she would laugh when she remembered the small amounts for which these called! Never again would she feel the slight quake of dismay which always overtook her when she saw words: "Miss Angèle Mory in account with,——" Outside of the regular monthly statement for gas she had never seen a bill in her father's house. Well, she'd have no difficulty in getting over her squeamish training.

Finally she opened Jinny's letter. Her sister had written:

"Angela I'm coming up for an exam. on the twenty-eighth. I'll arrive on the twenty-sixth or I could come the day before. You'll meet me, won't you? I know where I'm going to stay,"— she gave an address on 139th Street—" but I don't know how to get there; I don't know your school hours, write and tell me so I can arrive when you're free. There's no reason why I should put you out."

So Virginia was really coming to try her luck in New York. It would be nice to have her so near. "Though I don't suppose we'll be seeing so much of each other," she thought, absently reaching for her schedule. "Less than ever now, for I suppose Roger and I will live in Long Island; yes, that would be much wiser. I'll wear a veil when I go to meet her, for those coloured porters stare at you so and they never forget you."

The twenty-seventh came on Thursday; she had classes in the morning; well, Jinny would be coming in the afternoon anyway, and after twelve she had,—Oh heavens that was *the* day, the day she was to go out with Roger, the day that he

would put the great question. And she wrote
to Virginia:

"Come the twenty-sixth, Honey, any time after
four. I couldn't possibly meet you on the twenty-
seventh. But the twenty-sixth is all right. Let
me know when your train comes in and I'll be
there. And welcome to our city."

CHAPTER VI

THE week was one of tumult, almost of agony. After all, matters were not completely settled, you never could tell. She would be glad when the twenty-seventh had come and gone, for then, then she would be rooted, fixed. She and Roger would marry immediately. But now he was so far away, in Georgia; she missed him and evidently he missed her for the first two days brought her long telegrams almost letters. "I can think of nothing but next Thursday, are you thinking of it too?" The third day brought a letter which said practically the same thing, adding, "Oh, Angèle, I wonder what you will say!"

"But he could ask me and find out," she said to herself and suddenly felt assured and triumphant. Every day thereafter brought her a letter reiterating this strain. "And I know how he hates to write!"

The letter on Wednesday read, "Darling, when you get this I'll actually be in New York; if I can I'll call you up but I'll have to rush like mad so as to be free for Thursday, so perhaps I can't manage."

She made up her mind not to answer the telephone even if it did ring, she would strike one last note of indifference though only she herself would be aware of it.

It was the day on which Jinny was to arrive.

It would be fun to see her, talk to her, hear all the
news about the queer, staid people whom she had
left so far behind. Farther now than ever.
Matthew Henson was still in the post-office, she
knew. Arthur Sawyer was teaching at Sixteenth
and Fitzwater; she could imagine the sick distaste
that mantled his face every time he looked at
the hideous, discoloured building. Porter had
taken his degree in dentistry but he was not prac-
tising, on the contrary he was editing a small
weekly, getting deeper, more and more hopelessly
into debt she was sure. . . . It would be fun
some day to send him a whopping cheque; after
all, he had taken a chance just as she had; she
recognized his revolt as akin to her own, only he
had not had her luck. She must ask Jinny about
all this.

It was too bad that she had to meet her sister,
—but she must. Just as likely as not she'd be
car sick and then New York was terrifying for
the first time to the stranger,—she had known
an instant's sick dread herself that first day when
she had stood alone and ignorant in the great
rotunda of the station. But she was different
from Jinny; nothing about life ever made her
really afraid; she might hurt herself, suffer, meet
disappointment, but life could not alarm her;
she loved to come to grips with it, to force it to
a standstill, to yield up its treasures. But Jinny
although brave, had secret fears, she was really
only a baby. Her little sister! For the first
time in months she thought of her with a great
surge of sisterly tenderness.

It was time to go. She wore her most un-
obtrusive clothes, a dark blue suit, a plain white

155

silk shirt, a dark blue, bell-shaped hat—a *cloche*
—small and fitting down close over her eyes.
She pulled it down even farther and settled her
modish veil well over the tip of her nose. It
was one thing to walk about the Village with Miss
Powell. There were practically no coloured
people there. But this was different. Those
curious porters should never be able to recognize
her. Seymour Porter had worked among them
one summer at Broad Street station in Philadelphia. He used to say: "They aren't really
curious, you know, but their job makes them sick;
so they're always hunting for the romance, for
the adventure which for a day at least will take
the curse off the monotonous obsequiousness of
their lives."

She was sorry for them, but she could not
permit them to remedy their existence at her
expense.

    •   •   •   •   •

In her last letter she had explained to Jinny
about those two troublesome staircases which lead
from the train level of the New York Pennsylvania Railroad station to the street level.
"There's no use my trying to tell you which one
to take in order to bring you up to the right hand
or to the left hand side of the elevator because
I never know myself. So all I can say, dear, is
when you do get up to the elevator just stick to
it and eventually I'll see you or you'll see me as
I revolve around it. Don't you move, for it
might turn out that we were both going in the
same direction."

True to her own instructions, she was stationed

between the two staircases, jerking her neck now toward one staircase, now toward the other, stopping short to look at the elevator itself. She thrust up her veil to see better.

A man sprinted by in desperate haste, brushing so closely by her that the corner of his suit-case struck sharply on the thin inner curve of her knee.

"My goodness!" she exclaimed involuntarily.

For all his haste he was a gentleman, for he pulled off his hat, threw her a quick backward glance and began: "I beg your—why darling, darling, you don't mean to say you came to meet me!"

"Meet you! I thought you came in this morning." It was Roger, Roger and the sight of him made her stupid with fear.

He stooped and kissed her, tenderly, possessively. "I did,—oh Angela you *are* a beauty! Only a beauty can wear plain things like that. I did come in this morning but I'm trying to catch Kirby, my father's lawyer, he ought to be coming in from Newark just now and I thought I'd take him down to Long Island with me for the night. I've got a lot of documents for him here in this suitcase—that Georgia business was most complicated—that way I won't have to hunt him up in the morning and I'll have more time to—to arrange for our trip in the afternoon. What are you doing here?"

What was she doing there? Waiting for her sister Jinny who was coloured and who showed it. And Roger hated Negroes. She was lost, ruined, unless she could get rid of him. She told the first lie that came into her mind.

"I'm waiting for Paulette." All this could be fixed up with Paulette later. Miss Lister would think as little of deceiving a man, any man, as she would of squashing a mosquito. They were fair game and she would ask no questions.

His face clouded. "Can't say I'm so wild about your waiting for Paulette. Well we can wait together—is she coming up from Philadelphia? That train's bringing my man too from Newark." He had the male's terribly clarity of understanding for train connections.

"What time does your train go to Long Island? I thought you wanted to get the next one."

"Well, I'd like to but they're only half an hour apart. I can wait. Better the loss of an hour to-day than all of to-morrow morning. We can wait together; see the people are beginning to come up. I wish I could take you home but the minute he shows up I'll have to sprint with him."

"Now God be on my side," she prayed. Sometimes these trains were very long. If Mr. Kirby were in the first car and Jinny toward the end that would make all of ten minutes' difference. If only she hadn't given those explicit directions!

There was Jinny, her head suddenly emerging into view above the stairs. She saw Angela, waved her hand. In another moment she would be flinging her arms about her sister's neck; she would be kissing her and saying, "Oh, Angela, Angela darling!"

And Roger, who was no fool, would notice the name Angela—Angèle; he would know no coloured girl would make a mistake like this.

She closed her eyes in a momentary faintness, opened them again.

"What's the matter?" said Roger sharply, "are you sick?"

Jinny was beside her. Now, now the bolt would fall. She heard the gay, childish voice saying laughingly, assuredly:

"I beg your pardon, but isn't this Mrs. Henrietta Jones?"

Oh, God was good! Here was one chance if only Jinny would understand! In his astonishment Roger had turned from her to face the speaker. Angela, her eyes beseeching her sister's from under her close hat brim, could only stammer the old formula: "Really you have the advantage of me. No, I'm not Mrs. Jones."

Roger said rudely, "Of course she isn't Mrs. Jones. Come, Angèle." Putting his arm through hers he stooped for the suitcase.

But Jinny, after a second's bewildered but incredulous stare, was quicker even than they. Her slight figure, her head high, preceded them; vanished into a telephone booth.

Roger glared after her. "Well of all the damned cheek!"

.   .   .   .   .

For the first time in the pursuit of her chosen ends she began to waver. Surely no ambition, no pinnacle of safety was supposed to call for the sacrifice of a sister. She might be selfish,—oh, undoubtedly she had been selfish all these months to leave Jinny completely to herself—but she had never meant to be cruel. She tried to picture the tumult of emotions in her sister's mind, there must have been amazement,—oh she had seen it all on her face, the utter bewilderment, the incredulity and then the settling down on that face of a veil of dignity and pride—like a baby trying to harden its mobile features. She was in her apartment again now, pacing the floor, wondering what to do. Already she had called up the house in 139th Street, it had taken her a half-hour to get the number for she did not know the householder's name and "Information" had been coy, —but Miss Murray had not arrived yet. Were they expecting her? Yes, Miss Murray had written to say that she would be there between six and seven; it was seven-thirty now and she had not appeared. Was there any message? "No, no!" Angela explained she would call again.

But where was Jinny? She couldn't be lost, after all she was grown-up and no fool, she could ask directions. Perhaps she had taken a cab and in the evening traffic had been delayed,—or had met with an accident. This thought sent Angela to the telephone again. There was no Miss Murray as yet. In her wanderings back and forth across the room she caught sight of herself in the mirror. Her face was flushed, her eyes shining with remorse and anxiety. Her vanity reminded her: "If Roger could just see me now." Roger and to-morrow! He would have to speak words of gold to atone for this breach which for his sake she had made in her sister's trust and affection.

At the end of an hour she called again. Yes, Miss Murray had come in. So great was her relief that her knees sagged under her. Yes of course they would ask her to come to the telephone. After a long silence the voice rang again over the wire. "I didn't see her go out but she must have for she's not in her room."

"Oh all right," said Angela, "the main thing was to know that she was there." But she was astonished. Jinny's first night in New York and she was out already! She could not go to see her Thursday because of the engagement with Roger, but she'd make good the next day; she'd be there the first thing, Friday morning. Snatching up a sheet of note-paper she began a long letter full of apologies and excuses. "And I can't come to-morrow, darling, because as I told you I have a very important engagement, an engagement that means very much to me. Oh you'll understand when I tell you about it." She put a special delivery stamp on the letter.

Her relief at learning that Jinny was safe did not ease her guilty conscience. In a calmer mood she tried now to find excuses for herself, extenuating circumstances. As soon as Jinny understood all that was involved she would overlook it. After all, Jinny would want her to be happy. "And anyway," she thought to herself sulkily, "Mamma didn't speak to Papa that day that we were standing on the steps of the Hotel Walton." But she knew that the cases were not analogous; no principle was involved, her mother's silence had not exposed her husband to insult or contumely, whereas Roger's attitude to Virginia had been distinctly offensive. "And moreover," her thoughts continued with merciless clarity, "when a principle *was* at stake your mother never hesitated a moment to let those hospital attendants know of the true status of affairs. In fact she was not aware that she was taking any particular stand. Her husband was her husband and she was glad to acknowledge that relationship."

A sick distaste for her action, for her daily deception, for Roger and his prejudices arose within her. But with it came a dark anger against a country and a society which could create such an issue. And she thought: "If I had spoken to Jinny, had acknowledged her, what good would it have done me or her either? After it was all over she would have been exactly where she was before and I would have lost everything. And I do so want to be happy, to have a good time. At this very hour to-morrow I'll probably be one of the most envied girls in New York. And afterwards I can atone for it all. I'll be good to all sorts of people; I'll really help humanity, lots of coloured folks will be much better off on account of me. And if I had spoken to Jinny I could never have helped them at all." Once she murmured: "I'll help Jinny too, the darling! She shall have everything in the world she wants." But in her heart she knew already that Jinny would want nothing.

CHAPTER VII

THURSDAY came and Thursday sped as Thursdays
will. For a long time Angela saw it as a little
separate entity of time shut away in some hidden
compartment of her mind, a compartment whose
door she dreaded to open.

On Friday she called up her sister early in
the morning. "Is that you, Jinny? Did you
get my letter? Is it all right for me to come
up?"

"Yes," said Jinny noncommittally, to all
questions, then laconically: "But you'd better
come right away if you want to catch me. I take
the examination to-day and haven't much time."

Something in the matter-of-factness of her reply
disconcerted Angela. Yet there certainly was no
reason why her sister should show any enthusiasm
over seeing her. Only she did want to see her,
to talk to some one of her very own to-day.
She would like to burrow her head in
Virginia's shoulder and cry! But a mood
such as Jinny's voice indicated did not invite
confidences.

A stout brown-skinned bustling woman suggesting immense assurance and ability opened the
door. "Miss Murray told me that she was expecting someone. You're to go right on up.
Her's is the room right next to the third storey
front."

163

"She was expecting someone." Evidently Virginia had been discreet. This unexpected, unsought for carefulness carried a sting with it.

"Hello," said Jinny, casually thrusting a dishevelled but picturesque head out of the door. "Can you find your way in? This room's larger than any two we ever had at home, yet already it looks like a ship at sea." She glanced about the disordered place. "I wonder if this is what they mean by 'shipshape.' Here I'll hang up this suit, then you can sit down. Isn't it a sweetie? Got it at Snellenburg's."

She had neither kissed nor offered to shake hands with her sister, yet her manner was friendly enough, even cordial. "See I've bobbed my hair," she went on. "Like it? I'm wild about it even if it does take me forever to fix it." Standing before a mirror she began shaping the ends under with a curling iron.

Angela thought she had never seen any one so pretty and so colourful. Jinny had always shown a preference for high colours; to-day she was revelling in them; her slippers were high heeled small red mules; a deep green dressing-gown hung gracefully from her slim shoulders and from its open collar flamed the rose and gold of her smooth skin. Her eyes were bright and dancing. Her hair, black, alive and curling, ended in a thick velvety straightness like cut plush.

Angela said stiffly, "I hope I didn't get you up, telephoning so early."

Virginia smiled, flushing a little more deeply under the dark gold of her skin. "Oh dear no! I'd already had an earlier call than that this morning."

164

"You had!" exclaimed Angela, astonished. "I didn't know you knew anyone in New York." She remembered her sister's mysterious disappearance the first night of her arrival. "And see here, Jinny, I'm awfully sorry about what happened the other night. I wouldn't have had it happen for a great deal. I wish I could explain to you about it." How confidently she had counted on having marvellous news to tell Virginia and now how could she drag to the light yesterday's sorry memory? "But I called you up again and again and you hadn't arrived and then when they finally did tell me that you had come, it appeared that you had gone out. Where on earth did you go?"

Jinny began to laugh, to giggle in fact. For a moment she was the Virginia of her school days, rejoicing in some innocent mischief, full of it. "I wasn't out. There's a wash-room down the hall and I went there to wash my face,——" it clouded a moment. "And when I came back I walked as I thought into my room. Instead of that I had walked into the room of another lodger. And there he sat——"

"Oh," said Angela inattentively. "I'm glad you weren't out. I was quite worried. Listen, Virginia," she began desperately, "I know you think that what I did in the station the other day was unspeakable; it seems almost impossible for me to explain it to you. But that man with me was a very special friend,——"

"He must have been indeed," Jinny interrupted drily, "to make you cut your own sister." She was still apparently fooling with her hair, her head perched on one side, her eyes glued to the mirror. But she was not making much progress and her lips were trembling.

Angela proceeded unheeding, afraid to stop. "A special friend, and we had come to a very crucial point in our relationship. It was with him that I had the engagement yesterday."

"Well, what about it? Were you expecting him to ask you to marry him? Did he?"

"No," said Angela very low, "that 's just what he didn't do though he,—he asked everything else."

Virginia, dropping the hair-brush, swung about sharply. "And you let him talk like that?"

"I couldn't help it once he had begun,—I was so taken by surprise, and, besides, I think that his ultimate intentions are all right."

"His ultimate intentions! Why, Angela what are you talking about? You know perfectly well what his ultimate intentions are. Isn't he a white man? Well, what kind of intentions would he have toward a coloured woman?"

"Simple! He doesn't know I'm coloured. And besides some of them are decent. You must remember that I know something about these people and you don't, you couldn't, living that humdrum little life of yours at home."

"I know enough about them and about men in general to recognize an insult when I hear one. Some men bear their character stamped right on their faces. Now this man into whose room I walked last night by mistake,——"

"I don't see how you can do very much talking walking into strange men's rooms at ten o'clock at night."

166

The triviality of the retort left Jinny dumb.
It was their first quarrel.

.   .   .   .   .

They sat in silence for a few minutes, for several
minutes. Virginia, apparently completely composed, was letting the tendrils of her mind reach
far, far out to the ultimate possibilities of this
impasse in relationship between herself and her
sister. She thought: "I really have lost her,
she's really gone out of my ken just as I used to
lose her years ago when father and I would be
singing 'The Dying Christian.' I'm twenty-three
years old and I'm really all alone in the world."
Up to this time she had always felt she had
Angela's greater age and supposedly greater wisdom to fall back on, but she banished this
conjecture forever. "Because if she could cut me
when she hadn't seen me for a year for the sake
of a man who she must have known meant to
insult her, she certainly has no intention of
openly acknowledging me again. And I don't
believe I want to be a sister in secret. I hate
this hole and corner business."

She saw again the scene in the station, herself
at first so serene, so self-assured, Angela's
confused coldness, Roger's insolence. Something
hardened, grew cold within her. Even his arrogance had failed to bring Angela to her senses,
and suddenly she remembered that it had been
possible in slavery times for white men and women
to mistreat their mulatto relations, their own flesh
and blood, selling them into deeper slavery in the
far South or standing by watching them beaten,

167

almost, if not completely, to death. Perhaps
there was something fundamentally different between white and coloured blood after all. Aloud
she said: "You know before you went away that
Sunday morning you said that you and I were
different. Perhaps you're right, Angela; perhaps
there is an extra infusion of white blood in your
veins which lets you see life at another angle. If
that's the case I have no right to judge you. You
must forgive my ignorant comments."

She began slipping into a ratine dress of old blue
trimmed with narrow collars and cuffs and a tiny
belt of old rose. Above the soft shades the bronze
and black of her head etched themselves sharply;
she might have been a dainty bird of Paradise
cast in a new arrangement of colours but her
tender face was set in strange and implacable lines.

Angela looked at her miserably. She had not
known just what, in her wounded pride and
humiliation, she had expected to gain from her
sister, but certainly she had hoped for some balm.
And in any event not this cool aloofness. She had
forgotten that her sister might be suffering from
a wound as poignant as her own. The year had
made a greater breach than she had anticipated;
she had never been outspoken, as frank with
Virginia as the latter had been with her, but
there had always been a common ground between
them, a meeting place. In the household Jinny
had had something of a reputation for her willingness to hear all sides of a story, to find an excuse
or make one.

An old aphorism of Hetty Daniels returned to
her. "He who would have friends must show
himself friendly." And she had done anything

168

but that; she had neglected Jinny, had failed to answer her letters, had even planned,—was it only day before yesterday!—to see very little of her in what she had dreamed would be her new surroundings. Oh she had been shameful! But she would make it up to Jinny now—and then she could come to her at this, this crisis in her life which so frightened and attracted her. She was the more frightened because she felt that attraction. She would make her sister understand the desires and longings which had come to her in this strange, dear, free world, and then together they would map out a plan of action. Jinny might be a baby but she had strength. So much strength, said something within her, that just as likely as not she would say: "Let the whole thing go, Angela, Angela! You don't want to be even on the outskirts of a thing like this."

Before she could begin her overtures Jinny was speaking. "Listen, Angela, I've got to be going. I don't know when we'll be seeing each other again, and after what happened Wednesday you can hardly expect me to be looking you up, and as you doubtless are very busy you'd hardly be coming 'way up here. But there are one or two things I want to talk to you about. First about the house."

"About the house? Why it's yours. I've nothing more to do with it."

"I know, but I'm thinking of selling it. There is such a shortage of houses in Philadelphia just now; Mr. Hallowell says I can get at least twice as much as father paid for it. And in that case you've some more money coming to you."

If only she had known of this,—when?—
twenty-four hours earlier, how differently she
might have received Roger's proposition. If she
had met Virginia Wednesday and had had the
talk for which she had planned!

"Well of course it would be awfully nice to have
some more money. But what I don't understand
is how are you going to live? What are you
going to do?"

"If I pass this examination I'm coming over
here, my appointment would be only a matter
of a few months. I'm sure of that. This is May
and I'd only have to wait until September. Well,
I wouldn't be working this summer anyway. And
there's no way in the world which I could fail to
pass. In fact I'm really thinking of taking a
chance and coming over here to substitute. Mr.
Holloster, the University of Pennsylvania man,
has been investigating and he says there's plenty
of work. And I guess I'm due to have a change;
New York rather appeals to me. And there certainly is something about Harlem!" In spite of
her careless manner Angela knew she was thinking
about Matthew Henson. She stretched out her
hand, pulled Jinny's head down on her shoulder.
"Oh darling, don't worry about him. Matthew
really wasn't the man for you."

"Well," said Virginia, "as long as I think he
was, the fact that he wasn't doesn't make any real
difference, does it? At least not at first. But I
certainly shan't worry about it."

"No don't,—I,——" It was on the tip of her
tongue to say "I know two or three nice young
men whom you can play around with. I'll introduce you to them." But could she? Jinny

understood her silence; smiled and nodded. "It's all right, honey, you can't do anything; you would if you could. We've just got to face the fact that you and I are two separate people and we've got to live our lives apart, not like the Siamese twins. And each of us will have to go her chosen way. After all each of us is seeking to get all she can out of life! and if you can get more out of it by being white, as you undoubtedly can, why, why shouldn't you? Only it seems to me that there are certain things in living that are more fundamental even than colour,—but I don't know. I'm all mixed up. But evidently you don't feel that way, and you're just as likely to be right as me."

"Jinny!"

"My dear, I'm not trying to reproach you. I'm trying to look at things without sentiment. After all, in a negative way, merely by saying nothing, you're disclaiming your black blood in a country where it is an inconvenience,—oh! there's not a doubt about that. You may be proud of it, you may be perfectly satisfied with it—I am—but it certainly can shut you out of things. So why shouldn't you disclaim a living manifestation of that blood?"

Before this cool logic Angela was silent. Virginia looked at her sister, a maternal look oddly apparent on her young face. When she was middle-aged she would be the embodiment of motherhood. How her children would love her!

"Angela, you'll be careful!"

"Yes, darling. Oh if only I could make you understand what it's all about."

"Yes, well, perhaps another time. I've got to

171

fly now." She hesitated, took Angela by the arms and gazed into her eyes. "About this grand white party that you were in the station with. Are you awfully in love with him?"

"I'm not in love with him at all."

"Oh, pshaw!" said innocent Virginia, "you've got nothing to worry about! Why, what's all the shooting for?"

PLUM BUN

CHAPTER I

ANGELA wanted to ride downtown with her sister.
"Perhaps I might bring you luck." But on this
theme Jinny was adamant. "You'd be much
more likely to bring yourself bad luck. No,
there's no sense in taking a chance. I'll take the
elevated; my landlady said it would drop me
very near the school where I'm taking the examination. You go some other way." Down in
the hall Mrs. Gloucester was busy dusting, her
short bustling figure alive with housewifely ardour.
Virginia paused near her and held out her hand
to Angela. "Good-bye, Miss Mory," she said
wickedly, "it was very kind of you to give me so
much time. If you can ever tear yourself away
from your beloved Village, come up and I'll try
to show you Harlem. I don't think it's going to
take me long to learn it."

Obediently Angela let her go her way and walking over to Seventh Avenue mounted the 'bus,
smarting a little under Jinny's generous pre-
cautions. But presently she began to realize their
value, for at One Hundred and Fourteenth Street
Anthony Cross entered. He sat down beside her.
"I never expected to see you in my neighbor-
hood."

"Oh is this where you live? I've often wondered."

"As it happens I've just come here, but I've lived practically all over New York." He was thin, restless, unhappy. His eyes dwelt ceaselessly on her face. She said a little nervously:

"It seems to me I hardly ever see you any more. What do you do with yourself?"

"Nothing that you would be interested in."

She did not dare make the obvious reply and after all, though she did like him very much, she was not interested in his actions. For a long moment she sought for some phrase which would express just the right combination of friendliness and indifference.

"It's been a long time since we've had lunch together; come and have it to-day with me. You be my guest." She thought of Jinny and the possible sale of the house. "I've just found out that I'm going to get a rather decent amount of money, certainly enough to stand us for lunch."

"Thank you, I have an engagement; besides I don't want to lunch with you in public."

This was dangerous ground. Flurried, she replied unwisely: "All right, come in some time for tea; every once in a while I make a batch of cookies; I made some a week ago. Next time I feel the mood coming on me I'll send you a card and you can come and eat them, hot and hot."

"You know you've no intention of doing any such thing. Besides you don't know my address."

"An inconvenience which can certainly be rectified," she laughed at him.

But he was in no laughing mood. "I've no cards with me, but they wouldn't have the address anyway." He tore a piece of paper out of his

176

notebook, scribbled on it. "Here it is. I have to
get off now." He gave her a last despairing look.
"Oh, Angel, you know you're never going to send
for me!"

The bit of paper clutched firmly in one hand,
she arrived finally at her little apartment. Naturally of an orderly turn of mind she looked about
for her address book in which to write the street
and number. But some unexplained impulse led
her to smooth the paper out and place it in a
corner of her desk. That done she took off her
hat and gloves, sat down in the comfortable chair
and prepared to face her thoughts.

. . . . .

Yesterday! Even now at a distance of twenty-
four hours she had not recovered her equilibrium.
She was still stunned, still unable to realize the
happening of the day. Only she knew that she
had reached a milestone in her life; a possible
turning point. If she did not withdraw from her
acquaintanceship with Roger now, even though
she committed no overt act she would never be
the same; she could never again face herself with
the old, unshaken pride and self-confidence. She
would never be the same to herself. If she withdrew, then indeed, indeed she would be the same
old Angela Murray, the same girl save for a little
sophistication that she had been before she left
Philadelphia, only she would have started on an
adventure and would not have seen it to its finish,
she would have come to grips with life and would
have laid down her arms at the first onslaught.
Would she be a coward or a wise, wise woman?

She thought of two poems that she had read in
"Hart's Class-Book," an old, old book of her
father's,—one of them ran:

> 'He either fears his fate too much
>   Or his deserts are small,
> Who dares not put it to the touch
>   For fear of losing all.'

The other was an odd mixture of shrewdness
and cowardice:

> 'He who fights and runs away
>   Shall live to fight another day
> But he who is in battle slain
>   Has fallen ne'er to rise again.'

Were her deserts small or should she run away
and come back to fight another day when she was
older, more experienced? More experienced!
How was she to get that experience? Already she
was infinitely wiser; she would, if occasion required it, exercise infinitely more wariness than
she had yesterday with Roger. Yet it was
precisely because of that experience that she would
know how to meet, would even know when to
expect similar conditions.

She thought that she knew which verse she
would follow if she were Jinny, but, back once
more in the assurance of her own rooms, she knew
that she did not want to be Jinny, that she and
Jinny were two vastly different persons. "But,"
she said to herself, "if Jinny were as fair as I and
yet herself and placed in the same conditions as
those in which I am placed her colour would save

her. It's a safeguard for Jinny; it's always been
a curse for me."

    ·   ·   ·   ·   ·   ·

Roger had come for her in the blue car. There
were a hamper and two folding chairs and a rug
stored away in it. It was a gorgeous day. "If
we can," he said, "we'll picnic." He was extremely handsome and extremely nervous. Angela
was nervous too, though she did not show it
except in the loss of her colour. She was rather
plain to-day; to be so near the completion of her
goal and yet to have to wait these last few agon-
izing moments, perhaps hours, was deadly. They
were rather silent for a while, Roger intent on his
driving. Traffic in New York is a desperate
strain at all hours, at eleven in the morning it is
deadly; the huge leviathan of a city is breaking
into the last of its stride. For a few hours it
will proceed at a measured though never leisurely
pace and then burst again into the mad rush of
the homeward bound.

But at last they were out of the city limits and
could talk. For the first time since she had known
him he began to speak of his possessions. "Anything, anything that money can buy, Angèle, I
can get and I can give." His voice was charged
with intention. They were going in the direction
of Forest Hills; he had a cottage out there, perhaps she would like to see it. And there was a
grove not far away. "We'll picnic there," he
said, "and—and talk." He certainly was
nervous, Angela thought, and liked him the better
for it.

The cottage or rather the house in Forest Hills was beautiful, absolutely a gem. And it was completely furnished with taste and marked daintiness. "What do you keep it furnished for?" asked Angela wondering. Roger murmured that it had been empty for a long time but he had seen this equipment and it had struck him that it was just the thing for this house so he had bought it; thereby insensibly reminding his companion again that he could afford to gratify any whim. They drove away from the exquisite little place in silence. Angela was inclined to be amused; surely no one could have asked for a better opening than that afforded by the house. What would make him talk, she wondered, and what, oh what would he say? Something far, far more romantic than poor Matthew Henson could ever have dreamed of,—yes and far, far less romantic, something subconscious prompted her, than Anthony Cross had said. Anthony with his poverty and honour and desperate vows!

They had reached the grove, they had spread the rug and the tablecloth; Roger had covered it with dainties. He would not let her lift a finger, she was the guest and he her humble servant. She looked at him smiling, still forming vague contrasts with him and Matthew and Anthony.

Roger dropped his sandwich, came and sat behind her. He put his arm around her and shifted his shoulder so that her head lay against it.

"Don't look at me that way Angèle, Angèle! I can't stand it."

So it was actually coming. "How do you want me to look at you?"

He bent his head down to hers and kissed her.
"Like this, like this! Oh Angèle, did you like
the house?"

"Like it? I loved it."

"Darling, I had it done for you, you know. I
thought you'd like it."

It seemed a strange thing to have done without
consulting her, and anyway she did not want to
live in a suburb. Opal Street had been suburb
enough for her. She wanted, required, the noise
and tumult of cities.

"I don't care for suburbs, Roger." How
strange for him to talk about a place to live in
and never a word of love!"

"My dear girl, you don't have to live in a
suburb if you don't want to. I've got a place, an
apartment in Seventy-second Street, seven rooms;
that would be enough for you and your maid,
wouldn't it? I could have this furniture moved
over there, or if you think it too cottagey, you
could have new stuff altogether."

Seven rooms for three people! Why she
wanted a drawing-room and a studio and where
would he put his things? This sudden stinginess
was quite inexplicable.

"But Roger, seven rooms wouldn't be big
enough."

He laughed indulgently, his face radiant with
relief and triumph. "So she wants a palace,
does she? Well, she shall have it. A whole
ménage if you want it, a place on Riverside Drive,
servants and a car Only somehow I hadn't
thought of you as caring about that kind of thing.
After that little hole in the wall you've been living
in on Jayne Street I'd have expected you to find

the place in Seventy-second Street as large as
you'd care for."

A little hurt, she replied: "But I was thinking of you too. There wouldn't be room for
your things. And I thought you'd want to go on
living in the style you'd been used to." A sudden
welcome explanation dawned on her rising fear.
"Are you keeping this a secret from your father?
Is that what's the trouble?"

Under his thin, bright skin he flushed. "Keeping what a secret from my father? What are you
talking about, Angèle?"

She countered with his own question. "What
are *you* talking about, Roger?"

He tightened his arms about her, his voice
stammered, his eyes were bright and watchful.
"I'm asking you to live in my house, to live for
me; to be my girl; to keep a love-nest where I
and only I may come." He smiled shamefacedly
over the cheap current phrase.

She pushed him away from her; her jaw fallen
and slack but her figure taut. Yet under her
stunned bewilderment her mind was racing. So
this was her castle, her fortress of protection, her
refuge. And what answer should she make?
Should she strike him across his eager, half-
shamed face, should she get up and walk away,
forbidding him to follow? Or should she stay
and hear it out? Stay and find out what this man
was really like; what depths were in him and, she
supposed, in other men. But especially in this
man with his boyish, gallant air and his face as
guileless and as innocent apparently as her own.

.   .   .   .   .   .

That was what she hated in herself, she told
that self fiercely, shut up with her own thoughts
the next afternoon in her room. She hated herself for staying and listening. It had given him
courage to talk and talk. But what she most
hated had been the shrewdness, the practicality
which lay beneath that resolve to hear it out.
She had thought of those bills; she had thought
of her poverty, of her helplessness, and she had
thought too of Martha Burden's dictum: "You
must make him want you." Well here was a way
to make him want her and to turn that wanting
to account. "Don't," Martha said, "withhold too
much. Give a little." Suppose she gave him just
the encouragement of listening to him, of showing him that she did like him a little; while he
meanwhile went on wanting, wanting—men paid
a big price for their desires. Her price would be
marriage. It was a game, she knew, which wom-
en played all over the world although it had never
occurred to her to play it; a dangerous game at
which some women burned their fingers. "Don't
give too much," said Martha, "for then you lose
yourself." Well, she would give nothing and
she would not burn her fingers. Oh, it would be
a great game.

Another element entered too. He had wounded
her pride and he should salve it. And the only
unguent possible would be a proposal of marriage. Oh if only she could be a girl in a book
and when he finally did ask her for her hand, she
would be able to tell him that she was going to
marry someone else, someone twice as eligible,
twice as handsome, twice as wealthy.

.   .   .   .

Through all these racing thoughts penetrated the sound of Roger's voice, pleading, persuasive, seductive. She was amazed to find a certain shamefaced timidity creeping over her; yet it was he who should have shown the shame. And she could not understand either why she was unable to say plainly: "You say you care for me, long for me so much, why don't you ask me to come to you in the ordinary way?" But some pride either unusually false or unusually fierce prevented her from doing this. Undoubtedly Roger with his wealth, his looks and his family connections had already been much sought after. He knew he was an "eligible." Poor, unknown, stigmatized, if he but knew it, as a member of the country's least recognized group she could not bring herself to belong even in appearance to that band of young women who so obviously seek a "good match."

When he had paused a moment for breath she told him sadly: "But, Roger, people don't do that kind of thing, not decent people."

"Angèle, you are such a child! This is exactly the kind of thing people do do. And why not? Why must the world be let in on the relationships of men and women? Some of the sweetest unions in history have been of this kind."

"For others perhaps, but not for me. Relationships of the kind you describe don't exist among the people I know." She was thinking of her parents, of the Hallowells, of the Hensons whose lives were indeed like open books.

He looked at her curiously, "The people you know! Don't tell me you haven't guessed about Paulette!"

She had forgotten about Paulette! "Yes I know about her. She told me herself. I like her, she's been a mighty fine friend, but, Roger, you surely don't want me to be like her."

"Of course I don't. It was precisely because you weren't like her that I became interested. You were such a babe in the woods. Anyone could see you'd had no experience with men."

This obvious lack of logic was too bewildering. She looked at him like the child which, in these matters, she really was. "But,—but Roger, mightn't that be a beginning of a life like Paulette's? What would become of me after we, you and I, had separated? Very often these things last only for a short time, don't they?"

"Not necessarily; certainly not between you and me. And I'd always take care of you, you'd be provided for." He could feel her gathering resentment. In desperation he played a cunning last card: "And besides who knows, something permanent may grow out of this. I'm not entirely my own master, Angèle."

Undoubtedly he was referring to his father whom he could not afford to offend. It never occurred to her that he might be lying, for why should he?

.   .   .   .   .

To all his arguments, all his half-promises and implications she returned a steady negative. As twilight came on she expressed a desire to go home; with the sunset her strength failed her; she felt beaten and weary. Her unsettled future, her hurt pride, her sudden set-to with the realities of

the society in which she had been moving, bewildered and frightened her. Resentful, puzzled,
introspective, she had no further words for
Roger; it was impossible for him to persuade her
to agree or to disagree with his arguments. During the long ride home she was resolutely mute.

Yet on the instant of entering Jayne Street she
felt she could not endure spending the long evening hours by herself and she did not want to be
alone with Roger. She communicated this distaste to him. While not dishevelled they were not
presentable enough to invade the hotels farther
uptown. But, anxious to please her, he told her
they could go easily enough to one of the small
cabarets in the Village. A few turns and wind-
ings and they were before a house in a dark side
street knocking on its absurdly barred door, entering its black, mysterious portals. In a room
with a highly polished floor, a few tables and
chairs, some rather bizarre curtains, five or six
couples were sitting, among them Paulette, Jack
Hudson, a tall, rather big, extremely blonde girl
whose name Angela learned was Carlotta Parks,
and a slender, black-avised man whose name she
failed to catch. Paulette hailed him uproariously; the blonde girl rose and precipitately
threw her arms about Fielding's neck.

"Roger!"

"Don't," he said rather crossly. "Hello, Jack."
He nodded to the dark man whom he seemed to
know indifferently well. "What have they got to
eat here, you fellows? Miss Mory and I are tired
and hungry. We've been following the pike all
day." Miss Parks turned and gave Angela a
long, considering look.

186

"Sit here," said Paulette, "there's plenty of room. Jack, you order for them, the same things we've been having. You get good cooking here." She was radiant with happiness and content. Under the influence of the good, stimulating food Angela began to recover, to look around her.

Jack Hudson, a powerfully built bronze figure of a man, beamed on Paulette, saying nothing and in his silence saying everything. The dark man kept his eyes on Carlotta, who was oblivious to everyone but Roger, clearly her friend of long standing. She sat clasping one of his hands, her head almost upon his shoulder. "Roger it's so good to see you again! I've thought of you so often! I've been meaning to write to you; we're having a big house party this summer. You must come! Dad's asking up half of Washington; attachés, 'Prinzessen, Countessen and serene English Altessen;' he'll come up for week-ends."

A member of the *haut monde,* evidently she was well-connected, powerful, even rich. A girl of Roger's own set amusing herself in this curious company. Angela felt her heart contract with a sort of helpless jealousy.

The dark man, despairing of recapturing Carlotta's attention, suddenly asked Angèle if she would care to dance. He was a superb partner and for a moment or two, reinvigorated by the food and the snappy music, she became absorbed in the smooth, gliding motion and in her partner's pleasant conversation. Glancing over her shoulder she noted Carlotta still talking to Roger. The latter, however, was plainly paying the girl no attention. His eyes fixed on Angela, he was moodily following her every motion, almost

straining, she thought, to catch her words. His
eyes met hers and a long, long look passed between them so fraught, it seemed to her, with a
secret understanding and sympathy, that her
heart shook with a moment's secret wavering.

Her partner escorted her back to the table.
Paulette, flushed and radiant, with the mien of a
dishevelled baby, was holding forth while Hudson listened delightedly. As a *raconteuse* she had
a faint, delicious malice which usually made
any recital of her adventures absolutely irresis-
tible. "Her name," she was saying loudly, regardless of possible listeners, "was Antoinette
Spewer, and it seems she had it in for me from
the very first. She told Sloane Corby she wanted
to meet me and he invited both of us to lunch.
When we got to the restaurant she was waiting
for me in the lobby; Sloane introduced us and—
she pulled a lorgnette on me,—a lorgnette on
me!" She said it very much as a Westerner
might speak of someone "pulling" a revolver.
"But I fixed that. There were three or four
people passing near us. I drew back until they
were well within hearing range, and then I said
to her: 'I beg pardon but what did you say your
last name was?' Well, when a person's named
Spewer she can't shout it across a hotel lobby!
Oh, she came climbing down off her high horse;
she respects me to this day, I tell you."

Roger rose. "We must be going; I can't let
Miss Mory get too tired." He was all attention and courtesy. Miss Parks looked at her
again, narrowing her eyes.

In the car Roger put his arm about her. "Angèle, when you were dancing with that fellow

I couldn't stand it! And then you looked at me,—
oh such a look! You were thinking about me, I
felt it, I knew it."

Some treacherous barrier gave way within her.
"Yes, and I could tell you were thinking about
me."

"Of course you could! And without a word!
Oh, darling, darling, can't you see that's the way
it would be? If you'd only take happiness with
me there we would be with a secret bond, an
invisible bond, existing for us alone and no one
else in the world the wiser. But we should know
and it would be all the sweeter for that secrecy."

Unwittingly he struck a responsive chord within her,—stolen waters were the sweetest, she of
all people knew that.

Aloud she said: "Here we are, Roger. Some
of the day has been wonderful; thank you for
that."

"You can't go like this! You're going to let
me see you again?"

She knew she should have refused him, but
again some treacherous impulse made her assent.
He drove away, and, turning, she climbed the
long, steep flights of stairs, bemused, thrilled,
frightened, curious, the sense of adventure strong
upon her. To-morrow she would see Jinny, her
own sister, her own flesh and blood, one of her
own people. Together they would thresh this
thing out.

CHAPTER II

A CURIOUS period of duelling ensued. Roger was young, rich and idle. Nearly every wish he had ever known had been born within him only to be satisfied. He could not believe that he would fail in the pursuit of this baffling creature who had awakened within him an ardour and sincerity of feeling which surprised himself. The thought occurred to him more than once that it would have been a fine thing if this girl had been endowed with the name and standing and comparative wealth of—say Carlotta Parks,—but it never occurred to him to thwart in this matter the wishes of his father who would, he knew, insist immediately on a certified account of the pedigree, training and general fitness of any strange aspirant for his son's hand. Angela had had the good sense to be frank; she did not want to become immeshed in a tissue of lies whose relationship, whose sequence and inter-dependence she would be likely to forget. To Roger's few questions she had said quite truly that she was the daughter of "poor but proud parents;" —they had laughed at the hackneyed phrase,— that her father had been a boss carpenter and that she had been educated in the ordinary public schools and for a time had been a school teacher. No one would ever try to substantiate these statements, for clearly the person to whom they applied would not be falsifying such a simple account. There would be no point in so doing. Her little deceits had all been negative, she had merely neglected to say that she had a brown sister and that her father had been black.

Roger found her unfathomable. His was the careless, unreasoned cynicism of the modern, worldly young man. He had truly, as he acknowledged, been attracted to Angela because of a certain incurious innocence of hers apparent in her observations and in her manner. He saw no reason why he should cherish that innocence. If questioned he would have answered: "She's got to learn about the world in which she lives sometime; she might just as well learn of it through me. And I'd always look out for her." In the back of his mind, for all his unassuming even simple attitude toward his wealth and power, lurked the conviction that that same wealth and power could heal any wound, atone for any loss. Still there were times when even he experienced a faint, inner qualm, when Angela would ask him: "But afterwards, what would become of me, Roger?" It was the only question he could not meet. Out of all his hosts of precedents from historical Antony and Cleopatra down to notorious affinities discovered through blatant newspaper "stories" he could find for this only a stammered "There's no need to worry about an afterwards, Angèle, for you and I would always be friends."

Their frequent meetings now were little more than a trial of strength. Young will and determination were pitted against young will and determination. On both the excitement of the chase was strong, but each was pursuing a different quarry. To all his protestations, arguments and demands, Angela returned an insistent: "What you are asking is impossible." Yet she either could not or would not drive him away, and gradually, though she had no intention of yielding to his wishes, her first attitude of shocked horror began to change.

For three months the conflict persisted. Roger interposed the discussion into every talk, on every occasion. Gradually it came to be the *raison d'être* of their constant comradeship. His arguments were varied and specious. "My dearest girl, think of a friendship in which two people would have every claim in the world upon each other and yet no claim. Think of giving all, not because you say to a minister 'I will,' but from the generosity of a powerful affection. That is the very essence of free love. I give you my word that the happiest couples in the world are those who love without visible bonds. Such people are bound by the most durable ties. Theirs is a state of the closest because the freest, most elastic union in the world."

A singularly sweet and curious intimacy was growing up between them. Roger told Angela many anecdotes about his father and about his dead mother, whom he still loved, and for whom he even grieved in a pathetically boyish way. "She was so sweet to me, she loved me so. I'll never forget her. It's for her sake that I try to please my father, though Dad's some pumpkins on his own account." In turn she was falling into the habit of relating to him the little happenings of her every-day life, a life which she was begin-

ning to realize must, in his eyes, mean the last
word in the humdrum and the monotonous. And
yet how full of adventure, of promise, even of
mystery did it seem compared with Jinny's!

Roger had much intimate knowledge of people
and told her many and dangerous secrets. "See
how I trust you, Angèle; you might trust me a
little!"

If his stories were true, certainly she might just
as well trust him a great deal, for all her little
world, judging it by the standards by which she
was used to measuring people, was tumbling in
ruins at her feet. If this were the way people
lived then what availed any ideals? The world
was made to take pleasure in; one gained nothing
by exercising simple virtue, it was after all an
extension of the old formula which she had
thought out for herself many years ago. Roger
spent most of his time with her, it seemed. Anything which she undertook to do delighted him.
She would accept no money, no valuable presents.
"And I can't keep going out with you to dinners
and luncheons forever, Roger. It would be
different if,—if we really meant anything to each
other." He deliberately misunderstood her. "But
nothing would give me more pleasure than for
us to mean the world to one another." He sent
her large hampers of fruit and even the more
ordinary edibles; then he would tease her about
being selfish. In order to get rid of the food she
had asked him to lunch, to dinner, since nothing
that she could say would make him desist from
sending it.

Nothing gave her greater joy really than this
playful housekeeping. She was very lonely;

Jinny had her own happy interests; Anthony never came near her nor did she invite him to come; Martha Burden seemed engrossed in her own affairs, she was undergoing some secret strain that made her appear more remote, more strongly self-sufficient, more mysterious than ever. Paulette, making overt preparations to go to Russia with Hudson, was impossibly, hurtingly happy. Miss Powell,—but she could not get near her; the young coloured girl showed her the finest kind of courtesy, but it had about it a remote and frozen quality, unbreakable. However, Angela for the moment did not desire to break it; she must run no more risks with Roger, still she put Miss Powell on the list of those people whom she would some day aid,—when everything had turned out all right.

The result of this feeling of loneliness was, of course, to turn her more closely to Roger. He paid her the subtle compliment of appearing absolutely at home in her little apartment; he grew to like her plain, good cooking and the experiments which sometimes she made frankly for him. And afterwards as the fall closed in there were long, pleasant evenings before an open fire, or two or three last hours after a brisk spin in the park in the blue car. And gradually she had grown to accept and even inwardly to welcome his caresses. She perched with an air of great unconsciousness on the arm of the big chair in which he was sitting but the transition became constantly easier from the arm of the chair to his knee, to the steely embrace of his arm, to the sound of the hard beating of his heart, to his murmured: "This

is where you belong, Angèle, Angèle." He seemed
an anchor for her frail, insecure bark of life.

It was at moments like these that he told her
amazing things about their few common acquaintances. There was not much to say about Paulette.
"I think," said Roger judicially, "that tempera-
mentally she is a romantic adventurer. Something
in her is constantly seeking a change but she
will never be satisfied. She's a good sport, she
takes as she gives, asking nothing permanent
and promising nothing permanent." Angela
thought it rather sad. But Roger dismissed the
theme with the rather airy comment that there
were women as there were men "like that." She
wondered if he might not be a trifle callous.

More than once they had spoken of Martha
Burden; Angela confessed herself tremendously
intrigued by the latter, by that tense, brooding
personality. She learned that Martha, made of
the stuff which dies for causes, was constantly
being torn between theory and practice.

"She's full," said Roger, "of the most high-
falutin advanced ideas. Oh I've known old
Martha all my life, we were brought up together;
it's through her really that I began to know the
people in this part of town. She's always been a
sort of sister. More than once I've had to yank
her by the shoulders out of difficulties which she
herself created. I made her marry Starr."

"Made her marry him,—didn't she want
him?"

"Yes, she wanted him all right, but she doesn't
believe in marriage. She's got the courage of
her convictions, that girl. Why actually she

195

lived with Starr two years while I was away doing Europe. When I came back and found out what had happened I told Starr I'd beat him into pulp if he didn't turn around and make good."

"But why the violence? Didn't he want to?"

"Yes, only," he remembered suddenly his own hopes, "not every man is capable of appreciating a woman who breaks through the conventions for him. Some men mistake it for cheapness but others see it for what it is and love more deeply and gratefully." Softly, lingeringly he touched the soft hair shadowing her averted cheek. "I'm one of those others, Angèle."

She wanted to say: "But why shouldn't we marry? Why not make me safe as well as Martha?" But again her pride intervened. Instead she remarked that Martha did not seem always happy.

"No, well that's because she's got this fool idea of hers that now that they are bound the spontaneity is lacking. She wants to give without being obliged to give; to take because she chooses and not because she's supposed to. Oh she's as true as steel and the best fighter in a cause, but I've no doubt but that she leads old Starr a life with her temperament."

Angela thought that there were probably two sides to this possibility. A little breathlessly she asked Roger if he knew Anthony Cross.

"Cross, Cross! A sallow, rather thin fellow? I think I saw him once or twice at Paulette's. No, I don't really know him. A sullen, brooding sort of chap I should say. Frightfully self-absorbed and all that."

For some reason a little resentment sprang up in her. Anthony might brood, but his life had been lived on dark, troublesome lines that invited brooding; he had never known the broad, golden highway of Roger's existence. And anyway she did not believe, if Martha Burden had been Anthony's lifelong friend, almost his sister, that he would have told his sweetheart or his wife either of those difficult passages in her life. Well, she would have to teach Roger many things. Aloud she spoke of Carlotta Parks.

"She's an interesting type. Tell me about her."

But Roger said rather shortly that there was nothing to tell. "Just a good-hearted, high-spirited kid, that's all, who lets the whole world know her feelings."

.   .   .   .   .

According to Paulette there was more than this to be told about Miss Parks. "I don't know her myself, not being a member of that crowd. But I've always heard that she and Roger were childhood sweethearts, only they've just not pulled it off. Carlotta's family is as old as his. Her people have always been statesmen, her father's in the Senate. I don't think they have much money now. But the main thing is she pleases old man Fielding. Nothing would give him more pleasure than to see Carlotta Roger's wife. I may be mistaken, but I think nothing would give Carlotta more pleasure either."

"Doesn't he care for her?" Queer how her heart tightened, listening for the answer.

197

"Yes, but she likes him too much and shows it.
So he thinks he doesn't want her. Roger will
never want any woman who comes at his first
call. Don't you hate that sort of man? They
are really the easiest to catch; all you've got to
do provided they're attracted at all, is to give one
inviting glance and then keep steadily retreating.
And they'll come—like Bo Peep's sheep. But I
don't want a man like that; he'd cramp my
style. His impudence, expecting a woman to re-
press or evoke her emotions just as he wants
them! Hasn't a woman as much right to feel as
a man and to feel first? Never mind, some woman
is going to 'get' Roger yet. He doesn't think it
possible because he has wealth and position. He'll
be glad to come running to Carlotta then. I
don't care very much for her,—she's a little too
loud for me," objected the demure and conservative Miss Lister, "but I do think she likes Roger
for himself and not for what he can give her!"

. . . . . .

Undoubtedly this bit of knowledge lent a new
aspect; the adventure began to take on fresh
interest. Everything seemed to be playing into
her hands. Roger's interest and longing were
certainly undiminished. Martha Burden's advice,
confirmed by Paulette's disclosure, was bound to
bring results. She had only to "keep retreating."
But there was one enemy with whom she had
never thought to reckon, she had never counted
on the treachery of the forces of nature; she had
never dreamed of the unaccountable weakening of
those forces within. Her weapons were those

furnished by the conventions but her fight was
against conditions; impulses, yearnings which ante-
dated both those weapons and the conventions
which furnished them. Insensibly she began to
see in Roger something more than a golden way
out of her material difficulties; he was becoming
more than a means through which she should be
admitted to the elect of the world for whom all
things are made. Before her eyes he was changing to the one individual who was kindest,
most thoughtful of her, the one whose presence
brought warmth and assurance. Furthermore,
his constant attention, flatteries and caresses were
producing their inevitable effect. She was naturally cold; unlike Paulette, she was a woman
who would experience the grand passion only
once, perhaps twice, in her life and she would
always have to be kindled from without; in the
last analysis her purity was a matter not of morals,
not of religion, nor of racial pride; it was a
matter of fastidiousness. Bit by bit Roger had
forced his way closer and closer into the affairs
of her life, and his proximity had not offended
that fastidiousness. Gradually his demands
seemed to her to represent a very natural and
beautiful impulse; his arguments and illustrations
began to bear fruit; the conventions instead of
showing in her eyes as the codified wisdom based
on the experiences of countless generations of
men and women, seemed to her prudish and unnecessary. Finally her attitude reduced itself to
this: she would have none of the relationship
which Roger urged so insistently, not because
according to all the training which she had ever
received, it was unlawful, but because viewed in

the light of the great battle which she was wag-
ing for pleasure, protection and power, it was
inexpedient.

The summer and the early fall had passed. A
cold, rainy autumn was closing in; the disagree-
able weather made motoring almost impossible.
There were always the theatres and the cabarets,
but Roger professed himself as happy nowhere
else but at her fireside. And she loved to have
him there, tall and strong and beautiful, sometimes radiant with hope, at others sulking with
the assurance of defeat. He came in one day
ostensibly to have tea with her; he had an important engagement for the evening but he could
not let the day pass without seeing her. Angela
was tired and a little dispirited. Jinny had
sold the house and had sent her twelve hundred
dollars as her share, but the original three thousand was almost dissipated. She must not touch
this new gift from heaven; her goal was no nearer;
the unwelcome possibility of teaching, on the contrary, was constantly before her. Moreover, she
was at last realizing the danger of his constant
proximity, she was appalled by her thoughts and
longings. Upon her a great fear was creeping
not only of Roger but of herself.

Always watchful, he quickly divined her distrait mood, resolved to try its possibilities for
himself. In a tense silence they drank their tea
and sat gazing at the leaping, golden flames.
The sullen night closed in. Angela reminded
him presently that he must go but on he sat and
on. At eight o'clock she reminded him again;
he took out his watch and looked at it indifferently.

"It's too late for me to keep it now, besides I don't want to go. Angèle be kind, don't send me away."

"But you've had no dinner."

"Nor you either. I'm like the beasts of the field keeping you like this. Shall we go out somewhere?" But she was languid; she did not want to stir from the warm hearth out into the chilly night.

"No, I don't want to go. But you go, Roger. I can find something here in the house for myself, but there's not a thing for you. I hate to be so inhospitable."

"Tell you what, suppose I go around to one of these *delicatessens* and get something. Too tired to fix up a picnic lunch?"

In half an hour he returned, soaked. "It's raining in torrents! Why I never saw such a night!" He shook himself, spattering rain-drops all over the tiny apartment.

"Roger! You'll have to take off your coat!"

He sat in his shirt-sleeves before the fire, his hair curling and damp, his head on his hand. He looked so like a little boy that her heart shook within her. Turning he caught the expression in her eyes, sprang towards her. "Angèle you know, you *know* you like me a little!"

"I like you a very great deal." He put his arm about her, kissed her; her very bones turned to water. She freed herself, finding an excuse to go into the kitchenette. But he came and stood towering over her in the doorway, his eyes on her every motion. They ate the meal, a good one, almost as silently as they had drunk the tea; a terrible awareness of each other's presence was upon them, the air was charged with passion. Outside the rain and wind beat and screamed.

"It's a terrible night," she said, but he made no reply. She said again, "Roger, it's getting late, you must go home." Very reluctantly then, his eyes still on hers, he rose to his feet, got into his overcoat and, hat in hand, stooped to kiss her good-night. His arm stole about her, holding her close against him. She could feel him trembling, she was trembling herself. Another second and the door had closed behind him.

Alone, she sat looking at the fire and thinking: "This is awful. I don't believe anything is going to come of this. I believe I'll send him a note to-morrow and tell him not to come any more."

Someone tapped on the door; astonished that a caller should appear at such an hour, but not afraid, she opened it. It was Roger. He came striding into the room, flinging off his wet coat, and yet almost simultaneously catching her up in his arms. "It's such a terrible night, Angèle; you can't send me out in it. Why should I go when the fire is here and you, so warm and soft and sweet!"

All her strength left her; she could not even struggle, could not speak. He swept her up in his arms, cradling her in them like a baby with her face beneath his own. "You know that we were meant for each other, that we belong to each other!"

A terrible lassitude enveloped her out of which she heard herself panting: "Roger, Roger let me go! Oh, Roger, must it be like this? Can't it be any other way?"

And from a great distance she heard his voice
breaking, pleading, promising: "Everything will
be all right, darling, darling. I swear it. Only
trust me, trust me!"

. . . .

Life rushed by on a great, surging tide. She
could not tell whether she was utterly happy or
utterly miserable. All that she could do was to
feel; feel that she was Roger's totally. Her
whole being turned toward him as a flower to the
sun. Without him life meant nothing; with him
it was everything. For the time being she was
nothing but emotion; he was amazed himself at
the depth of feeling which he had aroused in her.

Now for the first time she felt possessive; she
found herself deeply interested in Roger's wel-
fare because, she thought, he was hers and she
could not endure having a possession whose qualities were unknown. She was not curious about
his money nor his business affairs but she thirsted
to know how his time away from her was spent,
whom he saw, what other places he frequented.
Not that she begrudged him a moment away
from her side, but she must be able to account
for that moment.

Yet if she felt possessive of him her feeling
also recognized his complete absorption of her, so
completely, so exhaustively did his life seem to en-
velop hers. For a while his wishes, his pleasure
were the end and aim of her existence; she told
herself with a slight tendency toward self-mock-
ery that this was the explanation of being, of her
being; that men had other aims, other uses but

that the sole excuse for being a woman was to be
just that,—a woman. Forgotten were her ideals
about her Art; her ambition to hold a salon; her
desire to help other people; even her intention of
marrying in order to secure her future. Only
something quite outside herself, something watchful, proud, remote from the passion and rapture
which flamed within her, kept her free and independent. She would not accept money, she would
not move to the apartment on Seventy-second
Street; she still refused gifts so ornate that they
were practically bribes. She made no explanations to Roger, but he knew and she knew too
that her surrender was made out of the lavish
fullness and generosity of her heart; there was no
calculation back of it; if this were free love the
freedom was the quality to be stressed rather than
the emotion.

Sometimes, in her inchoate, wordless intensity
of feeling which she took for happiness, she
paused to take stock of that other life, those other
lives which once she had known; that life which
had been hers when she had first come to New
York before she had gone to Cooper Union, in
those days when she had patrolled Fourteenth
Street and had sauntered through Union Square.
And that other life which she knew in Opal
Street,—æons ago, almost in another existence.
She passed easily over those first few months in
New York because even then she had been approaching a threshold, getting ready to enter on
a new, undreamed of phase of being. But sometimes at night she lay for hours thinking over her
restless, yearning childhood, her fruitless days at
the Academy, the abortive wooing of Matthew

Henson. The Hensons, the Hallowells, Hetty
Daniels,—Jinny! How far now she was beyond
their pale! Before her rose the eager, starved
face of Hetty Daniels; now she herself was cognizant of phases of life for which Hetty longed
but so condemned. Angela could imagine the
envy back of the tone in which Hetty, had she
but known it, would have expressed her disapproval of her former charge's manner of living.
"Mattie Murray's girl, Angela, has gone straight
to the bad; she's living a life of sin with some
man in New York." And then the final, blasting
indictment. "He's a white man, too. Can you
beat that?"

CHAPTER III

ROGER'S father, it appeared, had been greatly pleased with his son's management of the saw-mills in Georgia; as a result he was making more and more demands on his time. And the younger man half through pride, half through that steady determination never to offend his father, was always ready to do his bidding. Angela liked and appreciated her lover's filial attitude, but even in the period of her warmest interest she resented, secretly despised, this tendency to dependence. He was young, superbly trained; he had the gift of forming friendships whose strength rested on his own personality, yet he distrusted too much his own powers or else he was lazy— Angela could never determine which. During this phase of their acquaintanceship she was never sure that she loved him, but she was positive that if at this time he had been willing to fling aside his obsequious deference to his father's money, and had said to her: "Angèle, if you'll help me, we'll build up a life, a fortune of our own," she would have adored him.

Her strong, independent nature, buffeted and sickened and strengthened by the constant attrition of colour prejudice, was unable to visualize or to pardon the frame of mind which kept Roger from joining battle with life when the odds

were already so overwhelmingly in his favour.
Alone, possessed of a handicap which if guessed
at would have been as disabling as a game leg
or an atrophied body, she had dared enter the
lists. And she was well on the way to winning a
victory. It was to cost her, she was beginning to
realize, more than she had anticipated. But having entered she was not one to draw back,—unless indeed she changed her goal. Hers was a
curious mixture of materialism and hedonism,
and at this moment the latter quality was upper-
most in her life. But she supposed that in some
vague future she and Roger would marry. His
ardour rendered her complacent.

But she was not conscious of any of these inner
conflicts and criticisms; she was too happy. Now
she was adopting a curious detachment toward
life tempered by a faint cynicism,—a detachment
which enabled her to say to herself: "Rules are
for ordinary people but not for me." She remembered a verse from a poet, a coloured woman
about whom she had often wondered. The lines
ran:

> "The strong demand, contend, prevail.
> The beggar is a fool!"

She would never be a beggar. She would ask
no further counsel nor advice of anyone. She had
been lucky thus far in seeking advice only from
Paulette and Martha Burden, two people of
markedly independent methods of thought and
action. They had never held her back. Now she
would no longer consult even them. She would
live her life as an individualist, to suit herself
without regard for the conventions and estab-

¹ished ways of life. Her native fastidiousness, she
s sure, would keep her from becoming an of-
tence in her own eyes.

In spite of her increasing self-confidence and
self-sufficiency Roger's frequent absences left her
lonely. Almost then, without any conscious planning on her part, she began to work at her art
with growing vigour and interest. She was gaining in assurance; her technique showed an increased mastery; above all she had gained in the
power to compose, a certain sympathy, a breadth
of comprehension, the manifestation of that ability to interpret which she had long suspected lay
within her, lent themselves to her hand. Mr.
Paget, the instructor, spoke of her paintings with
increased respect; the attention of visitors was
directed thereto. Martha Burden and even Paulette, in the intervals of her ecstatic preparations,
admitted her to the freemasonry of their own
assured standing. Anthony Cross reminded her
of the possibilities for American students at
Fontainebleau. But she only smiled wisely; she
would have no need of such study, but she hoped
with all her heart that Miss Powell would be the
recipient of a prize which would enable her to
attend there.

"If she isn't," she promised herself, "I'll make
Roger give her her expenses. I'd be willing to
take the money from him for that."

To her great surprise her other interest besides
her painting lay in visiting Jinny. If anyone had
asked her if she were satisfied with her own life,
her reply would have been an instant affirmative.
But she did not want such a life for her sister. For
Virginia there must be no risks, no secrets, no

irregularities. Her efforts to find out how her
sister spent her free hours amazed herself; their
fruitlessness filled her with a constant irritation
which Virginia showed no inclination to allay.
The younger girl had passed her examination and
had been appointed; she was a successful and enthusiastic teacher; this much Angela knew, but
beyond this nothing. She gathered that Virginia
spent a good deal of time with a happy, intelligent, rather independent group of young coloured
men and women; there was talk occasionally of
the theatre, of a dance, of small clubs, of hikes,
of classes at Columbia or at New York City College. Angela even met a gay, laughing party,
consisting of Virginia and her friends *en route* to
Brooklyn, she had been later informed briefly.
The girls were bright birds of paradise, the men,
her artist's eye noted, were gay, vital fauns. In
the subway beside the laughing, happy groups,
white faces showed pale and bloodless, other coloured faces loomed dull and hopeless. Angela
began tardily to recognize that her sister had
made her way into that curious, limited, yet shifting class of the "best" coloured people; the old
Philadelphia phrase came drifting back to her,
"people that you know." She was amazed at
some of the names which Virginia let drop from
her lips in her infrequent and laconic descriptions
of certain evenings which she had spent in the
home of Van Meier, a great coloured American,
a littérateur, a fearless and dauntless apostle of
the rights of man; his name was known, Martha
Burden had assured her, on both sides of the
water.

Such information she picked up as best she

might for Virginia vouchsafed nothing; nor did
she, on the infrequent occasions on which she ran
across her sister, even appear to know her. This,
Angela pointed out, was silly. "You might just
as well speak," she told Jinny petulantly, remembering uncomfortably the occasion when she herself had cut her sister, an absolute stranger in
New York. "Plenty of white and coloured people
are getting to know each other and they always
acknowledge the acquaintanceship. Why shouldn't
we? No harm could come of it." But in Virginia's cool opinion no good could come of it
either. Usually the younger girl preserved a discreet silence; whatever resolves she might have
made with regard to the rupture between herself
and her sister, she was certainly able to keep her
own counsel. It was impossible to glean from
her perfect, slightly distrait manner any glimpse
of her inner life and her intentions. Frequently
she showed an intense preoccupation from which
she awakened to let fall a remark which revealed
to Angela a young girl's normal reactions to the
life about her, pleasant, uneventful and tinged
with a cool, serene happiness totally different
from the hot, heady, turgid rapture which at
present was Angela's life.

．　　．　　．　　．　　．　　．

The Jewish girl, Rachel Salting, who lived on
the floor above, took to calling on Angela. "We're
young and here by ourselves," she said smiling,
"it's stupid for us not to get acquainted, don't
you think so?" Hers was a charming smile and
a charming manner. Indeed she was a very

pretty girl, Angela thought critically. Her skin
was very, very pale, almost pearly, her hair jet
black and curling, her eyes large and almond-
shaped. Her figure was straight and slender but
bore none the less some faint hint of an exotic
voluptuousness. Her interests, she informed her
new friend, were all with the stage, her ideal
being Raquel Meller.

Angela welcomed her friendliness. A strange
apathy, an unusual experience for her, had invaded her being; her painting claimed, it is true,
a great deal of time and concentration; her hours
with Virginia, while not always satisfactory, were
at least absorbing; but for the first time in her
knowledge, her whole life was hanging on the
words, the moods, the actions of some one else—
Roger. Without him she was quite lost; not only
was she unable to order her days without him in
mind, she was even unable to go in quest of new
adventures in living as was once her wont. Consequently she received with outstretched arms
anything beyond the ordinary which might break
the threatening monotony of her life.

Rachel Salting was like a fresh breeze, a
curious mixture of Jewish conservatism and
modernity. Hers was a keen, clear mind, well
trained in the New York schools and colleges
with many branching interests. She spoke of
psychiatry, housing problems, Zionism, child wel-
fare, with a knowledge and zest which astounded
Angela, whose training had been rather superficial
and who had begun to adopt Paulette's cleverness
and Martha Burden's slightly professional,
didactic attitude toward things in general as
norms for herself. Rachel, except when dwelling

on the Jewish problem, seemed to have no particlar views to set forth. Her discussions, based on her wide reading, were purely academic, she had no desire to proselyte, she was no reformer. She was merely a "nice," rather jolly, healthy young woman, an onlooker at life which she had to get through with and which she was finding for the moment at any rate, extremely pleasant.

She was very happy; happy like Virginia with a happiness vastly different from what Angela was calling by that name; a breathless, constant, smiling happiness, palpable, transparent, for all the world to see. Within a few weeks after their acquaintanceship had started, Rachel with smiles and blushes revealed her great secret. She was going to be married.

"To the very best man in the world, Angèle."

"Yes, I'm sure of it."

"He's very good-looking, tall,——"

"As though I didn't know that."

"How could you know?"

"Darling child, haven't I seen him, at least the outline of him, often enough in the hall when I'd come in and turn on that wretched light? I didn't think you'd ever forgive me for it. It did seem as though I were doing it on purpose."

"Oh, I knew you weren't. Then you have seen him?"

"Yes, he's tall and blond. Quite a nice foil for your darkness. See, I'm always the artist."

"Yes," Rachel said slowly, "he is blond."

Angela thought she detected a faint undertone of worry in her hitherto triumphant voice but decided that that was unlikely.

But Rachel confirmed this impression by her next words: "If only everything will turn out all right."

Angela's rather material mind prompted her to ask: "What's the matter, is he very poor?"

Rachel stared. "Poor? As though that mattered. Yes, he's poor, but I don't care about that."

"Well, if you don't care about that, what's the trouble then? He's free, white and twenty-one, isn't he?"

"Yes, yes, it's only—oh you wouldn't understand, you lucky girl! It's nothing you'd ever have to bother about. You see we've got to get our parents' consent first. We haven't spoken of it yet. When we do, I'm afraid there'll be a row."

Some ritual inherent in her racial connections, Angela decided, and asked no further questions. Indeed, she had small chance, for Rachel, once launched, had begun to expound her gospel of marriage. It was an old, old story. Angela could have closed her eyes and imagined her own mother rhapsodizing over her future with Junius. They would be poor, very poor at first but only at first, and they would not mind poverty a bit. It would be fun together. There were little frame houses in the Bronx that rented comparatively cheap. Perhaps Angela knew of them.

Angela shuddering inwardly, acknowledged that she had seen them, dull brown, high-shouldered affairs, perched perilously on stoops. The rooms would be small, square, ugly,——

Rachel would help her John in every way. They would economize. "I won't wash and iron, for that is heart-breaking work, and I want to

213

keep myself dainty and pretty for him, so that
when we do become better off he won't have to be
ashamed of me. And all the time even in our
hardest days I'll be trying my luck at play-writing."
She spoke with the unquenchable ambition which
was her racial dowry. "I'll be attending lectures
and sitting up in the galleries of theatres where
they have the most successful plays. And some
day I'll land." Her fanciful imagination carried
her years ahead. "On our First Night, Angela,
you must be in our box and I'll have an ermine
coat. Won't it be wonderful? But nothing will
be more wonderful than those first few years
when we'll be absolutely dependent on each other;
I on what he makes, he on the way I run the
home. That will be heaven."

Confidences such as these left Angela unmoved
but considerably shaken. There must be something in the life of sacrifice, even drudgery which
Rachel had depicted. Else why should so many
otherwise sensible girls take the risk? But there,
it was silly for her to dwell on such pictures and
scenes. Such a life would never come to her. It
was impossible to conceive of such a life with
Roger. Yet there were times in her lonely room
when she pondered long and deeply, drawing
pictures. The time would be summer; she would
be wearing a white dress, would be standing in
the doorway of a house in the suburbs very, very
near New York. There'd be the best possible
dinner on the table. She did love to cook. And a
tall, strong figure would be hurrying up the walk:
"I had the best luck to-day, Angèle, and I brought
you a present." And presently after dinner she
would take him upstairs to her little work-room

and she'd draw aside the curtain and show him a portrait of a well-known society woman. "She's so pleased with it; and she's going to get me lots of orders,——" Somehow she was absolutely sure that the fanciful figure was not Roger.

. . . . . .

Her lover, back from a three weeks' trip to Chicago, dissipated that sureness. He was glad, overwhelmingly glad to be back and to see Angèle. He came to her apartment directly from the train, not stopping even to report to his father. "I can see him to-morrow. To-night is absolutely yours. What shall we do, Angèle? We can go out to dinner and the theatre or run out to the Country Club or stay here. What do you say?"

"We'll have to stay here, Roger; I'll fix up a gorgeous dinner, better than anything you've had to eat in any of your old hotels. But directly after, I'll have to cut and run because I promised Martha Burden faithfully to go to a lecture with her to-night."

"I never knew you to be interested in a lecture before."

She was worried and showed it. "But this is a different sort of lecture. You know how crazy Martha is about race and social movements. Well, Van Meier is to speak to-night and Martha is determined that a lot of her friends shall hear him. I'm to go with her and Ladislas."

"What's to keep me from going?"

"Nothing, only he's coloured, you know."

"Well, I suppose it won't rub off. I've heard

215

of him. They say he really has brains. I've never seen a nigger with any yet; so this bids fair to be interesting. And, anyway, you don't think I'm going to let my girl run off from me the very moment I come home, do you? Suppose I have Reynolds bring the big car here and we'll take Martha and Ladislas along and anyone else she chooses to bring."

The lecture was held in Harlem in East One Hundred and Thirty-fifth Street. The hall was packed, teeming with suppressed excitement and a certain surcharged atmosphere. Angela radiant, calmed with the nearness and devotion of Roger, looked about her with keen, observing eyes. And again she sensed that fullness, richness, even thickness of life which she had felt on her first visit to Harlem. The stream of living ran almost molten; little waves of feeling played out from groups within the audience and beat against her consciousness and against that of her friends, only the latter were without her secret powers of interpretation. The occasion was clearly one of moment. "I'd come any distance to hear Van Meier speak," said a thin-faced dark young man behind them. "He always has something to say and he doesn't talk down to you. To hear him is like reading a classic, clear and beautiful and true."

Angela, revelling in types and marshalling bits of information which she had got from Virginia, was able to divide the groups. There sat the most advanced coloured Americans, beautifully dressed, beautifully trained, whimsical, humorous, bitter, impatiently responsible, yet still responsible. In one section loomed the dark, eager faces

216

of West Indians, the formation of their features so markedly different from that of the ordinary American as to give them a wild, slightly feral aspect. These had come not because they were disciples of Van Meier but because they were earnest seekers after truth. But unfortunately their earnestness was slightly marred by a stubbornness and an unwillingness to admit conviction. Three or four coloured Americans, tall, dark, sleek young men sat within earshot, speaking with a curious didactic precision. "They're quoting all the sociologists in the world," Ladislas Starr told his little group in astonishment.

Martha, with her usual thoroughness, knew all about them. They were the editors of a small magazine whose chief bid to fame lay in the articles which they directed monthly against Van Meier; articles written occasionally in a spirit of mean jealousy but usually in an effort to gain a sort of inverted glory by carrying that great name on its pages.

Here and there a sprinkling of white faces showed up plainly, startlingly distinct patterns against a back-ground of patient, softly stolid black faces; faces beaten and fashioned by life into a mold of steady, rock-like endurance, of unshakable, unconquered faith. Angela had seen such faces before in the churches in Philadelpia; they brought back old pictures to her mind.

"There he is!" exclaimed Martha triumphantly. "That's Van Meier! Isn't he wonderful?" Angela saw a man, bronze, not very tall but built with a beautiful symmetrical completeness, cross the platform and sit in the tall, deep chair next

217

to the table of the presiding officer. He sat with a curious immobility, gazing straight before him like a statue of an East Indian idol. And indeed there was about him some strange quality which made one think of the East; a completeness, a superb lack of self-consciousness, an odd, arresting beauty wrought by the perfection of his fine, straight nose and his broad, scholarly forehead. One look, however casual, gave the beholder the assurance that here indeed was a man, fearless, dauntless, the captain of his fate.

He began to speak on a clear, deep, bell-like note. Angela thought she had never heard its equal for beauty, for resonance, for culture. And as the young man had said, he did not talk down. His English was the carefully sifted language of the savant, his periods polished, almost poetical. He was noted on two continents for his sociological and economic contributions, but his subject was racial sacrifice. He urged the deliberate introduction of beauty and pleasure into the difficult life of the American Negro. These objects should be theirs both as racial heritage and as compensation. Yet for a time, for a long time, there would have to be sacrifices, many sacrifices made for the good of the whole. "Our case is unique," the beautiful, cultured voice intoned; "those of us who have forged forward, who have gained the front ranks in money and training, will not, are not able as yet to go our separate ways apart from the unwashed, untutored herd. We must still look back and render service to our less fortunate, weaker brethren. And the first step toward making this a workable attitude is the acquisition not so much of a racial love as a racial pride. A

pride that enables us to find our own beautiful
and praiseworthy, an intense chauvinism that is
content with its own types, that finds completeness
within its own group; that loves its own as the
French love their country, because it is their own.
Such a pride can accomplish the impossible."
He quoted:

> "It is not courage, no, nor hate
> That lets us do the things we do;
> It's pride that bids the heart be great,—"

He sat down to a surge of applause that shook
the building. Dark, drooping faces took on an
expression of ecstatic uplift, it was as though they
suddenly saw themselves, transformed by racial
pride as princes in a strange land in temporary
serfdom, princes whose children would know
freedom.

Martha Burden and Ladislas went up to speak
to him; they were old friends. Angela, with
Roger, visibly impressed, stood on one side and
waited. Paulette and Hudson came pushing
through the crowd, the former flushed and excited.
Little groups of coloured people stood about,
some deeply content with a sort of vicarious pride,
some arguing; Angela caught sight of Virginia
standing with three young men and two girls.
They were for the most part gesticulating, lost
in a great excitement. But Jinny seemed listless
and aloof; her childish face looked thin and more
forlornly young than ever. Anthony Cross and
a tall man of undeniably Spanish type passed the
little party and spoke to one of the men, received
introductions. Presently Cross, swinging about,
caught sight of Angela and Roger. He bowed

hastily, flushing; caught his companion's arm and walked hurriedly from the hall, his head very straight, his slender figure always so upright, so *élancé*, more erect than ever.

Presently Martha's party was all out on the sidewalk; Roger in fine spirits invited Paulette and Hudson to ride down town in his car. Paulette was bubbling over with excited admiration of Van Meier. "He isn't a man, he's a god," she proclaimed. "Did you ever see such a superb personality? He's not a magnificent colour." She finished reflectively, "I wonder man; he is a man, just that; colour, race, conditions in his case are pure accidents, he over-rides them all with his ego. Made me feel like a worm too; I gave him my prettiest smile, grand white lady making up to an 'exceptional Negro' and he simply didn't see me; took my hand,—I did my best to make my grasp a clinging one—and he passed me right along disengaging himself as cool as a cucumber and making room for a lady of colour." She finished reflectively, "I wonder what he would be like alone."

"None of your nonsense, Paulette," said Roger frowning.

Hudson smiled. "Paulette's a mighty attractive little piece, I'll admit, but I'd back Van Meier against her every time; she'd present no temptation to him; the man's not only a prophet and the son of a prophet; he's pride incarnate."

Roger said meditatively, "I wonder what proportion of white blood he has in his veins. Of course that's where he gets his ability."

"You make me tired," said Martha. "Of course he doesn't get it from his white blood; he

gets it from all his bloods. It's the mixture that
makes him what he is. Otherwise all white people
would be gods. It's the mixture and the endurance which he has learned from being coloured
in America and the determination to see life
without bitterness,——"

"Oh help, help," exclaimed Roger. "No more
lectures to-night. Look, you're boring Angèle to
death."

"Nothing of the kind," said Angela, "on the
contrary I never was more interested in my life."
And reaching back she gave Martha's hand a
hearty squeeze.

.　　.　　.　　.　　.

Sometimes as on that first day at the art class,
the five of them, Miss Powell, Paulette, Cross,
Martha and Angela met before hours. Miss
Powell as always was silent—she came solely for
her work—but the others enjoyed a little preliminary chat. A week or so after the Van Meier
lecture all but Paulette were gathered thus on an
afternoon when she too came rushing in, starry
eyed, flushed, consumed with laughter.

"I've played the biggest joke on myself," she
announced, "I've been to see Van Meier."

Martha was instant attention. "A joke on Van
Meir?"

"No, on myself, I tell you."

It appeared that she had got Miss Powell to
introduce her to one of the clerks in the great
leader's office. Paulette then with deliberate intention had asked the girl to lunch and afterwards
had returned with her to the office expressing a

desire to meet her employer. Van Meier had
received her cordially enough but with the warning
that he was very busy.

"So I told him that I wouldn't sit down, thinking of course he'd urge me to. But he just raised
his eyebrows in the most quizzical way and said,
'Well'?"

"Of course I couldn't let matters rest like that
so I sat down and began talking to him, nothing
much you know, just telling him how wonderful
he was and letting him see that I'd be glad to
know him better. You should have seen him
looking at me and not saying a word. Presently
he reached out his hand and touched a bell and
Miss Thing-um-bob came in,—your friend, you
know, Miss Powell. He looked at her and nod-
ding toward me said: 'Take her away.' I never
felt such small potatoes in my life. I tell you he's
a personage. Wasn't it great?"

Martha replied crossly that the whole thing
seemed to her in dreadfully poor taste, while Miss
Powell, after one incredulous stare at the first
speaker, applied herself more sedulously to her
work. Even Anthony, shocked out of his habitual
moroseness pronounced the proceedings "a bit
thick, Miss Lister." Angela conscious of a swell-
ing pride, stowed the incident away as a tit-bit
for Virginia.

CHAPTER IV

LIFE had somehow come to a standstill; gone was its quality of high adventure and yet with the sense of tameness came no compensating note of assurance, of permanence. Angela pondered much about this; with her usual instinct for clarity, for a complete understanding of her own emotional life, she took to probing her inner consciousness. The fault, she decided, was bound up in her relationship with Roger. At present in a certain sense she might be said to be living for him; at least his was the figure about which her life resolved, revolved. Yet she no longer had the old, heady desire to feel herself completely his, to claim him as completely hers, neither for his wealth nor for the sense of security which he could afford nor for himself. For some reason he had lost his charm for her, much, she suspected, in the same way in which girls in the position which was hers, often lost their charm for their lovers.

And this realization instead of bringing to her a sense of relief, brought a certain real if somewhat fantastic shame. If there was to be no permanence in the relationship, if laying aside the question of marriage, it was to lack the dignity, the graciousness of an affair of long standing, of sympathy, of mutual need, then indeed according to the code of her childhood, according to every

223

code of every phase of her development, she had allowed herself to drift into an inexcusably vulgar predicament. Even when her material safety and security were at stake and she had dreamed vaguely of yielding to Roger's entreaties to en- sure that safety and security, there might have been some excuse. Life, she considered, came before creed or code or convention. Or if she had loved and there had been no other way she might have argued for this as the supreme ex- perience of her life. But she was no longer conscious of striving for marriage with Roger; and as for love—she had known a feeling of gratitude, intense interest, even intense possessive- ness for him but she did not believe she had ever known love.

But because of this mingling of shame and re- proach she found herself consciously striving to keep their relations on the highest plane possible in the circumstances. She wished now not so much that she had never left Jinny and the security of their common home-life, as that the necessity for it had never arisen. Now suddenly she found herself lonely, she had been in New York nearly three years but not even yet had she struck down deep into the lode of genuine friendship. Paulette was kind and generous; she desired, she said, a close woman friend but Paulette was still the adventuress. She was as likely to change her vo- cation and her place of dwelling as she was to change her lover. Martha Burden, at once more stable and more comprehending in the conduct of a friendship once she had elected for it, was, on the other hand, much more conservative in the expenditure of that friendliness; besides she was by her very nature as reserved as Paulette was expansive, and her native intenseness made it difficult for her to dwell very long on the needs of anyone whose problems did not centre around her own extremely fixed ideas and principles.

As for Anthony Cross,—by some curious, utterly inexplicable revulsion of feeling, Angela could not bring herself to dwell long on the possibilities of a friendship with him. Somehow it seemed to her sacrilegious in her present condition to bring the memory of that far-off day in Van Cortlandt Park back to mind. As soon as his image arose she dismissed it, though there were moments when it was impossible for his vision to come before her without its instantly bringing to mind Rachel Salting's notions of love and self sacrifice. Well, such dreams were not for her, she told herself impatiently. For her own soul's integrity she must make the most of this state in which she now found herself. Either she must effect through it a marriage whose excuse should be that of safety, assurance and a resulting usefulness; or she must resolve it by patience, steadfastness and affection into a very apotheosis of "free love." Of all possible *affaires du coeur* this must in semblance at any rate, be the ultimate desideratum, the finest flower of chivalry and devotion.

•   •   •   •   •   •

To this end she began then devoting herself again to the renewal of that sense of possessiveness in Roger and his affairs which had once been so spontaneous within her. But to this Roger

225

presented unexpected barriers; he grew restive
under such manifestations; he who had once
fought so bitterly against her indifference resented
with equal bitterness any showing of possessive
interest. He wanted no claims upon him, he
acknowledged none. Gradually his absences,
which at first were due to the business interests
of his father, occurred for other reasons or for
none at all. Angela could not grasp this all at
once; it was impossible for her to conceive that
kindness should create indifference; in spite of
confirmatory stories which she had heard, of
books which she had read, she could not make
herself believe that devotion might sometimes
beget ingratitude, loss of appreciation. For if
that were so then a successful relationship between
the sexes must depend wholly on the marriage tie
without reference to compatibility of taste, training or ideals. This she could scarcely credit. In
some way she must be at fault.

No young wife in the first ardour of marriage
could have striven more than she to please Roger.
She sought by reading and outside questions to
inform herself along the lines of Roger's training
—he was a mining engineer. His fondness for
his father prompted her to numerous inquiries
about the interest and pursuits of the older Fielding; she made suggestions for Roger's leisure
hours. But no matter how disinterested her
attitude and tone his response to all this was an
increased sullenness, remoteness, wariness. Roger
was experienced in the wiles of women; such
interest could mean only one thing,—marriage.
Well, Angela might just as well learn that he
had no thought, had never had any thought, of

marrying her or any other woman so far removed from his father's ideas and requirements.

Still Angela, intent on her ideals, could not comprehend. Things were not going well between them; affairs of this kind were often short-lived, that had been one of her first objections to the arrangement, but she had not dreamed that one withdrew when the other had committed no overt offense. She was as charming, as attractive, as pretty as she had ever been and far, far more kind and thoughtful. She had not changed, how could it be possible that he should be different?

A week had gone by and he had not dropped in to see her. Loneliness settled over her like a pall, frightening her seriously because she was realizing that this time she was not missing Roger so much as that a person for whom she had let slip the ideals engendered by her mother's early teaching, a man for whom she had betrayed and estranged her sister, was passing out of her ken. She had rarely called him on the telephone but suddenly she started to do so. For three days the suave voice of his man, Reynolds, told her that Mr. Fielding was "out, m'm."

"But did you give him my message? Did you ask him to call me as soon as he came in?"

"Yes, m'm."

"And did he?"

"That I couldn't tell you, m'm."

She could not carry on such a conversation with a servant.

On the fifth day Roger appeared. She sprang toward him. "Oh Roger, I'm so glad to see you. Did Reynolds tell you I called? Why have you been so long coming?"

"I'd have been still longer if you hadn't stopped 'phoning. Now see here, Angèle, this has got to stop. I can't have women calling me up all hours of the day, making me ridiculous in the eyes of my servants. I don't like it, it's got to stop. Do you understand me?"

Surprised, bewildered, she could only stammer: "But you call me whenever you feel like it."

"Of course I do, that's different. I'm a man." He added a cruel afterword. "Perhaps you notice that I don't call you up as often as I used."

.   .   .   .   .

Her pride was in arms. More than once she thought of writing him a brief note telling him that so far as she was concerned their "affair" was ended. But a great stubbornness possessed her; she was curious to see how this sort of thing could terminate; she was eager to learn if all the advice which older women pour into the ears of growing girls could be as true as it was trite. Was it a fact that the conventions were more important than the fundamental impulses of life, than generosity, kindness, unselfishness? For whatever her original motives, her actual relationship with Fielding had called out the most unselfish qualities in her. And she began to see the conventions, the rules that govern life, in a new light; she realized suddenly that for all their granite-like coldness and precision they also represented fundamental facts; a sort of concentrated compendium of the art of living and therefore as much to be observed and respected as warm, vital impulses.

Towards Roger she felt no rancour, only an apathy incapable of being dispersed. The conversation about the telephone left an effect all out of proportion to its actual importance; it represented for her the apparently unbridgeable difference between the sexes; everything was for men, but even the slightest privilege was to be denied to a woman unless the man chose to grant it. At least there were men who felt like that; not all men, she felt sure, could tolerate such an obviously unjust status. Without intent to punish with no set purpose in her mind, simply because she was no longer interested, she began to neglect Roger. She no longer let other engagements go for him; she made no attempt to be punctual in keeping such engagements as they had already made; in his presence she was often absorbed, absent-minded, lost in thought. She ceased asking him questions about his affairs.

Long before their quarrel they had accepted an invitation from Martha Burden to a small party. Angela was surprised that Roger should remember the occasion, but clearly he did; he was on hand at the correct date and hour and the two of them fared forth. During the brief journey he was courteous, even politely cordial, but the difference between his attitude and that of former days was very apparent. The party was of a more frivolous type than Martha usually sponsored, she was giving it for a young, fun-loving cousin of Ladislas; there was no general conversation, some singing, much dancing, much pairing off in couples. Carlotta Parks was present with Ralph Ashley, the slender, dark man who had appeared with Carlotta when Angela first met her. As soon as Roger appeared Carlotta came rushing toward him.

"I've been waiting for you!" She dragged at his hand and not unwillingly he suffered himself to be led to a small sofa. They chatted a few minutes; then danced; Roger simply must look at Martha's new etchings. The pair was inseparable for the evening. Try as she might Angela could discover no feeling of jealousy but her dignity was hurt. She could not have received less attention from her former lover if they had never met. At first she thought she would make up to Ashley but something malicious in Carlotta's glance deterred her. No, she was sick of men and their babyish, faithless ways; she did not care enough about Roger to play a game for him. So she sat quietly in a deep chair, smoking, dipping into the scattered piles of books which lent the apartment its air of cheerful disorder. Occasionally she chatted; Ladislas Starr perched on the arm of her chair and beguiled her with gay tales of his university days in pre-war Vienna.

But she would never endure such an indignity again. On the way home she was silent. Roger glanced at her curiously, raised his eyebrows when she asked him to come in. She began quietly: "Roger I'll never endure again the treatment—"

But he was ready, even eager for a quarrel. "It looks to me as though you were willing to endure anything. No woman with an ounce of pride would have stood for what you've been standing lately."

She said evenly: "You mean this is the end? We're through?"

"Well, what do you think about it? You certainly didn't expect it to last for ever."

His tone was unbelievably insulting. Eyeing him speculatively she replied: "No, of course I didn't expect it to last for ever, but I didn't think it would end like this. I don't see yet why it should."

The knowledge of his unpardonable manner lay heavy upon him, drove him to fresh indignity. "I suppose you thought some day I'd kiss your hand and say 'You've been very nice to me; I'll always remember you with affection and gratitude. Good-bye.' "

"Well, why shouldn't you have said that? Certainly I'd expected that much sooner than a scene of this sort. I never dreamed of letting myself in for this kind of thing."

Some ugly devil held him in its grasp. "You knew perfectly well what you were letting yourself in for. Any woman would know it."

She could only stare at him, his words echoing in her ears: "You knew perfectly well what you were letting yourself in for."

The phrase had the quality of a cosmic echo; perhaps men had been saying it to women since the beginning of time. Doubtless their biblical equivalent were the last words uttered by Abraham to Hagar before she fared forth into the wilderness.

CHAPTER V

LONG after Roger had left her she sat staring into the dark shadows of the room. For a long time the end, she knew, had been imminent; she had been curious to see how it would arrive, but the thought had never crossed her mind that it would come with harsh words and with vulgarity. The departure of Roger himself—she shut her hand and opened it—meant nothing; she had never loved, never felt for him one-tenth of the devotion which her mother had known for her father, of the spontaneous affection which Virginia had offered Matthew Henson. Even in these latter weeks when she had consciously striven to show him every possible kindness and attention she had done so for the selfish preservation of her ideals. Now she looked back on those first days of delight when his emotions and her own had met at full tide; when she dreamed that she alone of all people in the world was exempt from ordinary law. How, she wondered futilely, could she ever have suffered herself to be persuaded to tamper with the sacred mysteries of life? If she had held in her hand the golden key,—love! But to throw aside the fundamental laws of civilization for passion, for the hot-headed wilfulness of youth and to have it end like this, drably, vulgarly, almost in a brawl! How could she endure her-

232

self? And Roger and his promises of esteem and golden memories!

For a moment she hated him for his fine words and phrases, hated him for tricking her. No matter what she had said, how she had acted, he should have let her go. Better a wound to her passion than later this terrible gash in her proud assurance, this hurt in the core of herself "God!" she said, raging in her tiny apartment as a tiger in a menagerie rages in its inadequate cage, "God, isn't there any place where man's responsibility to woman begins?"

.   .   .   .   .

But she had grown too much into the habit of deliberately ordering her life, of hewing her own path, of removing the difficulties that beset that path, to let herself be sickened, utterly prostrated by what had befallen her. Roger, her companion, had gone; she had been caught up in an inexcusably needless affair without the pretext of love. Thank God she had taken nothing from Roger; she had not sold herself, only bestowed that self foolishly, unworthily. However upset and harassed her mind might be it could not dwell too long on this loss of a lover. There were other problems to consider; for Roger's passing meant the vanishing of the last hope of the successful marriage which once she had so greatly craved. And even though she had not actively considered this for some time, yet as a remote possibility it had afforded a sense of security. Now that mirage was dispelled; she was brought with a sudden shock back to reality. No longer

was it enough for her to plan how she could win
to a pleasant and happy means of existence, she
must be on the *qui vive* for the maintenance of
that very existence itself. New York had literally
swallowed her original three thousand dollars;
part of Virginia's gift was also dissipated. Less
than a thousand dollars stood between her and
absolute penury. She could not envisage turning
to Jinny; life which had seemed so promising, so
golden, had failed to supply her with a single
friend to whom she could turn in an hour of
extremity.

Such thoughts as these left her panic-stricken,
cold with fear. The spectre of possible want
filled her dreams, haunted her waking hours,
thrust aside the devastating shame of her affair
with Roger to replace it with dread and
apprehension. In her despair she turned more
ardently than ever to her painting; already she
was capable of doing outstanding work in
portraiture, but she lacked *cachet*; she was
absolutely unknown.

This condition of her mind affected her appearance; she began to husband her clothes, sadly
conscious that she could not tell where others
would come from. Her face lost its roundness,
the white warmness of her skin remained but
there were violet shadows under her eyes; her
forehead showed faint lines; she was slightly
shabby. Gradually the triumphant vividness so
characteristic of Angèle Mory left her, she was
like any one of a thousand other pitiful, frightened
girls thronging New York. Miss Powell glanced
at her and thought: "she looks unhappy, but

234

how can she be when she has a chance at
everything in the world just because she's
white?"

Anthony marked her fading brightness; he
would have liked to question her, comfort her,
but where this girl was concerned the rôle of
comforter was not for him. Only the instructor,
Mr. Paget guessed at her extremity. He had seen
too many students not to recognize the signs of
poverty, of disaster in love, of despair at the
tardy flowering of dexterity that had been mistaken for talent. Once after class he stopped
Angela and asked her if she knew of anyone
willing to furnish designs for a well-known journal
of fashion.

"Not very stimulating work, but the pay is
good and the firm reliable. Their last artist
was with them eight years. If you know of anyone,——"

She interrupted: "I know of myself. Do you
think they'd take me on?"

"I could recommend you. They applied to me,
you see. Doubtless they'd take my suggestions
into account."

He was very kind; made all the necessary
arrangements. The firm received Angela gladly,
offering her a fair salary for work that was a
trifle narrow, a bit stultifying. But it opened up
possibilities; there were new people to be met;
perhaps she would make new friends, form ties
which might be lasting.

"Oh," she said hopefully to herself, "life is
wonderful! It's giving me a new deal and I'll
begin all over again. I'm young and now I'm

sophisticated; the world is wide, somewhere
there's happiness and peace and a place for me.
I'll find it."

But her hope, her sanguineness, were a little
forced, her superb self-confidence perceptibly
diminished. The radiance which once had so
bathed every moment of her existence was fading
gently, inexorably into the "light of common
day."

HOME AGAIN

CHAPTER I

NEW YORK, it appeared, had two visages. It could offer an aspect radiant with promise or a countenance lowering and forbidding. With its flattering possibilities it could elevate to the seventh heaven, or lower to the depths of hell with its crushing negations. And loneliness! Loneliness such as that offered by the great, noisy city could never be imagined. To realize it one would have to experience it. Coming home from work Angela used to study the people on the trains, trying to divine what cause had engraved a given expression on their faces, particularly on the faces of young women. She picked out for herself four types, the happy, the indifferent, the preoccupied, the lonely. Doubtless her classification was imperfect, but she never failed, she thought, to recognize the signs of loneliness, a vacancy of expression, a listlessness, a faintly pervading despair. She remembered the people in Union Square on whom she had spied so blithely when she had first come to New York. Then she had thought of them as being "down and out," mere idlers, good for nothing. It had not occurred to her that their chief disaster might be loneliness. Her office was on Twenty-third Street and often at the noon-hour she walked down to the dingy Square and looked again on the

239

sprawling, half-recumbent, dejected figures. And between them and herself she was able to detect a terrifying relationship. She still carried her note-book, made sketches, sitting watching them and jotting down a line now and then when their vacant, staring eyes were not fixed upon her. Once she would not have cared if they had caught her; she would have said with a shrug: "Oh they wouldn't mind, they're too far gone for that." But since then her sympathy and knowledge had waxed. How fiercely she would have rebelled had anyone from a superior social plane taken her for copy!

In the evenings she worked at the idea of a pic-ture which she intended for a masterpiece. It was summer and the classes at Cooper Union had been suspended. But she meant to return in the fall, perhaps she would enter the scholarship contest and if successful, go abroad. But the urge to wander was no longer in the ascendant. The prospect of Europe did not seem as alluring now as the prospect of New York had appeared when she lived in Philadelphia. It would be nice to stay put, rooted; to have friends, experiences, memories.

·　　　·　　　·　　　·　　　·

Paulette, triumphant to the last, had left with Hudson for Russia. Martha and Ladislas were spending the summer with Martha's people on Long Island. Roger had dropped into the void, but she could not make herself miss him; to her he was the symbol of all that was most futile in her

existence, she could forgive neither him nor herself for their year of madness. If the experience,
she told herself, had ended—so-beit—everything
ends. If it had faded into a golden glow with a
wealth of memories, the promise of a friendship,
she would have had no qualms; but as matters had
turned out it was an offense in her nostrils, a
great blot on the escutcheon of her fastidiousness.

She wished that Martha had asked her to spend
week-ends with her but the idea had apparently
never crossed the latter's mind. "Good-bye until
fall," she had said gaily, "do you know, I'm
awfully glad to go home this time. I always have
my old room; it's like beginning life all over
again. Of course I wouldn't give up New York
but life seems so much more real and durable
down there. After all it's where my roots are."

Her roots! Angela echoed the expression to
herself on a note that was wholly envious. How
marvellous to go back to parents, relatives,
friends with whom one had never lost touch!
The peace, the security, the companionableness
of it! This was a relationship which she had
forfeited with everyone, even with Jinny. And
as for her other acquaintances in Philadelphia,
Henson, Butler, Kate and Agnes Hollowell, so
completely, so casually, without even a ripple had
she dropped out of their lives that it would have
been impossible for her to re-establish their old,
easy footing even had she so desired.

Virginia, without making an effort, seemed
overwhelmed, almost swamped by friendships,
pleasant intimacies, a thousand charming interests.
She and Sara Penton, another teacher, had taken

241

an apartment together, a three room affair on the top floor of a house on 139th Street, in "Striver's Row," explained Jinny. Whether or not the nickname was deserved, it seemed to Angela well worth an effort to live in this beautiful block with its tree-bordered pavements, its spacious houses, its gracious neighbourliness. A doctor and his wife occupied the first two floors; they were elderly, rather lonely people, for their two children had married and gone to other cities. They had practically adopted Virginia and Sara; nursing them when they had colds, indulgently advising them as to their callers. Mrs. Bradley, the doctor's wife, occasionally pressed a dress for them; on stormy days the doctor drove them in his car around to "Public School 89" where they both taught. Already the two girls were as full of intimacies, joyous reminiscences, common plans as though they had lived together for years. Secrets, nick-names, allusions, filled the atmosphere. Angela grew sick of the phrases: "Of course you don't understand that; just some nonsense and it would take too long to explain it. Besides you wouldn't know any of the people." Even so, unwelcome as the expression was, she did not hear it very often, for Jinny did not encourage her visits to the apartment even as much as to the boarding house.

"Sara will think it strange if you come too often."

"We might tell her," Angela rejoined, "and ask her to keep it a secret."

But Jinny opined cooly that that would never do; it was bad to entrust people with one's secrets. "If you can't keep them yourself, why should

242

they?" she asked sagely. Her attitude showed
no malice, only the complete acceptance of the
stand which her sister had adopted years ago.

. . . . .

In her sequestered rooms in the Village lying in
the summer heat unkempt and shorn of its
glamour Angela pondered long and often on her
present mode of living. Her life, she was pretty
sure, could not go on indefinitely as it did now.
Even if she herself made no effort it was unlikely
that the loneliness could persist. Jinny, she
shrewdly suspected, had known something of this
horrible condition when she, the older sister had
left her so ruthlessly to go off and play at adventure. This loneliness and her unfortunate
affair with Henson had doubtless proved too much
for her, and she had deliberately sought change
and distraction elsewhere. There were depths
upon depths of strength in Jinny and as much
purpose and resource as one might require. Now
here she was established in New York with
friends, occupation, security, leading an utterly
open life, no secrets, no subterfuges, no goals to
be reached by devious ways.

Jinny had changed her life and been successful.
Angela had changed hers and had found pain and
unhappiness. Where did the fault lie? Not, certainly, in her determination to pass from one race
to another. Her native good sense assured her
that it would have been silly for her to keep on
living as she had in Philadelphia, constantly,
through no fault of her own, being placed in
impossible positions, eternally being accused and

243

hounded because she had failed to placard herself, forfeiting old friendships, driven fearfully to the establishing of new ones. No, the fault was not there. Perhaps it lay in her attitude toward her friends. Had she been too coldly deliberate in her use of them? Certainly she had planned to utilize her connection with Roger, but on this point she had no qualms; he had been paid in full for any advantages which she had meant to gain. She had not always been kind to Miss Powell, "but," she murmured to herself, "I was always as kind to her as I dared be in the circumstances and far, far more attentive than any of the others." As for Anthony, Paulette, and Martha, her slate was clear on their score. She was struck at this point to realize that during her stay of nearly three years these five were the only people to whom she could apply the term friends. Of these Roger had dropped out; Miss Powell was negative; Paulette had gone to Russia. There remained only Martha and Anthony. Martha was too intensely interested in the conduct of her own life in connection with Ladislas to make a friend, a satisfying, comfortable, intimate friend such as Sara Penton seemed to be with Virginia. There remained then only Anthony—yes, and her new acquaintance, Rachel Salting.

.   .   .   .   .

She began then in her loneliness to approach Rachel seeking for nothing other than those almost sisterly intimacies which spring up between solitary women cut off in big cities from their homes and from all the natural resources which add so much to the beauty and graciousness of young womanhood. "If anything comes out of this friendship to advance me in any way," she told herself solemnly, "it will happen just because it happens but I shall go into this with clean hands and a pure heart—merely because I like Rachel."

After the fever and fret of her acquaintanceship with Roger, the slight unwholesomeness attendant on Paulette, the didactic quality lurking in Martha's household, it was charming, even delicious to enter on a friendship with this simple, intelligent, enthusiastic girl. Rachel, for all her native endowment, her wide reading and her broad scholastic contacts, had the straightforward utter sincerity and simplicity of a child; at times Angela felt quite sophisticated, even blasé beside her. But in reality they were two children together; Angela's brief episode with Roger had left no trace on her moral nature; she was ashamed now of the affair with a healthy shame at its unworthiness; but beyond that she suffered from no morbidness. Her sum total of the knowledge of life had been increased; she saw men with a different eye, was able to differentiate between the attitudes underlying the pleasantries of the half dozen young men in her office; listening, laughing, weighing all their attentions, accepting none. In truth she had lost to a degree her taste for the current type of flirtations. She might marry some day but all that was still in the dim future. Meanwhile the present beckoned; materially she was once more secure, her itching ambition was temporarily lulled; she had a friend. It was just as well to let time slide by for a while.

The two girls spent their evenings together.

245

Rachel's fiancé, John Adams, was a travelling
salesman and nearly always out of town. When
he was home Angela was careful to have an engagement, though Rachel assured her, laughing
and sparkling, that the two were already so used
to each other that a third person need not feel *de
trop*. Occasionally the three of them went during
the hot summer nights to Coney Island or Far
Rockaway. But this jaunt took on the proportions
more of an ordeal than a pleasure trip; so packed
were the cars with helpless humanity, so crowded
the beaches, so nightmarish the trip home.
Fortunately Angela came face to face one day
with Ralph Ashley, Carlotta's former friend.
Low-spirited, lonely, distrait, he asked Angela
eagerly to allow him to call occasionally. He
seemed a rather bookish, serious young man who
had failed to discover the possibilities of his inner
resources. Without an acquaintance or a book
he was helpless. Angela's self-reliance and cleverness seemed to offer a temporary harbour.
Apparently with Carlotta out of town, he was at
loose ends. By some tacit understanding he was
taken into the little group and as he possessed a
car which he was willing and eager to share the
arrangement was a very happy one.

．　　　．　　　．　　　．　　　．

These were pleasant days. Long afterwards,
Angela, looking back recalled them as among the
happiest she had known in New York. In particular she liked the hours when she and Rachel
were together busied with domestic, homely
affairs. They advised each other on the subject

246

of dress; Angela tried out new recipes. In the late
evenings she worked on the sketches, recalling
them from her note-book while Rachel, sitting
sidewise in the big chair, her legs dangling
comfortably over its arm, offered comments and
suggestions. She had had "courses in art," and on
a trip to France and Italy at the age of eighteen had
visited the Louvre, the Pitti and Uffizi Galleries.
All this lent a certain pithiness and authority to
the criticisms which she poured forth for her
friend's edification; her remarks rarely produced
any effect on Angela, but both girls felt that
Rachel's knowledge gave a certain effect of
"atmosphere."

Usually Rachel's talk was on John and their
approaching marriage, their unparalleled courtship. Many years later Angela could have re-
lated all the details of that simple, almost sylvan
wooing, the growing awareness of the two lovers,
their mutual fears and hopes, their questionings,
assurances and their blissful engagement. She
knew to a penny what John made each week, how
much he put by, the amount which thrifty Rachel
felt must be in hand before they could marry.
Once this recital, so unvarying, so persistent,
would have bored her, but she was more sympathetic in these days; sometimes she found herself
making suggestions, saving the house wifely
clippings culled from newspapers, proposing
decorations for the interior of one of the ugly
little houses on which Rachel had so inexplicably
set her heart. She was a little older than her
friend, she had had experience in keeping house
and in shopping with her mother in those far-off
days; she ventured occasionally to advise Rachel

in her rare purchases very much as though the latter were her own sister instead of a chance acquaintance whom she had known less than a year.

It was a placid, almost ideal existence. Only one thread of worry ran through its fabric, the thought that Rachel and John would soon be marrying and again Angela would be left on the search for a new friend. With one of them in the Bronx and the other in Greenwich Village, frequent communication would be physically impossible. But, curiously enough, whenever Angela lamented over this to her friend, a deep sombreness would descend on the latter; she would remark gloomily: "Time enough to worry about that; after all we might not get married. You never can tell." This was too enigmatic for Angela and finally she grew to look on it as a jest, a rather poor one but still a jest.

CHAPTER II

INTO the midst of this serenity came a bolt from the blue. Rachel, a librarian, was offered the position of head librarian in a far suburb of Brooklyn. Furthermore a wealthy woman from Butte, Montana, desiring to stay in New York for a few months and taking a fancy to the dinginess of Jayne Street and to the inconveniences of Rachel's apartment found she must live there and not otherwhere. No other location in the whole great city would do; she was willing to sublet at any figure. Unwillingly Rachel named a price which she secretly considered in the nature of highway robbery, but none of this matter to Mrs. Denver, who was used to paying for what she wanted. And Rachel could not refuse, for both offers meant a substantial increase in the nest-egg which was to furnish the little brown house in the Bronx. In reality it meant to her extraordinary, unhoped for luck whose only flaw consisted in the enforced separation from her new friend. But to Angela it brought the awfulness of a catastrophe, though not for one moment would she let her deep dismay be suspected. After her first involuntary exclamation of consternation she never faltered in her complete acquiescence in the plan. But at heart she was sick.

The sudden flitting entailed much work and

bustle. Rachel was as untidy as Angela was neat;
everything she possessed had to be collected sepa-
rately; there were no stacks of carefully folded
clothing to be lifted wholesale and placed in
gaping trunks. To begin with the trunks themselves were filled with dubious odds and ends
which required to be sorted, given or even thrown
away. There was no question of abandoning the
débris, for the apartment must be left habitable
for Mrs. Denver.

A nightmare then of feverish packing ensued;
hasty meals, general house-cleaning. In order to
assuage the sinking of her heart Angela plunged
into it with great ardour. But at night, weary as
she would be from the extra activity of the day,
she could not fight off the sick dismay which over-
flowed her in great, submerging waves. It seemed
to her she could not again endure loneliness; she
could never summon the strength to seek out new
friends, to establish fresh intimacies. She was
twenty-six years old and the fact that after having
lived all those years she was still solitary appalled
her. Perhaps some curse such as one reads of in
mediæval legends had fallen upon her. "Perhaps
I'm not meant to have friends," she told herself
lying face downwards in her pillows on the
sweltering June nights. And a great nostalgia
for something real and permanent swept upon
her; she wished she were either very, very young,
safe and contented once more in the protection
of her father's household or failing that, very,
very old.

. . . . .

A nature as strong, as self-reliant as hers could

not remain long submerged; she had seen too many bad beginnings convert themselves into good endings.   One of her most valuable native endowments lay in her ability to set herself and her difficulties objectively before her own eyes; in this way she had solved more than one problem.   On the long ride in the subway back from Brooklyn whither she had accompanied Rachel on the night of the latter's departure she resolved to pursue this course that very night.   Mercifully the terrible heat had abated, a little breeze came sifting in her open windows, moving the white sash curtains, even agitating some papers on the table.   Soberly she set about the business of getting supper.   Once she thought of running up to Rachel's former apartment and proffering some hospitality to Mrs. Denver.   Even if the rich new tenant should not accept she'd be pleased doubtless; sooner or later she would be offering a return of courtesies, a new friendship would spring up.   Again there would be possibilities.   But something in her rebelled against such a procedure; these intimacies based on the sliding foundation of chance sickened her; she would not lend herself to them—not ever again.   From this day on she'd devote herself to the establishing of permanencies.

Supper over, the dishes cleared away, she sat down and prepared to think.   Callers were unlikely; indeed there was no one to call, since Ashley was out of town for the week-end, but the pathos of this fact left her untouched.   To-night she courted loneliness.

An oft heard remark of her mother's kept running through her mind: "You get so taken up with the problem of living, with just life itself,

that by and by being coloured or not is just one
thing more or less that you have to contend with."
It had been a long time since she had thought
about colour; at one time it had seemed to
complicate her life immensely, now it seemed to
her that it might be of very little importance. But
her thoughts skirted the subject warily for she
knew how immensely difficult living could be made
by this matter of race. But that should take a
secondary place; at present life, a method of living was the main thing, she must get that problem
adjusted and first she must see what she wanted.
Companionship was her chief demand. No more
loneliness, not even if that were the road that led
to the fulfilment of vast ambition, to the realization of the loftiest hopes. And for this she was
willing to make sacrifices, let go if need be of her
cherished independence, lead a double life, move
among two sets of acquaintances.

For deep in her heart she realized the longing
to cast in her lot once more with Virginia, her
little sister whom she should never have left.
Virginia, it is true, showed no particular longing
for her; indeed she seemed hardly cognizant of
her existence; but this attitude might be a forced
one. She thought, "I didn't want her, the darling,
and so she just made herself put me out of her
life." Angela was well aware of the pluck, the
indomitableness that lay beneath Jinny's babyish
exterior, but there was a still deeper stratum of
tenderness and love and loyalty which was the
real Virginia. To this Angela would make her
appeal; she would acknowledge her foolishness,
her selfishness; she would bare her heart and
crave her sister's forgiveness. And then they

252

would live together, Jinny and she and Sara
Penton if need be; what a joke it would all be on
Sara! And once again she would know the bliss
and happiness of a home and the stabilities of
friendships culled from a certain definite class
of people, not friendships resulting from mere
chance. There would be blessed Sunday mornings
and breakfasts, long walks; lovely evenings in the
autumn to be filled with reminiscences drawn
from these days of separation. How Virginia
would open her eyes at her tales of Paulette and
Martha! She would never mention Roger. And
as for colour; when it seemed best to be coloured
she would be coloured; when it was best to be
white she would be that. The main thing was,
she would know once more the joys of ordinary
living, home, companionship, loyalty, security,
the bliss of possessing and being possessed. And
to think it was all possible and waiting for her;
it was only a matter of a few hours, a few miles.

A great sense of peace, of exaltation descended
upon her. Almost she could have said: "I will
arise and go unto my father."

On Sunday accordingly she betook herself to
her sister's apartment in 139th Street. Miss
Penton, she thought, would be out; she had
gathered from the girls' conversation many
pointed references to Sara's great fondness, of
late, for church, exceeded only by her interest in
the choir. This interest in the choir was ardently
encouraged by a member of that body who
occasionally walked home with Sara in order more

fully to discuss the art of music. Virginia no longer went to church; Sunday had become her "pick-up day," the one period in the week which she devoted to her correspondence, her clothes and to such mysterious rites of beautifying and revitalizing as lay back of her healthy, blooming exquisiteness. This would be the first time in many months that the sisters would have been alone together and it was with high hopes that Angela, mounting the brown stone steps and ringing the bell, asked for Virginia.

Her sister was in, but so was Sara, so was a third girl, a Miss Louise Andrews. The room was full of the atmosphere of the lightness, of the badinage, of the laughter which belong to the condition either of youth or of extreme happiness. In the middle of the room stood a large trunk from whose yawning interior Jinny lifted a glowing, smiling face. Angela was almost startled at the bright ecstasy which radiated from it. Sara Penton was engaged rather negligently in folding clothes; Miss Andrews perched in magnificent ease on the daybed, struck an occasional tune from a ukelele and issued commands which nobody heeded.

"Hello," said Virginia carelessly. "Can you get in? I was thinking of writing to you."

"Oh," Angela's hopes fluttered, fell, perished. "You're not going away?" Her heart echoed Jinny's old cry: "And leave me—when I'm all ready to come back to you, when I need you so terribly!"

But of all this Virginia was, of course, unaware. "Nothing different," she said briskly. "I'm going away this very afternoon to Philadel-

phia, Merion, points south and west, going to
stay with Edna Brown."

Angela was aghast. "I wanted to see you
about something rather important, Virginia—at
least," she added humbly, "important to me."
Rather impatiently she glanced at the two girls
hoping they would take the hint and leave them,
but they had not even heard her, so engrossed
were they in discussing the relative merits of one-
and two-piece sports clothes.

Her sister was kind but not curious. "Unless
it's got something to do with your soul's salvation
I'm afraid it'll have to wait a bit," she said gaily.
"I'm getting a two o'clock train and I must finish
this trunk— Sara's such a poor packer or I'd leave
it for her. As it is she's going to send it after me.
Aren't you, darling?" Already Angela's request
was forgotten. "After I finish this," the gay
voice went on, "I've got some 'phoning to do and
—oh a million things."

"Let me help you," said Angela suddenly
inspired, "then we'll call a taxi and we can go
down to the station together and we'll have a long
talk so I can explain things."

Virginia was only half-attentive. "Miss Mory
wants to go to the station with me," she said
throwing a droll look at her friends. "Shall I
take her along?" She vanished into the bedroom,
Louise Andrews at her heels, both of them overwhelmed with laughter bubbling from some secret
spring.

Cut and humiliated, Angela stood silent. Sara
Penton who had been looking after the vanishing
figures turned and caught her expression. "Don't
mind her craziness. She's not responsible to-day."

She came closer. "For heaven's sake don't let on I told you; she's engaged."

This was news. "Engaged? To whom?"

"Oh somebody she's always been crazy about." The inevitable phrase followed: "You wouldn't know who he was."

Not know who he was, not know Matthew! She began to say "Why I knew him before Virginia," but remembering her rôle, a stupid and silly one now, caught herself, stood expectantly.

"So you see," Sara went on mysteriously, one eye on the bedroom, "you mustn't insist on going to the station with her; he's going to take her down."

"Why, is he here?"

"Came yesterday. We've been threatening all morning to butt in. That's the reason she spoke as she did about your going down. She expressed herself to us, you bet, but she probably wouldn't feel like doing that to you."

"Probably not," said Angela, her heart cold. Her little sister was engaged and she was learning of it from strangers. It was all she could do to hold back the tears. "But you've only yourself to blame," she reminded herself valiantly.

The two girls came back; Virginia still laughing but underneath the merriment Angela was able to detect a flurry of nervousness. After all, Jinny was just a child. And she was so happy, it would never do to mar that happiness by the introduction of the slightest gloom or discomfort. Her caller rose to her feet. "I guess I'll be going."

256

Virginia made no effort to detain her, but the glance which she turned on her sister was suddenly very sweet and friendly. "Here, I'll run down to the door with you. Sara, be a darling and pick out the best of those stockings for me, put in lots. You know how hard I am on them."

Out in the hall she flung an impulsive arm about her sister. "Oh, Angela, I'm so happy, so happy. I'm going to write you about it right away, you'll be so surprised." Astonishingly she gave the older girl a great hug, kissed her again and again.

"Oh," said Angela, the tears welling from her eyes, "Oh Jinny, you do forgive me, you do, you do? I'm so sorry about it all. I've been wretched for a long time. I thought I had lost you, Virginia."

"I know," said Jinny, "I'm a hard-hearted little wretch." She giggled through her own tears, wiped them away with the back of her childish bronze hand. "I was just putting you through; I knew you'd get sick of Miss Anne's folks and come back to me. Oh Angela, I've wanted you so. But it's all right now. I won't be back for ten weeks, but then we will talk! I've got the most marvellous plans for both of us—for all of us." She looked like a wise baby. "You'll get a letter from me in a few days telling you all about it. Angela, I'm so happy, but I must fly. Good-bye, darling."

They clung for a moment in the cool, dim depths of the wide hall.

. . . . .

257

Angela could have danced in the street. As it was she walked gaily down Seventh Avenue to 110th Street and into the bosky reaches of the park. Jinny had forgiven her. Jinny longed for her, needed her; she had known all along that Angela was suffering, had deliberately punished her. Well, she was right, everything was right this glorious memorable day. She was to have a sister again, some one of her own, she would know the joy of sharing her little triumphs, her petty woes. Wise Jinny, wonderful Jinny!

And beautiful Jinny, too, she thought. How lovely, how dainty, how fresh and innocent her little sister seemed. This brought her mind to Matthew and his great good fortune. "I'd like to see him again," she mused, smiling mischievously. "Doubtless he's forgotten me. It would be great fun to make him remember." Only, of course, now he was Jinny's and she would never get in the way of that darling. "Not even if he were some one I really wanted with all my heart and soul. But I'd never want Matthew." It would be fun, she thought, to see him again. He would make a nice brother, so sturdy and kind and reliable. She must be careful never to presume on that old youthful admiration of his. Smiling and happy she reached her house, actually skipped up the steps to her rooms. Her apartment no longer seemed lonely; it was not beautiful and bright like Jinny's but it was snug and dainty. It would be fun to have Virginia and Sara down; yes, and that new girl, that Miss Andrews, too. She didn't care what the other people in the house thought. And the girls themselves, how astonished they would be to learn the true state of affairs. Suddenly remembering Mrs. Denver, she ran up to see her; that lady, in spite of her wealth and means for self-indulgence, was palpably lonely. Angela cheered her up with mirthful accounts of her own first days in New York; she'd been lonely too, she assured her despondent hostess, sparkling and fascinating.

"I don't see how anybody with a disposition like yours could ever be lonely," said Mrs. Denver enviously. She'd been perilously near tears all day.

Gone, gone was all the awful melancholy, the blueness that had hung about her like a palpable cloud. She was young, fascinating; she was going to be happy,—again. *Again!* She caught her breath at that. Oh, God was good! This feeling of lightness, of exaltation had been unknown to her so long; not since the days when she had first begun to go about with Roger had she felt so free, bird-like. In the evening Ralph Ashley came with his car and drove her halfway across Long Island, or so it seemed. They stopped at a gorgeous hotel and had a marvellous supper. Ashley was swept off his feet by her gay vitalness. In the doorway of the Jayne Street house she gave him her hand and a bewitching smile. "You can't imagine how much I've enjoyed myself. I'll always remember it." And she spoke sincerely, for soon this sort of thing would be far behind her.

"You're a witch," said Ashley, his voice shaking a little. "You can have this sort of thing whenever you want it and you know it. Be kind to me, Angèle. I'm not a bad fellow."

Frightened, she pushed him away, ran in and slammed the door. No, no, no, her heart pounded. Roger had taught her an unforgettable lesson. Soon she'd be with Jinny and Matthew, safe, sheltered.

CHAPTER III

In the middle of the night she found herself sitting up in bed. A moment before she had been asleep, but a sudden thought had pierced her consciousness so sharply that the effect was that of an icy hand laid suddenly on her shoulder. Jinny and Matthew marry—why, that meant—why, of course it meant that they would have to live in Philadelphia. How stupid she had been! And she couldn't go back there—never, never. Not because of the difficulties which she had experienced as a child; she was perfectly willing to cast in her lot again with coloured people in New York. But that was different; there were signal injustices here, too—oh, many, many of them—but there were also signal opportunities. But Philadelphia with its traditions of liberty and its actual economic and social slavery, its iniquitous school system, its prejudiced theatres, its limited offering of occupation! A great, searing hatred arose in her for the huge, slumbering leviathan of a city which had hardly moved a muscle in the last fifty years. So hide-bound were its habits that deliberate insult could be offered to coloured people without causing the smallest ripple of condemnation or even consternation in the complacent commonwealth. Virginia in one of her expansive moments had told her of a letter received from Agnes Hallo-

261

well, now a graduate of the Women's Medical
College. Agnes was as fair as Angela, but she
had talked frankly, even with pride, of her racial
connections. "I had nothing to be ashamed of,"
Angela could imagine her saying, her cheeks flushing, her black eyes snapping. On her graduation
she had applied for an interneship at a great hospital for the insane; a position greatly craved by
ardent medical graduates because of the unusually
large turnover of pathological cases. But the man
in charge of such appointments, looking Agnes
hard in the eye told her suavely that such a position would never be given to her "not if you
passed ahead of a thousand white candidates."

As for Angela, here was the old problem of
possible loneliness back on her hands. Virginia,
it was true, would hardly marry at once, perhaps
they would have a few happy months together.
But afterwards. . . . She lay there, wide awake
now, very still, very straight in her narrow bed,
watching the thick blackness grow thinner, less
opaque. And suddenly as on a former occasion,
she thought of marriage. Well, why not? She
had thought of it once before as a source of relief
from poverty, as a final barrier between herself
and the wolves of prejudice; why not now as a
means of avoiding loneliness? "I must look
around me," her thoughts sped on, and she blushed
and smiled in the darkness at the cold-bloodedness
of such an idea. But, after all, that was what men
said—and did. How often had she heard the expression—"he's ready to settle down, so he's looking around for a wife." If that were the
procedure of men it should certainly be much more
so the procedure of women since their fate was so

much more deeply involved. The room was growing lighter; she could see the pictures a deeper
blur against the faint blur of the wall. Her passing shame suddenly spent itself, for, after all, she
knew practically no men. There was Ashley—
but she was through with men of his type. The
men in her office were nearly all impossible but
there were three, she told herself, coldly, unen-
thusiastic, who were not such terrible pills.

"But no," she said out loud. "I'd rather stay
single and lonely, too, all my life than worry along
with one of them. There must be someone else."
And at once she thought of Anthony Cross. Of
course there was Anthony. "I believe I've always
had him in the back of my mind," she spoke again
to the glimmering greyness. And turning on her
pillow she fell, smiling, asleep.

.   .   .   .   .   .

Monday was a busy day; copy must be prepared for the engraver; proofs of the current
edition of the magazine had to be checked up;
some important French fashion plates for which
she was responsible had temporarily disappeared
and must be unearthed. At four-thirty she was
free to take tea with Mrs. Denver, who immediately thereafter bore her off to a "movie" and
dinner. Not until nine o'clock was she able to
pursue her new train of thought. And even when
she was at liberty to indulge in her habit of introspection she found herself experiencing a certain
reluctance, an unexpected shyness. Time was
needed to brood on this secret with its promise of
happiness; this means of salvation from the prob-

lems of loneliness and weakness which beset her.
For since the departure of Roger she frequently
felt herself less assured; it would be a relief to
have some one on whom to lean; some one who
would be glad to shield and advise her,—and
love her! This last thought seemed to her marvellous. She said to herself again and again:
"Anthony loves me, I know it. Think of it, he
loves me!" Her face and neck were covered with
blushes; she was like a young girl on the eve of
falling in love, and indeed she herself was entering
on that experience for the first time. From the
very beginning she had liked Anthony, liked him
as she had never liked Roger—for himself, for his
sincerity, for his fierce pride, for his poverty, for
his honest, frantic love. "And now," she said
solemnly, "I believe I'm going to love him; I believe I love him already."

There were many things to be considered. His
poverty,—but she no longer cared about that; insensibly her association with Rachel Salting, her
knowledge of Rachel's plans and her high flouting
of poverty had worked their influence. It would
be fun, fun to begin at the beginning, to save and
scrape and mend. Like Rachel she would do no
washing and ironing, she would keep herself
dainty and unworn, but everything else, everything else she would do. Cook—and she could
cook; she had her blessed mother to thank for
that. For a moment she was home again on Opal
Street, getting Monday dinner, laughing with
Virginia about Mrs. Henrietta Jones. There they
were at the table, her pretty mother, her father
with his fine, black face—his black face, she had
forgotten that.

Colour,—here the old problem came up again. Restlessly she paced the room, a smouldering cigarette in her fingers. She rarely smoked but sometimes the insensate little cylinder gave her a sense of companionship. Colour, colour, she had forgotten it. Now what should she do,—tell Anthony? He was Spanish, she remembered, or no, —since he came from Brazil he was probably Portuguese, a member of a race devoid, notoriously devoid of prejudice against black blood. But Anthony had lived in America long enough to become inoculated; had he ever spoken about coloured people, had the subject ever come up? Wait a minute, there was Miss Powell; she remembered now that his conduct towards the young coloured woman had always been conspicuously correct; he had placed chairs for her, opened doors, set up easels; once the three of them had walked out of Cooper Union together and Anthony had carefully helped Miss Powell on a car, removing his hat with that slightly foreign gesture which she admired so much. And so far as she knew he had never used any of Roger's cruelly slighting expressions; the terms "coon," "nigger," "darky" had never crossed his lips. Clearly he had no conscious feeling against her people—"my people" she repeated, smiling, and wondered herself which people she meant, for she belonged to two races, and to one far more conspicuously than the other. Why, Anthony had even attended the Van Meier lecture. And she wondered what Van Meier would say if she presented her problem to him. He had no brief, she knew, against intermarriage, though, because of the high social forfeit levied, he did not advocate its practice in America. For

265

a moment she considered going to him and asking
his advice. But she was afraid that he would
speak to her about racial pride and she did not
want to think of that. Life, life was what she
was struggling for, the right to live and be happy.
And once more her mother's dictum flashed into
her mind. "Life is more important than colour."
This, she told herself, was an omen, her mother
was watching over her, guiding her. And, burying
her face in her hands, she fell on her knees and
wept and prayed.

Virginia sent a gay missive: "As soon as you
left that wretch of a Sara told me that she had
let you in on the great news. I wish I'd known it,
I'd have spoken to you about it there in the hall;
only there was so much to explain. But now you
know the main facts, and I can wait until I see
you to tell you the rest. But isn't it all wonderful? Angela, I do believe I'm almost the happiest
girl alive!

"It's too lovely here. Edna is very kind and
you know I always did like Pennsylvania country.
Matthew is out almost every day. He tells me it
renews his youth to come and talk about old times,
—anyone to hear us reminiscing, starting every
other sentence with 'do you remember——?'
would think that we averaged at least ninety years
apiece. It won't pique your vanity, will it, if I
tell you that he seems to have recovered
entirely from his old crush on you? Maybe he
was just in love with the family and didn't
know it.

"We go into Philadelphia every day or two.
The city has changed amazingly. But after the
hit or miss method of New York society there is
something very restful and safe about this tight
organization of 'old Philadelphians.' In the short
time I've been here I've met loads of first families,
people whose names we only knew when we were
children. But they all seem to remember father
and mother; they all begin: 'My dear, I remember when Junius Murray——' I meet all these
people, old and young, through Matthew, who
seems to have become quite the beau here and
goes everywhere. He really is different. Even
his hair in some mysterious way is changed. Not
that I ever minded; only he's so awfully nice that
I just would like all the nice things of the world
added unto him. We were talking the other day
about the wedding, and I was thinking what a
really distinguished appearance he would make.
Dear old Matt, I'm glad I put off marriage until
he could cut a fine figure. Write me, darling, if
you feel like it, but don't expect to hear much
from me. I'm so happy I can't keep still long
enough to write. The minute I get back to New
York though we'll have such a talk as never
was."

.   .   .   .   .

Mrs. Denver was growing happier; New York
was redeeming itself and revealing all the riches
which she had suspected lay hidden in its ware-
houses. Through one letter of introduction forced
into her unwilling hands by an officious acquaintance on her departure from Butte she had gained

an *entrée* into that kindest and happiest of New York's varied groups, the band of writers, columnists, publishers and critics. The lady from the middle West had no literary pretensions herself, but she liked people who had them and lived up to them; she kept abreast of literary gossip, read *Vanity Fair,* the *New Yorker,* and *Mercury.* As she was fairly young, dainty, wealthy and generous and no grinder of axes, she was caught up and whirled right along into the galaxy of teas, luncheons, theatre parties and "barbecues" which formed the relaxations of this joyous crowd. Soon she was overwhelmed, with more invitations than she could accept; to those which she did consider she always couched her acceptance in the same terms. "Yes I'll come if I may bring my young friend, Angèle Mory, along with me. She's a painter whom you'll all be glad to know some day." Angela's chance kindness to her in her days of loneliness and boredom had not fallen on barren ground.

Now indeed Angela was far removed from the atmosphere which she had known in Greenwich Village; the slight bohemianism which she had there encountered was here replaced by a somewhat bourgeois but satisfying sophistication. These people saw the "Village" for what it was, a network of badly laid off streets with, for the most part, uncomfortable, not to say inconvenient dwellings inhabited by a handful of artists in the midst of a thousand *poseurs.* Her new friends were frankly interested in the goods of this world. They found money an imperative, the pre-eminent, concomitant of life; once obtained, they spent it on fine apartments, beautiful raiment, delicate

viands, and trips to Paris and Vienna. Conversation with them was something more than an
exchange of words; "quips and jests" passed
among them, and, though flavoured with allusions
to stage and book, so that Angela was at times
hard put to it to follow the trend of the talk, she
half suspected that she was in this company assist-
ing more nearly at the restoration of a lost art
than in any other circles in the world save in the
corresponding society of London.

Once again her free hours could be filled to
overflowing with attention, with gaiety, with intellectual excitement; it came to her one day that
this was the atmosphere of which she once had
dreamed. But she was not quite happy, her economic condition interfered here. Constantly she
was receiving every conceivable manifestation of
an uncalculating generosity at the hands not only
of Mrs. Denver but of her new acquaintances.
And she could make no adequate return; her little
apartment had turned too shabby for her to have
guests of this calibre, even in to tea. Her rich
friend, making short shrift of such furniture as
Rachel Salting had left behind, had transformed
her dwelling into a marvel of luxury and elegance;
tiny but beautiful. Mrs. Denver was the soul of
real and delicate kindness but Angela could not
accept favours indefinitely; besides she was afraid
to become too used to this constant tide from a
horn of plenty on which she had absolutely no
claim. If there were any one thing which the
harsh experiences of these last three years had
taught her it was the impermanence of relationships; she must, she felt, lay down and follow a
method of living for herself which could never

269

betray her when the attention of the rich and
great should be withdrawn. Gradually she ceased
accepting Mrs. Denver's invitations; she pleaded
the necessity of outside work along the lines of her
employment; she was busy, too, on the portrait
of her mother, stimulating her vivid memory with
an old faded photograph. Her intention was to
have it as a surprise for Virginia upon the latter's
return.

But before withdrawing completely she made
the acquaintance of a young married woman and
her husband, a couple so gifted, so genuine and
sincere that she was unable to keep to the letter
her spartan promise of cutting herself entirely
adrift from this fascinating cross-section of New
York society. The husband, Walter Sandburg,
was a playwright; his name was a household
word; the title of one or another of his dramas
glittered on Broadway every night. His wife,
Elizabeth, reviewed books for one of the great
New York weeklies. Their charming apartment
in Fifty-fifth Street was the centre for many clever
and captivating people. Between these two and
Angela something of a real friendship awakened;
she was not ashamed to have them see the shabbi-
ness of her apartment. The luncheons to which
she treated Elizabeth in the Village tea-rooms and
in department stores brought as great satisfaction
as the more elaborate meals at the Algonquin, the
favourite rendezvous of many of these busy,
happy, contented workers.

Ashley, too, had returned to a town still devoid
of Carlotta, and in his loneliness was again constantly seeking Angela. His attitude was perfect;
never by word or look did he revive the unpleasant

impression which he had once made; indeed, in a
sober, disillusioned sort of way, she was growing
to like him very much. He was shy, sensitive,
sympathetic and miserably lonely. It was not
likely that his possessions were as fabulously great
as Roger's but it was certain that he belonged to
Roger's social group with all that such a ranking
implies. But in spite of this he was curiously
diffident; lacking in pep, the girls in his "set"
coldly classified him, and let him alone. Outside
his group ambitious Amazons dubbed him "easy"
and made a mad rush for him and his fabled
millions. The two verdicts left him ashamed and
frightened; annually he withdrew farther and
farther into his shell, emerging only in response
to Carlotta's careless and occasional beckoning or
to Angela's genuine and pre-occupied indifference.

But this was not her world; for years she had
craved such a *milieu,* only to find herself, when
once launched into it, outwardly perfectly at ease,
inwardly perturbed and dismayed. Although she
rarely thought of colour still she was conscious of
living in an atmosphere of falseness, of tangled
implications. She spoke often of Martha Burden
and her husband; Walter Sandburg the playwright, knew Ladislas Starr; Elizabeth had met
Paulette Lister in some field of newspaper activity, and Ashley of course had seen Roger in Angela's company. Behind these three or four names
and the background which familiarity with them
implied, she did not dare venture and in her gay-
est moments she was aware of the constant
stirring within of a longing for someone real and
permanent with whom she could share her life.
She would, of course make up with Jinny, but

Jinny was going to live in Philadelphia, where she herself would never sojourn again. That aftermath was the real consideration.

Her thoughts went constantly winging to Anthony; her determination became static. Saving only this invisible mixture of dark blood in her veins they, too, could meet on a par. They were both young, both gifted, ambitious, blessedly poor. Together they would climb to happier, sunnier heights. To be poor with Anthony; to struggle with him; to help him keep his secret vow; to win his surprised and generous approbation; finally to reach the point where she, too, could open her home to poor, unknown, struggling geniuses, —life could hold nothing more pleasing than these possibilities. And how kind she would be to these strangers! How much she hoped that among them there would be some girl struggling past the limitations of her heritage even as she herself had done. Through some secret, subtle bond of sympathy she would, she was sure, be able to recognize such a girl; and how she would help her and spur her on! To her communings she said humbly, "I am sure that this course will work out all right for me for see, I am planning chiefly for Anthony and for helpless, harassed people; hardly anything for myself but protection and love. I am willing to work for success and happiness." And even as she spoke she knew that the summit of her bliss would be reached in the days while she and Anthony were still poor and struggling and when she would be giving of her best to make things so.

Elizabeth Sandburg reminiscing about the early married days of herself and Walter gave a fillip to her thought. Said Elizabeth: "Walt and I were just as poor as we could be, we only made twenty dollars a week, and half of that went for a room in a cheap hotel. Meals even at the punkest places were awfully expensive, and half the time I used to cook things over the gas-jet. I didn't know much about cooking, and I imagine the stuff was atrocious, but we didn't mind. There were we with no one to interfere with us; we had each other and we didn't give a damn."

Smiling, glowing, she gave Angela a commission to paint hers and her Walter's portraits. "We'll leave the price to you and if you really put the job over I'll get you a lot of other sitters. No, don't thank me. What are friends for? That's what I always say."

CHAPTER IV

SOMETIMES this thought confronted her: "Perhaps
Anthony no longer needs me; has forgotten me."
And at the bare idea her heart would contract
with an actual, palpable movement. For by now
he was representing not only surcease from loneliness but peace and security; a place not merely in
society but in the world at large. Marriage appeared, too, in a different light. Until she had
met Roger she had not thought much about the
institution except as an adventure in romance or
as a means to an end; in her case the method of
achieving the kind of existence which once had
been her ideal. But now she saw it as an end in
itself; for women certainly; the only, the most
desirable and natural end. From this state a
gifted, an ambitious woman might reach forth and
acquit herself well in any activity. But marriage
must be there first, the foundation, the substratum.
Of course there were undoubtedly women who,
like men, took love and marriage as the sauce of
existence and their intellectual interests as the
main dish. Witness for instance, Paulette. Now
that she came to think of it, Paulette might vary
her lovers but she never varied in the manifestation of her restless, clever mental energy. At no
time did she allow her "love-life," as the psycho-
analyst termed it, to interfere with her mental
interests. Indeed she made no scruple of fur-

thering these same interests by her unusual and
pervasive sex charm. But this was Paulette, a
remarkable personage, a woman apart. But for
most women there must be the safety, the assurance of relationship that marriage affords. Indeed, most women must be able to say as did men,
"You are mine," not merely, "I am yours."

A certain scorching humility thrust itself upon
her. In all her manifestations of human relationships, how selfish she had been! She had left
Virginia, she had taken up with Roger to further
her own interests. For a brief interval she had
perhaps loved Roger with the tumultuous, heady
passion of hot, untried youth. But again when,
this subsiding, she had tried to introduce a note of
idealism, it had been with the thought of saving
her own soul. She thought of her day in the park
with Anthony, his uncomplaining acceptance of
her verdict; his wistfully grateful: "I almost
touched happiness." How easily she might have
made him happy if she had turned her thoughts
to his needs. But she had never thought of that;
she had been too intent always on happiness for
herself. Her father, her mother and Jinny had
always given and she had always taken. Why was
that? Jinny had sighed: "Perhaps you *have* more
white blood than Negro in your veins." Perhaps
this selfishness was what the possession of white
blood meant; the ultimate definition of Nordic
Supremacy.

Then she remembered that Anthony was white
and, bewildered; she ceased trying to cogitate, to
unravel, decipher, evaluate. She was lonely, she
loved. She meant to find a companion; she meant
to be beloved.

She must act.

None of her new friends was acquainted with Anthony. Ralph Ashley in response to a tentative question could not recall ever having seen him. The time was August, consequently he could not be at the school. Telephone books revealed nothing. "Lost in a great city!" she told herself and smiled at the cheap novel flavour of the phrase. She sent her thoughts fluttering back to the last time she had really seen Anthony, to their last intimate conversation. They had met that day after she had cut Jinny; she remembered, smiling now in her superior knowledge, the slight panic which she had experienced at his finding her in a 'bus in Harlem. There had been some chaffing about tea and he had given her his address and she had put it,—where? It was not in her address book. A feverish search through her little desk revealed it in the pages of her prayer book, the one which she had used as a child. This she considered a good omen. The bit of paper was crinkled and blurred but she was able to make out an address on One Hundred and Fourteenth Street. Suppose he were no longer there! She could not brook the thought of another night of uncertainty; it was ten o'clock but she mounted a 'bus, rode up to One Hundred and Fourteenth and Seventh Avenue. Her heart beat so loudly as she turned the corner,—it seemed as though the inhabitants of the rather shabby block hearing that human dynamo would throng their windows. The street, like many others in New York, possessed the pseudo elegance and impressiveness which comes from an equipment of brown stone houses with their massive fronts, their ostentatious regularity and simplicity, but a second glance revealed its down-at-heel condition; gaping windows disclosed the pitiful smallness of the rooms that crouched behind the pretentious outsides. There was something faintly humorous, ironical, about being cooped up in these deceptive palaces; according to one's temperament one might laugh or weep at the thought of how these structures, the product of human energy could yet cramp, imprison, even ruin the very activity which had created them.

Angela found her number, mounted the steps, sought in the dim, square hall feverishly among the names in the bells. Sullivan, Brown, Hendrickson, Sanchez,—and underneath the name of Sanchez on the same card, five small, neat characters in Anthony's inimitably clear printing—Cross. She almost fainted with the relief of it. Her fingers stole to the bell,—perhaps her one-time fellow-student was up in his room now,—how strange that this bit of gutta percha and its attendant wires should bridge all the extent of time and space that had so long lain between them! But she could not push it; Anthony, she was sure, was real enough, close enough to the heart of living to refuse to be shocked by any mere breach of the conventionalities. Even so, however, to seek at eleven o'clock at night and without preliminary warning admission to the rooms of a man whom one has not noticed for a year, was, as he himself would have put it, "a bit thick."

The little note which she sent was a model of demureness and propriety. "Dear Anthony," it read, "Do you remember my promising to ask you in for tea the next time I made a batch of cookies?

Well, to-morrow at 5.30 will be the next time. Do come!"

He had changed; her interested, searching eyes descried it in a moment. Always grave, always austere, always responsible, there was now in his manner an imponderable yet perceptible increment of each quality. But this was not all; his old familiar tortured look had left him; a peace, a quality of poise hovered about him, the composure which is achieved either by the attainment or by the relinquishment of the heart's desire. There is really very little difference, since each implies the cessation of effort.

All this passed rapidly through Angela's mind. Aloud she said: "How do, Anthony? you're really looking awfully well. It's nice to see you again."

"It's nice to see you," he replied. Certainly there was nothing remarkable about their conversation. After the bantering, the jests and allusions which she had been used to hearing at the Sandburgs,—compared with the snappy jargon of Mrs. Denver's "crowd" this was trivial, not to say banal. She burst out laughing. Anthony raised his eyebrows.

"What's so funny? Is it a secret joke?"

"No,—only I've been thinking hard about you for a long time." She made a daring stroke. "Presumably you've thought occasionally about me. Yet when we meet we sit up like a dandy and a dowager with white kid gloves on and exchange comments on our appearances. I suppose the next step in order would be to talk about the weather. Have you had much rain up in One Hundred and Fourteenth Street, Mr. Cross?"

Some of his poise forsook him. The pervasive

peacefulness that sat so palpably upon him deserted him like a rended veil. "You've been thinking about me for a long time? Just how long?"

"I couldn't tell you when it began." She ventured another bold stroke. "But you've been in the back of my mind,—oh for ages, ages."

The poise, the composure, the peace were all fled now. Hastily, recklessly he set down his glass of tea, came and towered over her. She bit her lips to hide their trembling. Oh he was dear, dearer than she had ever imagined, so transparent, so honest. Who was she to deserve him?

His face quivered. He should never have come near this girl! As suddenly as he had left his chair he returned to it, settled himself comfortably and picked up his glass. "I've been away from you so long I had forgotten."

"Forgotten what?"

"Forgotten how dangerous you are. Forgotten how a woman like you plays with poor fools like me. Why did you send for me? To set me dancing once more to your tune?"

His bitterness surprised and frightened her. "Anthony, Anthony don't talk like that! I sent for you because I wanted to see you, wanted to talk to my old friend."

Appeased, he lounged back in the famous and unique easy chair, lit a cigarette. She brought out some of her sketches, displayed her note-book. He was especially interested in the "Fourteenth Street Types," was pleased with the portrait of her mother. "She doesn't look like you, though I can see you probably have her hair and that pearly tint of her skin. But you must have got your nose from your father. You know all the

279

rest of your face," he dwelt on her features dreamily, "your lips, your eyes, your curly lashes are so deliciously feminine. But that straight nose of yours betokens strength." The faded, yet striking photograph lay within reach. He picked it up, studying it thoughtfully. "What a beautiful woman;—all woman I should say. Did she have much effect on your life?"

"N-no, I can't say she did." She remembered those Saturday excursions and their adventures in "passing," so harmless, yet so far-reaching. "Oh yes, in one respect she influenced me greatly, changed my whole life."

He nodded, gazing moodily at the picture. "My mother certainly affected me."

Angela started to say glibly; "She made you what you are to-day;" but a glance at his brooding countenance made her think better of it.

"What's this?" He had turned again to the sketch book and was poring upon a mass of lightly indicated figures passing apparently in review before the tall, cloaked form of a woman, thin to emaciation, her hands on her bony hips, slightly bent forward, laughing uproariously yet with a certain chilling malevolence. "I can't make it out."

With something shamefaced in her manner she took it from him. "I'm not sure yet whether I'll develop it. I,—it's an idea that has slowly taken possession of me since I've been in New York. The tall woman is Life and the idea is that she laughs at us; laughs at the poor people who fall into the traps which she sets for us."

Sorrow set its seal on his face as perceptibly as though it had been stamped there. He came closer. "You've found that out too? If I could have managed it you would never have known it. I wanted so to keep it from you." His manner suddenly changed. "I must go. This afternoon has been perfect; I can't thank you enough,—but I'm not coming again."

"Not coming again! What nonsense! Why, why ever not? Now, Anthony, don't begin that vow business. To-day has been perfect, marvellous. You don't suppose I'm going to let my friend go when I'm really just discovering him!"

Weakly he murmured that it was foolish for them to take up each other's time; he was going away.

"All the more reason, then, why we should be seeing each other."

His glance fell on the formless sketch. "If I could only get one laugh on life. . . . When are you going to let me see you again? I'm my own man just now; my time is at your disposal."

The next afternoon they met outside her office building and dined together. On Friday they sailed to the Atlantic Highlands. Saturday, Sunday, Monday, Tuesday flashed by, meaning nothing to either except for the few hours which they spent in each other's company. Thursday was a slack day; she arranged her work so as to be free for the afternoon, and they passed the hurrying, glamorous hours in Van Cortlandt Park, laughing, jesting, relating old dreams, relapsing into silences more intimate than talk, blissfully aware of each other's presence, still more throbbingly aware of a conversation held in this very Park years ago. Back again in the little hall on Jayne Street he took her in his arms and kissed her slowly, with rapture,

281

with adoration and she returned his kisses. For a
long time he held her close against his pounding
heart; she opened her languid eyes to meet his
burning gaze which she could feel rather than see.
Slowly he took her arms from his neck, let them
drop.

"Angel, Angel, I shall love you always. Life
cannot rob me of that. Good-bye, my sweetest."

He was lost in the shadowy night.

The next day passed and the next. A week
sped. Absolute silence. No sign of him by either
word or line.

. . . . .

At the end of ten days, on a never to be forgotten Sunday afternoon, she went to see him. Without conscious volition on her part she was one
moment in her apartment on Jayne Street; and at
the end of an hour she was pressing a button
above the name Cross in a hall on One Hundred
and Fourteenth Street, hearing the door click,
mounting the black well of a stair-way, tapping on
a door bearing the legend "Studio."

A listless voice said "Come in."

Presently the rather tall, slender young man
sitting in his shirt sleeves, his back toward her,
staring dejectedly but earnestly at a picture on
the table before him asked: "What can I do for
you?"

The long and narrow room boasted a rather
good parquet floor and a clean plain wall paper
covered with unframed pictures and sketches. In
one corner stood an easel; the furniture for the
most part was plain but serviceable and comfort-

able, with the exception of an old-fashioned horse-hair sofa which Angela thought she had never seen equalled for its black shininess and its promise of stark discomfort.

On entering the apartment she had felt perturbed, but as soon as she saw Anthony and realized that the picture at which he was gazing was an unfinished sketch of herself, her worry fled. He had asked his question without turning, so she addressed his back:

"You can tell me where you found that terrible sofa; I had no idea there were any in existence. Thought they had died out with the Dodo."

The sound of her voice brought him to her side. "Angèle, tell me what are you doing here?"

She tried to keep the light touch: "Not until you have told me about the sofa." But his dark, tormented face and the strain under which she had been suffering for the past week broke down her defence. Swaying, she caught at his hand. "Anthony, Anthony, how could you?"

He put his arm about her and led her to the despised sofa; looked at her moodily. "Why did you come to see me, Angèle?"

Ordinarily she would have fenced, indulged in some fancy skirmishing; but this was no ordinary occasion; indeed in ordinary circumstances she would not have been here. She spoke gravely and proudly.

"Because I love you. Because I think you love me." A sudden terrible fear assailed her. "Oh, Anthony, don't tell me you were only playing!"

"With you? So little was I playing that the moment I began to suspect you cared,—and I never dreamed of it until that last day in the park,

283

—I ran away from you. I knew you had so many resources; men will always adore you, want you, that I thought you'd soon forget; turn to someone else just as you had turned for a sudden whim to me from God knows how many admirers."

She shook her head, but she was frightened; some nameless fear knocking at her heart. "I turned to you from no one, Anthony. I've had only one 'admirer' as you call it in New York and I had long, long since ceased thinking of him. No, Anthony, I came to you because I needed you; you of all men in New York. I think in the world. And I thought you needed me."

They sat in silence on the terrible sofa. He seized her hand and covered it with kisses; started to take her in his arms, then let them fall in a hopeless gesture.

"It's no good, Angel; there's no use trying to buck fate. Life has caught us again. What you're talking about is absolutely impossible."

"What do you mean, impossible?" The little mute fear that had lain within her for a long time as a result of an earlier confidence of his bestirred itself, spoke.

"Anthony, those men, those enemies that killed your father,—did you kill one of them?" She had her arms about him. "You know it's nothing to me. Don't even tell me about it. Your past belongs to you; it's your future I'm interested in, that I want."

He pushed her from him, finally, even roughly. "No, I've never killed a man. Though I've wanted to. But I was little boy when it all happened and afterwards I wouldn't go back because of my mother." He went over to a drawer and took out a revolver, "I've half a mind to kill my-self now, now before I go mad thinking how I've broken my promise, broken it after all these years." He looked at her wistfully, yet implac-ably. "I wish that I had died long before it was given to me to see that beautiful, loving look on your face change into one of hatred and dread and anger."

She thought he must be raving; she tried to sooth him. "Never mind, Anthony; I don't care a rap about what you've done. Only tell me why do you say everything's impossible for us? Why can't we mean everything to each other, be mar-ried——"

"Because I'm coloured." In her bewildered relief she fell away from him.

"Yes, that's right, you damned American! I'm not fit for you to touch now, am I? It was all right as long as you thought I was a murderer, a card sharp, a criminal, but the black blood in me is a bit too much, isn't it?" Beside himself he rushed to the windows, looked on the placid Sun-day groups festooning the front steps of the brown stone houses. "What are you going to do, alarm the neighbourhood? Well, let me tell you, my girl, before they can get up here I'll be dead." His glance strayed to the revolver. "They'll never catch me as they did my father."

It was on the point of her tongue to tell him her great secret. Her heart within her bubbled with laughter to think how quickly she could put an end to this hysteria, how she could calm this black madness which so seethed within him, poisoning the very spring of his life. But his last words turned her thoughts to something else, to another

need. How he must have suffered, loving a girl
who he felt sure would betray him; yet scorning
to keep up the subterfuge.

She said to him gently: "Anthony, did you think
I would do that?"

His answer revealed the unspeakable depths of
his acquaintance with prejudice; his incurable
cynicism. "You're a white American. I know
there's nothing too dastardly for them to attempt
where colour is involved."

A fantastic notion seized her. Of course she
would tell him that she was coloured, that she was
willing to live with coloured people. And if he
needed assurance of her love, how much more
fully would he believe in her when he realized
that not even for the sake of the conveniences to
be had by passing would she keep her association
with white people secret from him. But first she
must try to restore his faith in human goodness.
She said to him gently: "Tell me about it, Anthony."

And sitting there in the ugly, tidy room in the
sunshot duskiness of the early summer evening,
the half-subdued noises of the street mounting up
to them, he told her his story. An old story it
was, but in its new setting, coupled with the fact
that Angela for years had closed her mind to the
penalty which men sometimes pay for being "different," it sounded like some unbelievable tale
from the Inquisition.

His father, John Hall, of Georgia, had been a
sailor and rover, but John's father was a well-
known and capable farmer who had stayed in his
little town and slowly amassed what seemed a
fortune to the poor and mostly ignorant whites
by whom he was surrounded. In the course of

John's wanderings he had landed at Rio de Janeiro and he had met Maria Cruz, a Brazilian with the blood of many races in her veins. She herself was apparently white, but she looked with favour on the brown, stalwart sailor, thinking nothing of his colour, which was very much the same as that of her own father. The two married and went to many countries. But finally John, wearying of his aimless life, returned to his father, arriving a month before it was time to receive the old man's blessing and his property. Thence all his troubles. Certain white men in the neighbourhood had had their eyes turned greedily on old Anthony Hall's possessions. His son had been a wanderer for many years; doubtless he was dead. Certainly it was not expected that he would return after all these years to his native soil; most niggers leaving the South left for ever. They knew better than to return with their uppity ways.

Added to the signal injustice of John Hall's return and the disappointment caused thereby, was the iniquity of his marriage to a beautiful and apparently white wife. Little Anthony could remember his father's constant admonition to her never to leave the house; the latter had, in his sudden zeal for home, forgotten what a sojourn in Georgia could mean. But his memory was soon refreshed and he was already making every effort to dispose of his new possessions without total loss. This required time and patience, but he hoped that only a few months need elapse before they might shake off the dust of this cursed hole for ever.

"Just a little patience, Maria," he told his lovely wife.

But she could not understand. True, she never

ventured into the town, but an infrequent visit to the little store was imperative and she did not mind an occasional admiring glance. Indeed she attributed her husband's admonitions to his not unwelcome jealousy. Anthony, always a grave child, constituted himself her constant guardian; his father, he knew, had to be away in neighbouring townships where he was trying to put through his deal, so the little boy accompanied his silly trusting mother everywhere. When they passed a group of staring, mouthing men he contrived to hurt his finger or stub his toe so as to divert his mother's attention. In spite of his childish subterfuges, indeed because of them, his mother attracted the notice of Tom Haley, son of the magistrate. Anthony apparently had injured his hand and his beautiful mother, bending over it with great solicitude, made a picture too charming, too challenging to be overlooked. Haley stepped forward, actually touched his cap. "Can I do anything to help you, ma'am?" She looked at him with her lovely, melting eyes, spoke in her foreign liquid voice. He was sure he had made a conquest. Afterwards, chagrined by the gibes of the bystanders who jeered at him for his courtesy to a nigger wench "for that's all she is, John Hall's wife," he ground his heel in the red dust; he would show her a thing or two.

In the hot afternoon, awakened from her siesta by a sudden knock, she came to the door, greeted her admirer of the early morning. She was not quite pleased with the look in his eyes, but she could not suspect evil. Haley, who had done some wandering on his own account and had picked up a few words of Spanish, let fall an insulting phrase or two. Amazed and angry she struck him across his face. The boy, Anthony, uneasily watching, screamed; there was a sudden tumult of voices and Haley fled, forgetting for the moment that these were Negro voices and so need not be dreaded. An old coloured man, mumbling and groaning "Gawd forgive you, Honey; we'se done fer now" guided the child and the panic-stricken mother into the swamp. And lying there hidden at night they could see the sparks and flames rising from the house and buildings, which represented the labour of Anthony Hall's sixty years. In a sudden lull they caught the sounds of the pistol shots which riddled John Hall's body.

"Someone warned my father," said Anthony Cross wearily, "but he would go home. Besides, once back in town he would have been taken any-way, perhaps mobbed and burned in the public square. They let him get into his house; he washed and dressed himself for death. Before nightfall the mob came to teach this man their opinion of a nigger who hadn't taught his wife her duty toward white men. First they set fire to the house, then called him to the window. He stepped out on a little verandah; Haley opened fire. The body fell over the railing, dead before it could touch the ground, murdered by the bullets from twenty pistols. Souvenir hunters cut off fin-gers, toes, his ears,—a friend of my grandfather found the body at night and buried it. They said it was unlike anything they had ever seen before, totally dehumanized. After I heard that story I was unable to sleep for nights on end. As for my mother,——"

Angela pressed his head close against her shoulder. There were no words for a thing like this, only warm human contact.

He went on wanly. "As for my mother, she was like a madwoman. She has gone all the rest of her life haunted by a terrible fear."

"Of white people," Angela supplemented softly. "Yes, I can see how she would."

He glanced at her sombrely. "No, of coloured people. She believes that we, particularly the dark ones, are cursed, otherwise why should we be so abused, so hounded. Two years after my father's death she married a white man, not an American—that was spared me,—but a German who, I believe, treats her very kindly. I was still a little boy but I begged and pleaded with her to leave the whole race alone; I told her she owed it to the memory of my father. But she only said women were poor, weak creatures; they must take protection where they could get it."

Horrified, mute with the tragedy of it all, she could only stare at him white-lipped.

"Don't ask me how I came up. Angèle, for a time I was nothing, worthless, only I have never denied my colour; I have always taken up with coloured causes. When I've had a special point to make I've allowed the world to think of me as it would but always before severing my connections I told of the black blood that was in my veins. And then it came to me that for my father's sake I would try to make something of myself. So I sloughed off my evil ways, they had been assumed only in bravado,—and came to New York where I've been living quietly, I hope usefully, keeping my bitterness within myself where it could harm no one but me.

"I made one vow and kept it,—never by any

chance to allow myself to become entangled with
white people; never to listen to their blandish-
ments; always to hate them with a perfect hate.
Then I met you and loved you and somehow healing began. I thought, if she loves me she'll be
willing to hear me through. And if after she
hears me she is willing to take me, black blood and
all,—but mind," he interrupted himself fiercely,
"I'm not ashamed of my blood. Sometimes I
think it's the leaven that will purify this Nordic
people of their cruelty and their savage lust of
power."

She ignored this. "So you were always going
to tell me."

"Tell you? Of course I would have told you.
Oh, I'm a man, Angel, with a man's record. When
I was a sailor,—there're some pages in my life I
couldn't let your fingers touch. But *that* I'd have
told you, it was too vital, too important. Not
that I think it really means anything, this mixture
of blood, as life goes, as God meant the world to
go. But here in America it could make or mar
life. Of course I'd have told you."

Here was honour, here was a man! So would
her father have been. Having found this comparison her mind sought no further.

A deep silence descended upon them; in his
case the silence of exhaustion. But Angela was
thinking of his tragic life and of how completely,
how surprisingly she could change it. Smiling,
she spoke to him of happiness, of the glorious
future. "I've something amazing to tell you, but
I won't spring it on you all at once. Can't we
go out to Van Cortlandt Park to-morrow evening?"

He caught her hand. "No matter what in the

goodness of your heart you may be planning, there is no future, none, none, Angel, for you and me. Don't deceive yourself,—nor me. When I'm with you I forget sometimes. But this afternoon has brought it all back to me. I'll never forget myself and my vow again."

A bell shrilled three, four times.

He looked about frowning. "That's Sanchez; he's forgotten his key again. My dear girl, my Angel, you must go,—and you must not, must not come back. Hurry, hurry! I don't want him to see you here." He guided her towards the door, stemming her protestations. "I'll write you at once, but you must go. God bless and keep you."

In another moment she was out in the dim hall, passing a dark, hurrying figure on the stairs. The heavy door swung silently behind her, thrusting her inexorably out into the engulfing summer night; the shabby pretentious house was again between her and Anthony with his tragic, searing past.

CHAPTER V

ALL the next day and the next she dwelt on Anthony's story; she tried to put herself in his place, to force herself into a dim realization of the dark chamber of torture in which his mind and thoughts had dwelt for so many years. And she had added her modicum of pain, had been so unsympathetic, so unyielding; in the midst of the dull suffering, the sickne₅ of life to which perhaps his nerves had become accustomed she had managed to inject an extra pinprick of poignancy. Oh, she would reward him for that; she would brim his loveless, cheated existence with joy and sweetness; she would cajole him into forgetting that terrible past. Some day he should say to her: "You have brought me not merely new life, but life itself." Those former years should mean no more to him than its pre-natal existence means to a baby.

Her fancy dwelt on, toyed with all the sweet offices of love; the delicate bondage that could knit together two persons absolutely *en rapport*. At the cost of every ambition which she had ever known she would make him happy. After the manner of most men his work would probably be the greatest thing in the world to him. And he should be the greatest thing in the world to her. He should be her task, her "job," the fulfilment of her ambition. A phrase from the writings of Anatole France came drifting into her mind.

293

"There is a technique of love." She would discover it, employ it, not go drifting haphazardly,
carelessly into this relationship. And suddenly
she saw her affair with Roger in a new light; she
could forgive him, she could forgive herself for
that hitherto unpardonable union if through it she
had come one iota nearer to the understanding
and the need of Anthony.

His silence—for although the middle of the
week had passed she had received no letter,—
worried her not one whit. In the course of time
he would come to her, remembering her perfect
sympathy of the Sunday before and thinking that
this woman was the atonement for what he considered her race. And then she would surprise
him, she would tell him the truth, she would make
herself inexpressibly dearer and nearer to him
when he came to know that her sympathy and her
tenderness were real, fixed and lasting, because
they were based and rooted in the same blood, the
same experiences, the same comprehension of this
far-reaching, stupid, terrible race problem. How
inexpressibly happy, relieved and overwhelmed he
would be! She would live with him in Harlem,
in Africa, anywhere, any place. She would label
herself, if he asked it; she would tell every member of her little coterie of white friends about her
mixed blood; she would help him keep his vow
and would glory in that keeping. No sacrifice of
the comforts which came to her from "passing,"
of the assurance, even of the safety which the mere
physical fact of whiteness in America brings,
would be too great for her. She would withdraw
where he withdrew; hate where he hated.

. . . . . .

His letter which came on Thursday interrupted her thoughts, her fine dreams of self-immolation which women so adore. It was brief and stern, and read:

"Angèle, don't think for one moment that I do not thank you for Sunday. . . . My heart is at your feet for what you revealed to me then. But you and I have nothing in common, have never had, and now can never have. More than race divides us. I think I shall go away. Meanwhile you are to forget me; amuse yourself, beautiful, charming, magnetic Angel with the men of your own race and leave me to my own.

"ANTHONY."

It was such a strange letter; its coldness and finality struck a chill to her heart. She looked at the lonely signature, "Anthony,"—just that, no word of love or affection. And the phrase: "More than race divides us." Its hidden significance held a menace.

The letter was awaiting her on her return from work. She had come in all glowing with the promise of the future as she conceived it. And then here were these cold words killing her high hopes as an icy blast kills the too trusting blossoms of early spring. . . . Holding the letter she let her supper go untasted, unregarded, while she evolved some plan whereby she could see Anthony, talk to him. The tone of his letter did not sound as though he would yield to ordinary persuasion. And again in the midst of her bewilderment and suffering she was struck afresh with the difficulties inherent in womanhood in conducting the most

295

ordinary and most vital affairs of life. She was
still a little bruised in spirit that she had taken it
upon herself to go to Anthony's rooms Sunday;
it was a step she felt conventionally, whose justi-
fication lay only in its success. As long as she had
considered it successful, she had been able to rele-
gate it to the uttermost limbo of her self-consciousness. But now that it seemed to avail nothing it
loomed up before her in all its social significance.
She was that creature whom men, in their selfish
fear, have contrived to paint as the least attractive
of human kind,—"a girl who runs after men."
It seemed to her that she could not stand the application of the phrase, no matter how unjustly,
how inaptly used in her own case.

Looking for a word of encouragement she re-
read the note. The expression "My heart is at
your feet" brought some reassurance; she remembered, too, his very real emotion of Sunday, only
a few days before. Men, real men, men like
Anthony, do not change. No, she could not let
him go without one last effort. She would go to
Harlem once more to his house, she would see him,
reassure him, allay his fears, quench his silly ap-
prehensions of non-compatability. As soon as he
knew that they were both coloured, he'd succumb.
Now he was overwrought. It had never occurred
to her before that she might be glad to be coloured. . . . She put on her hat, walked slowly
out the door, said to herself with a strange fore-
boding: "When I see this room again, I'll either
be very happy, or very, very sad. . . ." Her
courage rose, braced her, but she was sick of
being courageous, she wanted to be a beloved
woman, dependent, fragile, sought for, feminine;

after this last ordeal she would be "womanly" to
the point of ineptitude. . . .

During the long ride her spirits rose a little.
After all, his attitude was almost inevitable. He
thought she belonged to a race which to him
stood for treachery and cruelty; he had seen her
with Roger, Roger, the rich, the gay; he saw her
as caring only for wealth and pleasure. Of
course in his eyes she was separated from him by
race and by more than race.

For long years she was unable to reconstruct
that scene; her mind was always too tired, too
sore to re-enact it.

As in a dream she saw Anthony's set, stern face,
heard his firm, stern voice: "Angel-girl,—Angèle
I told you not to come back. I told you it was
all impossible."

She found herself clutching at his arm, blurting
out the truth, forgetting all her elaborate plans,
her carefully pre-concerted drama. "But, Anthony, Anthony, listen, everything's all right.
I'm coloured; I've suffered too; nothing has to
come between us."

For a moment off his guard he wavered. "Angèle, I didn't think you'd lie to me."

She was in tears, desperate. "I'm not lying,
Anthony. It's perfectly true."

"I saw that picture of your mother, a white
woman if I ever saw one,——"

"Yes, but a white coloured woman. My father
was black, perfectly black and I have a sister,
she's brown. My mother and I used to 'pass'
sometimes just for the fun of it; she didn't mind
being coloured. But I minded it terribly,—until

very recently. So I left my home,—in Philadelphia,—and came here to live,—oh, going for
white makes life so much easier. You know it,
Anthony." His face wan and terrible frightened
her. "It doesn't make you angry, does it? You've
passed yourself, you told me you had. Oh
Anthony, Anthony, don't look at me like that!
What is it?"

She caught at his hand, following him as he
withdrew to the shiny couch where they both sat
breathless for a moment. "God!" he said suddenly; he raised his arms, beating the void like a
madman. "You in your foolishness, I in my care-
lessness, 'passing, passing' and life sitting back
laughing, splitting her sides at the joke of it. Oh,
it was all right for you,—but I didn't care whether
people thought I was white or coloured,—if we'd
only known,——"

"What on earth are you talking about? It's
all right now."

"It isn't all right; it's worse than ever." He
caught her wrist. "Angel, you're sure you're not
fooling me?"

"Of course I'm not. I have proof, I've a sister
right here in New York; she's away just now. But
when she comes back, I'll have you meet her. She
is brown and lovely,—you'll want to paint her
. . . don't you believe me, Anthony?"

"Oh yes, I believe you," he raised his arms
again in a beautiful, fluid gesture, let them fall.
"Oh, damn life, damn it, I say . . . isn't there
any end to pain!"

Frightened, she got on her knees beside him.
"Anthony, what's the matter? Everything's going to be all right; we're going to be happy."

"You may be. I'll never be happy. You were the woman I wanted,—I thought you were white. For my father's sake I couldn't marry a white girl. So I gave you up."

"And I wouldn't stay given up. See, here I am back again. You'll never be able to send me away." Laughing but shamefaced, she tried to thrust herself into his arms.

"No, Angel, no! You don't understand. There's, there's somebody else——"

She couldn't take it in. "Somebody else. You mean,—you're married? Oh Anthony, you don't mean you're married!"

"No, of course not, of course not! But I'm engaged."

"Engaged, engaged and not to me,—to another girl? And you kissed me, went around with me? I knew other men did that, but I never thought that of you! I thought you were like my father!" And she began to cry like a little girl.

Shamefaced, he looked on, jamming his hands tightly into his pockets. "I never meant to harm you; I never thought until that day in the park that you would care. And I cared so terribly! Think, I had given you up, Angèle,—I suppose that isn't your name really, is it?—and all of a sudden, you came walking back into my life and I said, 'I'll have the laugh on this damned mess after all. I'll spend a few days with her, love her a little, just a little. She'll never know, and I'll have a golden memory!' Oh, I had it coming to me, Angel! But the minute I saw you were beginning to care I broke off short."

A line from an old text was running through her head, rendering her speechless, inattentive.

She was a little girl back in the church again in Philadelphia; the minister was intoning "All we like sheep have gone astray." He used to put the emphasis on the first word and Jinny and she would look at each other and exchange meaning smiles; he was a West Indian and West Indians had a way of misplacing the emphasis. The line sounded so funny: "*All* we like sheep,——" but perhaps it wasn't so funny after all; perhaps he had read it like that not because he was a West Indian but because he knew life and human nature. Certainly *she* had gone astray,—with Roger. And now here was Anthony, Anthony who had always loved her so well. Yet in his background there was a girl and he was engaged.

This brought her to a consideration of the unknown fiancée,—her rival. Deliberately she chose the word, for she was not through yet. This unknown, unguessed at woman who had stolen in like a thief in the night. . . .

"Have you known her long?" she asked him sharply.

"Who? Oh my,—my friend. No, not as long as I've known you."

A newcomer, an upstart. Well at least she, Angela, had the advantage of precedence.

"She's coloured, of course?"

"Of course."

They sat in a weary silence. Suddenly he caught her in his arms and buried his head in her neck. A quick pang penetrated to the very core of her being. He must have been an adorable baby. . . . Anthony and babies!

"Now God, Life, whatever it is that has power,

this time you must help me!" cried her heart.
She spoke to him gently.

"Anthony, you know I love you. Do you still
love me?"

"Always, always, Angel."

"Do you—Oh, Anthony, I don't deserve it,
but do you by any chance worship me?"

"Yes, that's it, that's just it, I worship you. I
adore you. You are God to me. Oh, Angèle, if
you'd only let me know. But it's too late now."

"No, no don't say that, perhaps it isn't too late.
It all depends on this. Do you worship *her*,
Anthony?" He lifted his haggard face.

"No—but she worships *me*. I'm God to *her*
do you see? If I fail her she won't say anything,
she'll just fall back like a little weak kitten, like a
lost sheep, like a baby. She'll die." He said as
though unaware of his listener. "She's such a
little thing. And sweet."

Angela said gently: "Tell me about her. Isn't
it all very sudden? You said you hadn't known
her long."

He began obediently. "It was not long after
I—I lost you. She came to me out of nowhere,
came walking to me into my room by mistake;
she didn't see me. And she put her head down
on her hands and began to cry terribly. I had
been crying too—in my heart, you understand,—
and for a moment I thought she might be the
echo of that cry, might be the cry itself. You see,
I'd been drinking a little,—you were so far removed, white and all that sort of thing. I couldn't
marry a white woman, you know, not a white
American. I owed that to my father.

301

"But at last I saw it was a girl, a real girl and I went over to her and put my hand on her shoulder and said: 'Little girl, what's the matter?'

"And she lifted her head, still hidden in the crook of her arm, you know the way a child does and said: 'I've lost my sister.' At first I thought she meant lost in the street and I said 'Well, come with me to the police station, I'll go with you, we'll give them a description and you'll find her again. People don't stay lost in this day and time.' I got her head on my shoulder, I almost took her on my knee, Angèle, she was so simple and forlorn. And presently she said: 'No, I don't mean lost that way; I mean she's left me, she doesn't want me any more. She wants other people.' And I've never been able to get anything else out of her. The next morning I called her up and somehow I got to seeing her, for her sake, you know. But afterwards when she grew happier,—she was so blithe, so lovely, so healing and blessed like the sun or a flower,—then I saw she was getting fond of me and I stayed away.

"Well, I ran across you and that Fielding fellow that night at the Van Meier lecture. And you were so happy and radiant, and Fielding so possessive,—damn him!—damn him!—he—you didn't let him hurt you, Angèle?"

As though anything that had ever happened in her life could hurt her like this! She had never known what pain was before. White-lipped, she shook her head. "No, he didn't hurt me."

"Well, I went to see her the next day. She came into the room like a shadow,—I realized she was getting thin. She was kind and sweet and far-off; impalpable, tenuous and yet there. I could

302

see she was dying for me. And all of a sudden it
came to me how wonderful it would be to have
someone care like that. I went to her; I took her
in my arms and I said: 'Child, child, I'm not
bringing you a whole heart but could you love
me?' You see I couldn't let her go after that."

"No," Angela's voice was dull, lifeless. "You
couldn't. She'd die."

"Yes, that's it; that's just it. And I know you
won't die, Angel."

"No, you're quite right. I won't die."

An icy hand was on her heart. At his first
words: "She came walking into my room,——"
an icy echo stirred a memory deep, deep within
her inner consciousness. She heard Jinny saying:
"I went walking into his room,——"

Something stricken, mortally stricken in her
face fixed his attention. "Don't look like that,
my girl, my dear Angel. . . . There are three of
us in this terrible plight,—if I had only known.
. . . I don't deserve the love of either of you but
if one of you two must suffer it might as well be
she as you. Come, we'll go away; even unhappiness, even remorse will mean something to us as
long as we're together."

She shook her head. "No, that's impossible,—
if it were someone else, I don't know, perhaps—
I'm so sick of unhappiness,—maybe I'd take a
chance. But in her case it's impossible."

He looked at her curiously. "What do you
mean 'in her case'?"

"Isn't her name Virginia Murray?"

"Yes, yes! How did you guess it? Do you
know her?"

"She's my sister. Angèle Mory,—Angela Murray, don't you see. It's the same name. And it's all my fault. I pushed her, sent her deliberately into your arms."

He could only stare.

"I'm the unkind sister who didn't want her. Oh, can't you understand? That night she came walking into your room by mistake it was because I had gone to the station to meet her and Roger Fielding came along. I didn't want him to know that I was coloured and I,—I didn't acknowledge her, I cut her."

"Oh," he said surprised and inadequate. "I don't see how you could have done that to a little girl like Virginia. Did she know New York?"

"No." She drooped visibly. Even the loss of him was nothing compared to this rebuke. There seemed nothing further to be said.

Presently he put his arm about her. "Poor Angèle. As though you could foresee! It's what life does to us, leads us into pitfalls apparently so shallow, so harmless and when we turn around there we are, caught, fettered,——"

Her miserable eyes sought his. "I was sorry right away, Anthony. I tried my best to get in touch with her that very evening. But I couldn't find her,—already you see, life was getting even with me, she had strayed into your room."

He nodded. "Yes, I remember it all so plainly. I was getting ready to go out, was all prepared as a matter of fact. Indeed I moved that very night. But I loitered on and on, thinking of you.

"The worst of it is I'll always be thinking of you. Oh Angèle, what does it matter, what does anything matter if we just have each other? This damned business of colour, is it going to ruin all chances of happiness? I've known trouble, pain, terrible devastating pain all my life. You've suffered too. Together perhaps we could find peace. We'd go to your sister and explain. She is kind and sweet; surely she'd understand."

He put his arms about her and the two clung to each other, solemnly, desperately, like children.

"I'm sick of pain, too, Anthony, sick of longing and loneliness. You can't imagine how I've suffered from loneliness."

"Yes, yes I can. I guessed it. I used to watch you. I thought you were probably lonely inside, you were so different from Miss Lister and Mrs. Starr. Come away with me and we'll share our loneliness together, somewhere where we'll forget,——"

"And Virginia? You said yourself she'd die,——"

"She's so young, she—she could get over it." But his tone was doubtful, wavering.

She tore herself from him. "No, I took her sister away from her; I won't take her lover. Kiss me good-bye, Anthony."

They sat on the hard sofa. "To think we should find one another only to lose each other! To think that everything, every single thing was all right for us but that we were kept apart by the stupidity of fate. I'd almost rather we'd never learned the truth. Put your dear arms about me closer, Angel, Angel. I want the warmth, the sweetness of you to penetrate into my heart. I want to keep it there forever. Darling, how can I let you go?"

She clung to him weeping, weeping with the heart-broken abandonment of a child.

A bell shrilled four times.

He jumped up. "It's Sanchez, he's forgotten his key; thank God he did forget it. My darling, you must go. But wait for me. I'll meet you,— we'll go to your house, we'll find a way. We can't part like this!" His breath was coming in short gasps; she could see little white lines deepening about his mouth, his nostrils. Fearfully she caught at her hat.

"God bless you; good-bye Anthony. I won't see you again."

Halfway down the black staircase she met the heedless Sanchez, tall, sallow, thin, glancing at her curiously with a slightly amused smile. Politely he stood aside to let her pass, one hand resting lightly against his hip. Something in his attitude made her think of her unfinished sketch of Life. Hysterical, beside herself, she rushed down the remaining steps afraid to look around lest she should see the thin dark figure in pursuit, lest her ears should catch the expansion of that faint meaning smile into a guffaw, uproarious, menacing.

CHAPTER VI

ONCE long ago in the old days in the house on
Opal Street she had been taken mysteriously ill.
As a matter of fact she had been coming down
with that inglorious disease, the mumps. The expense of having a doctor was a consideration, and
so for twenty-four hours she was the object of
anxious solicitude for the whole house. Her
mother had watched over her all night; her father
came home twice in the day to see how she felt;
Jinny had with some reluctance bestowed on her
an oft-coveted, oft-refused doll. In the midst of
all her childish pain and suffering she had realized
that at least her agony was shared, that her tribu-
lation was understood. But now she was ill with
a sickness of the soul and there was no one with
whom she could share her anguish.

For two days she lay in her little room; Mrs.
Denver, happening in, showered upon her every
attention. There was nothing, nothing that Angela could suggest, the little fluttering lady said
sincerely, which she might not have. Angela
wished that she would go away and leave her
alone, but her experiences had rendered her highly
sensitive to the needs of others; Mrs. Denver, for
all her money, her lack of responsibility, her almost childish appetite for pleasure, was lonely
too; waiting on the younger, less fortunate woman
gave her a sense of being needed; she was pathe-

tically glad when the girl expressed a desire for anything no matter how expensive or how trivial. Angela could not deprive her entirely of those doubtful pleasures. Still there were moments, of course, when even Mrs. Denver for all her kindly officiousness had to betake herself elsewhere and leave her willing patient to herself and her thoughts.

Minutely, bit by bit, in the long forty-eight hours she went over her life; was there anything, any overt act, any crime which she had committed and for which she might atone? She had been selfish, yes; but, said her reasoning and unwearied mind, "Everybody who survives at all is selfish, it is one of the pre-requisites of survival." In "passing" from one race to the other she had done no harm to anyone. Indeed she had been forced to take this action. But she should not have forsaken Virginia. Here at this point her brain, so clear and active along all other lines, invariably failed her. She could not tell what stand to take; so far as leaving Philadelphia was concerned she had left it to seek her fortune under more agreeable circumstances; if she had been a boy and had left home no one would have had a word of blame, it would have been the proper thing, to be expected and condoned. There remained then only the particular incident of her cutting Jinny on that memorable night in the station. That was the one really cruel and unjust action of her whole life.

"Granted," said something within her rooted either in extreme hard common sense or else in a vast sophistry, "granted, but does that carry with it as penalty the shattering of a whole life, or even the suffering of years? Certainly the punishment

308

is far in excess of the crime." And it was then
that she would lie back exhausted, hopeless, bewildered, unable to cope further with the mysterious
and apparently meaningless ferocity of life. For
if this were a just penalty for one serious misde-
meanour, what compensation should there not be
for the years in which she had been a dutiful
daughter, a loving sister? And suddenly she found
herself envying people possessed of a blind religious faith, of the people who could bow the head
submissively and whisper: "Thy will be done."
For herself she could see how beaten and harried,
one might subside into a sort of blind passivity,
an acceptance of things as they are, but she would
never be able to understand a force which gave
one the imagination to paint a great desire, the
tenacity to cling to it, the emotionalism to spend
on its possible realization but which would then
with a careless sweep of the hand wipe out the
picture which the creature of its own endowment
had created.

More than once the thought came to her of
dying. But she hated to give up; something in-
nate, something of the spirit stronger than her
bodily will, set up a dogged fight, and she was too
bruised and sore to combat it. "All right," she
said to herself wearily, "I'll keep on living." She
thought then of black people, of the race of her
parents and of all the odds against living which a
cruel, relentless fate had called on them to endure.
And she saw them as a people powerfully, almost
overwhelmingly endowed with the essence of life.
They had to persist, had to survive because they
did not know how to die.

Not because she felt like it, but because some day she must begin once more to take up the motions of life, she moved on the third day from her bed to the easy chair, sat there listless and motionless. To-morrow she would return to work,—to work and the sick agony of forcing her mind back from its dolorous, painful, vital thoughts to some consideration of the dull, uninteresting task in hand. God, how she hated that! She remembered studying her lessons as a girl; the intense absorption with which she used to concentrate. Sometimes she used to wonder: "Oh what will it be like when I am grown up; when I won't be studying lessons . . ." Well, this was what it was like. Or no, she was still studying with the same old absorption,—an absorption terribly, painfully concentrated,—the lessons set down by life. It was useless to revolve in her head the causes for her suffering, they were so trivial, so silly. She said to herself, "There is no sorrow in the world like my sorrow," and knew even as she said it that some one else, perhaps only in the next block, in the next house, was saying the same thing.

Mrs. Denver tapped lightly, opened the door, came in closing mysteriously behind her.

"I've a great surprise for you." She went on with an old childish formula: "Will you have it now, or wait till you get it?"

Angela's features twisted into a wan smile. "I believe I'd better have it now. I'm beginning to think I don't care for surprises."

"You'll like this one." She went to the door and ushered in Rachel Salting.

"I know you two want to talk," Mrs. Denver

called over her shoulder. "Cheer her up, Rachel, and I'll bring you both a fine spread in an hour or so." She closed the door carefully behind her.

Angela said, "What's the matter, Rachel?" She almost added, "I hardly knew you." For her friend's face was white and wan with grief and hopelessness; gone was all her dainty freshness, her pretty colour; indeed her eyes, dark, sunken, set in great pools of blackness, were the only note, —a terrible note,—of relief against that awful whiteness.

Angela felt her strength leaving her; she rose and tottered back to the grateful security of her bed, lay down with an overwhelming sense of thankfulness for the asylum afforded her sudden faintness. In a moment, partly recovered, she motioned to Rachel to sit beside her.

"Oh," said Rachel, "you've been ill,—Mrs. Denver told me. I ought not to come bothering you with my worries. Oh, Angèle, I'm so wretched! Whatever shall I do?"

Her friend, watching her, was very gentle. "There're lots of awful things that can happen. I know that, Rachel. Maybe your trouble isn't so bad that it can't be helped. Have you told John about it?" But even as she spoke she sensed that the difficulty in some way concerned John. Her heart contracted at the thought of the pain and suffering to be endured.

"Yes, John knows,—it's about him. Angèle, we can't marry."

"Can't marry. Why, is he,—it can't be that he's—involved with some one else!"

A momentary indignation flashed into Rachel's face bringing back life and colour. For a small

space she was the Rachel Salting of the old happy
days. "Involved with some one else!" The indignation was replaced by utter despair. "How
I wish he were! That at least could be arranged.
But this can never be altered. He,—I, our parents
are dead set against it. Hadn't you ever noticed,
Angèle? He's a Gentile and I'm a Jew."

"But lots of Jews and Gentiles marry."

"Yes, I know. Only—he's a Catholic. But
my parents are orthodox—they will never consent
to my marriage. My father says he'd rather see
me dead and my mother just sits and moans. I
kept it from her as long as I could,—I used to
pray about it, I thought God must let it turn out
all right, John and I love each other so. But I
went up to Utica the other day, John went with
me, and we told them. My father drove him out
of the house; he said if I married him he'd curse
me. I am afraid of that curse. I can't go against
them. Oh, Angèle, I wish I'd never been born."

It was a delicate situation; Angela had to feel
her way; she could think of nothing but the trite
and obvious. "After all, Rachel, your parents
have lived their lives; they have no business trying
to live yours. Personally I think all this pother
about race and creed and colour, tommyrot. In
your place I should certainly follow my own
wishes; John seems to be the man for you."

But Rachel weeping, imbued with the spirit of
filial piety, thought it would be selfish.

"Certainly no more selfish than their attempt
to regulate your life for you."

"But I'm afraid," said Rachel shivering, "of
my father's curse." It was difficult for Angela to
sympathize with an attitude so archaic; she was

surprised to find it lurking at the bottom of her
friend's well-trained intelligence.

"Love," she said musing to herself rather than
to her friend, "is supposed to be the greatest thing
in the world but look how we smother and confine
it. Jews mustn't marry Catholics; white people
mustn't marry coloured——"

"Oh well, of course not," Rachel interrupted in
innocent surprise. "I wouldn't marry a nigger
in any circumstances. Why, would you?"

But Angela's only answer was to turn and,
burying her head in her pillow, to burst into un-
restrained and bitter laughter. Rachel went flying to call Mrs. Denver.

"Oh come quick, come quick! Angèle's in
hysterics. I haven't the ghost of an idea what to
do for her!"

.   .   .   .   .

Once more the period of readjustment. Once
more the determination to take life as she found
it; bitter dose after sweet, bitter after sweet. But
it seemed to her now that both sweetness and bitterness together with her high spirit for adventure
lay behind her. How now was she to pass through
the tepid, tasteless days of her future? She was
not quite twenty-seven, and she found herself
wondering what life would be like in ten, five, even
one years' time. Changes did flow in upon one,
she knew, but in her own case she had been so
used herself to give the impetus to these changes.
Now she could not envisage herself as making a
move in any direction. With the new sullenness
which seemed to be creeping upon her daily, she

313

said "Whatever move I make is always wrong.
Let life take care of itself." And she saw life,
even her own life, as an entity quite outside her
own ken and her own directing. She did not care
greatly what happened; she would not, it was true,
take her own life, but she would not care if she
should die. Once if her mind had harboured such
thoughts she would have felt an instant self-pity.
"What a shame that I so young, so gifted, with
spirits so high should meet with death!" But now
her senses were blunting; so much pain and confusion had brought about their inevitable attrition.
"I might just as well be unhappy, or meet death as
anyone else," she told herself still with that mounting sullenness.

Mrs. Denver, the Sandburgs and Ashley were
the only people who saw her. It did seem to Mrs.
Denver that the girl's ready, merry manner was
a little dimmed; if her own happy, sunny, voca-
bulary had known the term she would have
dubbed her cynical. The quasi-intellectual atmosphere at the Sandburgs suited her to perfection;
the faint bitterness which so constantly marred
her speech was taken for sophistication, her frequent silences for profoundness; in a small way,
aided by her extraordinary good looks and the
slight mystery which always hung about her, she
became quite a personage in their entourage; the
Sandburgs considered her a splendid find and
plumed themselves on having "brought her out."

.   .   .   .   .

The long golden summer, so beautiful with its
promise of happiness, so sickening with its actual-

PLUM BUN

ity of pain ripened into early, exquisite September.
Virginia was home again; slightly more golden,
very, very faintly plumper, like a ripening fruit
perfected; brimming with happiness, excitement
and the most complete content, Angela thought,
that she had ever seen in her life.

Jinny sent for the older girl and the two sat on
a Sunday morning, away from Sara Penton and
the other too insistent friends, over on Riverside
Drive looking out at the river winding purple and
alluring in the soft autumn haze.

"Weren't you surprised?" asked Jinny. Laconically, Angela admitted to no slight amazement.
She still loved her sister but more humbly, less
achingly than before. Their lives, she thought
now would never, could never touch and she was
quite reconciled. Moreover, in some of Virginia's
remarks there was the hint of the acceptance of
such a condition. Something had brought an irre-
vocable separation. They would always view each
other from the two sides of an abyss, narrow but
deep, deep.

The younger girl prattled on. "I don't know
whether Sara told you his name,—Anthony
Cross? Isn't it a dear name?"

"Yes, it's a nice name, a beautiful name," said
Angela heartily; when she had learned it was of
no consequence. She added without enthusiasm
that she knew him already; he had been a member
of her class at Cooper Union.

"You don't talk as though you were very much
taken with him," said Jinny, making a face. "But
never mind, he suits me, no matter whom he
doesn't suit." There was that in her countenance
which made Angela realize and marvel again at

315

the resoluteness of that firm young mind. No curse of parents could have kept Virginia from Anthony's arms. As long as Anthony loved her, was satisfied to have her love, no one could come between them. Only if he should fail her would she shrivel up and die.

On the heels of this thought Virginia made an astounding remark: "You know it's just perfect that I met Anthony; he's really been a rock in a weary land. Next to Matthew Henson he will, I'm sure, make me happier than any man in the world." Dreamily she added an afterthought: "And I'll make him happy too, but, oh, Angela, Angela, I always wanted to marry Matthew!"

. . . . .

The irony of that sent Angela home. Virginia wanting Matthew and marrying Anthony; Anthony wanting Angela and marrying Virginia. Herself wanting Anthony and marrying, wanting, no other; unable to think of, even to dream of another lover. The irony of it was so palpable, so ridiculously palpable that it put her in a better mood; life was bitter but it was amusingly bitter; if she could laugh at it she might be able to outwit it yet. The thought brought Anthony to mind: "If I could only get a laugh on life, Angèle!"

Sobered, she walked from the 'bus stop to Jayne Street. Halfway up the narrow, tortuous staircase she caught sight of a man climbing, climbing. He stopped outside her door. "Anthony?" she said to herself while her heart twisted with pain. "If it is Anthony,— —" she breathed, and stopped. But something within her, vital, cruel, persistent, completed her thought. "If it is An-

thony,—after what Virginia said this morning,—
if he knew that he was not the first, that even as
there had been one other there might still be
others; that Virginia in her bright, hard, shallow
youthfulness would not die any more than she had
died over Matthew,—would console herself for
the loss of Anthony even as she had consoled herself for the loss of Matthew!" But no, what
Jinny had told her was a confidence, a confidence
from sister to sister. She would never break faith
with Jinny again; nor with herself.

"But Anthony," she said to herself in the few
remaining seconds left on the staircase, "you were
my first love and I think I was yours."

However, the man at the door was not Anthony;
on the contrary he was, she thought, a complete
stranger. But as he turned at her footsteps, she
found herself looking into the blue eyes of Roger.
Completely astounded, she greeted him, "You
don't mean it's you, Roger?"

"Yes," he said humbly, shamefacedly, "aren't
you going to let me in, Angèle?"

"Oh yes, of course, of course;" she found herself hoping that he would not stay long. She
wanted to think and she would like to paint; that
idea must have been in the back of her head ever
since she had left Jinny. Hard on this thought
came another. "Here's Roger. I never expected
to see him in these rooms again; perhaps some
day Anthony will come back. Oh, God, be kind!"

But she must tear her thoughts away from
Anthony. She looked at Roger curiously, search-
ingly; in books the man who had treated his sweetheart unkindly often returned beaten, dejected,
even poverty-stricken, but Roger, except for a

slight hesitation in his manner, seemed as jaunty, as fortunate, as handsome as ever. He was even a trifle stouter.

Contrasting him with Anthony's hard-bitten leanness, she addressed him half absently. "I believe you're actually getting fat!"

His quick high flush revealed his instant sensitiveness to her criticism. But he was humble. "That's all right, Angèle. I deserve anything you choose to say if you'll just say it."

She was impervious to his mood, utterly indifferent, so indifferent that she was herself unaware of her manner. "Heavens, I've sort of forgotten, but I don't remember your ever having been so eager for criticism heretofore!"

He caught at one phrase. "Forgotten! You don't mean to say you've forgotten the past and all that was once so dear to us?"

Impatience overwhelmed her. She wished he would go and leave her to her thoughts and to her picture; such a splendid idea had come to her; it was the first time for weeks that she had felt like working. Aware of the blessed narcotic value of interesting occupation, she looked forward to his departure with a sense of relief; even hoped with her next words to precipitate it.

"Roger, you don't mean to say that you called on me on a hot September Sunday just to talk to me in that theatrical manner? I don't mind telling you I've a million things to do this afternoon; let's get down to bed rock so we can both be up and doing."

She had been sitting, almost lolling at ease in the big chair, not regarding him, absently twisting a scarf in her fingers. Now she glanced up and

something in the hot blueness of his eyes brought
her to an upright position, alert, attentive.

"Angèle, you've got to take me back."

"Back! I don't know what you're talking
about. Between you and me there is no past, so
don't mention it. If you've nothing better to say
than that, you might as well get out."

He tried to possess himself of her hands but she
shook him off, impatiently, angrily, with no pretence at feeling. "Go away, Roger. I don't want
to be bothered with you!" This pinchbeck emotionalism after the reality of her feeling for
Anthony, the sincerity of his feeling for her! "I
won't have this sort of thing; if you won't go
I will." She started for the door but he barred
her way, suddenly straight and serious.

"No listen, Angèle, you must listen. I'm in
earnest this time. You must forgive me for the
past, for the things I said. Oh, I was unspeakable! But I had it in my head,—you don't know
the things a man has borne in on him about de-
signing women,—if he's got anything, family,
money,——" she could see him striving to hide
his knowledge of his vast eligibility. "I thought
you were trying to 'get' me, it made me suspicious,
angry. I knew you were poor,——"

"And nobody! Oh say it, say it!"

"Well, I will say it. According to my father's
standards, nobody. And when you began to take
an interest in me, in my affairs,——"

"You thought I was trying to marry you. Well,
at first I was. I was poor, I was nobody! I
wanted to be rich, to be able to see the world, to
help people. And then when you and I came so
near to each other I didn't care about marriage at

319

all—just about living! Oh, I suppose my attitude
was perfectly pagan. I hadn't meant to drift into
such a life, all my training was against it, you can't
imagine how completely my training was against
it. And then for a time I was happy. I'm afraid
I didn't love you really, Roger, indeed I know now
that in a sense I didn't love you, but somehow life
seemed to focus into an absolute perfection. Then
you became petulant, ugly, suspicious, afraid of
my interest, of my tenderness. And I thought, 'I
can't let this all end in a flame of ugliness; it must
be possible for people to have been lovers and yet
remain friends.' I tried so hard to keep things so
that it would at least remain a pleasant memory.
But you resented my efforts. What I can't understand is—why shouldn't I, if I wanted to, either
try to marry you or to make an ideal thing of our
relationship? Why is it that men like you resent
an effort on our part to make our commerce decent? Well, it's all over now. . . . Theoretically
'free love' or whatever you choose to call it, is all
right. Actually, it's all wrong. I don't want any
such relationship with you or with any other man
in this world. Marriage was good enough for
my mother, it's good enough for me."

"There's nothing good enough for you, Angèle;
but marriage is the best thing that I have to offer
and I'm offering you just that. And it's precisely
because you were honest and frank and decent
and tried to keep our former relationship from
deteriorating into sordidness that I am back."

Clearly she was staggered. Marriage with
Roger meant protection, position, untold wealth,
unlimited opportunities for doing good. Once
how she would have leapt to such an offer!

"What's become of Carlotta?" she asked
bluntly.

"She's on the eve of marrying Tom Estes, a
fellow who was in college with me. He has heaps
more money than I. Carlotta thought she'd better take him on."

"I see." She looked at him thoughtfully, then
the remembrance of her great secret came to her,
a secret which she could never share with Roger.
No! No more complications and their consequent
disaster! "No, no, we won't talk about it any
more. What you want is impossible; you can't
guess how completely impossible."

He strode toward her, seized her hands. "I'm
in earnest, Angèle; you've no idea how tired I am
of loneliness and uncertainty and,—and of seeking
women; I want someone whom I can love and
trust, whom I can teach to love me,—we could
get married to-morrow. There's not an obstacle
in our way."

His sincerity left her unmoved. "What would
your father say?"

"Oh, we wouldn't be able to tell him yet; he'd
never consent! Of course we'd have to keep
things quiet, just ourselves and one or two friends,
Martha and Ladislas perhaps, would be in the
know."

More secrets! She pulled her hands away from
him. "Oh Roger, Roger! I wouldn't consider
it. No, when I marry I want a man, a man, a real
one, someone not afraid to go on his own!" She
actually pushed him toward the door. "Some
people might revive dead ashes, but not you and
I. . . . I'd never be able to trust you again and
I'm sick of secrets and playing games with human

321

relationships. I'm going to take my friendships straight hereafter. Please go. I've had a hard summer and I'm very tired. Besides I want to work."

Baffled, he looked at her, surprise and indignation struggling in his face. "Angèle, are you sure you know what you're doing? I've no intention of coming back, so you'd better take me now."

"Of course you're not coming back! I'm sure I wouldn't want you to; my decision is final." Not unsympathetically she laughed up into his doleful face, actually touched his cheek. "If you only knew how much you look like a cross baby!"

. . . .

Her newly developed sympathy and understanding made her think of Ashley. Doubtless Carlotta's defection would hit him very hard. Her conjecture was correct although the effect of the blow was different from what she had anticipated. Ashley was not so perturbed over the actual loss of the girl as confirmed in his opinion that he was never going to be able to form and keep a lasting friendship. In spite of his wealth, his native timidity had always made him distrustful of himself with women of his own class; a veritable Tony Hardcastle, he spent a great deal of time with women whom he did not actually admire, whom indeed he disliked, because, he said to Angela wistfully, they were the only ones who took him seriously.

"No one but you and Carlotta have ever given me any consideration, have ever liked me for myself, Angèle."

They were seeing a great deal of each other; in a quiet, unemotional way they were developing a real friendship. Angela had taken up her painting again. She had re-entered the classes at Cooper Union and was working with great zest and absorption on a subject which she meant to enter in the competition for scholarships at the school at Fontainebleau. Ashley, who wrote some good verse in the recondite, falsely free style of the present day, fell into the habit of bringing his work down to her little living-room, and in the long tender autumn evenings the two worked seriously, with concentration. Ashley had travelled widely and had seen a great deal of life, though usually from the side-lines; Angela for all her lack of wandering, "had lived deeply," he used to tell her, pondering on some bit of philosophy which she let fall based on the experiences of her difficult life.

"You know, in your way you're quite a wonder, Angèle; there's a mystery hanging about you; for all your good spirits, your sense of humour, you're like the Duse, you seem to move in an aura of suffering, of the pain which comes from too great sensitivity. And yet how can that be so? You're not old enough, you've had too few contacts to know how unspeakable life can be, how damnably she can get you in wrong,——"

An enigmatic smile settled on her face. "I don't know about life, Ralph? How do you think I got the idea for this masterpiece of mine?" She pointed to the painting on which she was then engaged.

"That's true, that's true. I've wondered often about that composition; lots of times I've meant to ask you how you came to evolve it. But keep your mystery to yourself, child; it adds to your charm."

About this she had her own ideas. Mystery might add to the charm of personality but it certainly could not be said to add to the charm of living. Once she thought that stolen waters were sweetest, but now it was the unwinding road and the open book that most intrigued.

Ashley, she found, for all his shyness, possessed very definite ideas and convictions of his own, was absolutely unfettered in his mode of thought, and quite unmoved by social traditions and standards. An aristocrat if ever there were one, he believed none the less in the essential quality of man and deplored the economic conditions which so often tended to set up superficial and unreal barriers which make as well as separate the classes.

With some trepidation Angela got him on the subject of colour. He considered prejudice the greatest blot on America's shield. "We're wrong, all wrong about those people; after all they did to make America habitable! Some day we're going to wake up to our shame. I hope it won't be too late."

"But you wouldn't want your sister to marry a nigger!"

"I'm amazed, Angèle, at your using such a word as an exclusive term. I've known some fine coloured people. There're hardly any of unmixed blood in the United States, so the term Negro is usually a misnomer. I haven't a sister; if I had I'd advise her against marriage with an American coloured man because the social pressure here would probably be too great, but that would be

324

absolutely the only ground on which I'd object
to it.   And I can tell you this; I wouldn't care to
marry a woman from the Congo but if I met a
coloured woman of my own nationality, well-bred,
beautiful, sympathetic, I wouldn't let the fact of
her mixed blood stand in my way, I can tell you."

.   .   .   .   .

A sort of secondary interest in living was creeping into her perspective.   The high lights, the high
peaks had faded from her sight.   She would
never, she suspected, know such spontaneity of
feeling and attitude again as she had felt toward
both Roger and Anthony.   Nor would she again
approach the experiences of existence with the
same naïve expectation, the same desire to see
how things would turn out.   Young as she was she
felt like a battle-scarred veteran who, worn out
from his own strenuous activities, was quite content to sit on the side-lines gazing at all phases
of warfare with an equal eye.
Although she no longer intended to cast in her
lot with Virginia, she made no further effort to
set up barriers between herself and coloured people.   Let the world take her as it would.   If she
were in Harlem, in company with Virginia and
Sara Penton she went out to dinner, to the noisy,
crowded, friendly "Y" dining room, to "Gert's"
tea-room, to the clean, inviting drug-store for rich
"sundaes."   Often, too, she went shopping with
her sister and to the theatre; she had her meet
Ashley and Martha.   But she was careful in this
company to avoid contact with people whose attitude on the race question was unknown, or definitely antagonistic.

Harlem intrigued her; it was a wonderful city; it represented, she felt, the last word in racial pride, integrity and even self-sacrifice. Here were people of a very high intellectual type, exponents of the realest and most essential refinement living cheek by jowl with coarse or ill-bred or even criminal, certainly indifferent, members of their race. Of course some of this propinquity was due to outer pressure, but there was present, too, a hidden consciousness of race-duty, a something which if translated said: "Perhaps you do pull me down a little from the height to which I have climbed. But on the other hand, perhaps, I'm helping you to rise."

There was a hair-dresser's establishment on 136th Street where Virginia used to have her beautiful hair treated; where Sara Penton, whose locks were of the same variety as Matthew's, used to repair to have their unruliness "pressed." Here on Saturdays Angela would accompany the girls and sit through the long process just to over-hear the conversations, grave and gallant and gay, of these people whose blood she shared but whose disabilities by a lucky fluke she had been able to avoid. For, while she had been willing for the sake of Anthony to re-enlist in the struggles of this life, she had never closed her eyes to its dis-advantages; to its limitedness! What a wealth of courage it took for these people to live! What high degree of humour, determination, steadfast-ness, undauntedness were not needed,—and poured forth! Maude, the proprietress of the business, for whom the establishment was laconi-cally called "Maude's" was a slight, sweet-faced woman with a velvety seal-brown skin, a charming

voice and an air of real refinement. She was from
Texas, but had come to New York to seek her
fortune, had travelled as ladies' maid in London
and Paris, and was as thoroughly conversant with
the arts of her calling as any hairdresser in the
vicinity of the Rue de la Paix or on Fifth Avenue.
A rare quality of hospitality emanated from her
presence; her little shop was always full not only
of patrons but of callers, visitors from "down
home," actresses from the current coloured
"show," flitting in like radiant birds of paradise
with their rich brown skins, their exotic eyes and
the gaily coloured clothing which an unconscious
style had evolved just for them.

In this atmosphere, while there was no coarse-
ness, there was no restriction; life in busy Harlem
stopped here and yawned for a delicious moment
before going on with its pressure and problems.
A girl from Texas, visiting "the big town" for a
few weeks took one last glance at her shapely,
marvellously "treated" head, poised for a second
before the glass and said simply, "Well, good-bye,
Maude; I'm off for the backwoods, but I'll never
forget Harlem." She passed out with the sinuous
elegant carriage acquired in her few week's
sojourn on Seventh Avenue.

A dark girl, immaculate in white from head to
foot, asked: "What's she going back South for?
Ain't she had enough of Texas yet?"

Maude replied that she had gone back there because of her property. "Her daddy owns most
of the little town where they live."

"Child, ain't you learned that you don't *never*
own no property in Texas as long as those white
folks are down there too? Just let those Ku

Kluxers get it into their heads that you've got something they want. She might just as well leave there first as last; she's bound to have to some day. I know it's more'n a notion to pull up stakes and start all over again in a strange town and a strange climate, but it's the difference between life and death. I know I done it and I don't expect ever to go back."

She was a frail woman, daintily dressed and shod. Her voice was soft and drawling. But Angela saw her sharply as the epitome of the iron and blood in a race which did not know how to let go of life.

MARKET IS DONE

CHAPTER I

THE eternal routine of life went on,—meals, slumber, talk, work—and all of it meaning nothing; a void starting nowhere and leading nowhither; a "getting through" with the days. Gradually however two points fixed themselves in her horizon, and about these her life revolved. One was her work,—her art. Every week found her spending three or four of its nights at her easel. She was feverishly anxious to win one of the prizes in the contest which would be held in May; if successful she would send in her application for registration in the Fountainebleau School of Fine Arts which was financed by Americans and established, so read the circular, "as a summer school for American architects, painters and sculptors." If she were successful in winning this, she would leave the United States for a year or two, thus assuring herself beyond question of a new deal of the cards. The tenacity with which she held to this plan frightened her a little until she found out that there were also possible funds from which she could, with the proper recommendation, borrow enough money to enable her to go abroad with the understanding that the refund was to be made by slow and easy payments. Ashley discovered this saving information, thus relieving

331

her of the almost paralyzing fear which beset her from time to time. It both amused and saddened her to realize that her talent which she had once used as a blind to shield her real motives for breaking loose and coming to New York had now become the greatest, most real force in her life.

Miss Powell, with whom Angela in her new mood had arranged a successful truce, knew of her ambition, indeed shared it. If she herself should win a prize, that money, combined with some small savings of her own and used in connection with the special terms offered by the American Committee, would mean the fruition of her dearest dreams. All this she confided to Angela on two Sunday mornings which the latter spent with her in her rather compressed quarters up in 134th Street. A dwelling house nearby had been converted into a place of worship for one of the special divisions of religious creed so dear to coloured people's hearts. Most of the service seemed to consist of singing, and so the several hours spent by the two girls in earnest talk were punctuated by the outbursts of song issuing from the brazen-coated throats of the faithful.

The other point about which her thoughts centred was her anomalous position. Yet that clear mind of hers warned her again and again that there was nothing inherently wrong or mean or shameful in the stand which she had taken. The method thereof might come in perhaps for a little censure. But otherwise her harshest critics, if unbiased, could only say that instead of sharing the burdens of her own group she had elected to stray along a path where she personally could find the greatest ease, comfort and expan-

332

sion. She had long since given up the search
for happiness. But there were moments when a
chance discussion about coloured people couched
in the peculiarly brutal terms which white America
affects in the discussion of this problem made her
blood boil, and she longed to confound her
vis-à-vis and his tacit assumption that she, being
presumably a white woman, would hold the same
views as he, with the remark: "I'm one of them,
—do you find me worthless or dishonest or
offensive in any way?" Such a *dénouement* would
have, she felt, been a fine gesture. But life she
knew had a way of allowing grand gestures to go
unremarked and unrewarded. Would it be worth
while to throw away the benefits of casual whiteness in America when no great issue was at stake?
Would it indeed be worth while to forfeit them
when a great issue was involved? Remembering
the material age in which she lived and the material nation of which she was a member, she was
doubtful. Her mother's old dictum recurred:
"Life is more important than colour."

.   .   .   .   .

The years slipped by. Virginia seemed in no
haste to marry. Anthony whom Angela saw
occasionally at the Art School shared apparently
in this cool deliberateness. Yet there was nothing
in his action or manner to make her feel that he
was anticipating a change. Rather, if she judged
him correctly he, like herself, tired of the snarl
into which the three of them had been drawn, had
settled down to a resigned acceptance of fate.
If conceivable, he was quieter, more reserved than

ever, yet radiating a strange restfulness and the peace which comes from surrender.

In May the prizes for the contest were announced. Angela received the John T. Stewart Prize for her "Fourteenth Street Types;" her extreme satisfaction was doubled by the knowledge that the Nehemiah Sloan Prize, of equal value, had been awarded Miss Powell for her picture entitled "A Street in Harlem." The coloured girl was still difficult and reserved, but under Angela's persistent efforts at friendship her frank and sympathetic interest and comprehension of her class-mate's difficulties, the latter had finally begun to thaw a little. They were not planning to live together in France, their tastes were not sufficiently common for that closeness, but both were looking forward to a year of pleasure, of inspiring work, to a life that would be "different." Angela was relieved, but Miss Powell was triumphant; not unpleasantly, she gave the impression of having justified not only her calling but herself and, in a lesser degree, her race. The self-consciousness of colour, racial responsibility, lay, Angela had discovered, deep upon her.

The passage money to France was paid. Through the terms offered by the committee of the School for Americans at Fontainebleau, an appreciable saving had been affected. The girls were to sail in June. As the time drew nearer Angela felt herself becoming more and more enthusiastic. She had at first looked upon her sojourn abroad as a heaven-sent break in the monotony and difficulties of her own personal problems, but lately, with the involuntary reaction to youth, she was beginning to recover her

sense of embarking on a great adventure. Her
spirits mounted steadily.

One evening she went around to Martha Burden's to discuss the trip; she wanted information
about money, clothes, possible tips.

"Everything you can think of, Martha," she
said with something of her former vital manner.
"This is an old story to you,—you've been abroad
so many times you ought to write an encyclopædia
on 'What to take to Europe.' I mean to follow
your advice blindly and the next time I see Miss
Powell I'll pass it along to her."

"No need to," said Martha laconically and
sombrely. "She isn't going."

"Not going! Why she was going two weeks
ago."

"Yes, but she's not going this week nor any
other week I'm afraid; at least not through the
good offices of the American Committee for the
Fontainebleau School of Fine Arts. They've
returned her passage money. Didn't you know
it? I thought everybody had heard of it."

Angela fought against a momentary nausea.
"No, I didn't know it. I haven't seen her for
ages. I'm so busy getting myself together.
Martha, what's it all about? Is it because she's
coloured? You don't mean it's because she's
coloured?"

"Well, it is. They said they themselves were
without prejudice, but that they were sure the
enforced contact on the boat would be unpleasant
to many of the students, garnered as they would
be from all parts of the United States. Furthermore they couldn't help but think that such contact would be embarrassing to Miss Powell too.

335

Oh, there's no end to the ridiculous piffle which they've written and said. I've had a little committee of students and instructors going about, trying to stir up public sentiment. Mr. Cross has been helping and Paget too. I wish Paulette were here; she'd get some yellow journal publicity. Van Meier has come out with some biting editorials; he's shown up a lot of their silly old letters. I shouldn't be surprised but what if we kept at it long enough we'd get somewhere."

She reflected a moment. "Funny thing is we're having such a hard time in making Miss Powell show any fight. I don't understand that girl."

Angela murmured that perhaps she had no hope of making an impression on prejudice. "It's so unreasonable and far-reaching. Maybe she doesn't want to sacrifice her peace of mind for what she considers a futile struggle."

"That's what Mr. Cross said. He's been wonderful to her and an indefatigable worker. Of course you'll be leaving soon since none of this touches you, but come into a committee meeting or two, won't you? We're meeting here. I'll give you a ring."

"Well," said Angela to herself that night after she had regained her room. "I wonder what I ought to do now?" Even yet she was receiving an occasional reporter; the pleasant little stir of publicity attendant on her prize had not yet died away. Suppose she sent for one of them and announced her unwillingness to accept the terms of the American Committee inasmuch as they had withdrawn their aid from Miss Powell. Suppose she should finish calmly: "I, too, am a Negro."

336

What would happen? The withdrawal of the assistance without which her trip abroad, its hoped for healing, its broadening horizons, would be impossible. Evidently, there was no end to the problems into which this matter of colour could involve one, some of them merely superficial, as in this instance, some of them gravely physical. Her head ached with the futility of trying to find a solution to these interminable puzzles.

As a child she and Jinny had been forbidden to read the five and ten cent literature of their day. But somehow a copy of a mystery story entitled "Who killed Dr. Cronlin?" found its way into their hands, a gruesome story all full of bearded men, hands preserved in alcohol, shadows on window curtains. Shivering with fascination, they had devoured it after midnight or early in the morning while their trusting parents still slumbered. Every page they hoped would disclose the mystery. But their patience went unrewarded for the last sentence of the last page still read: "Who killed Dr. Cronlin?"

Angela thought of it now, and smiled and sighed. "Just what is or is not ethical in this matter of colour?" she asked herself. And indeed it was a nice question. Study at Fontainebleau would have undoubtedly changed Miss Powell's attitude toward life forever. If she had received the just reward for her painstaking study, she would have reasoned that right does triumph in essentials. Moreover the inspiration might have brought out latent talent, new possibilities. Furthermore, granted that Miss Powell had lost out by a stroke of ill-fortune, did that necessarily call for Angela's loss? If so, to what end?

337

Unable to answer she fell asleep.

Absorbed in preparations she allowed two weeks to pass by, then, remembering Martha's invitation, she went again to the Starr household on an evening when the self-appointed committee was expected to meet. She found Anthony, Mr. Paget, Ladislas and Martha present. The last was more perturbed than ever. Indeed an air of sombre discouragement lay over the whole company.

"Well," asked the newcomer, determined to appear at ease in spite of Anthony's propinquity, "how are things progressing?"

"Not at all," replied Mr. Paget. "Indeed we're about to give up the whole fight."

Ladislas with a sort of provoked amusement explained then that Miss Powell herself had thrown up the sponge. "She's not only withdrawn but she sends us word to-night that while she appreciates the fight we're making she'd rather we'd leave her name out of it."

"Did you ever hear anything to equal that?" snapped Martha crossly. "I wonder if coloured people aren't natural born quitters. Sometimes I think I'll never raise another finger for them."

"You don't know what you're talking about," said Anthony hotly. "If you knew the ceaseless warfare which most coloured people wage, you'd understand that sometimes they have to stop their fight for the trimmings of life in order to hang on to the essentials which they've got to have and for which they must contend too every day just as hard as they did the first day. No, they're not quitters, they've merely learned to let

338

go so they can conserve their strength for another
bad day. I'm coloured and I know."

There was a moment's tense silence while the
three white people stared speechless with surprise. Then Martha said in a still shocked voice:
"Coloured! Why, I can't believe it. Why, you
never told us you were coloured."

"Which is precisely why I'm telling you
now," said Anthony, coldly rude. "So you won't
be making off-hand judgments about us." He
started toward the door. "Since the object for
which this meeting has been called has become
null and void I take it that we are automatically
dismissed. Good-night."

Martha hastened after him. "Oh, Mr. Cross,
don't go like that. As though it made any difference! Why should this affect our very real regard
for each other?"

"Why should it indeed?" he asked a trifle
enigmatically. "I'm sure I hope it won't. But I
must go." He left the room, Paget and Ladislas
both hastening on his heels.

Martha stared helplessly after him. "I suppose
I haven't said the right thing. But what could I
do? I was so surprised!" She turned to Angela:
"And I really can't get over his being coloured,
can you?"

"No," said Angela solemnly, "I can't . . ,"
and surprised herself and Martha by bursting into
a flood of tears.

•   •   •   •   •

For some reason the incident steadied her determination. Perhaps Anthony was the vicarious

339

sacrifice, she told herself and knew even as she said
it that the supposition was pure bunk. Anthony
did not consider that he was making a sacrifice;
his confession or rather his statement with regard
to his blood had the significance of the action of
a person who clears his room of rubbish. Anthony
did not want his mental chamber strewn with the
chaff of deception and confusion. He did not
label himself, but on the other hand he indulged
every now and then in a general house-cleaning
because he would not have the actions of his life
bemused and befuddled.

As for Angela she asked for nothing better than
to put all the problems of colour and their attendant difficulties behind her. She could not meet
those problems in their present form in Europe;
literally in every sense she would begin life all
over. In France or Italy she would speak of her
strain of Negro blood and abide by whatever consequences such exposition would entail. But the
consequences could not engender the pain and
difficulties attendant upon them here.

Somewhat diffidently she began to consider the
idea of going to see Miss Powell. The horns of
her dilemma resolved themselves into an unwillingness to parade her own good fortune before
her disappointed classmate and an equal
unwillingness to depart for France, leaving behind
only the cold sympathy of words on paper. And,
too, something stronger, more insistent than the
mere consideration of courtesy urged her on.
After all, this girl was one of her own. A whim
of fate had set their paths far apart but just the
same they were more than "sisters under the skin."
They were really closely connected in blood, in

racial condition, in common suffering. Once again she thought of herself as she had years ago when she had seen the coloured girl refused service in the restaurant: "It might so easily have been Virginia."

Without announcement then she betook herself up town to Harlem and found herself asking at the door of the girl's apartment if she might see Miss Powell. The mother whom Angela had last seen so proud and happy received her with a note of sullen bafflement which to the white girl's consciousness connoted: "Easy enough for you, all safe and sound, high and dry, to come and sympathize with my poor child." There was no trace of gratitude or of appreciation of the spirit which had inspired Angela to pay the visit.

To her inquiry Mrs. Powell rejoined: "Yes, I guess you c'n see her. There're three or four other people in there now pesterin' her to death. I guess one mo' won't make no diffunce."

Down a long narrow hall she led her, past two rooms whose dark interiors seemed Stygian in contrast with the bright sunlight which the visitor had just left. But the end of the hall opened into a rather large, light, plain but comfortable dining-room where Miss Powell sat entertaining, to Angela's astonishment, three or four people, all of them white. Her astonishment, however, lessened when she perceived among them John Banky, one of the reporters who had come rather often to interview herself and her plans for France. All of them, she judged angrily, were of his profession, hoping to wring their half column out of Miss Powell's disappointment and embarrassment.

Angela thought she had never seen the girl one half so attractive and exotic. She was wearing a thin silk dress, plainly made but of a flaming red from which the satin blackness of her neck rose, a straight column topped by her squarish, somewhat massive head. Her thin, rather flat dark lips brought into sharp contrast the dazzling perfection of her teeth; her high cheek bones showed a touch of red. To anyone whose ideals of beauty were not already set and sharply limited, she must have made a breathtaking appeal. As long as she sat quiescent in her rather sulky reticence she made a marvellous figure of repose; focussing all the attention of the little assemblage even as her dark skin and hair drew into themselves and retained the brightness which the sun, streaming through three windows, showered upon her.

As soon as she spoke she lost, however, a little of this perfection. For though a quiet dignity persisted, there were pain and bewilderment in her voice and the flat sombreness of utter despair. Clearly she did not know how to get rid of the intruders, but she managed to maintain a poise and aloofness which kept them at their distance. Surely, Angela thought, listening to the stupid, almost impertinent questions put, these things can mean nothing to them. But they kept on with their baiting rather as a small boy keeps on tormenting a lonely and dispirited animal at the Zoo.

"We were having something of an academic discussion with Miss Powell here," said Banky, turning to Angela. "This," he informed his co-workers, "is Miss Mory, one of the prize-winners of the Art Exhibit and a class-mate of Miss Powell. I believe Miss Powell was to cross

342

with you,—as—er—your room-mate did you
say?"

"No," said Angela, flushing a little for Miss
Powell, for she thought she understood the
double meaning of the question, "we weren't in-
tending to be room-mates. Though so far as I
am concerned," she heard herself, to her great
surprise, saying: "I'd have been very glad to share
Miss Powell's state-room if she had been willing."
She wanted to get away from this aspect.
"What's this about an academic discussion?"

Miss Powell's husky, rather mutinous voice
interrupted: "There isn't any discussion, Miss
Mory, academic or otherwise. It seems Mr.
Paget told these gentlemen and Miss Tilden here,
that I had withdrawn definitely from the fight to
induce the Committee for the American Art
School abroad to allow me to take advantage of
their arrangements. So they came up here to get
me to make a statement and I said I had none to
make other than that I was sick and tired of the
whole business and I'd be glad to let it drop."

"And I," said Miss Tilden, a rangy young lady
wearing an unbecoming grey dress and a peculiarly straight and hideous bob, "asked her if she
weren't really giving up the matter because in her
heart she knew she hadn't a leg to stand on."

Angela felt herself growing hot. Something
within her urged caution, but she answered
defiantly: "What do you mean she hasn't a leg
to stand on?"

"Well, of course, this is awfully plain speaking
and I hope Miss Powell won't be offended,"
resumed Miss Tilden, showing only too plainly
that she didn't care whether Miss Powell were

343

offended or not, "but after all we do know that a great many people find the—er—Negroes objectionable and so of course no self-respecting one of them would go where she wasn't wanted."

Miss Powell's mother hovering indefinitely in the background, addressing no one in particular, opined that she did not know that "that there committee owned the boat. If her daughter could only afford it she'd show them how quickly she'd go where she wanted and not ask no one no favours either."

"Ah, but," said Miss Tilden judicially, "there's the fallacy. Something else is involved here. There's a social side to this matter, inherent if not expressed. And that *is* the question." She shook a thin bloodless finger at Miss Powell. "Back of most of the efforts which you people make to get into schools and clubs and restaurants and so on, isn't there really this desire for social equality? Come now, Miss Powell, be frank and tell me."

With such sharpness as to draw the attention of everyone in the room Angela said: "Come, Miss Tilden, that's unpardonable and you know it. Miss Powell hadn't a thought in mind about social equality. All she wanted was to get to France and to get there as cheaply as possible."

Banky, talking in a rather affected drawl, confirmed the last speaker. "I think, too, that's a bit too much, Miss Tilden. We've no right to interpret Miss Powell's ideas for her."

A short, red-faced young man intervened: "But just the same *isn't* that the question involved? Doesn't the whole matter resolve itself into this: Has Miss Powell or any other young

344

coloured woman knowing conditions in America
the right to thrust her company on a group of
people with whom she could have nothing in
common except her art? If she stops to think she
must realize that not one of the prospective group
of students who would be accompanying her on
that ship would really welcome her presence.
Here's Miss Mory, for instance, a fellow student.
What more natural under other circumstances
than that she should have made arrangements to
travel with Miss Powell? She knows she has to
share her cabin with some one. But no; such a
thought apparently never entered her head.
Why? The answer is obvious. Very well then.
If she, knowing Miss Powell, feels this way, how
much more would it be the feeling of total
strangers?"

A sort of shocked silence fell upon the room.
It was an impossible situation. How, thought
Angela desperately, knowing the two sides, could
she ever explain to these smug, complacent people
Miss Powell's ambition, her chilly pride, the
remoteness with which she had treated her fellow-
students, her only too obvious endeavour to share
their training and not their friendship? Hastily,
almost crudely, she tried to get something of this
over, ashamed for herself, ashamed for Miss
Powell whose anguished gaze begged for her
silence.

At last the coloured girl spoke. "It's wonderful of you to take my part in this way, Miss Mory.
I had no idea you understood so perfectly. But
don't you see there's no use in trying to explain
it? It's a thing which one either does see or
doesn't see." She left her soft, full, dark gaze

345

rest for a second on her auditors. "I'm afraid it is not in the power of these persons to grasp what you mean."

The stocky young man grew a little redder. "I think we do understand, Miss Powell. All that Miss Mory says simply confirms my first idea. For otherwise, understanding and sympathizing with you as she does, why has she, for instance, never made any very noticeable attempt to become your friend? Why shouldn't she have asked you to be her side-partner on this trip which I understand you're taking together? There would have been an unanswerable refutation for the committee's arguments. But no, she does nothing even though it means the thwarting for you of a life-time's ambition. Mind, I'm not blaming you, Miss Mory. You are acting in accordance with a natural law. I'm just trying to show Miss Powell here how inevitable the workings of such a law are."

It was foolish reasoning and fallacious, yet containing enough truth to make it sting. Some icy crust which had formed over Angela's heart shifted, wavered, broke and melted. Suddenly it seemed as though nothing in the world were so important as to allay the poignancy of Miss Powell's situation; for this, she determined quixotically, no price would be too dear. She said icily in tones which she had never heard herself use before: "It's true I've never taken any stand hitherto for Miss Powell for I never thought she needed it. But now that the question has come up I want to say that I'd be perfectly willing to share my state-room with her and to give her as much of my company as she could stand. However, that's all out of the question now because Miss Powell isn't going to France on the American Committee Fund and I'm not going either." She stopped a second and added quietly: "And for the same reason."

Someone said in bewilderment: "What do you mean when you say you're not going? And for the same reason?"

"I mean that if Miss Powell isn't wanted, I'm not wanted either. You imply that she's not wanted because she's coloured. Well, I'm coloured too."

One of the men said under his breath, "God, what a scoop!" and reached for his hat. But Banky, his face set and white, held him back.

"I don't believe you know what you're saying, Miss Mory. But anyway, whether it's true or untrue, for God's sake take it back!"

His tone of horror added the last touch. Angela laughed in his face. "Take it back!" She could hardly contain herself. "Do you really think that being coloured is as awful as all that? Can't you see that to my way of thinking it's a great deal better to be coloured and to miss—oh—scholarships and honours and preferments, than to be the contemptible things which you've all shown yourselves to be this morning? Coming here baiting this poor girl and her mother, thrusting your self-assurance down their throats, branding yourselves literally dogs in the manger?" She turned to the coloured girl's mother. "Mrs. Powell, you surely don't want these people here any longer. Have I your permission to show them out?" Crossing the room superbly she opened the door. "This way, please, and don't come back any more.

You can rest assured we'll find a way to keep you out."

Silently the little line filed out. Only Miss Tilden, laying her hand on Angela's arm paused to say avidly: "You'll let me come to see you, surely? I can give you some fine publicity, only I must have more data. How about an exclusive interview?"

Angela said stonily: "Mrs. Powell will show you the front door." Then she and her former class-mate stood regarding each other. The dark girl crossed the room and caught her hands and kissed them. "Oh," she said, "it was magnificent —I never guessed it,—but you shouldn't have done it. It's all so unjust, so—silly—and so tiresome. You, of course, only get it when you bring it upon yourself. But I'm black and I've had it all my life. You don't know the prizes within my grasp that have been snatched away from me again because of colour." She turned as her mother entered the room. "Mother, wasn't she magnificent?"

"She was a fool," Mrs. Powell replied shortly.

Her words brought the exalted Angela back to earth. "Yes," she said, smiling whimsically, "I am just that, a fool. I don't know what possessed me. I'm poor, I was in distress; I wanted a new deal. Now I don't know which way to turn for it. That story will be all over New York by to-morrow morning." She burst out laughing. "Think of my choosing four reporters before whom to make my great confession!" Her hand sought Miss Powell's. "Good-bye, both of you. Don't worry about me. I never dreamed that anything like this could happen, but the mere fact

348

that it has shows that the truth was likely to come out any day. So don't blame yourselves for it. Good-bye."

.   .   .   .   .

Banky was waiting for her in the vestibule downstairs. "I'm so sorry about the whole damned business, Miss Mory," he said decently. "It's a damned shame. If there's anything I can do——"

Rather shortly she said there was nothing. "And you don't need to worry. As I told you upstairs, being coloured isn't as awful as all that. I'll get along." Ignoring his hand she passed by him into the street. It was Saturday afternoon so there was a chance of her finding Jinny at home.

"And if she isn't there I can wait," she told herself, and thanked God in her heart for the stability implied in sisterhood.

Jinny was home, mulling happily over the small affairs which kept her a little girl. Her sister, looking at the serene loveliness of her face, said irrelevantly: "You make me feel like an old woman."

"Well," replied Jinny, "you certainly have the art of concealing time's ravages, for you not only look young but you have the manner of someone who's just found a million dollars. Come in and tell me about it."

"Found a million dollars! H'm, lost it I should say!" But a sudden wave of relief and contentment broke over her. "Oh, Jinny, tell me, have I been an utter fool! I've thrown away every chance I've ever had in the world,—just

349

for a whim." Suddenly close in the full tide of sisterliness, they sat facing each other on the comfortable couch while Angela told her story. "I hadn't the faintest idea in the world of telling it. I was thinking only the other day how lucky I was compared to Miss Powell, and the first thing I knew there it all came tripping off my tongue. But I had to do it. If you could just have seen those pigs of reporters and Miss Powell's face under their relentless probing. And old Mrs. Powell, helpless and grunting and sweating and thinking me a fool; she told me so, you know. . . . Why, Jinny, darling, you're not ever crying! Darling, there's nothing to cry about; what's the matter, Honey!"

"It's because you *are* a fool that I am crying," said Jinny sobbing and sniffling, her fingers in her eyes. "You're a fool and the darlingest girl that ever lived, and my own precious, lovely, wonderful sister back again. Oh, Angela, I'm so happy. Tell them to send you your passage money back; say you don't want anything from them that they don't want to give; let them go, let them all go except the ones who like you for yourself. And dearest, if you don't mind having to skimp a bit for a year or two and not spreading yourself as you planned, we'll get you off to Europe after all. You know I've got all my money from the house. I've never touched it. You can have as much of that as you want and pay me back later or not at all."

Laughing and crying, Angela told her that she couldn't think of it. "Keep your money for your marriage, Jinny. It'll be some time before— Anthony will make any real money, I imagine.

But I will take your advice and go to Europe after
all. All this stuff will be in the paper to-morrow,
I suppose, so I'll write the American Committee
people to-night. As for the prize money, if they
want that back they can have it. But I don't think
they will; nothing was said about Miss Powell's.
That's a thousand dollars. I'll take that and go
to Paris and live as long as I can. If I can't have
the thousand I'll use the few hundreds that I have
left and go anyway. And when I come back I'll
go back to my old job or—go into the schools.
But all that's a long way off and we don't know
what might turn up."

There were one or two matters for immediate
consideration. The encounter with the reporters
had left Angela a little more shaken than was at
first apparent. "I don't want to run into them
again," she said ruefully. Her lease on the little
apartment in Jayne Street had still a month to
run. She would go down this very evening, get
together her things, and return to Jinny, with
whom she would live quietly until it was time for
her to sail. Her mail she could leave with the
janitor to be called for. Fortunately the furniture
was not hers; there were only a few pictures to be
removed. After all, she had very few friends to
consider,—just the Sandburgs, Martha Burden,
Mrs. Denver, Ralph Ashley and Rachel Salting.

"And I don't know what to do about them,"
she said, pondering. "After all, you can't write
to people and say: 'Dear friend:—You've always
thought I was white. But I'm not really. I'm
coloured and I'm going back to my own folks to
live.' Now can you? Oh, Jinny, Jinny, isn't it a
great old world?"

In the end, after the story appeared, as it assuredly did, in the next morning's paper, she cut out and sent to each of her former friends copies of Miss Tilden's story whose headlines read: "Socially Ambitious Negress Confesses to Long Hoax."

．　　　．　　　．　　　．　　　．

With the exception of Banky's all the accounts took the unkindest attitude possible. The young Hungarian played up the element of self-sacrifice and the theory that blood after all was thicker than water. Angela guessed rightly that if he could have he would have preferred omitting it, and that he had only written it up to offset as far as possible the other accounts. Of the three other meanly insinuating stories Miss Tilden's was the silliest and most dangerous. She spoke of mixed blood as the curse of the country, a curse whose "insidiously concealed influence constantly threatens the wells of national race purity. Such incidents as these make one halt before he condemns the efforts of the Ku Klux Klan and its unceasing fight for 100 per cent. Americanism."

The immediate effect of this publicity was one which neither of the sisters had foreseen. When Angela reported for work on the following Monday morning she found a note on her desk asking her immediate appearance in the office. The president returning her good-morning with scant courtesy, showed her a clipping and asked if she were the Miss Mory of the story. Upon her assurance that she was none other, he handed her a month's salary in lieu of notice and asked her to consider her connection with the firm at an end.

"We have no place for deceit in an institution such as this," he said augustly.

The incident shook both girls to a degree. Virginia particularly was rendered breathless by its cruel immediacy. Never before had she come so close to the special variation of prejudice manifested to people in Angela's position. That the president of the concern should attribute the girl's reticence on this subject to deceit seemed to her the last ounce of injustice. Angela herself was far less perturbed.

"I've seen too much of this sort of thing to feel it as you do, Virginia. Of course, as you see, there are all kinds of absurdities involved. In your case, showing colour as you do, you'd have been refused the job at the very outset. Perhaps they would have said that they had found coloured people incompetent or that other girls had a strong natural aversion toward working beside one of us. Now here I land the position, hold it long enough to prove ability and the girls work beside me and remain untainted. So evidently there's no blind inherent disgust to be overcome. Looking just the same as I've ever looked I let the fact of my Negro ancestry be known. Mind, I haven't changed the least bit, but immediately there's all this holding up of hands and the cry of deceit is raised. Some logic, that! It really would be awfully funny, you see, Jinny, if it couldn't be fraught with such disastrous consequences for people like, say, Miss Powell."

"Don't mention her," said Jinny vehemently. "If it hadn't been for her you wouldn't have been in all this trouble."

Angela smiled. "If it hadn't been for her, you

353

and I probably never would have really found each other again. But you mustn't blame her. Sooner or later I'd have been admitting,—'confessing,' as the papers say,—my black blood. Not that I myself think it of such tremendous importance; in spite of my efforts to break away I really don't, Virginia. But because this country of ours makes it so important, against my own conviction I was beginning to feel as though I were laden down with a great secret. Yet when I begin to delve into it, the matter of blood seems nothing compared with individuality, character, living. The truth of the matter is, the whole business was just making me fagged to death."

She sat lost intently in thought. "All of the complications of these last few years,—and you can't guess what complications there have been, darling child,—have been based on this business of 'passing.' I understand why Miss Powell gave up the uneven fight about her passage. Of course, in a way it would have been a fine thing if she could have held on, but she was perfectly justified in letting go so she could avoid still greater bitterness and disappointment and so she could have something left in her to devote to her art. You can't fight and create at the same time. And I understand, too, why your Anthony bestirs himself every little while and makes *his* confession; simply so he won't have to be bothered with the trappings of pretence and watchfulness. I suppose he told you about that night down at Martha Burden's?"

"Yes," said Jinny, sighing, "he has terrible ideals. There's something awfully lofty about Anthony. I wish he were more like Matthew,

354

comfortable and homey. Matt's got some ideals,
too, but he doesn't work them overtime. Anthony's
a darling, two darlings, but he's awfully, awfully
what-do-you-call-it, ascetic. I shouldn't be at all
surprised but what he had a secret canker eating
at his heart."

Angela said rather sternly, "Look here, Jinny,
I don't believe you love him after all, do you?"

"Well now, when I get right down to it sometimes I think I do. Sometimes I think I don't. Of
course the truth of the matter is, I'd hardly have
thought about Anthony or marriage either just
now, if I hadn't been so darn lonely. You know
I'm not like you, Angela. When we were children
I was the one who was going to have a career,
and you were always going to have a good time.
Actually it's the other way round; you're the one
who's bound to have a career. You just gravitate
to adventure. There's something so forceful and
so strong about you that you can't keep out of the
battle. But, Angela, I want a home,—with you
if you could just stand still long enough, or failing
that, a home with husband and children and all
that goes with it. Of course I don't mind admitting that at any time I'd have given up even you
for Matthew. But next to being his wife I'd
rather live with you, and next to that I'd like to
marry Anthony. I don't like to be alone; for
though I can fend for myself I don't want to."

Angela felt herself paling with the necessity of
hiding her emotion. "So poor Anthony's only
third in your life?"

"Yes, I'm afraid he is . . . Darling, what do
you say to scallops for dinner? I feel like cooking
to-day. Guess I'll hie me to market."

She left the room, and her sister turned to the large photograph of Cross which Virginia kept on the mantel. She put her fingers on the slight youthful hollows of his pictured cheeks, touched his pictured brow. "Oh Anthony, Anthony, is Life cheating you again? You'll always be first in my life, dearest."

Perhaps Virginia's diagnosis of her character was correct. At any rate she welcomed the present combination of difficulties through which she was now passing. Otherwise this last confession of Jinny's would have plunged her into fresh unhappiness. But she had many adjustments to make and to face. First of all there was her new status in the tiny circle in which she had moved. When at the end of two weeks she went down to her old apartment in Jayne Street to ask for her mail, she was, in spite of herself amazed and hurt to discover a chilled bewilderment, an aloofness, in the manner of Mrs. Denver, with whom she had a brief encounter. On the other hand there were a note and a calling card from Martha Burden, and some half dozen letters from Elizabeth and Walter Sandburg.

Martha's note ran: "Undoubtedly you and Mr. Cross are very fine people. But I don't believe I could stand another such shock very soon. Of course it was magnificent of you to act as you did. But oh, my dear, how quixotic. And after all *à quoi bon?* Will you come to see me as soon as you get this, or send me word how I may see you? And Angèle, if you let all this nonsense interfere with your going to Europe I'll never forgive you. Ladislas and I have several thousand dollars stored away just begging to be put out at interest."

Elizabeth Sandburg said nothing about the matter, but Angela was able to read her knowledge between the lines. The kind-hearted couple could not sufficiently urge upon her their unchanging regard and friendship. "Why on earth don't you come and see us?" Elizabeth queried in her immense, wandering chirography, five words to a page. "You can't imagine how we miss you. Walter's actually getting off his feed. Do take a moment from whatever masterpiece you're composing and give us a week-end."

But from Rachel Salting and from Ashley not one single word!

CHAPTER II

MORE than ever her determination to sail became fixed. "Some people," she said to Jinny, "might think it the thing to stay here and fight things out. Martha, for instance, is keenly disappointed because I won't let the committee which had been working for Miss Powell take up my case. I suspect she thinks we're all quitters. But I know when I've had enough. I told her I wanted to spend my life doing something besides fighting. Moreover, the Committee, like myself, is pretty sick of the whole affair, though not for the same reason, and I think there'd be even less chance for a readjustment in my case than there was in Miss Powell's."

An interview with Clarke Otter, Chairman of the Advisory Board of the American Committee, had given her this impression. Mr. Otter's attitude betokened a curious admixture of resentment at what he seemed to consider her deceit in "passing" and exasperation at her having been quixotic enough to give the show away. "We think you are quite right in expressing your determination not to take advantage of the Committee's arrangements. It evidences a delicacy of feeling quite unusual in the circumstances." Angela was boiling with anger when she left.

A letter to the donor of the prize brought back

358

the laconic answer that the writer was interested
"not in Ethnology but in Art."

"I'd like to see that party," said Angela, revert-
ing to the jargon of her youth. "I'll bet he's nowhere near as stodgy as he sounds. I shouldn't
wonder but what he was just bubbling over with
mirth at the silliness of it all."

Certainly she herself was bubbling over with
mirth or with what served for that quality. Virginia could not remember ever having seen her
in such high spirits, not since the days when they
used to serve Monday's dinner for their mother
and play at the *rôles* in which Mrs. Henrietta
Jones had figured so largely. But Angela herself
knew the shallowness of that mirth whose reality,
Anthony, unable to remain for any length of time
in her presence and yet somehow unable to stay
away, sometimes suspected.

Her savings, alas! including the prize money,
amounted roughly to 1,400 dollars. Anthony had
urged her to make the passage second class on one
of the large, comfortable boats. Then, if she
proved herself a good sailor, she might come back
third class.

"And anyway don't put by any more than
enough for that," said Jinny maternally, "and if
you need any extra money write to me and I'll
send you all you want."

From stories told by former foreign students
who had sometimes visited the Union it seemed as
though she might stretch her remaining hundreds
over a period of eight or nine months. "And by
that time I'll have learned enough to know
whether I'm to be an honest-to-God artist or a
plain drawing teacher."

"I almost hope it will be the latter," said Jinny
with a touching selfishness, "so you'll have to come
back and live with us. Don't you hope so, Anthony?"

Angela could see him wince under the strain of
her sister's artlessness. "Eight or nine months
abroad ought to make a great difference in her
life," he said with no particular relevance. "Indeed in the lives of all of us." Both he and Angela had only one thought these days, that the
time for departure would have to arrive. Neither
of them had envisaged the awfulness of this pull
on their self-control.

.   .   .   .   .

Now there were only five days before her departure on Monday. She divided them among
the Sandburgs, Anthony and Jinny who was coming down with a summer cold. On Saturday the
thought came to her that she would like to see
Philadelphia again; it was a thought so persistent
that by nine o'clock she was in the train and by
11.15 she was preparing for bed in a small side-
room in the Hotel Walton in the city of her birth.
Smiling, she fell asleep vaguely soothed by the
thought of being so close to all that had been once
the scene of her steady, unchecked life.

The propinquity was to shake her more than
she could dream.

In the morning she breakfasted in her room,
then coming downstairs stood in the portico of
the hotel drawing on her gloves as she had done
so many years before when she had been a girl
shopping with her mother. A flood of memories

rushed over her, among them the memory of that
day when her father and Virginia had passed them
on the street and they had not spoken. How
trivial the reason for not speaking seemed now!
In later years she had cut Jinny for a reason
equally trivial.

She walked up toward Sixteenth Street. It was
Sunday and the beautiful melancholy of the day
was settling on the quiet city. There was a freshness and a solemnity in the air as though even the
atmosphere had been rarified and soothed. A
sense of loneliness invaded her; this was the city
of her birth, of her childhood and of most of her
life. Yet there was no one, she felt, to whom she
could turn this beautiful day for a welcome; old
acquaintances might be mildly pleased, faintly
curious at seeing her, but none of them would
show any heart-warming gladness. She had left
them so abruptly, so completely. Well, she must
not think on these things. After all, in New York
she had been lonely too.

The Sixteenth Street car set her down at Jefferson Street and slowly she traversed the three long
blocks. Always quiet, always respectable, they
were doubly so in the sanctity of Sunday morning.
What a terrible day Sunday could be without
friends, ties, home, family. Only five years ago,
less than five years, she had had all the simple,
stable fixtures of family life, the appetizing breakfast, the music, the church with its interesting,
paintable types, long afternoons and evenings
with visitors and discussions beating in the void.
And Matthew Henson, would he, she wondered,
give her welcome? But she thought that still she
did not want to see him. She was not happy, but

361

she was not through adventuring, through tasting
life. And she knew that a life spent with Matthew
Henson would mean a cessation of that.   After
all, was he, with his steadiness, his uprightness, his
gift for responsibility any happier than she?   She
doubted it.

Oh, she hoped Sundays in Paris would be gay!

Opal Street came into her vision, a line, a mere
shadow of a street falling upon the steadfastness
of Jefferson.   Her heart quickened, tears came
into her eyes as she turned that corner which she
had turned so often, that corner which she
had once left behind her forever in order to taste
and know life.   In the hot July sun the street lay
almost deserted.   A young coloured man, immaculate in white shirt sleeves, slim and straight,
bending in his doorway to pick up the bulky Sunday paper, straightened up to watch her advancing
toward him.   Just this side of him stood her
former home,—how tiny it was and yet how full
of secrets, of knowledge of joy, despair, suffering,
futility—in brief Life!   She stood a few moments
in front of it, just gazing, but presently she went
up and put her hand on the red brick, wondering
blindly if in some way the insensate thing might
not communicate with her through touch.   A coloured woman sitting in the window watching her
rather sharply, came out then and asked her sus-
piciously what she wanted.

"Nothing," Angela replied dully.   "I just
wanted to look at the house."

"It isn't for sale, you know."

"No, no, of course not.   I just wanted to look
at it again.   I used to live here, you see.   I wondered——" Even if she did get permission to

go inside, could she endure it? If she could just stand once in that little back room and cry and cry—perhaps her tears would flood away all that mass of regret and confusion and futile memories, and she could begin life all over with a blank page. Thank God she was young! Suddenly it seemed to her that entering the house once more, standing in that room would be a complete panacea. Raising her eyes expectantly to the woman's face she began: "Would you be so kind——?"

But the woman, throwing her a last suspicious look and muttering that she was "nothing with poor white trash," turned and, slamming the door behind her, entered the little square parlour and pulled down the blinds.

.   .   .   .   .   .

The slim young man came running down the street toward her. Closer inspection revealed his ownership of a pleasant brown freckled face topped by thick, soft, rather closely cropped dark-red hair.

"Angela," he said timidly, and then with more assurance: "It *is* Angela Murray."

She turned her stricken face toward him. "She wouldn't let me in, Matthew. I'm going to France to-morrow and I thought I'd like to see the old house. But she wouldn't let me look at it. She called me,"—her voice broke with the injustice of it,—"poor white trash."

"I know," he nodded gravely. "She'd do that kind of thing; she doesn't understand, you see." He was leading her gently toward his house. "I think you'd better come inside and rest a moment. My father and mother have gone off for their

363

annual trip to Bridgeton; mother was born there, you know. But you won't mind coming into the house of an old and tried friend."

"No," she said, conscious of an overwhelming fatigue and general sense of let-downness, "I should say I wouldn't." As they crossed the threshold she tried faintly to smile but the effort was too much for her and she burst into a flood of choking, strangling, noisy tears.

Matthew removed her hat and fanned her; brought her ice-water and a large soft handkerchief to replace her own sodden wisp. Through her tears she smiled at him, understanding as she did so, the reason for Virginia's insistence on his general niceness. He was still Matthew Henson, still freckled and brown, still capped with that thatch of thick bad hair. But care and hair-dressings and improved toilet methods and above all the emanation of a fine and generous spirit had metamorphosed him into someone still the old Matthew Henson and yet someone somehow translated into a quintessence of kindliness and gravity and comprehending.

She drank the water gratefully, took out her powder puff.

"I don't need to ask how you are," he said, uttering a prayer of thanks for averted hysterics. "When a lady begins to powder her nose, she's bucking up all right. Want to tell me all about it?"

"There's nothing to tell. Only I wanted to see the house and suddenly found myself unexpectedly homesick, lonely, misunderstood. And when that woman refused me so cruelly, it was just too much." Her gaze wavered, her eyes filled again.

"Oh," he said in terror, "for God's sake don't cry again! I'll go over and give her a piece of my mind; I'll make her turn the whole house over to you. I'll bring you her head on a charger. Only 'dry those tears'." He took her handkerchief and dried them himself very, very gently.

She caught his hand. "Matthew, you're a dear."

He shrugged negligently, "You haven't always thought that."

This turn of affairs would never do. "What were you planning to do when I barged in? Getting ready to read your paper and be all homey and comfortable?"

"Yes, but I don't want to do that now. Tell you what, Angela, let's have a lark. Suppose we have dinner here? you get it. Remember how it used to make me happy as a king in the old days if you'd just hand me a glass of water? You said you were sailing to-morrow; you must be all packed. What time do you have to be back? I'll put you on the train."

The idea enchanted her. "I'd love it! Matthew, what fun!" They found an apron of his mother's, and in the ice-box, cold roast beef, lettuce which Philadelphians call salad, beets and corn. "I'll make muffins," said Angela joyously, "and you take a dish after dinner and go out and get some ice-cream. Oh, Matthew, how it's all coming back to me! Do you still shop up here in the market?"

They ate the meal in the little dark cool diningroom, the counterpart of the dining-room in Junius Murray's one-time house across the way. But somehow its smallness was no longer irksome;

365

rather it seemed a tiny island of protection reared out of and against an encroaching sea of troubles. In fancy she saw her father and mother almost a quarter of a century ago coming proudly to such a home, their little redoubt of refuge against the world. How beautiful such a life could be, shared with some one beloved,—with Anthony! Involuntarily she sighed.

Matthew studying her thoughtfully said: "You're dreaming, Angela. Tell me what it's all about."

"I was thinking what a little haven a house like this could be; what it must have meant to my mother. Funny how I almost pounded down the walls once upon a time trying to get away. Now I can't think of anything more marvellous than having such a place as this, here, there, anywhere, to return to."

Startled, he told her of his surprise at hearing such words from her. "If Virginia had said them I should think it perfectly natural; but I hadn't thought of you as being interested in home. How, by the way, is Virginia?"

"Perfect."

With a wistfulness which barely registered with her absorption, he queried: "I suppose she's tremendously happy?"

"Happy enough."

"A great girl, little Virginia." In his turn he fell to musing, roused himself. "You haven't told me of your adventures and your flight into the great world."

"There's not much to tell, Matthew. All I've seen and experienced has been the common fate of most people, a little sharpened, perhaps, a little

366

vivified. Briefly, I've had a lot of fun and a
measure of trouble. I've been stimulated by adventure; I've known suffering and love and pain."

"You're still surprising me. I didn't suppose
a girl like you could know the meaning of pain."
He gave her a twisted smile. "Though you certainly know how to cause it. Even yet I can get
a pang which no other thought produces if I let
my mind go back to those first few desperate days
after you left me. Heavens, can't you suffer when
you're young!"

She nodded, laid her hand on his. "Terribly.
Remember, I was suffering too, Matthew, though
for different causes. I was so pushed, so goaded
. . . well, we won't talk about that any more.
. . . I hope you've got over all that feeling. Indeed, indeed I wasn't worth it. Do tell me you
haven't let it harass you all these years."

His hand clasped hers lightly, then withdrew.
"No I haven't. . . . The suddenness, the in-
evitableness of your departure checked me, pulled
me up short. I suffered, oh damnably, but it was
suffering with my eyes open. I knew then you
weren't for me; that fundametally we were too
far apart. And eventually I got over it. Those
days!" He smiled again wryly, recalling a
memory. "But I went on suffering just the same,
only in another way. I fell in love with Jinny."

Her heart in her breast stopped beating. "Matthew, you didn't! Why on earth didn't you ever
say so?"

"I couldn't. She was such a child, you see; she
made it so plain all the time that she looked on
me as her sister's beau and therefore a kind of
dependable brother. After you went I used to go

to see her, take her about. Why she'd swing on
my arm and hold up her face for a good-night
kiss! Once, I remember, we had been out and
she became car-sick,—poor little weak thing! She
was so ashamed! Like a baby, you know, playing
at being grown-up and then ashamed for revert-
ing to babyhood. I went to see her the next day
and she was so little and frail and confiding! I
stayed away then for a long time and the next
thing I knew she was going to New York. I mis-
judged you awfully then, Angela. You must forgive me. I thought you had pulled her away. I
learned later that I was wrong, that you and she
rarely saw each other in New York. Do you
know why she left?"

There was her sister's pride to shield but her
own need to succour; who could have dreamed
of such a dilemma? "I can't betray Jinny," she
said to herself and told him that while she personally had not influenced her sister the latter had
had a very good reason for leaving Philadelphia.

"I suppose so. Certainly she left. But she'd
write me, occasionally, letters just like her dear
self, so frank and girlish and ingenuous and making it so damnably plain that any demonstration
of love on my part was out of the question. I said
to myself: 'I'm not going to wreck my whole life
over those Murray girls.' And I let our friendship
drift off into a nothingness. . . . Then she came
to visit Edna Brown this summer. I fairly leaped
out to Merion to see her. The moment I laid
eyes on her I realized that she had developed,
had become a woman. She was as always, kind
and sweet, prettier, more alluring than ever. I
thought I'd try my luck . . . and Edna told me

she was engaged. What's the fellow like Angela?"

"Very nice, very fine."

"Wild about her, I suppose?"

Desperately she looked at him. "He's a rather undemonstrative sort. I suppose he's wild enough. Only,—well they talk as though they had no intention of marrying for years and years and they both seem perfectly content with that arrangement."

He frowned incredulously. "What! If I thought they weren't in earnest!"

Impulsively she broke out: "Oh, Matthew, don't you know,—there's so much pain, such suffering in the world,—a man should never leave any stone unturned to achieve his ultimate happiness. Why don't you—write to Jinny, go to New York to see her?"

Under his freckles his brown skin paled. "You think there's a chance?"

"My dear, I wouldn't dare say. I know she likes you very, very much. And I don't think she regards you as a brother."

"Angela, you wouldn't fool me?"

"Why should I do that? And remember after all I'm giving you no assurance. I'm merely saying it's worth taking a chance. Now let's see, we'll straighten up this place and then we must fly."

At the station she kissed him good bye. "Anyway you're always a brother to me. Think of what I've told you, Matthew; act on it."

"I shall. Oh, Angela, suppose it should be that God sent you down here to-day?"

"Perhaps He did." They parted solemnly.

Three hours later found her entering her sister's apartment. Jinny, her cold raging, her eyes inflamed and weeping, greeted her plaintively. "Look at me, Angela. And you leaving tomorrow! I'll never be able to make that boat!" The telephone rang. "It's been ringing steadily for the last hour, somebody calling for you. Do answer it."

The message was from Ashley. He had been away in New Orleans. "And I came back and found that clipping. I knew you sent it. Girl, the way I've pursued you this day! Finally I caught up with Martha Burden, she told me where you were staying. May I come up? Be there in half an hour."

"Not to-night, Ralph. Would you like to come to the boat to-morrow?"

"So you're going anyhow? Bully! But not before I've seen you! Suppose I take you to the boat?"

"Awfully nice of you, but I'm going with my sister."

Here Jinny in a voice full of misplaced consonants told her she was going to do nothing of the sort. "With this cold!"

Angela spoke into the receiver again. "My sister says she isn't going, so I will fall back on you if I may." She hung up.

Virginia wanted to hear of the trip. The two sisters sat talking far into the night, but Angela said no word about Matthew.

. . . . . .

Monday was a day of surprise. Martha and Ladislas Starr, unable to be on hand for the sailing of the boat, came up to the house to drive down town with the departing traveller. Secretly Angela was delighted with this arrangement, but it brought a scowl to Ashley's face.

Virginia, miserable with the wretchedness attendant on a summer cold, bore up bravely. "I don't mind letting you go like this from the house; but I couldn't stand the ship! Angela, you're not to worry about me one bit. Only come back to me,—happy. I know you will. Oh how different this is from that parting years ago in Philadelphia!"

"Yes," said Angela soberly. "Then I was to be physically ninety miles away from you, but we were really seas apart. Now—darling, three thousand miles are nothing when there is love and trust and understanding. And Jinny, listen! Life is full of surprises. If a chance for real happiness comes your way don't be afraid to grasp at it."

"Cryptic," wheezed Jinny, laughing. "I don't know what you're talking about, but I'll do my best to land any happiness that comes drifting toward me." They kissed each other gravely, almost coldly, without tears. But neither could trust herself to say the actual good-bye.

Angela was silent almost all the way down to the dock, answering her friends only in monosyllables. There, another surprise awaited her in the shape of Mrs. Denver, who remained, however, only for a few moments. "I couldn't stand having you go," she said pitifully, "without seeing you for one last time." And, folding the girl in a close embrace, she broke down and murmured sadly of a lost daughter who would have been "perhaps like you, dear, had she lived."

Elizabeth Sandburg, the gay, the complacent, the beloved of life, clung to her, weeping, "I can't bear to lose you, Angèle." Walter put his arm about her. "Kiss me, old girl. And mind, if you need anything, *anything*, you're to call on us. If you get sick we'll come over after you,— am I right, Lizzie?"

"Yes, of course, of course . . . and don't call me Lizzie. . . . Come away, can't you, and leave them a moment together. Don't you see Ashley glaring at you?"

They withdrew to a good point of vantage on the dock.

Angela, surprised and weeping, remembering both Mrs. Denver's words and the manifestations of kindness in her state-room said: "They really did love me after all, didn't they?"

"Yes," said Ashley earnestly, "we all love you. I'm coming over to see you by and by, Angèle, may I? You know we've a lot of things to talk about, some things which you perhaps think mean a great deal to me but which in reality mean nothing. Then on the other hand there are some matters which actually do mean something to me but whose value to you I'm not sure of."

"Oh," she said, wiping her eyes and remembering her former secret. "You aren't coming over to ask me to marry you, are you? You don't have to do that. And anyway 'it is not now as it hath been before.' There's no longer a mystery about me, you know. So the real attraction's gone. Remember, I'm not expecting a thing of

you, so please, please don't ask it. Ralph, I can't
placard myself, and I suppose there will be lots of
times when in spite of myself I'll be 'passing.'
But I want you to know that from now on, so far
as sides are concerned, I am on the coloured side.
And I don't want you to come over on that side."
She shook her head finally. "Too many complications even for you."

For though she knew he believed in his brave
words, she was too sadly experienced to ask an
American to put them to the test.

"All right," he said, smiling at her naïve
assumptions. "I won't ask you to marry me,—
at least not yet. But I'm coming over just the
same. I don't suppose you've got a lien on
Paris."

"Of course I haven't," she giggled a little.
"You know perfectly well I want you to come."
Her face suddenly became grave. "But if you
do come you won't come to make love without
meaning anything either, will you? I'd hate that
between you and me."

"No," he said gently, instantly comprehending.
"I won't do that either."

"You'll come as a friend?"

"Yes, as a friend."

A deck hand came up then and said civilly that
in a few minutes they would be casting off and all
visitors must go ashore.

CHAPTER III

AMONG her steamer-letters was a brief note from
Anthony:

"Angela, my angel, my dear girl, good-bye.
These last few weeks have been heaven and hell.
I couldn't bear to see you go,—so I've taken myself off for a few hours . . . don't think I'll
neglect Jinny. I'll never do that. Am I right in
supposing that you still care a little? Oh Angela,
try to forget me,—but don't do it! I shall never
forget you!"

There were letters and flowers from the Burdens, gifts of all sorts from Ashley and Mrs. Denver, a set of notes for each day out from Virginia.
She read letters, examined her gifts and laid them
aside. But all day long Anthony's note reposed
on her heart; it lay at night beneath her head.

． ● ● ● ● ●

Paris at first charmed and wooed her. For a
while it seemed to her that her old sense of joy
in living for living's sake had returned to her. It
was like those first few days which she had spent
in exploring New York. She rode delightedly in
the motor-buses on and on to the unknown, unpre-
dictable terminus; she followed the winding Seine;
crossing and re-crossing the bridges each with its

distinctive characteristics. Back of the Panthéon, near the church of St. Geneviève she discovered a Russian restaurant where strange, exotic dishes were served by tall blond waiters in white, stiff Russian blouses. One day, wandering up the Boulevard du Mont Parnasse, she found at its juncture with the Boulevard Raspail the Café Dome, a student restaurant of which many returned students had spoken in the Art School in New York. On entering she was recognized almost immediately by Edith Martin, a girl who had studied with her in Philadelphia.

Miss Martin had lived in Paris two years; knew all the gossip and the characters of the Quarter; could give Angela points on pensions, cafés, tips and the Gallic disposition. On all these topics she poured out perpetually a flood of information, presented her friends, summoned the new comer constantly to her studio or camped uninvited in the other girl's tiny quarters at the Pension Franciana. There was no chance for actual physical loneliness, yet Angela thought after a few weeks of persistent comradeship that she had never felt so lonely in her life. For the first time in her adventuresome existence she was caught up in a tide of homesickness.

Then this passed too with the summer, and she found herself by the end of September engrossed in her work. She went to the Academy twice a day, immersed herself in the atmosphere of the Louvre and the gallery of the Luxembourg. It was hard work, but gradually she schooled herself to remember that this was her life, and that her aim, her one ambition, was to become an acknowledged, a significant painter of portraits. The instructor, renowned son of a still more renowned father, almost invariably praised her efforts.

With the coming of the fall the sense of adventure left her. Paris, so beautiful in the summer, so gay with its thronging thousands, its hosts bent on pleasure, took on another garb in the sullen greyness of late autumn. The tourists disappeared and the hard steady grind of labour, the intent application to the business of living, so noticeable in the French, took the place of a transient, careless freedom. Angela felt herself falling into line; but it was good discipline as she herself realized. Once or twice, in periods of utter loneliness or boredom, she let her mind dwell on her curiously thwarted and twisted life. But the ability for self-pity had vanished. She had known too many others whose lives lay equally remote from goals which had at first seemed so certain. For a period she had watched feverishly for the incoming of foreign mail, sure that some word must come from Virginia about Matthew, but the months crept sullenly by and Jinny's letters remained the same artless missives prattling of school-work, Anthony, Sara Penton, the Movies and visits to Maude the inimitable.

"Of course not everything can come right," she told herself. Matthew evidently had, on second thought, deemed it wisest to consult the evidence of his own senses rather than be guided by the hints which in the nature of things she could offer only vaguely.

Within those six months she lost forever the blind optimism of youth. She did not write Anthony nor did she hear from him.

.   .   .   .   .

Christmas Eve day dawned or rather drifted
greyly into the beholder's perception out of the
black mistiness of the murky night. In spite of
herself her spirits sank steadily. Virginia had
promised her a present,—"I've looked all over
this whole town," she wrote, "to find you something good enough, something absolutely perfect.
Anthony's been helping me. And at last I've
found it. We've taken every possible precaution
against the interference of wind or rain or
weather, and unless something absolutely un-
predictable intervenes, it will be there for you
Christmas Eve or possibly the day before. But
remember, don't open it until Christmas."

But it was now six o'clock on Christmas Eve
and no present had come, no letter, no remembrance of any kind. "Oh," she said to herself,
"what a fool I was to come so far away from
home!" For a moment she envisaged the possibility of throwing herself on the bed and sobbing
her heart out. Instead she remembered Edith
Martin's invitation to make a night of it over at
her place, a night which was to include dancing
and chaffing, a trip just before midnight to hear
Mass at St. Sulpice, and a return to the studio for
doubtless more dancing and jesting and laughter,
and possibly drunkenness on the part of the American male.

At ten o'clock as she stood in her tiny room
rather sullenly putting the last touches to her
costume, the maid, Héloise, brought her a cable.
It was a long message from Ashley wishing her
health, happiness and offering to come over at a
week's notice. Somehow the bit of blue paper
cheered her, easing her taut nerves. "Of course

377

they're thinking about me. I'll hear from Jinny
any moment; it's not her fault that the delivery
is late. I wonder what she sent me."

Returning at three o'clock Christmas morning
from the party she put her hand cautiously in
the door to switch on the light for fear that a
package lay near the threshold, but there was no
package there. "Well, even if it were there I
couldn't open it," she murmured, "for I'm too
sleepy." And indeed she had drugged herself
with dancing and gaiety into an overwhelming
drowsiness. Barely able to toss aside her pretty
dress, she tumbled luxuriously into bed, grateful
in the midst of her somnolence for the fatigue
which would make her forget. . . . In what seemed
to her less than hour, she heard a tremendous
knocking at the door.

"*Entrez*," she called sleepily and relapsed
immediately into slumber. The door, as it happened, was unlocked; she had been too fatigued
to think of it the night before. Héloise stuck in
a tousled head. "My God," she told the cook
afterwards, "such a time as I had to wake her!
There she was asleep on both ears and the gentleman downstairs waiting!"

Angela finally opened bewildered eyes. "A
gentleman," reiterated Héloise in her staccato
tongue. "He awaits you below. He says he has
a present which he must put into your own hands.
Will Mademoiselle then descend or shall I tell
him to come back?"

"Tell him to come back," she murmured, then
opened her heavy eyes. "Is it really Christmas,
Héloise? Where is the gentleman?"

"As though I had him there in my pocket,"

said Héloise later in her faithful report to the cook.

But finally the message penetrated. Grasping a robe and slippers, she half leaped, half fell down the little staircase and plunged into the five foot square drawing-room. Anthony sitting on the mendously disproportionate tan and maroon a rose to meet her.

His eyes on her astonished countenance, he began searching about in his pockets, slapping his vest, pulling out keys and handkerchiefs. "There ought to be a tag on me somewhere," he remarked apologetically, "but anyhow Virginia and Matthew sent me with their love."

THE END

Jessie Redmon Fauset (1882–1961), novelist and literary editor, was born in what is now Lawnside, New Jersey. Among the most prolific writers of the Harlem Renaissance, her published works include four novels — *There Is Confusion* (1924), *Plum Bun* (1929), *The Chinaberry Tree* (1931), and *Comedy, American Style* (1933) — and a series of essays, poems, and short stories. *Plum Bun* is considered her best novel.